A DEATHLESS EMPIRE

A DEATHLESS EMPIRE

A DEATHLESS EMPIRE
BOOK ONE

KAYLA MCGRATH

CONTENT WARNINGS

This book includes content that may be disturbing to some readers, discretion is advised. Content includes graphic violence (blood, gore, body mutilation, decapitation, murder, death, death of family), sexually explicit scenes, knife play, mentions and attempts of sexual assault, mention of rape, brief substance abuse from side characters (drugs), mention of abortion and abortifacients (historical and off the page), thalassophobia, religious bigotry, depictions of slavery, animal death, and arachnophobia.

ENNEIVE
CUUEVOTA
(BLACK MARKET)
SELYNDYR
TALLOH
THE MURAVO MOUNTAIN PASS
RTHA
PRAVO
BASTIA
LUNETH
CYDRA
RUNELL
OPHETTE
GALLAE

IXAITHA
MELUSDA
ASTRA
VALENCYA
NYXIA
ADRAALI
FAYLA
THYCCA
VALOS
CURRAM
DUBON

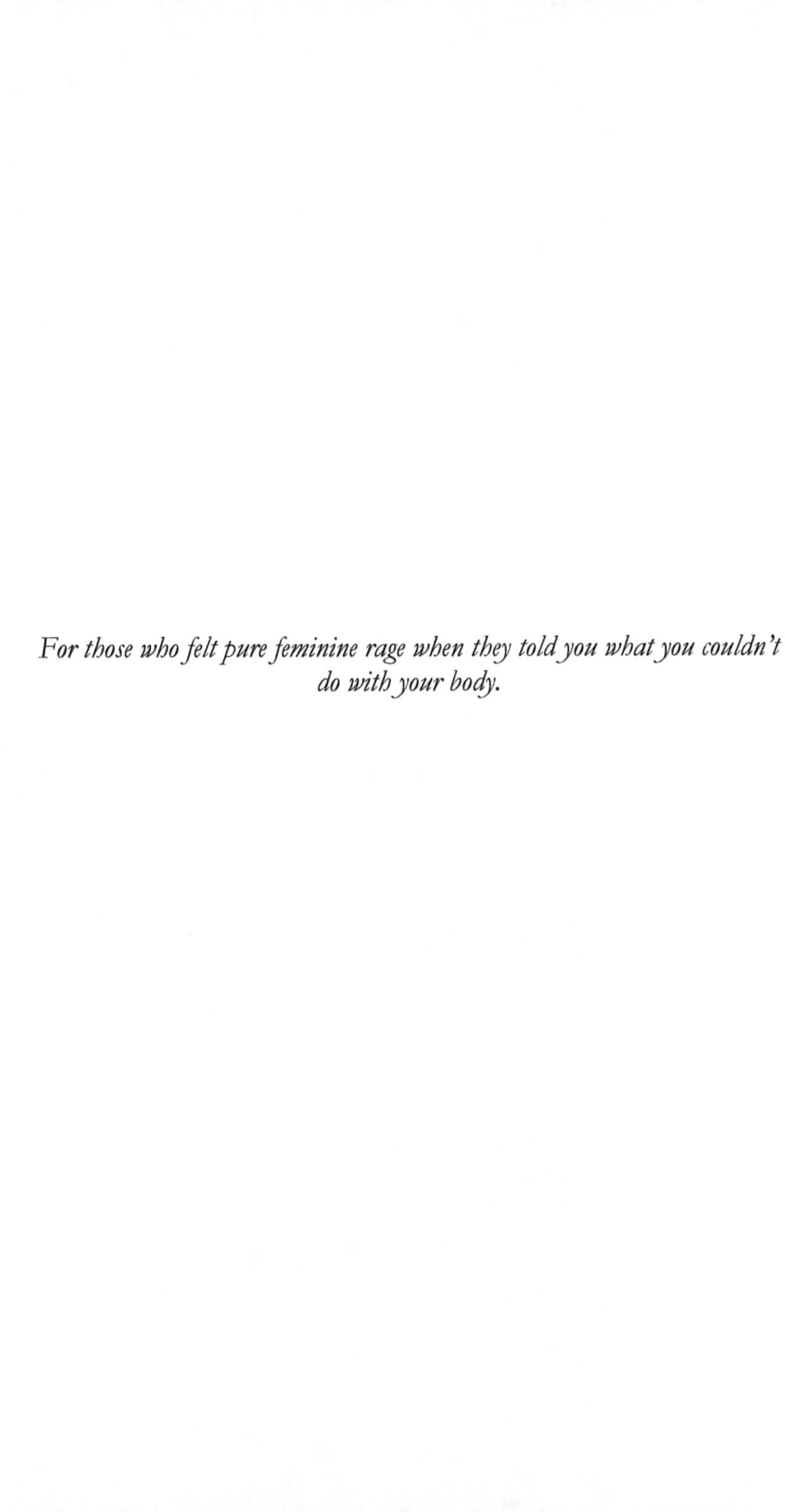

*For those who felt pure feminine rage when they told you what you couldn't
do with your body.*

PART ONE

CHAPTER ONE

There was little Valine considered more predictable than the folly of men and their truly astounding ability to think only with their cocks.

Even the most stalwart of soldiers found difficulty forming coherent thoughts and following simple logic when the sway of hips or jiggle of tits were present. It was why she felt disappointed now, in the forgotten-named, bawdry tavern located at Astra's Edge, with the sour stench of ale and male sweat permeating her nose. All it took was donning her most coquettish smile paired with a shy flutter of lashes over her bare shoulder, and her mark was done for.

Inside, the tavern was warm, bathed in golden candlelight from the stubs dripping on tables and the massive antler chandeliers fashioned above their heads. The walls were paneled ironwood and stone, both hewn from the Laskava Mountains on the south-eastern border and surrounding territory. Women perched, and men leered at the far end of the liquor-soiled bar. Some men were drinking to drown their sorrows, others drinking to be merry, and others drinking to fuck.

By the massive hearth lounged Valine's mark, Captain Ishaq. He was a grizzled soldier with a thin scar bisecting his left brow, stark white against the olive of his skin and the black of his hair. Thick, rubbery lips were hidden beneath a poorly groomed beard, and the beginnings of crow's feet radiated from his cold eyes. Valine knew implicitly, like she knew the north-western Kingdom of Talloh had a triad of moons, that those lines were not from smiling.

Disregarding her unpleasant notions, she approached the man and fought her rising gorge after catching sight of his sharpened teeth. Such was the style of the former Ixaithan Empire during the Tri-Region War twenty years before, only further affirming her suspicions about why she'd been hired and what crimes he'd been pardoned for. Tri-Region War veterans were considered heroes, but as a foreigner in the conquering lands, she knew the victors of that war were anything but.

Ixaitha had lost sovereignty over the independent kingdom of Melusda, the eastern half of Adraali, and the northern border of Dubon. The northern desert country had turned into one of the weakest nations, while Adraali was steadily becoming increasingly influential, thanks to the power of the west side liberating all three countries during the war.

"I've heard a man in uniform is to women what a whore's lingerie is to men. I'd never believed it before, but now it's starting to make sense," she said coyly. It was a lie, of course; the man was repugnant.

He laughed gruffly as she twirled a lock of her dark hair around her fingers—it was similar to spinning a blade. "Not from around here if this old lout is the first uniform to tickle your fancy. What is that accent? Dubonian?"

It was true. She wasn't from Adraali, and her cool white complexion only further betrayed her southern heritage. Observing all her exposed skin with lust darkening his mossy gaze, his eyes traveled her form. He took in everything from her creamy thigh slipping from the high slit in her skirt to her cleavage and the full breasts begging to spill from the top of her corset.

"Thyccan, actually," she corrected. "And on the contrary, I enjoy my men older."

More lies.

"Thyccan," he nearly purred, reaching for her hand and pulling her into his lap. She let him. "You make it sound like you've bedded a man or two."

"Perhaps I have," she simpered, running a beringed hand down his chest. Ishaq had the start of a gut, soft from lack of battles, and below, she could see a rather unimpressive erection tenting his trousers.

Ishaq tightened his meaty grip on her ribs while his thumb stroked the underside of her breast, possessiveness growing on him. Valine swallowed back the nausea his touch evoked and shifted her weight into him, biting her lip softly. She pretended that, for a moment, nothing mattered but his stale breath at her neck, his broad, hairy chest beneath her fingertips, and his rotten gaze devouring her generous decolletage. In reality, she was pulling into herself, focusing on the ruffians in the corner singing the pirate ballad about Veronyka's freckles, the clinking of metal tankards, and the high-pitched giggles of courtesans.

"That's a beautiful ring. Only beautiful things for such a lovely girl." He was gesturing to her teardrop-shaped emerald, many golden claws holding it in place. It was modest and it adorned the middle finger of her left hand. It was one of her many rings.

"It *is* quite special."

"What's your name, pet?" he drawled.

"Jemma."

It continued like that for some time. Captain Ishaq would inquire, and Valine would lie. He would stroke, and she would caress, careful to tease and scintillate without being too transparent. Sickness roiled in her belly, but she held her façade, and the captain was none the wiser. She was quite an excellent actress, and had her situation been different, she may have found her calling in the theatre. Alas, it was not her life, and the way of shadows was her future.

It took moments to convince him to take her to his room. Leading him up the stairs, she let him fantasize, let him leer. It was the least she could give him in his final moments.

Producing the bronze key, she playfully snatched it from him, holding it to her nose in a child-like way. His creature grin deepened, and that spark of lust in his eyes became a deadly inferno.

"What wonderful things this key will unlock for you," she lilted as she grazed it down her bodice, resting just below her navel. "So many treasures to be discovered."

She turned to unlock the door as his large arms wrapped around her waist, his face in her mahogany waves, nuzzling below her ear. She forced a contented sigh as she opened the door, pulling out of his grip and flouncing into his room. Spinning on her toes, she coaxed him to enter with all but a finger. He dutifully followed, locking the door and his fate behind him.

The room was modest. A bed, a wardrobe, a washbasin, a chest, and a chair. The chair in question sat in the center of the room. She pushed him into it. Eagerly, he let her as she trailed her fingers across his chest and circled him. Her fingers traced his throat, and he reveled in the touch of a woman more than twenty years his junior.

His inclinations were his ruin as she pulled a thin wire from her jeweled ring, and wrapped it around the deceptively delicate—and hooked—filigree of another. Yanking the wire taut against his throat, she used the leverage of her boot on the back of his chair to haul the bigger man up and plunged the hidden spike into the soft bit of flesh below his ear.

What he didn't know about that beautiful ring was that it hid both half of a garrote and a poisoned barb. It was laughable, that he had complimented the instrument of his death.

His movements became wild and animalistic. Any thoughts he had of sex evaporated the same instant that his realization of impending doom solidified. Ishaq was spitting, reaching to claw her, but she was well out of the way, and her leather vambraces protected her from his filthy nails.

"I'm not going to kill you yet," she growled, dropping her false accent as he thrashed. "But soon."

She still had an accent, but it was not Thyccan as she had faked and he had assumed. It was more lyrical, the flowing tones of Runell. There was a lilt of their highborn she couldn't seem to obscure completely in the roll of her tongue—proper enunciation and slow, languid speeches.

"The toxin won't kill you right away. It paralyzes first. You wouldn't believe how difficult it was to draw venom from a silvered viper—bastard bit me a time, too. But the lovely thing about this venom is that it allows you to speak for a short time and experience all sensations—some accounts say, in a heightened manner."

Even now, the captain's movements were slowing, growing sluggish. Drool seeped from his mouth; blood boiled beneath his skin. Seconds later, as Valine was rounding the chair, Ishaq began to still and freeze, but his eyes maintained a murderous hatred. His arms dangled uselessly beside his legs, and his back began to slump. Now, in front of the captain, Valine pushed him against the chair with the thick sole of her booted foot, forcing him while the toxin completely incapacitated him.

She leaned into her knee, luxuriating in the fact she had such a vile man beneath her boot. "You're going to die tonight," she told him simply. "Now, it's your choice whether it be quickly or slowly." Her eyes drifted down to his crotch as she wrapped the garrote back into her ring. "And you can choose if you lose your favorite little toy."

"Fucking bitch," he spit. It was hardly discernable under the poison's duress, but Valine understood perfectly.

"What limited vocabulary, I'm disappointed. I was hoping for something a little more creative than that."

"Wicked cunt."

"Ahh, there's an improvement, Captain. You had me worried, I'll admit."

Taking a jeweled blade from her boot, admiring the amethyst hilt and golden inlay, Valine brandished it before them. Quite casually. Ishaq's eyes widened ever so, just enough for the whites to show.

"I have questions and I kindly request you give answers. The more truthful I deem your responses, the less pain I elicit. Do you comprehend?" She emphasized this by setting the tip of her blade beneath his nail and *pushed*. His eyes lit with pain and he began to spew hardly discernable vitriol laced with panic. "Am I clear?"

"Yes," he growled.

"Delightful!" Valine pulled back and sat upon the bed the captain had thought he was going to get lucky on. Crossing her legs, she leaned forward as the captain was of no threat to her now. "During the Tri-Region War, you were serving under a General Azad until you murdered him because he found you raping and pillaging, correct?"

"Yes."

"Why?"

"Those little vixens had it coming, running from me in those tiny dresses. A man has needs, and the chase makes it all the better." There was no shame in this monster's eyes, no remorse in his soul. Valine felt sick, felt her stomach roiling. It made all that she had to do easier.

She slammed her booted feet to the floorboards. "They were *children*."

"They had tits, didn't they? I hardly call fourteen Harvest Seasons a child."

"Do you remember how many?"

"No."

"You're a twisted motherfucker."

Ishaq tried to shrug but only succeeded in moving his jaw, which caused an indecent amount of drool to slip from his mouth. "I've seen your type before. You're going to kill me either way, and no amount of begging or pleading will save me, so I'd rather go quick. You want me to lie? Say I didn't enjoy those fresh little flowers? Their screams? Their soft little noises before I tore out their throats?" He grins, showing those *fucking teeth*. "All of that made me harder than the willing cunt of any whore."

In that moment, Valine didn't care that she lost her composure. There were other missions, other jobs where she could restrain herself, be a little less impulsive. But it wasn't this one, and she reassured herself that the torture she would give this monster would be repeated over and over tenfold until he pled for death. Until the toxin left his soulless corpse, and even then, begged to disappear into the afterlife. She would not let him, not until she knew how many needed justice. Not until she got their vengeance. He was too cocky, too proud; she would have to bring him down to a level deserving of his filth.

"Thank you for your cooperation. True death will be swift."

It was a flash, and she was across the room with an even longer blade she'd stashed beneath the bed. It was seconds, and she'd removed his favorite weapon. It was a breath, and he was screaming. It was blood that covered the floor in crimson and the scent of copper. It was anger when she pummeled his face and squashed his nose beneath the blows. It was warranted as she tore every single one of those demonic fangs from his mouth. It was a pity when he fell unconscious while she pulled his nails from their beds. It was righteousness when he woke up to her carving *RAPIST* into his chest.

It *might* have been overkill when she gouged out his left eye.

Valine yanked back his head by his greasy hair and grinned demonically at him, pouring all her fury into her black gaze. He was a blubbering, bloody, drooling mess. Blood and gore leaked from the mess of his eye socket. Scarlet ran rivulets from the pockets in his gums, streams from his nailbeds. The scent of piss and shit was acrid in her nostrils.

"Please, p-p-please let me go this time. Please let me die," he begged and sniveled. He'd already died thrice.

"I thought you said you knew my type? That no amount of pleading or begging will save you?" Valine asked sweetly, knowing the tone was ruined by the blood that spattered her pale complexion.

"*Please!* Please stop bringing me back, you promised me!" he sobbed, tears running from his one good eye.

"I promised you only a quick true death. I said nothing of the others. Dear Captain Ishaq, have your previous passings become permanent?"

"*You fucking witch!*" he shrieked, spraying spit and blood everywhere. He screamed and sobbed in fury and agony. "You hateful fucking *bitch.*" His last word broke, ending in a choking breath. "I didn't know you were a fucking necromancer when I said that!"

Caressing his face with the tip of a knife, ruby following in its wake, she cocked her head to the side. "I will let you go this time, but only because *I'm* out of time."

He hung his head in her grasp and sobbed, equal parts relief and despair. Taking the blade from his face, she pulled back, extricated her magic from his reanimated body, and sliced him from ear to ear. A gout of claret red spilled across his front and splattered onto her boots and long skirt.

Before the sounds of Ishaq's comrades coming up the stairs could reach the landing, Valine was throwing open the window, the scent of cool night air blasting her as she dashed outside. Balancing on the desiccated flowerbed, she launched herself across the alley and onto the trellis of climbing wisteria on the building opposite. She scaled the structure and pulled herself up over the lip of the bakery's roof. Seconds later, she was gone from sight before the dismayed yells of Ishaq's discovery could implicate her.

Captain Ishaq's final death was swift as she'd promised, but evidence of his previous demises was anything but. She grew tired of bringing him back. Truly, she wondered how the man had survived so many battles when he died with the first cut. Granted, the first slice had been the removal of his cock—and the nicking of an artery—but the monster deserved the castration. The second was when she'd jammed his nose into his brain—that was a tricky one. Head injuries were so much harder to pull the strings of the spirit back from.

From one moment to the next, she was night and shadows, darkness and death. As she crossed the roof, there was another moment, and a figure stepped out from behind a brick chimney. A breath later, lancing pain struck her skull, and oblivion overtook her.

CHAPTER TWO

A bucket full of icy water to the face and a spike of pain through the skull brought Valine to. She awoke spluttering, discovering herself strapped to a wooden chair with leather manacles. Blood caked the back of her head, matting the dark locks, and nausea accompanied her blurry vision. She was dripping wet, hair soaked to her scalp, and her flimsy dress was now near sheer.

"Mother*fucker*," she hissed through the pain.

Valine tried wiggling around, but the restraints held fast. Not only were they tight, but they highlighted the fact that she'd been stripped bare of her weaponry. All ten of her blades, pistol, and bladed barrette. They'd even plucked her garrote rings from her fingers.

Bastards.

"Ahh, the little assassin awakens," a melodic male voice chortled, and a thrill of familiarity stole through her.

Valine squinted past the pain and the hazy light filtering in through a basement window. There were bars on it, and a mix of streetlight and moonlight filtered in—good. It was still night. The walls were stone, as were the floors, and past the dim lighting, the only other structure she could make out was a set of stairs leading up to a wooden door. It was musty and smelled of it, dust coating the corners of the room. This was not a well-used place—not a good sign. There were three tall figures surrounding her, but they were shapeless forms.

The one who'd spoken stepped forward, close enough for her to define more features.

Before her stood a man with crossed arms, and she was taken aback at the astounding shade of magenta he wore. The cloak was clasped with a golden brooch, inset with a large topaz in the shape of a sun. Above, his hair was perfectly coiffed and a shocking shade of red—a deep auburn she could hardly recall seeing in her life.

At his feet sat a wet, wooden bucket.

"Sorry about that knock to the head, love," he continued in the same accent as hers. The accent of a place she once called home. "But you've been a difficult one to get a hold of. Desperate times and all that mess."

"You're from Runell," she deadpanned.

She could hear the evergreens and peach orchards in his voice. She could see the silver statues of Runellian saints and turquoise ocean on his face. She could smell the blackberry fields and humid sunshine on his clothes. He embodied the best memories of home. It was almost enough to convince her to forget the worst.

"As are you."

Runell was at the south-western end of the continent. The mass of the country curved around a narrow bay framed by two crescent islands. Virtually every city, village, and town occupied coastline. It was jewel bright and cool, monsoons and lightning storms common, but it was also sprawling greens, lush forests, and orchards. Runell didn't possess mountains or lakes, but it had one strong river at its border and ocean as far as the eye could see.

"What are you doing in Adraali? And who are you?"

He chuckled, and the sound was oddly comforting to her cold heart. "Alastair Whitechurch. And I could ask you the same thing, but to skip the games; I'm a dignitary, permanently stationed here. Personally, I think it was just that my parents desired my drinking and debauchery as far from their estate as possible."

Valine remembered the Whitechurch family from long ago. They were one of the larger names, notable and rich, with a glorious penchant for luxury and a strict code of image. If Alastair was participating in entertainment of the boozy and licentious variety, then it was no surprise he was sent off.

Runell was strictest of all the kingdoms; customs unwaveringly enforced and rights stripped, with fair-skinned, older men holding all the power and decision-making abilities. Women were little more than brood mares and pretty baubles on arms, and access to many herbs and substances like contraceptives or recreational drugs—including alcohol, aside from sanctified wine—was forbidden under punishment of dismemberment or death. It was not a forgiving place, especially for someone like Valine.

As she blinked a bit more of her fogginess away, more of Alastair's features came into focus. He looked somewhere in his twenties—still youthful, but the solid lines of his jaw indicated his maturity. His cheekbones were high and elegantly curved, and his eyes were like the summer skies of the Valassa Beach at midday—clear and endlessly blue. He was possibly one of the most handsome men she'd laid eyes on, with a long, straight nose, full lips, and a touch of highlighting cosmetics on his pale features,.

"What do you want from me? Money? Names? Secrets?" she demanded, searching the men in the barren room. "I'm afraid I'm fresh out of diamonds."

"Your services, actually, Valine."

Valine whipped her gaze to the dark voice beyond the flamboyant man and zeroed in. Heat and panic flooded her face because she *knew* him.

He was the king.

Valine tilted her chin up, trying to regain some semblance of dignity and composure. Her lip curled in a sneer, and she knew the look on her face could only be described as haughty.

"King Malik Jirani Amir."

King Malik had only recently obtained the crown and throne a mere five years ago. In that time, Adraali had become the wealthiest kingdom on the continent and the strongest in military. It was no surprise when the newest Amir developed a lust for greed and power, beginning the conquering of lands. Already, he had the entire east side of the continent—aside from Ixaitha—allied and in the palm of his hand. Yet, all he seemed to want was more and more. She had to give him credit however, he punished crimes like Captain Ishaq's to the severest degree, and poverty in Astra and Nyxia were at an all-time low. Although, those may be his only redeeming qualities.

He chuckled softly as he approached, and his face came into light. His complexion was a light brown, sculpted with an artist's hand. His strong jaw held a groomed shadow of a beard. Hair, heavy on top and shorter on the sides, black as night fell over his brow. But his eyes…oh, his eyes. They were lined in gold and framed with full lashes. They were an unnamable shade. They were the lightest of blues and the softest of golds. They were piercing and captivating.

"You say my name like I'm in trouble."

All the fine hairs on her body were raised at the sound of his voice. It was lilting and lyrical, smooth and melodic. It was a lethal calm and a soft chide.

"I disagree, Your Majesty. I say your name in reverence and acknowledgment."

He scoffed, showing off his white teeth. "What a pretty little liar you are."

Her lip curled. "I try."

King Malik now stood before her, and she took in his frame. He was lean, yet muscles showed through his fine ebony clothing. His boots were jet and clasped with gold, the thick soles of which only added to his already impressive height. She stared up at him, daring him toward his next move.

"Why is it that I had to resort to a courtesan hiring you rather than regular channels? You ignored my previous summons."

Valine hid her surprise. She hadn't realized Nallia had hired her so that the king could access her. To know *exactly* where she would be and when. It was a slight blow knowing she hadn't been hired to mete out Nallia's justice but rather turned into another pawn on the king's chessboard.

"Apologies. I suppose I never got the letters." A lie, of course.

The redheaded man from home—Alastair—chortled behind the king, knocking elbows with the darker figure next to him. The other man smirked but remained silent.

Malik leaned toward her, and she could see his eyes taking her in. Soaked as she was, she knew she was a beauty. Long hair, creamy skin, luscious curves, an ample bosom. She knew with the cold and the wet that her nipples were erect, and she dared not consider it might also be due to the king's hungry gaze. He was slow in devouring her person, and a thrill shot through her. She contemplated if she would taunt him.

She would.

Ever so slightly, she parted her legs and shook out her hair.

Malik immediately noticed and placed a hand directly on her bare thigh. His touch was hot, and wetness seeped between her legs. His other hand came to rest on her throat, and he applied an expert amount of pressure. And she knew two things at once.

One, he knew just the right amount of pressure to expend where to heighten sexual desire.

And two, he knew just the right amount of pressure to expend where to strangulate.

She didn't care that two others were in the room; her pulse went wild with Malik's touch, and he *knew it*. The bastard even smirked.

"As much as we both might enjoy *those* services, they are not the ones I am referring to," King Malik teased, and she flamed.

Releasing her from his spell, he backed up and paced.

"I'm in need of an assassin that I may retain in my employ. After careful consideration, word of mouth, and frequenting of the seediest establishments Astra has to offer, your name was consistently on everyone's tongue."

"Well, how sweet of you to think of me. Truly, I'm honored to be your selection, but I don't do repeat business, and I don't work for royals." Valine shrugged. "It's dangerous in my line of work."

Royalty notoriously paid well, but it was always messy. It was always siblings, cousins, and parents, and they were not the sort of clients she preferred to prey on. Small hits on lords and ladies were a gray area to her, but she drew the line at princes, princesses, and regent rulers. Besides, more often than not, kings could make you disappear with the right words—a wealthy mistress had only the reach of her money. It was smart business, Valine had reasoned.

"Don't flatter yourself. You possess a certain skill set and presence I need, but I could hire many other assassins. Though, to be frank, yes, you were my first choice." Pivoting toward her. "And you do now. I own you. You will only work for me. Only do the jobs I place before you, and you will be happy to perform such duties."

"And if I don't? You'll kill me? Or am I just to be your slave?"

The prospect was terrifying to her. To be at such a mercy. There were reasons why she chose to use her body for death rather than sex. Simply, it was an easier choice with her predisposition towards the darker of the two—with her necromantic abilities—but even so, the idea was horrifying. Horrifying enough that she debated assassinating the king and his men right then and there.

She tried.

She reached out with her magic, a charcoal smoke visible only to her, and coiled it up the king's legs, circling his form and twining its tendrils up around his throat. Then, with the slightest conscious decision, she *squeezed.*

And nothing happened.

Malik raised a groomed brow in question. "If you're trying something, you'll be disappointed. I'm protected from all magics." A breath. "My men are, too, if you were considering."

She was.

It wasn't worth the risk of attempting to harm his men if the king could not be touched. That was a surefire way to end up positively dead.

Sighing, she loosened her hold, and the smoke slithered from him, crawling back to her over the floor and bleeding back into her skin. It filled her with the coolness of night and the scent of cinnamon. She didn't see a Veritasium Medallion, but that didn't mean that he didn't have the magic-repelling silver somewhere on his person.

"You're a despicable fucking asshole," she spit.

He only grinned. "You don't get to be king by playing nice, Little Liar. Although, you never let me finish. You won't be a slave, rather, you will be an esteemed employee and paid handsomely, I assure you."

Valine's interest was piqued. "How much exactly?"

He named a sum.

"Monthly," he added.

Valine was floored. It was an astronomical amount. More than she dared to hope for in her lifetime and it was a *monthly* fee. It was enough for her to obliterate her self-imposed line in the sand and leap over it. With that amount she could pay off all her debts and then some. With so much money she could live comfortably. Forever.

Valine grinned.

"Now, why didn't you start with that, dear king?" She jingled the buckles on her restraints. "If we have an agreement, is there any chance these can be removed?"

Malik cocked his head to the side and signaled to the third figure in the room, the one she'd yet to interact with. He stepped forward, and this man embodied everything about a Valmotti warrior.

The years of training Valmotti had to go through were grueling and intense, shaping them into the finest weapons the continent had to offer. From near infancy to early adulthood, they were trained in every weapon from each kingdom until they were proficient enough to best a master. Their education included identification of poisons and their following symptoms, in addition to survival in all climes. First and foremost, they were protectors of the innocent, but they were more dangerous than the Ōrdinem or the Vanguard. Both of which were prestigious societies dedicated to the training and enlisting of assassins and warriors.

The Valmotti had a short, well-groomed beard, sculpted brows, fine lips, and a vivid set of amber eyes narrowed in concentration. It was clear he was the tallest of the three and the most muscular. His skin was warm brown, several shades darker than the king's, but his hair was the same raven black—albeit longer, the length brushing his shoulders.

"Sarim, care to help the lady?"

"You're a pain in my ass, prince, you know that?" Sarim's voice was gravelly but playful, and a light glittered in his eyes, unfitting for the current circumstances.

Malik's mouth twitched, and at first, Valine thought there was a rift between the two—one she considered driving a wedge between to further her means and potentially gain the upper hand—but she was mistaken. Sarim was teasing Malik, and Malik was letting him because they were *friends*. She inwardly sighed.

"Careful there, Mal, you almost cracked a smile that time," Alastair announced, bumping shoulders with the king before he turned his attention towards her. "He hates when Sarim calls him 'prince,' but that just makes him want to do it more."

The king flipped him off.

Sarim took Valine's wrists in his large hands and looked her dead in the face, his amber eyes burning. "If you attempt to harm me, these go back on with a black eye and a broken nose to accompany it."

Valine feigned innocence. "I would never! Besides, don't you have codes about beating women as a Valmotti Warrior?"

Sarim smirked with amusement. "If you know I'm Valmotti, then you know that we do not consider female warriors lesser. Therefore, your status as an assassin places you safely within my ethics."

"Well shit," she muttered, and Sarim laughed low in his throat. The rumbling noise sent shivers down her body and through her core. She chastised herself; she didn't need to be sexually aware of two of her should-be captors, but again, Sarim was very attractive as well. Frankly, they all were.

Pulling her wrist towards him, she attempted to cool herself while his fingers expertly worked the straps. They loosened, and as he bent to her ankles, he stared up at her from heavy lids. She quite liked the view.

"Kick me, and I swear—"

"Worry not, Sarim. I feel no need to get any more blood on these boots." Captain Ishaq's blood still stained the leather—and her skirt, too.

He removed the last of the manacles and stood. Valine also got to her feet, reaching only to Sarim's chest. She crossed her arms, stared up at him, and skirted around him.

With a confident stride, she crossed the room to Malik, and he watched her with amusement. The moonlight hit his eyes, and for a second, they glittered silver. She took in this man, the King of Adraali, holding so much power in his grasp, her life in his hand. But in them, she knew he saw her, too. Saw her not as an adversary, or a tool he now possessed, but as a woman who could bring him the world.

Her lips pulled up.

"When do we start?"

CHAPTER THREE

Life and Death

Blind trust was something Valine never understood, and it seemed she and the king had that in common. He warned her, as he handed her a thin shawl that future attempts on his life would not be appreciated, and he hoped that his generous payment would be enough for her to joyfully stay in his employ. She wasn't a fool; she knew this was the best thing she was ever going to get. Even then, she knew her word wasn't going to be enough. Malik informed her there were servants she'd encounter that wouldn't simply be chambermaids or cooks but rather spies, and she'd be checked in on. She expected nothing less of the dark monarch.

Surprisingly enough, they returned her stolen weapons to her without a word. Seems some form of trust was at present—she'd remember that for the future.

Alastair led them out, followed by Malik and then herself, with Sarim taking up the rear. Once they were out on the cobbles, a fifth shadow joined their ensemble, and Malik nodded to them. They formed a cage around Valine, hoods up with Alastair whistling without a care. To her right, the king's face was turned to her, the shadows from the hood obscuring those mysterious eyes. But she felt him watching.

The night was cold, just on the cusp of the Cold Season, and frost threatened to coat the trees. Even then, the shawl they'd given her was nowhere near warm enough, especially in her soaking-wet state. Instead of shivering and chattering her teeth like she wanted to, she gritted and powered through.

"I don't suppose we'll be announcing my placement at the palace as an assassin."

"No," Malik chuckled. "You'll be posing as an unattached companion to the hopeful brides next year."

"You're betrothed?"

"Saints, no." He was aghast. "But I've been receiving pressure from neighboring kingdoms to commit and solidify alliances, so they're sending their daughters in hopes of winning my heart and fealty. We have not confirmed who yet will arrive.

"You will be learning their secrets and seeing where it gets us. Perhaps the Princess of Valencya prefers to fuck women? Or the Duchess of Ophette has a terrible drug addiction? Whatever gets them out of my home and their father's coins in my pockets."

"Or their kingdoms under your thumb?" she commented dryly.

Malik smiled. "You learn fast."

They walked in silence for a few moments, their footsteps and Alastair's whistling the only sound from the quintet. Around them were townhouses shuttered against the night, taverns and pubs quietly hosting only the most committed or desolate of drinkers. Oil lamps glowed gold over the street, some luxmancer and pyromancer-powered lighting reflecting the previous night's rainfall on the black rocks. Night-blooming jasmine scented the air, the tiny white flowers nestled in beds along the walk, short wrought iron fences guarding them. Tall deciduous trees surrounded them, allowing only a sliver of starlight to penetrate the canopy above. They were in Astra, the old quarter where King Malik's father, Saalim Halil Amir, swore to protect the old growth and integrity of heritage buildings.

Astra and Nyxia were twin cities, most establishments congregating on the line between the two, known as the Edge—or Astra's Edge, and the reverse towards Nyxia's in the case of being in the perspective of the latter. The most notable differences were that Astra was older and seedier, and Nyxia was traditional and contained the palace.

Under Saalim's peaceful rule, this area flourished. The entire city prospered, but after his untimely death and the several years since, Astra fell into corruption. Now, it boasted a large amount of organized crime, devious associations, and cabals—associations and cabals that Valine now realized Malik had his fingers in.

In the distance sat the castle. It was a massive gothic structure of obsidian, granite, and slate, tall spires stretching into the star-scattered sky. Stained glass windows in emerald, gold, and ruby adorned the towers, diamond-pane windows glowed with warmth from the many rooms and halls boasted throughout. The roofs were tiled in the deepest sage, and gargoyle statues perched on the eves, watching over the city. Towers and turrets hanging onto the fringes of the structure like fingers of a beast.

Valine had never been inside the palace herself, but she'd heard it was dark and beautiful. Brutal and lovely. She'd heard that cruelty streaked the walls as sure as gold dripped from the ceilings.

"In addition to your companion status, I'll also require you to leave the kingdom on occasion. Certain kings and lords will not bend to my rule, and I'll need them taken care of."

Valine nearly stopped in her tracks. "That was never part of the deal."

"For the amount I'm paying you, I could be asking you to scrub chamber pots."

She wrinkled her nose. "The castle doesn't have plumbing?"

Ever since hydromancers existed, people have used hydromancer-powered plumbing, but some kingdoms have shunned the use of magic, refusing the new and upholding archaic and ridiculous practices on the foundation of tradition. Runell was one such kingdom—she hadn't anticipated Adraali would also be one of them. Especially since most of the establishments—if they were not questionable locations—had it.

"Of course, it does. But that's not my point," Malik answered, nearly offended.

"I have a rule against working with royals. I drew the line at working for you."

This time, he actually stopped, and their entourage continued as if this was something they expected. Malik backed her up against the stone pillar of a bridge they were about to cross. He was so close she could smell the cloves on his breath, feel the heat from his body. He pressed her against the stone, his hands hot and rough on her shoulders.

"I don't give a fuck if you have any qualms. You made a line? Draw a new one. There are certain things I will allow you to refuse me. You choose not to use sex as a weapon? Fine. If you know a better way to get the job done, then, by all means, do it. If you prefer to use poison rather than a blade? Great. If you think we should wait to target a mark for a different time? I understand; I defer to you because death is your area of expertise. But if you try to tell me you won't kill a sniveling duke when I know you pulled every single one of Ishaq's teeth from his mouth, then you're full of shit. You want to be known as a coward and an embarrassment?"

Valine's worst trait erupted from her. Her hot-headedness.

"Fuck you."

Without thinking, without consideration, she shoved the king. He stumbled back a step, and she took the moment to punch him square in the jaw. Surprise lit them both up, and he returned to her with higher intensity and fervor, his arm pinned against her neck and his body flush against her. His hood had fallen back, and she saw the raw fury in his beguiling gaze—the blood dripping from the cut on his lip.

She realized it wasn't just his arm he had against her throat, but a short blade.

"Don't you *ever*—" he said with lethal calm, and panic flickered through her, "—lay a finger on me again. Or I will ensure you lose that finger, and any further transgressions will be punished accordingly." He was so composed.

Blood leaked down his mouth and his chin. She watched it disappear into the stubble that was turning into a beard, and she held her breath, containing her ire. She felt her lungs expand, her heart race. Blood rushed her face and burned beneath her skin.

"Is that a promise?" she taunted.

"Don't play coy, assassin. You speak freely because you are afraid, and you think by acting boldly it will protect you. Not only are you a coward, but you are impulsive. The only reason you have those self-imposed rules is because you have something to hide." His voice was low, careful as his hand ghosted down her body. "If you want to keep those highborn roots of yours hidden," he paused, searching her gaze as her breath caught. "Try harder."

He released her, and she felt stripped. He'd seen right through her, and she felt naked and vulnerable before him. Her façade had been thin as tissue. Malik's words were wind against it, and it took so little for him to unveil her. The only solace was that she kept the worst of her secrets buried inside, beneath the dirt over her grave and inside the casket of her soul.

"What gave me away?"

A slight twitch of his lips indicated that he didn't quite *know*, but she'd confirmed it. She cursed herself for slipping up again and strengthening his suspicions.

Malik swiped the blood on his mouth with the pad of his thumb, and the movement captivated her. He stared at it for a moment before continuing.

"The cadence of your words, you speak softer than commonfolk. Not to mention, all of your blades are *very* expensive, so you have a penchant for luxury born either of wealth or the lack thereof." As he said this, he tossed her the jeweled blade she'd used to kill Ishaq—the one that *was* hidden in her boot.

It seemed the king was talented in the arts of sleight-of-hand. It irked her.

Valine caught her thieved property in the air and snarled. The blade was special. Amethyst, opal, and gold, held in a filigree design of blackberry. Leaves, thorns, berries and all. It was her first and most treasured. It also had imbued properties that detected poisons, turning the blade to a sickly green-violet shade.

"Stay on your toes, Little Liar."

He turned on his heel, pulled up his hood, and continued walking with the rest of the group. The golden lamps caught his silhouette and ringed it with an aura. It made him look regal. Powerful. Like the coronas that circled the heads of saints. Malik held his back straight and walked with the grace of power, wealth, and status. It was filled with confidence, and even from their distance, she knew a smug grin caught his mouth.

Valine was furious that he was so sure she would follow him. The wrath flowed hot and red through her because not only did he hold her entire career at his mercy, but it was humiliation to trail after him like a beaten dog for its master.

Mustering all the dignity she could and ignoring the cold penetrating her bones, she stepped onto the bridge and continued the trek to Malik and her fate.

They entered through the waterways. A large wooden wheel churned up the water from the river—a backup in case the hydromancer-powered machinery failed—and they slipped behind it one by one and through the hidden passage there. It was dark, but what little she could see was rock. They were surrounded by stone and the thrumming of the waterwheel. The vibrations sent tremors through her body and made the already slick stones near treacherous. The tunnel was wet and dank, filled with the scent of damp stone and iron. A whispered word and the gloom was illuminated by a ball of sapphire light conjured by Alastair.

Because, of course, the Runellian was a mage.

She wondered what his affinity was. Luxmancy? Pyromancy?

Alistair caught her eyeing this magic, and he grinned. "Vitamancer."

Dread hit her like a lead block.

Not a simple light mage or even a fire mage, but a fucking *life* mage.

Valine's stomach sank. What a sick joke. He was her opposite. A vitamancer. She'd never encountered her mirror equal in all of her twenty-six years. Valine couldn't afford a complication like that. Not only was he able to nullify her abilities, but his magic stemmed from life. Therefore, he was constantly powered by the vitality of animals, of the people around him, of his own damned *self*. Death was only in so many places, and she had to ensure those tools were at her disposal. She had a certain level of reserves within her, but if she had access to instruments of death and decay, then she had to pull less from herself and take from them. If those were unavailable, then her magic drew *her* closer to the afterlife.

The only comfort she felt from this was that she nullified his abilities as well.

A common misconception was that vitamancers took life from themselves and others, but that wasn't the case. In fact, the opposite was true. They were charged by life. That life circled through them and they then poured more of it out. There had been cases of people living two centuries from prolonged contact with a vitamancer.

They magnified life.

It made sense why Malik kept him around. However, what didn't make sense was why his family sent him away, even if he was out whoring and drinking. To shun a vitamancer, even in Runell was the epitome of stupidity. Either they must not have known, or it was a cover. Or even Malik had enough blackmail to retain the mage's presence at his side.

Alastair began leading them further into the bowels of the castle, and Malik followed closely behind him. Valine remained rooted in place, still reigning in her shock as Sarim prodded her forward with an elbow. She shook herself out of it as a feminine giggle startled her. She had assumed the figure that had joined their entourage was a lean male, but evidently, it was a tall and willowy woman.

She shook off her hood, and being in her presence was like taking a personal blow to her self-esteem. This woman was magnificent. She was sun-kissed with long, sleek blonde hair the color of starlight. Her eyes were fierce and long-lashed, bright green-gold and cunning. Her features were exquisite; full red lips, high and regal cheekbones, a jaw so sharp it could cut glass, brows perfectly arched and severe on her beautiful face.

Valine had never found herself particularly attracted to women, but this one had her questioning herself.

"Freyja Nahara," the woman introduced. Her accent was the lilting tone of Thycca, the same that Valine herself had donned to con Ishaq with.

"Valine Hardgrave."

Freyja's mouth twitched as if prepared to call her lie. They both knew Hardgrave was a pseudonym. An assassin with the last name containing "grave"? It was bullshit.

"Charmed," she said instead.

Turning back to the others, Valine picked up the pace and traversed the remainder of the tunnel. They ascended several flights of stairs. Each stair brought them to progressively drier and warmer air and stones, lit only by Alastair's indigo vitamancy. The scent of cinnamon, black orchid, and tobacco caught Valine's attention, and she was surprised to see lanterns hanging on the walls on the seventh landing.

At the end of the tunnel—which Valine now realized had turned into a hallway with several others attached—was not a dead-end like she thought, but the back of a very large tapestry. Pulling the tapestry back, Alastair ushered them all through, and as Valine entered, she was taken aback.

Not only were they well within the palace…they were in the throne room.

Valine took in her surroundings, awestruck.

The room was like a cathedral. A tall, arched ceiling reached to a golden point, gold leaf on the filigree designs, skylights of emerald stained glass ruled over them. Walls of deepest and gleaming obsidian, pillars of gilt black marble. The floor was a massive expanse of jet inset with an enormous motif of a fanged serpent and orchids. At the tail of the snake, as if the monster were protecting it, stood a grand throne. Plush viridian velvet, black iron, and bright gold. It sat on a three-tiered dais, alternating from onyx to more of that auric metal. Wrought iron chandeliers dripped emeralds, diamonds, and rubies, flouting the lavishness of the royal wealth. Crimson, petaled sconces on the walls held candles that smelled of cloves, and cinnamon, black orchid bouquets graced each of the statues of the patrons. The tapestry they'd entered from behind was deep evergreen emblazoned with a massive pair of leathery daemon wings. They were illustrated in ebony and gilded with details. Fine florals and forest illustrations graced it, blackberries wrought in an aura, wolves gleaming, mountains glittering. Across from it was its mirror, the same depiction only with a golden corona haloing clasped hands.

Valine was so caught up in the grandeur she nearly jumped out of her skin when an explosion erupted from the tunnel.

CHAPTER FOUR

Valine didn't think. She just moved. Tackling Freyja to the floor, she wrapped her arms around the other woman's head and shielded her body with her own. For a moment, she didn't breathe. For a moment, she only locked eyes with Freyja, hazel meeting Earth.

"Are you okay?" Valine whispered.

"I'm fine," Freyja answered, slightly breathless. Her eyes searched Valine's face, and she scrambled to get off the other woman.

Valine got to her feet and was prepared to offer Freyja her hand, but the other woman was already up. She glanced behind Valine, and she followed her gaze. Behind them, Malik leaned against his throne, and his expression was...amused.

"Mayhap I should have mentioned that Freyja is a ruin-mancer and that she would be destroying the tunnel behind us.

Too many people know about it. But not to worry, a new passage will be constructed in due time."

Malik had a smirk about him, his light eyes predatory and interested. Valine realized with a start that she was seeing attraction. That something about her on Freyja had spiked something in the dark ruler. Interesting. Valine made a mental note to file that away for future experimentation.

Freyja was perilously close to the explosion. Had Valine known that the ruinmancer—a destruction mage—was aware of the distance needed from the ruin, she would have acted differently.

The tapestry hardly billowed, and the dust had already settled behind it. The sound had been much larger than the actual explosion. It hadn't shaken the foundations or even the room. The hanging jewels on the chandeliers jittered the slightest as if a breeze had passed by, but otherwise, the palace was unscathed and unaffected. Even then, Freyja had been able to contain it so well, Valine doubted anyone even woke from their beds.

"That information may have benefited all parties present," she replied curtly.

"On the contrary," the king demurred, thumbing his lip, "I'm quite entertained by this outcome."

His eyes were hungry, and Valine flushed.

"Alistair, Freyja, Sarim, you may retire for the night. Get some rest," Malik commanded.

"Are you sure, Mal?" Sarim asked carefully, amber eyes flitting to Valine. She resisted the urge to react.

"I am," Malik confirmed with a flick of his head. "We'll be all right."

The trio acquiesced and disappeared through the enormous arched door, the obsidian and gold blending in with the rest of the throne room. The door opened and closed with a squeal of hinges. With the slamming of it a final sound to their departure, Malik turned to Valine.

They were silent in their regarding of each other. With the slightest lift of his head, Malik sat himself on the dais steps, bringing a knee up and stretching his other out. The king was actually *lounging*. He was at ease, and his dark cloak spread out behind him, his black vest tight against his abdomen—a garment she knew was popular in Adraali—with a corseted back. It only enhanced the king's good looks and trim waist.

"I will show you to your rooms shortly, but I wish to speak with you freely here."

"I am at your service, My King."

Malik's lips pulled up in the corner. "I see you've changed your attitude since the bridge."

"I have," Valine bit out.

"Glad to see it. What do you know of the Thyccan royal family?"

Valine answered immediately. "The king has two daughters, one married to a lord in the north-east—Melusda, I believe. The younger of the two went to university to study botany and herbalism, but now her father's coffers are running dry, and her apothecary isn't bringing in the revenue he wished. He's hoping to marry her off rich to pay off his debts when he made some poor public investments."

"Very good. That would be Liesl. She is one of the hopeful brides being sent to the palace." He tapped his fingers on his knees. "Being fiscally irresponsible is not enough to bring her father to bend the knee. We need a little more than that."

"I shall work on it."

"Delightful."

Valine shifted her weight. She was still wet and very much cold from the midnight jaunt and bucket bath courtesy of Alastair. The king noticed her discomfort. Unclipping his cloak from his shoulders, he beckoned her closer. She was too cold to fight much, but she did huff for good measure.

"I don't do apologies very well, but I regret punching you," Valine ground out.

"I never asked for one, but the sentiment is appreciated, nonetheless."

Without the cloak, she could confirm that the vest was, in fact, corseted, with burgundy boning and restraints. The rings, of course, were gold.

Approaching the king, she sat next to him, and he wrapped her in the swath of fabric. It was warm and scented with black orchids, tobacco, and cloves—she wondered if that scent was from cigarettes or perhaps the candles. Beside her, the king's body heat was like an open fire, and she forced herself not to lean into him.

"Dubon?"

Valine pulled the cloak up to her mouth, warming her fingers in the fabric. Another eastern country. "Not much on the king and queen. They're quite boring. Three children, two boys, and a daughter. The crown prince is the dutiful son, the second son promised to take over lands to the north-east with a political marriage to the Ixaithan princess. I'm assuming the daughter is set to be another bride hopeful?"

"Correct, but so is the Ixiathan princess. Your intel is a few days late. The marriage was called off due to the second son admitting he preferred to never procreate. How do you know so much about the continent's politics?"

Valine shrugged, attempting to deflect. "When you're an assassin, it pays to know who to avoid and what blood wars not to become involved in."

She could feel Malik's burning gaze on her. Reaching out, he clasped her jawline in his hand, forcing her to look at him. He was firm, his eyes intense. "What do you know about the city of Cydra?"

Panic flared through her, setting her heart racing. Ice plunged through her veins, and blood ran from her face. She knew she was caught. Malik quite literally held her in place, and she knew the quick shot of alarm that had widened her eyes was not missed.

Valine swallowed. "This one feels like a trick question."

"It's not. You and I both know the answer to this one, so why don't you just tell me."

"Cydra is my family's lands," she finally admitted.

Malik quirked a brow, interest piqued, his face open for her to continue.

"My father was a cruel beast. Sired more illegitimate children than legitimate. I was his first daughter, the fourth child by my mother. I was an embarrassment. He's not missed. My eldest brother now rules Cydra with his wife. I've never met her." Her answers were ticked off, automatic.

Cydra was second only to Gallae, the capital city of Runell. She was hardly removed from royalty, but she'd done everything possible to make the world forget it.

"Did you kill your father?"

Valine stared him hard in the eyes, his strong grip still clutched her. She said without flinching, without blinking. "Yes."

"Why?" Was all Malik asked, his hand dropping.

"He was a bastard. He would beat us, and any daughter born of his marriage after me was killed." Valine swallowed, forcing down her fury. That hot temper she'd inherited from the brute rising. She fought it by standing before the king, shaking out her damp hair. He watched her, and she saw him look her up and down, drinking in the wet fabric clinging to her cold skin, the bare flesh that remained exposed.

"He shouldn't have been so surprised when I murdered him. But oh, he was. Perhaps he'd thought me so weak and inconsequential that I'd never have the power to silence his continued siring. To me, he was the inconsequential one, not even important enough to be the first man I'd killed. Nor lucky number three, or even magical number seven." She chuckled darkly. "No, he was basic and simple number four."

Malik got to his feet and stood before her. "What did you tell him before he died?"

The assassin smiled. "I told him that all his hopes and dreams would die with me. That I was never going to be the pure and chaste daughter he wanted me to be. I told him that I would fuck all the men I wanted, that I would be a whore if that's what I desired. I told him I would burn down the Desdemon name, bury it beneath shame and disgrace. I told him that I would ensure his legacy ends with despair."

Malik's hand came to rest on her waist, his fingers tightened, pulling her closer. "Did you?" he whispered, lust darkening his eyes. "Did you fuck all the men you wanted? Burn down the Desdemon name?"

Her eyes flickered to his lips. To the wound she'd given him. From beneath her lashes, she rasped, "Not yet, but I am not finished."

His fingers drifted beneath her breast, and she shuddered—not in revulsion like what Ishaq had elicited, but in pleasure. Her eyelids fluttered. "I'd like to help you with those plans. Would that interest you?"

She knew the double entendre he was giving her, and the prospect of bedding a king was incredibly alluring, but she had rules she wouldn't break. "I must be clear; my services as an assassin are the only ones to be paid for. I do not sell my body, and I do not fuck the men who employ me."

"I would not dream of buying anything else," he breathed, his other hand cupping her chin. "Your boundaries are noted, though I must admit, I am disappointed."

"I am open to flirtation," she managed, her desire warring against her values.

He grinned. "Then, I look forward to the wonderful and terrible future we will wreak."

"As will I."

They stayed like that for a minute. Frozen and electric. She didn't know what had come over her. What possessed her to stay in the king's arms, when only an hour before, she'd punched him in the face, and he'd held a blade to her throat, pinning her to the bridge. When she quite literally told him, she wasn't going to sleep with him, despite the stirrings in her wanting to. Perhaps it *was* raw sexual energy. Perhaps it was lust. Perhaps it was animal attraction. Or maybe even it was the draw of a hate fuck. She didn't know the king, nor did she particularly like him. But sex…sex was definitely a desire.

Malik broke from her.

"I will show you to your room. You are cold and require rest."

They left the throne room and the king escorted her through the viridian and onyx and golden halls. The palace was dark and beautiful, luxurious and ornate. Guards in dark livery and armor patrolled. With a simple nod from the monarch, they were unbothered. Ascending three floors, they came to a wing lighter than others—walls of diamond-pane windows were set into the stone, ironwood doors opposite. He brought her to the third door.

"These are your quarters. If you require anything, please let me know. You will be assigned servants in the morning. You are not to tell anyone what your role is here. If you do, I'm sure I don't need to remind you, your life will be forfeit."

Valine smirked, cocking her head. "Now, why would I ever consider a foolish task like that?"

"Spies and assassins are a fickle bunch."

"Ah, but you did choose me."

The king grinned, backing her against the door, a hand above her head. "Oh, I certainly did. And I'd choose you again." Stepping back, he nodded politely. "Goodnight, Little Liar."
"Goodnight, My King."

CHAPTER FIVE

Valine was born on the death date of her grandmother. She noted this because it was the anniversary, and she felt like her heart had struggled to restart today. The day marked Valine's twenty-sixth year. It was a day she never celebrated.

Her mother told her she was a vicious woman; therefore, Valine was cursed with the sinister nature of the Desdemon matriarch. Because, of course, she was a bad omen, an ill portent if her body and soul shared such an anniversary with as a cruel creature as her. It mattered little that Valine was one of her father's few legitimate children, and it mattered even less to her mother that even as a babe, she'd been born with beauty and lacked a colicky cry. No, she was foisted onto the family's wet nurse rather than her own mother's breast. The plethora of her father's offspring had been nourished by the woman, bastard and legitimate alike, and how her mother tolerated her father's infidelity, she'd never know. She was proud, and he was wealthy. Perhaps that was enough for a woman of high bearing who valued her image and glamorous finery.

Valine would not have submitted to a man like that.

Her mother was very different than her wet nurse. Her mother was sharp, slender, and cool, while the woman was soft, plump, and warm. She also had tired brown eyes to her mother's vibrant jade. This brokered no surprise by the fact that her father's entire brood had been latched onto her like a disease. Valine had never been permitted to know her name. She'd been treated like little more than a slave to the Desdemon household, yet for many years she'd been Valine's whole world.

Because Valine was born female, she was her father's most grievous embarrassment and she was treated worse than her father's male bastards. Last she was able to count, his seed produced fifteen, nine of which were male. And those were only the ones she knew of.

It mattered no more; his death ended her father's sleazy ways.

Valine thought of this not only because it was her birth date but because she woke wrapped in a bed of emerald satin, golden midmorning light cast across the sheets, heavy wood furniture standing proudly in the room, with a servant standing at the door. This servant was like her wet nurse. A slave to the crown rather than the Desdemon name.

"Miss Valine, the king requests your presence in the library. I will assist you in getting ready."

Valine blinked the sleep from her eyes. "Yes, of course."

She'd not bothered with a bath last night; she was much too tired. Instead, she'd stripped off all her ruined clothes, left the leather on the floor, and threw the fabric in the grand fireplace. After washing her hands and face in the attached bathroom, she'd collapsed into the bed naked, half wishing the king would join her.

Shaking the thoughts from her head, she shucked off the covers and motioned for the maid to enter the room. From the wardrobe, the woman pulled out a garment of storm silk and dark leather. It was a long-sleeved, wrapped style tunic and leggings. In addition, the woman gathered heavy socks and thigh-high boots of gleaming black, as well as one of the corsets that were singular to Adraali. It was sculpted to the female form, the breasts covered in silver filigree, the hard case of it like a frosted ocean.

The ivory and ebony tiles were cold against her bare feet, but Valine was guided to the adjoining bathroom, where a large porcelain tub sat in the center. Within moments, the servant was filling the bath with hot water and scented oils of lemongrass and citrus.

Valine took a second to admire herself in the large, gilt, floor-length mirror. She was slender with all the right curves, a contrast of starlight and midnight with her rich dark hair and creamy skin. Her eyes were a bruised sky, dark brown with the barest hint of lilac, just enough to question their depth and truth.

Of course, she could have been lovely and blemish-free, but the life of an assassin was not kind, and scars scattered her flesh with knife marks and burns and slashes and bites. There were old claw tracks and even a bullet wound, signs of a hard-worn life. How different things could have been had her father not been such a prick. Had she not been born with death magic.

Valine could see the servant adjusting the bath in the background, paying no mind to the naked assassin. It was pointless when Valine covered an ugly scar upon her ribs.

When Valine stepped into the tub, she nearly moaned with pleasure. The heat was glorious, and the smell wondrous. Sinking into the hot bath, Valine leaned back, closed her eyes, and enjoyed the sensation for a moment. The coils of steam, the smell of the oils, the fog on the stained glass windows.

The servant brought over a silver pitcher and washed her hair, but even as Valine relaxed into the bath and the woman's touch, she didn't truly *relax*. No adept assassin really could. Assassins had enemies, and Malik had made it no secret that servants and maids were spies. As the woman massaged lavender soap into Valine's hair, she tilted her gaze to her.

The woman was perhaps a decade younger than her mother, putting her close to forty. She had soft, red hair, nothing like Alastair's burning waves, but rather a cinnamon blend of a shade. It was tied at the nape of her neck in an elegant twist. It was a pretty look, and it showcased the woman's slender neck. Her eyes were earthen brown, like the soil beneath the hawthorn tree at Desdemon Manor. They were wide, open and inviting, much like the tree's shade on a mild, Hot Season day.

"What is your name?" Valine inquired, letting scented water fall from her cupped hand.

The woman smiled lightly, politely. "Diana, Miss Valine."

"Just Valine is fine."

"As you wish, Valine."

Diana continued in her ministrations, massaging lemon oil into her hair and twisting Valine's long locks away from her damp skin and over the lip of her bathtub. Producing a file, Diana took Valine's hand and cleaned beneath her nails, despite her best efforts last night, grime and blood still caked beneath them. Diana did not comment. Once the nails were shaped and cleaned, Diana took up a sponge and set to work on Valine's sore back, scrubbing and working the strained muscles. As much as she was adept at climbing buildings, it was not kind to the body. As Diana continued, Valine felt the knots releasing and sighed softly.

"Thank Malik for me," Valine exhaled.

"What for?"

"For sending such a talented woman to keep watch on me."

"It is my duty, Valine."

"Not just that. It's not every day the king appoints one of the Ōrdinem to watch over you."

"I beg your pardon?"

Valine smiled indulgently. "You must learn to keep your weapons hidden better. Use colored glass to obscure the vibrancy of poisons, and tuck your moonstone blade deeper within your boot."

Diana flushed, embarrassment staining her cheeks. "I did not poison you."

"Oh, I know," Valine assured her. "I would've realized it immediately. You carry such tools with self-import but hide them with afterthought. They are a point of pride but also a last resort. I'll give you no reason to require them if you give me no threats to my person."

Diana breathed softly. "On my honor."

Valine nodded and lifted her foot from the hot water, examining her battered feet. They were a sight and not a pleasant one. Bruised, broken, and rough, she knew it would take pains to refine them back into what they once were in her youth.

"When did you graduate?" Valine asked as she poured more lavender oil into the bath.

"Twenty-four years ago," Diana responded as she took up a pumice stone and set to work on Valine's horrendous feet.

So, Diana was forty-two. Graduates of the Ōrdinem trained until their eighteenth year, beginning from the age of six. They studied a balance of healing and killing. It was said that learning both earned their acolytes a higher sense of morals and judgment. Upon their tenth year, they chose their path: the ending or continuing of life. Apothecary or mithridatism. Salves or poisons. Bandages or blades. More often than not, students chose the light. As revealed by her moonstone dagger, Diana had not.

Moonstone, opal, and silver for death.

Sunstone, amber, and bronze for life.

They continued the rest of the bath in some companionable silence, interspersed with conversation, Valine luxuriating while Diana labored. The women circled tentative lines of communication; Valine knew Diana's history, but Valine did not divulge her own. Malik had urged her into secrecy, and without crossing him, she was not willing to reveal any more than what Diana probably knew. Diana likely knew she was an unsavory sort—it didn't take much wisdom to see scars like hers did not come from a life of luxury.

Diana dressed her and styled her hair, adding a braid and a twist and pulling the mass over her shoulder. With an added touch of cosmetics—a shadow of smoke on her eyes, a slash of liquid black across the lids, pigment for her lashes, berry on her lips—she was a sight more appealing than the sodden and dirty mess she became after the king and his trio's visit.

On a chaise lounge were her weapons, and Valine grinned as she armed herself.

As they exited the room, a set of two young maids—one blonde, the other brunette—slipped into the room and immediately began stripping the sheets and re-dressing the bed. The heavy doors shut as Valine caught the timid eyes of the blonde. Valine realized it was likely just as many of her ladies were spies as many as others weren't.

The halls were different in the daylight, less enticing for romantic and salacious interludes and more exposed, easier for eavesdroppers and flirtations. The stone was still dark, the diamond panes and stained glass still beautiful and intricate. The gold was even more vibrant, the viridian even more bold. The gothic palace was just as stunning under the sun as it was below the moon.

Descending a staircase with Diana leading the way, nodding to passing servants and maids, Valine took it all in. In awe and to strategize. Everyone was so busy, bustling, and hurrying. Most kept their heads down, others stood proud. It was easy to pluck out which were seniors in their posts or new as a babe to others. Valine had always prided herself on her perception. It was a skill she'd gleaned back home. When she was a lady, and servants were at her every beck and call.

There was once a maid her father had fired when Valine was twelve. She had been blamed for stealing the sugared plums when it had actually been Valine. The maid had taken it with grace and with her head high. The girl was only five years older than her but had worked for the Desdemons for ten years. Part of an ancestry whose mother and father had been part of the manor for years. It was a generation, and Valine had squandered it. She should have felt guilty, and she did in pangs and twinges, but not enough to face one of her father's beatings. More so, if she thought about that young woman's fate, questioned if the young girl she'd seen at the brothel two years later was really her.

Squealing hinges brought Valine back to the present, and she found herself entering a grand room. A glass ceiling, a grand marble fireplace with a chestnut mantle, fanged beasts flanking it. Heavy bookcases lined the walls and ran in stacks across the checkered floor. There was a second level, filled with sofas and tea tables, lighted with jewel-toned lamps, the floors scattered with rich rugs—likely stolen from Ixaitha during the war and pilfered from artists' quarters. The walls were paneled in more chestnut wood or papered in lush florals, royal sapphire and deep emerald, sconces and chandeliers dripping with even more finery. This room was spectacular and opulent. It was the epitome of luxury, a wild boasting of wealth and wisdom. It was bragging rights and righteousness. It was pride and vanity.

And Valine loved it.

In a saffron armchair by the hearth lounged Malik, clothed in burgundy and ebony, utterly at ease, legs thrown over the arm, a book in hand, an arm pulled behind his head. It was a regal and yet careless pose. He looked haughty and aloof, academic and privileged, uncaring and controlled. He looked exquisite.

Catching sight of the assassin, the king placed the book down and rose. Crossing the room, he met them, a lazy smile on his handsome face.

"Thank you, Diana, you are dismissed."

Diana dipped slightly and turned on her heel, leaving Valine alone with Malik.

"So, little assassin. What magic do you possess?"

CHAPTER SIX

"Don't try to hedge this," the king began with irritation after Valine's failure to answer. "I know you're a mage. What I don't know, is exactly what sort. And do not lie, I will discover it."

Valine shifted and hid her fear and uncertainty under the pretense of leaning against a desk. "Do I have your word that you will not share this information?"

Malik raised a brow. "I am your king. You do not get to make demands of me, if I feel fit to hold a ball and announce your status, I will. But regardless, yes you have my word. You are my advantage. I'd not sully it by giving away our secrets."

There was something about the way he said "our" that sent butterflies through her core, even when he was nearly threatening her.

Valine sighed and pressed two fingers to her forehead. "I've never told anyone living this." She looked up at him, meeting his inscrutable gaze, her voice the barest of whispers. "I'm a necromancer."

Malik gave no indication of shock if he felt any. He did not startle; his mouth did not drop. The only sign that he'd truly heard her was the arching of a brow—he seemed to do that a lot. A touch of lightheadedness struck her, and she wavered from the flash of anxiety.

"You're powerful, then. Much more than I'd anticipated." A feral smile spread across his handsome face. "Valine, you have made me quite the happy man today."

Her lip curled. "Pleased to have had the privilege, Your Majesty."

"Do you have to touch to kill?"

She was silent for a beat. "No."

"Interesting. And how many times can you bring a soul back from the threshold?"

This time, a sinister smile tampered with her features. "As many times as I want."

Memories of Captain Ishaq fluttered through her, along with previous marks and kills. Her father was among those prior thoughts—she could still remember the way he'd begged. Men were awfully pathetic in those final moments, blubbery messes upon their faces and soiled linens in their pants. It was the women who'd surprised her. Women saw a resolve in her, and with that came their calm resignation.

"Show me."

"And how do you wish to see this?"

"I have a few prisoners in need of questioning."

"Of course, My King."

Malik approached her, a careful sauntering step in his fancy black boots. He came close enough that he was all she could smell. Black orchid. Tobacco. Cinnamon. Cloves. Leather. He was in her senses, in her lungs. He reached above her, and there, balanced on a bust of a long-dead queen, was an ebony crown, heavily spiked with obsidian and black diamonds, the latter only found and hewn from the Laskava Mountains.

Placing the expensive piece upon his brow, he collected an onyx velvet cloak from a solidary armchair and tossed it onto his shoulders, attached by spider-shaped epaulets. Sweeping an arm elegantly to encourage Valine to join pace with him, several guards melted from the shadows and silently led the way.

It was no small thing to say, Valine startled. She had not noticed the guards surrounding them, but truthfully, she couldn't be surprised. She was an assassin, and he was a king—a king who did not yet trust her. What did reassure her, though, was the fact that they were much too far away from the saffron chair to have heard her reveal her identity. Even so, he leaned into her.

"They did not hear our conversation." His voice was barely a breath.

She nodded, and Valine kept these small anxieties to herself. She followed the procession of guards out and down. And down. They delved further into the depths of the opulent castle until the gloom permeated, and not even the valiant rays of sun bathed the depths of the lower levels. She was guided silently, the king striding powerfully beside her, and she knew that, despite her reservations, she also appeared powerful. These guards didn't quite know what to make of her, but they knew she was no simple guest. It was also an aura she'd perfected: a low thrum of danger that pulsed against instincts, her sharp eyes, her cutting smiles, the too-clever looks, the hands that were best at ease with a blade in hand.

The flights of stairs turned from carpeted stone and glossy wood to damp cobble beneath their feet. A guard in front of them snapped their fingers, and sparks of gold erupted and formed into a molten ball—a luxmanxer. Light mages were low on the risk scale, but they did have a penchant and ability to blind. Valine recoiled at the thought.

One of the guards hurried ahead, coming to the bottom of the staircase and pushing open a set of vertical bars. The dungeon doors. Valine squared her shoulders and sauntered through with the king at her back and guards on her heels.

Malik leaned into one guard, hushed conversation following, bitter tones flowing between the two. It was strange—she couldn't hear what they were saying, but Malik's whole demeanor had her neck prickling with unease as he bit out each word. He was ensuring the guard knew he was in command, and it was only moments more before the guard hung his head in shame and acquiescence.

"Valine and I will be visiting the prisoner alone. Do not follow. Am I clear?" Malik announced, and she didn't show the surprise that gripped her.

"Understood," the three guards chorused.

With a roguish smirk, the king welcomed her forward with an upturned hand. She grinned a daemon's signature and took it, walking through the gates and holding hands with a devil.

The further they traversed into the dungeons, the more permeating the cold and dark became. Valine still held the king's fingertips but only did so because Malik had not parted them, and the guards were still within eyesight. The luxmancer had gingerly passed the light to the king, and now the fluctuating ball of light followed the king and assassin. It was a temporary magic, and the flickering and intermittent waning proved it.

Without further informing, Malik took a left-hand turn and then began the sounds of prisoners. Reedy breathing, thin words, whispers of prayers, and shouts of delusions. As they passed, dirty vagrants pressed themselves against vertical iron bars interspersed with embossed Robursium Medallions— amulets that made the wearer or bound impervious to physical harm. Valine wondered what they did for prisoners with magic—perhaps laced their food and drink with mage shade. A filthy, bearded man howled, spitting with yellow teeth. She couldn't begin to debate the man's age, but his clothing was once finery, the cerulean velvet crumbling and stained.

"You worthless fucks, you'll be in here next, and we'll see how fucking smug you are then!" The voice was gravel and spite. "I'll piss in your stew and spit on your corpses."

Malik paused and turned his head towards the prisoner. It was then the prisoner blanched and took in the man before him. Valine watched his eyes rove up and down, staring pointedly and fearfully at the treacherous crown, and Malik's coolly burning eyes.

"Darling Valine," Malik purred dangerously, and that sound embedded itself in Valine's heart as he squeezed her fingers. "Would you care for a trial run with this cretin?"

Valine cocked her head, and the man caught sight of her, startling. "Oh, I'll be much obliged, My King."

"V—Valine?" the man stuttered, and confusion struck Valine.

"Do I know you?" she asked, stepping forward in front of the king. She pulled that hand from him and twisted her fingers. It was then, as the darkness crept from her fingertips, that the unkempt ginger hair and icy eyes registered. Recognition flooded her, and she smirked, her voice turning throaty. "Oh, Lord Bayliss, how the mighty fall."

Lord Bayliss was a loud, gambling oaf, that Valine's father had favored. He was rich, charming, and once handsome. It was a façade. What crept beneath the surface was a slimy smile, a slick and untouchable attitude, and a sense of entitlement that rivaled a king's throne. He was handsy with the barmaids and servants, and word warned that he preferred girls little older than his own adolescent daughters. Valine remembered those pale eyes because, too often, they had watched her with a hunger that struck fear into her soul.

"You do remember me!"

"That I do."

"Please, dear girl, help me."

Valine cocked her head, her fingers dancing by her brow, smoke she made material threading through them. "And why would I do that?"

"I was your father's closest friend. I've known you since you were a babe. I sought justice when he was murdered."

The listed reasons were not compelling.

She cackled. "That doesn't put you in my good graces. My father was a disgusting disease of a man."

Lord Bayliss blinked rapidly, disbelief lining his haggard features. "I don't understand…you are his daughter."

"Let me put this simply." She approached the bars and let her monstrous side leap to the surface. "You, like my father, are a predatory beast that cannot be tamed nor trained. You both are rabid dogs that must be put down. You and he did not care a whit for anything but your own pursuits and gain." She bared her teeth with a manic gleam. "Because you are so like him, I will show you everything I did before I severed his soul from his body."

For a moment, Lord Bayliss did not comprehend, but when it did, true horror and terror poured from every tremor of his body. She saw the moment he caught sight of her magic when he realized it wasn't natural shadows. It was the brightness in his eyes and the stiffening of his limbs. It was the rod in his spine and the piss that ran down his leg. It was the sour scent of body odor, adrenaline, sweat, and urine. It was the first notes of death.

Finally, Valine reached through the bars—just enough that, should she have wanted to, she could touch him. She did not want, though. Instead, she swirled her middle finger down, her littlest finger arced out to the side, twisting her wrist inward as her index finger directed her necromancy to Lord Bayliss's throat. The black magic lunged out and coiled around the lord's throat.

His tongue bulged as she sank the hooks of her necromancy into him, his fingers clawing at the non-corporeal magic, unable to pry the noose from his neck. As she pulled her pointer finger in, the smoke tightened. Lord Bayliss's face turned purple, his eyes bloodshot. He began to choke, spittle leaking. It was quick when he collapsed to the soiled floor, and his life left him, but Valine still had her hooks in.

Valine felt Malik approach her, the heat from him burning her back, his tall frame towering over her shoulder, utterly enthralled. As she curled all her fingers inward, rotating her wrist with her palm down, she slowly released her fingers. The magic uncoiled from Lord Bayliss's neck and poured down his throat. Immediately, he gasped.

Bayliss's eyes widened, and he didn't just see death before him, he saw a master over it.

Malik reached up and circled her waist with a hand, the heat thrilling her as it burned through the silk and leather. His fingers tightened; his thumb circled. "Do it again, you beautiful monster," he whispered, the sound seductive.

She turned her head, and his face was right there, his eyes hungry, his luscious mouth parted. Valine looked up at him with heavy-lidded eyes, only breaths separating them.

"As you wish, My King."

CHAPTER SEVEN

Valine displayed her necromantic abilities over and over for Malik, subjecting Lord Bayliss to deaths upon deaths. He was begging after every time, and every repetition brought her back to the memories of her father's end. They cried such similar sentiments. They crowed the same curses. They whimpered identical pleas. They screamed the same useless, cruel vitriol.

When it was truly done and Malik's curiosity sated, Valine ended the performance with a swift cut, and the lord was no more. It was so simple to end him, and it was just as simple for Malik to call a guard to dispose of the body. It was clear they had heard the torture of the prisoner, but they did not know the extent or the method in which was deployed. They nodded and silently tended to their duties.

They had returned to the library, and Malik was once again in the saffron chair while Valine leaned against the hearth, staring into the eyes of a fanged daemon—Nylantia, the patroness of the night and stars. Valine favored the daemons to the saints. Their darkness answered to hers, their desires understood hers.

"Did he hurt you?" Malik asked softly.

Valine spun on her heel, and she found the king with his head bowed, crown discarded, but he was looking up at her. His hands were clutching his knees, the knuckles turning white. Beneath his short beard, his jaw was clenched, and he had difficulty swallowing. She startled because she recognized that look. He cared but was trying to contain it and whatever emotion was trying to escape.

"Did he touch you?" He paused. "Before."

She inhaled through her nose. "No. But I know there were others."

Relief deflated him in the slightest of shrugs. "I suspected as much. It's why he was down there. He attempted on Freyja during a festival in the Frost Season."

Valine calculated Lord Bayliss had been there for more than half the year. If imprisoned in the Frost Season, he'd been rotting all the way through the Blooming, Rain, Hot, and now Harvest Season. She wondered if he would have made it to the Cold Season had her necromancy not intervened. She wondered if he would have been forgotten for years in the depths of the Adraali palace.

"I'm not sorry for what I've done," Valine declared, lifting her chin.

"I never want you to be sorry for your nature. You are in my service, and you are my ally. It's what makes you irreplaceable."

Valine's heart raced, but she did not speak. She didn't think her words would come without a waver. She couldn't help but want to feel Malik's touch on her waist again, to feel those fingertips trace her skin, to stroke and wander, to feel the shape of her breasts. Her breath became thin, and arousal surged in her core, her center aching.

"Is there anything that can harm you?"

Valine laughed. "I am mortal. I can be killed."

"Can you?"

Valine stayed silent.

"Will poison affect you?" he questioned, pulling out a small vial and fiddling with it. It was an inky liquid, of what, Valine could not tell for certain—but she had a theory.

"No, and I can recognize any from sight, scent, or taste. I've studied extensively."

"Do you know what this is?" He presented the vial, and she caught the opalescent shimmer in the dark liquid.

She did. "Nylantia's Tears."

"What would happen if one was to drink it?"

She licked her lips. "A drop to help sleep, three for eternal slumber."

It was one of the gentler poisons, and it was readily used by apothecaries for sleep disturbances or merciful deaths when patients were beyond saving. A single drop in a cup of tea, and the drinker would sleep for a day and a night. Three drops spelled a silent death that painted lips black. Two drops was always an accident.

"And if you drank it?"

"Nothing."

"Prove it." And he tossed her the vial.

Valine caught it. It was warm from his palm, and Valine never lifted her eyes from his as she uncorked the vial and downed the contents without breaking their gaze. The taste was sweet, but the undertones were sour—just like blackberries. It was undeniably Nylantia's Tears, and it was unmistakably useless on her.

Moments passed. The poison coursed through her, and her necromancy destroyed it. Her lips did not blacken, she did not fall. She tossed the vial into the fire, and it exploded against the hot stone.

The king got up from his perch, and strut over to her. Before her, he towered, an enigmatic, and wild light in his eyes. "What an incredible treasure I've discovered." A hand came up to cup her cheek, fingers trailing her jaw, so dangerously close to her poisonous mouth. "And in such an exquisite form."

Valine's heart raced in her chest as his scent overwhelmed her—black orchid, tobacco, cloves. Whatever this was, it was leaving her unbalanced. She was not a lover of the king; she should not have entertained the idea of such a tryst. She was a tool, a pawn, a slave, a prisoner to the Amir throne. And yet she did not care. Her life was cut into moments and forced into cages. When one cell no longer suited her, she bent the bars and slipped to the next. This was the first time she'd been plucked from one, only to be deposited in the loosest of restraints.

It might have been an illusion.

It might have been an oubliette.

It was all she could have hoped for.

"What do you want from me?" she whispered.

"In what way?" he breathed back.

"The grand picture. I am a necromancer and an assassin. You knew this. What do you truly need from me?"

She had broken the moment, but it was deliberate and worth the flaring of his eyes. He'd been caught off guard and given her such an ability.

"You see too much."

"No, I just see more than you like. Whatever you want, let me help you. Whatever you want to achieve, let me give it to you. If you can promise me a modicum of security as a key person within these walls and to tell me the truth, I will give you the world."

"Oh, dear Valine, that's exactly what I want."

She paused, the gears turning in her head. "You want to rule the realm."

He leaned in, a glint in his eye. "I *need* to rule the realm. Runell is spreading its plague of ideals, and I am the only one who can stop it. Their plans are egregious transgressions and will only put us centuries in the past. I will be a liberator, and if that makes me a tyrant to some, then I will wear the badge with honor."

"What use will I be to you in this endeavor?"

"The most important detail. Use murder, threats, extortion. If it is within your arsenal, employ it. Eventually, every kingdom will bow to and serve me."

A gear clicked. "You cannot outright attack because of your alliances in the east; they won't allow you without breaking off. That's why you need me."

Malik nods. "Precisely. So, until I can overpower or sway them, I need you."

Self-preservation flared within Valine. "What about after? When you don't need me?"

Malik sighed. "Oh, I think I'll need you very much."

Heat squirmed in her belly, and she felt the fire of his gaze burning through her, burning through the clothes that Diana selected for her, burning into her core and seeing into the depths of her. Of her want.

"Having an assassin nearby is the best threat and security I could imagine. If there's something I want dealt with under the table then you will serve those duties as needed. As you know, running a kingdom requires much more underhanded deals than those written in the ledgers."

Valine brushed aside her growing sensations. The king had to marry a royal for appearances and alliances, fooling around with her would not be wise. Unfortunately, her latest dry spell had her toes curling in her boots.

"I want to be on more than a need-to-know basis. I know I cannot be in the council chambers due to my false position as the bridal companion, but I would like to be informed the night a meeting has concluded and filled in."

Malik acquiesced. "Acceptable."

She paused, weighing what she wanted and what she could viably ask of the king. She sought an ending. "And I want Runell to burn. I want that saints-damned kingdom destroyed."

"Once I have my empire, we will raze the ground on which it stood."

"Good." Valine grinned and it was a feral thing.

A glint of gold on the wall caught Valine's attention, and before she could spare a thought, she'd taken a step towards it. It was a solid gold pistol; the grip had a snake winding around it, and its eyes were rubies. Rose thorns wrapped the barrel, and the flower was embossed on the chamber. Below it were three ruined bullets.

"Do you have any talent for marksmanship, or are you just admiring the craftsmanship?" Malik inquired, sidling up to her.

"Both," she answered swiftly, a hand lifting towards it. A hand that she quickly dropped.

Malik seemed to have none of her reservations, and he picked up the gun, and handed it to her. She took it gingerly as he shuffled through a small box with pearl inlay nearby, from it he produced two whole bullets. He gave them to her. Tentatively, she plucked them from his palm, and slowly loaded them.

"This was my great-grandmother's pistol," Malik told her, crossing his arms behind his back. "Back when Adraali was ruled by sets of siblings, my great-grandmother was the prospective bride for my great-grandfather, and she used this gun— those bullets—to kill his three brothers. They did not want to share the throne or crown with anyone but the other."

Valine stared at the piece of history in her hands and the markers of death displayed on the wall. Bullets that had lodged inside bodies and stripped souls from their hosts. How quickly lives were snuffed out with the pulling of a golden trigger. How quickly Valine was the same.

"I've heard stories of her, Aaliyah Amir. She was a poisoner before she was queen, was she not?"

"She was. She was also a divinamancer."

Valine quirked a brow. "You have clairvoyant blood in your veins?"

"Among others." He smirked as he slid behind her, skirting his fingers along the underside of her arms, gently prodding them upward to aim. "You see the map of the continent across the room?"

She squinted until she made out the horseshoe shape on the parchment, stretching the length of a wall between two stained glass windows. It was artfully done with phoenixes, arachne, kraken, basilisks, and sand serpents bordering the edges, hemmed in with stars and flora. Parts of it were gilt, and others were touched with watercolors. It was a hundred feet away.

"I do."

His breath feathered against her hair, tickling her throat. "I want you to shoot Cydra on that map."

Valine pulled in a breath, steadying herself as she removed the safety. With Malik's long fingers still upon her, she took aim, zeroing in on the lower left quadrant of the map. She breathed again, and then she fired.

The gunshot was a crack in the air, the scent of powder sharp in her nose. Smoke coiled from the end of the ornate barrel. Two guards leaped from their posts but backed down after a wave from Malik. She didn't have to approach the map to know that she hit the mark, but Malik crossed the room and leaned down, tracing over a hole exactly where Cydra sat. She had not failed.

Malik returned and took the golden weapon from her, staring at her in wonder.

"Does anyone rival you?"

She laughed. "I must admit, my closest brother, Acanthus, is the only marksman to ever beat me. He is accurate with a pistol at two hundred yards and even more deadly with a rifle. But in other matters? No, I've not tested myself against another."

Memories of Acanthus punched her heart, the loss of that connection a physical ache. She hadn't seen her older brother in more than six years, but prior to that, not much more than a year of age had separated them. When they were children, they had raced in the Runellian fields together, ate wild blackberries till their mouths and fingers were dyed, and their bellies ached. When they were older, they practiced marksmanship together, gaining proficiency with bow and firearm. They taught each other how to fight with a blade—even though she was forbidden to do so. When they were forced to attend balls and galas, they disappeared from the courtiers with a bottle of wine and got drunk with the servants. None of her brothers had understood her like him.

"Where is he now?"

Valine pulled herself from the recesses of her memory. "Last I'd heard, he was serving as captain of the guard in Gallae."

"A prestigious position."

"Yes, it truly is." She inhaled sharply and changed the subject. "When do your prospective brides arrive?"

Malik seemed to understand immediately, and something about it nudged a feathering sensation in her chest. "Not until the Blooming Season, though we have no confirmed date. But first, I'm sending you and Sarim to Talloh ahead of our retinue. We've been invited to their blessed Tri-Moon Festival."

Valine crossed her wrists behind her back, rocking carefully on her heels. "And just why must I depart beforehand?"

Malik's stunning eyes turned hard, and a wicked smile twisted his lips.

"Because you are going to kill a king."

And without removing his gaze from hers, he lifted the gun behind him and shot Talloh on the map.

CHAPTER EIGHT

It had only been hours and a day in the palace before Valine had been sent off. After Malik informed her of her first assassination assignment, he gave her directions to divert suspicion, as well as why she and Sarim would be stopping in Luneth. She, however, did not appreciate the fact that they were being sent across the Twilight Sands to do so.

"Are you mad?" she'd crowed at the king. "Have you ever encountered sand serpents?"

Sand serpents were not typical snakes. They were massive serpentine creatures with two arms, claws, fangs, and a secondary mouth in addition to their rotating maw. Such beasts travelled beneath vast expanses of sand, able to camouflage among their surroundings, and detect vibrations in the ground. Not to mention a single one of their bites was deadly—whether that death entailed the rapid torture of their venom or being ripped to shreds.

Valine was immune to the former and had no interest in experiencing the latter.

Malik had only inclined his head. "I have not."

"Neither have I, but I have met men who've lost limbs and eyes and friends to them. They were forever haunted by the encounters."

"But they were not you. We cannot risk you being seen through the Muravo Mountain Pass before us, and going through Pravo will add weeks to the journey we cannot afford."

"But *you* are going through the pass."

"I am, which is why *you* cannot."

"It's insanity."

"Are you on good terms with any discreet basilisk riders, then?"

She thinned her lips, and shook her head.

"Then you're out of options."

And that was that. She began packing the necessary belongings in a fuss, her hot temper burning beneath her skin, and the desire to slap the king tingled in her palm. Somehow, Malik had obtained the location of where she'd been previously inhabiting, and had her things sent over. She should've been concerned; she'd been so cautious of her comings and goings, but she was too angry to much care. Besides, they were now on the same side.

The only thing that had softened her ire was a small wrapped package on her bed. She disregarded the attached note, ripping the twine free. When she tore through the parchment to the present beneath, she held her breath. It was a golden hilted dagger with a viridian blade, the design that of a basilisk in flight. The gift shone viciously in the light and Valine held it up, watching the lines of the blade gleam. Her eye had caught on the note, and she picked it up, reading.

For your twenty-sixth year. May your birthdate be merry, Little Liar.

M

It was the shock of a lifetime, yet she couldn't have beat the grin off her face with a mace.

The chestnut stallion beneath her cantered to a stop. It had been six days since she'd departed from the palace, and beside her Sarim was holding a recently drawn map of their continent, Enneive, stretched out before him. It was a jagged horseshoe-shaped landmass with Valencya and Thycca stacked at the base of the curve. After a careful consult, Sarim traced their path. They'd just crossed the borders into Luneth, and Valine resisted the urge to look southwest to Runell. Instead, she peered further into the golden dunes of sand before them. This close to the border, sand serpents were unheard of due to the impenetrable rock wall fathoms beneath the sand, but one could never be too cautious.

Terramancers had tried to recreate this wall erected by Dunia, but for some reason they never held—whether it was the serpents crashing through them, or the magic failing.

"We should reach Bastia this afternoon," Valine told him, her newly ink-stained locks escaping the white linen wrap covering her head. The heat of the morning was already aggressive, making thoughts sluggish and agitating attitudes.

Sarim's kohl-lined eyes slid to hers, dubiously. "Do you really think you can pull this off?"

Valine shrugged away his doubts. "I don't see why I can't."

He snorted. "Infiltrating Luneth's capital city and posing as—"

She silenced him with a look, her eyes daggers. There was no reason the rest of the retinue needed to know the true purpose of stopping in Bastia. Perhaps she was being paranoid. The riders were more than five yards away, and in no danger of overhearing conversation spoken in normal levels. Even so, she wasn't taking chances. This was the first mission assigned by the king, and she wasn't fucking it up.

Under the guise of acquiring supplies to cross the Twilight Sands—Luneth had deserts and stores of practicalities for such environments, but Adraali was not so prepared—the three soldiers accompanying them had a list to fill while they had alibis to secure and compromise. There was a reason she'd dyed her hair with ink, and that reason was the same one that had her carrying jewels in her satchel.

"There is a river before we reach Bastia, is there not?" Valine inquired, eyes peering at the map Sarim still had before him.

"Yes, here," he said, indicating a thin ribbon that snaked by a mountain range. "The Lazuli, it branches from the great Lapis River. We can set up camp nearby before we depart for Talloh tomorrow."

"Lady Hardgrave?"

Valine turned to one of the soldiers approaching on her left. His complexion was reddened by the sun and pockmarked, while what little of his eyes she could see beneath the draping linen were a hazy blue. She scrutinized him for a moment, attempting to recall his name.

"Yes, Olivander?"

"I do not wish to question the motives of our king, but I can't help but think it ill-advised to—"

"Do you really think you should impart the wisdom you think you speak?" Valine cut; her dark eyes shrewd. She knew what he was going to ask and she was not going to allow such ponderings. "Your king gave you an order. Do not disobey it."

He hung his head in shame. "It sounds treasonous, but I fear the Twilight Sands only spell our doom."

Valine drew in a slow breath, the hot air and dry sand burning her throat. "King Malik assigned you to this mission. Do not insult him by refusing this out of cowardice."

Olivander inhaled sharply, his brows drawing closer. "Of course, My Lady, my apologies."

"If it will assuage your concerns, you may be in charge of selecting our weapons for the journey. The bladesmith is located in the city center and I have heard tell of a flute whose notes are so piercing they are silent. Such sounds we cannot hear, but the sand serpents scream in agony from them."

A light blinked alive within Olivander's eyes.

"Here," Valine said, tossing a pouch of silver at him, "find that flute."

Olivander clutched the coins to his chest, greedily. "I will not fail my task."

"See that you don't."

Two hours later they crested a dune, and found the city of Bastia sprawling in an oasis below. The streets were strung with linens and silks, blocking out the worst of the overbearing midday sun. The buildings were squat sandstone, no taller than four floors with open air windows in curved arches, and balconies encased in hand-worked iron. Terracotta roofs glowed warmly in the sun, palms arcing across the sky and sat in clay pots. The city opened from the dunes straight into the verdant grass that was welcomed by a fountain before the city square and a bustling market. It was one of the few cities that wasn't encased within walls—its walls were somewhere underground, miles away to prevent sand serpents from entry if they managed to cross the river—it simply ceased at some point in the sand, constantly expanding along the landscape.

Except for the palace that stood proudly at the western edge of the city. Its surrounding walls were sun-bleached stone, blocks painted gold and white, some carved with depictions of saints and daemons, others displaying legends and rulers long gone. The palace itself was golden stone and ivory pillars and sapphire tiles; the roofs and windows were done up in luxurious shades of the gemstone, and those apertures that weren't made up of glass were open to the air. Waving proudly from the battlements were a series of Luneth flags, the orange background rippling, the circular series of the moon cycles blinding white under the harsh sun. Beyond, orchards and groves took up the most fertile of land and whatever greenery was left went to the wealthy denizens of the city, selfishly boasting lawns of green and flora that backed onto mansions and manors of grandeur.

Because of its proximity to the Lazuli River, the breeze carried a hint of fresh coolness. But deep within the heart of the Luneth palace fortress and worlds away from the teeming city was an expansive natural pool, rimmed with bright pink bougainvillea, shining daffodils, and the wildest array of peonies wealth and magic could buy. Paintings existed solely to capture the wonder of Luneth's most treasured garden, the Bowl of the Saints. Royals flocked to Bastia celebrations desperate for just a glimpse of the trove, commoners pledged service to the crown just to pass a flicker of it, people killed just to bear witness to it if only once.

Valine had been one of the lucky few to behold it. She had never forgotten it.

Pulling herself from the past, Valine directed four of their entourage to set up camp at the bank of the river that ribboned around the city. A mile out there was a spot that offered palms and reeds, reasonable shade, and support from the thin trees. They separated while Valine, Sarim, Olivander, and another soldier took on the city.

The slope of the dune was a sharp degree and it caused Valine to practice a careful rotation of her hips to keep saddled, and it was then when she noticed the fourth soldier staring at her lewdly. She gave him a venomous smile, and as if she had bit him, he flinched and trotted ahead.

"I imagine he wanted to sleep with you," Sarim commented from beside her.

The smile she tossed him was more playful. "I imagine his plight will end in vain."

"It's the folly of men, truly."

She couldn't help the mirth that crept into her voice. "Oh, it truly is."

When they arrived, their group divided once more, Olivander and the soldier in search of the flute, and Valine and Sarim towards their own goal. They stabled their horses for a copper and tipped a silver each for generous treatment of their steeds. The stable hand didn't seem to know what to do with two silvers to rub together, but he quickly set the horses troughs with fresh water, and a clean brush.

On foot, Valine and Sarim weaved through the packed streets, sounds of the market around them; a plethora of languages, the shuffle of feet, the yells of hawkers. The scent of roasting meat was thick in the air, and Valine even caught the luxurious scent of honeysuckle and citrus from a perfumery. The further they traversed the market, the seedier the clientele and enterprises became. Street urchins ducked elbows and cut purses, whores beckoned from brothel doors, a gambling den threw a drunk from its entrance. Closer to their destination the more potent the scent of piss and unwashed bodies became. Valine was suddenly very grateful for the required disguise, her nose and mouth covered by linen to filter the worst of the smells.

Their destination was at the final line of Enders Alley, and here even the dregs of Bastia's citizens didn't dare linger. These were opium dens and mortuaries, sick rooms and abandoned jail houses. The roads were filthy and the air just as bad.

"My father told me that Astra and Nyxia smelled like this before Malik's father's rule," Sarim told her, the scrunching of his nose evident even beneath the navy linen wrap. "It was before indoor plumbing had become commonplace and shit had run in the streets. Even still, apparently it took years for the stench to leave."

"I miss ten seconds ago when I didn't have that mental image."

Sarim laughed and clapped her on the shoulder. "You're telling me an assassin is squeamish about—"

"We are not having this conversation. Besides, I think this is the place."

Sarim's entire demeanor shifted, straightening and focusing. Valine steered them towards a hollow section of brick, squeezing into the space with little room to spare. Valine's side was pressed against Sarim's front as she fished out her brass timepiece. They had minutes for their opportunity.

They waited, Sarim's breathing controlled, his muscles taut. Valine held still, her body coiling, preparing to strike. Minutes later, the shush of leather-soled slippers met her awareness.

The mark was arriving.

As the uncoordinated shuffling continued, Valine twisted her fingers beside her, coiling that dark magic that resided in her, pulling the tendrils out, and weaving them between slender fingers. The invisible blackness wrapped her wrist—ready. She remained poised until her target emerged.

He was around her age, garbed in orange silk, gaudy with golden medallions strewn across the tunic and threaded through his greasy dark hair. She couldn't believe how unbelievably idiotic this man was, to wear *gold* and *silk* on Enders Alley. The man was *begging* to be robbed.

Once he was in range, she let loose her necromantic magic, and shot it at the unsuspecting drug lord in a deadly arrow.

It hit a barrier, and her magic scattered across the dome of protection like ash.

Her mark startled, and his dark eyes widened as he looked around for the threat that had just tried to end his weaselly existence. As he spun in place, a silver necklace swung from his neck, the labyrinth pattern the bane of Valine's existence.

"Fuck!" she seethed.

"What? What's wrong?" Sarim whispered, panic edging his tone.

"He has a Veritasium Medallion. My magic can't touch him." She pulled her magic back in. "Okay, alternate plan."

She prayed he didn't have a Robursium Medallion, too.

With that, she launched herself out of the ruined alcove, pulling out a plain dagger from her thigh sheath. She was upon him in seconds, stabbing and gutting without precision—as if she didn't know what she was doing. But she did know what she was doing, and she knew how to ensure she didn't get a drop of blood on her clothes. He fell to the ground, blood pooling around him before he'd even had a chance to scream.

The man slipped from this world with a gurgle, and Valine quickly set to work, cutting the gold chains from the drug lord and swathes of unbloodied silk. She internally thanked herself for packing a spare satchel as she began stuffing the items into it.

"You were supposed to make it look like his heart gave out, Valine." Sarim gaped at the massacre she'd created in only a handful of breaths.

"That was the plan," she grunted as the blade caught. "But plans sometimes fail. Now it looks like he was mugged. You can't tell me it's an unreasonable assumption in this area. The man was wearing *silk*, for fuck's sake." As she sliced the Veritasium Medallion from his neck, she rose and stuffed it into her pocket. It was then she caught Sarim's disbelieving expression.

She examined her blood caked hand with displeasure while Sarim continued his frozen observation, a hint of fear entering his eyes. She didn't blame him. She'd severed the man's soul from his body with hardly a second thought, and despite the fact that it was her norm, and she'd completed acts like this many times, the distanced brutality startled her. Lost in thought, Valine scrubbed her hands free of blood on some of the ruined silk, and donned a pair of dark gloves.

"Malik really doesn't understand what he got into with you," Sarim finally said.

"I'd like to believe I surpass expectations." She surveyed her arms and torso. "Any blood?"

Sarim raised his brows and searched her. His brows furrowed. "Surprisingly no."

"Lovely. Let's go. We're not done this job yet."

CHAPTER NINE

They left the body in the alley and covered him with the barest of consideration in refuse before they disappeared from the scene like ghosts. Sarim seemed to hold some reservations, but Valine squandered them as she guided him back through the market and into less-seedy—but certainly still seedy—establishments.

Ducking into a communal bathroom, Valine checked the stalls—empty—and reassessed her appearance while Sarim stood watch just inside the doorway. Sarim hadn't lied, Valine couldn't find a speck of blood on her person as she gazed into the mirror hanging over the sink, the edges of it chipped, and the whole murky. She was a bit dusty, so she wafted the worst of it from the linen, but a small bit would aid her endeavors today. She removed her gloves, and washed the still-imbedded blood from her nail beds, the chai and amber scented soap lightly dying her palms darker—better to hide any bloodstains, then. Tugging a few locks of her temporarily jet hair from its wrap, she arranged them over a shoulder, careful to tuck behind her ears. Smudging her heavy eye makeup into a deliberate style, she applied balm to her dry lips, and stuck in a pair of dangling earrings. The stones were golden topaz, citrine, and sapphire, set in pure silver. They hung heavy from her lobes as she ensured their visibility, swishing her head from side to side.

White linen. Citrus-toned jewels. Dark eyes. Black hair. Creamy skin. Lithe build.

"Passable?" she asked Sarim.

He canted his head in her direction, the golden sun catching the hard warrior planes of his face, revealing hollows and highlighting his arched cheekbones. As if lit from within by the burning star outside, his dark eyes glowed, discovering striations of gold and bronze. He truly was handsome, and even if she could only see half of the strong line of his nose and the barest hint of a widow's peak from beneath the dark linen, it was undeniable.

"I would certainly mistake you—and I have met her myself."

"It helps when your father whores about. You end up having one of those faces. See hints of yourself in every girl about your age, wondering if just maybe, those brown eyes are the same shade as yours, or the shape of your jaw is too like hers. Saints know I have at least nine illegitimate siblings, surely there are more."

Sarim's face turned questioning. "I didn't realize you were legitimate."

Valine cursed herself internally, but refused to let it show on her face, hiding it with a false smile she prayed reached her eyes. "My mother and father were married—I just don't think he understood his vows. He was fond of other women."

"He has since passed?"

Valine wondered if Malik had informed Sarim of her identity after all. This conversation was veering a little too close to one she'd already disclosed with the king.

"He has."

"I am sorry."

Valine smiled wickedly, a closed lip smirk as she looked down. "I'm not."

Sarim held out his arm. "My father was a real piece of work, too."

She took it. "Oh, do tell me, I wouldn't mind bonding over shitty parents."

Sarim threw his head back, and gave a hearty laugh; it warmed Valine's heart to evoke such a warm and genuine sound from the warrior. She squeezed his arm in support as they exited the bathrooms together, and she felt a sheathed blade beneath her hand. If anyone noticed them, she thought they could imagine what they wanted about it. It would only serve her purposes better. She raised her chin at a superior angle.

"My mother died in childbirth, and saddled my father with four children he never wanted. He sold me to the Valmotti when I was three. I saw him only twice after that, and one of those times was a fluke. The other was for a lesson on family lore and Adraalian history—so I didn't forget my heritage, supposedly. My being sold was the only way he thought he could pay off his gambling debts."

Valine tsked. "Those pesky habits have a way of biting a person."

Sarim shared a secret smile. "They do, don't they?" He gazed ahead. "I don't know what he did with my older brother, but he sent my sisters to live at a convent in Runell. At least that's what I was told." He sighed. "Frankly, I don't know what to believe. I've never checked to see if this information is true."

"Then why don't you see?" Valine didn't reveal her startle at the mention of her home country. "I'm certain Malik could arrange it if you wanted."

Sarim scoffed. "He may be king, but sending a Valmotti warrior to a country we're struggling to maintain peace with does not send a reassuring message."

Valine narrowed her eyes. "I thought our tentative alliance with Runell was secure." Runell and Adraali were both power hungry kingdoms, but one sought oppression, while the other, liberation.

"For a couple of years, it was. Until a week ago when the Gallaen princess was found dead and desecrated."

Valine stopped in her tracks, peering up at Sarim in disbelief. "Princess Gloriana is dead?" Her voice was a low hiss, but she still leveled her eyes at the crowd, ensuring she was not overheard. The person she was supposed to be would already know this information.

"That's why this plan was moved up—I thought you knew."

She cursed herself. She was so focused on Nallia's justice, and the assassination of Captain Ishaq that she'd neglected this vital piece of information. The puzzle that made up the royals was falling apart, old pieces disintegrating before new ones could be formed. If Crown Princess Gloriana was no longer, then that meant her younger sister, Princess Elliandra was now heir.

"I suppose I was otherwise engaged."

Sarim measured her carefully, his eyes carefully calculating, and she could see doubt begin to creep into his expression. Not only had she botched the drug lord kill, but she was evidently lacking in the gathering of crucial information. She switched gears.

"Look, I was doing a job for a friend, and it took up a lot of my time. Normally, I don't help friends this way, and normally, I keep an ear out for all avenues of gossip, but this is the one time I didn't."

Casting his gaze aside, Sarim seemed to struggle internally. "I worry for Malik, and as bad as it sounds, I was against him hiring you." He held up a hand in protest. "Not for the reasons you think. Yes, you are a woman, but the only problem with that is that you are a clever, vicious woman, and Malik will like that too much."

"Dear Sarim, I do believe you've paid me a compliment," she teased, leaning into him and squeezing his arm tighter. He couldn't see it, but she was grinning beneath her wrap.

He took a deep breath. "It's dangerous being the object of a king's affections. I've seen him become enamored, and then lose interest just as quickly, but this is the first time someone has equaled him, and aligned with him on so many levels."

"What are you trying to say?"

"I'm trying to tell you that everything you are, is everything he wants, and you should think carefully about what that means to you."

She met his eyes meaningfully, ensuring her conviction was conveyed. "I will."

The conversation ended with a nod as they traversed into a thickening crowd, where Valine instantly sought out the woman and urchins. The particular street kids she was looking for were obvious, eyes eager with not only the glint of hunger, but anticipation. They knew coin was coming, and someone who looked like a royal would be the bringer of it.

As they passed, Valine discreetly flicked the three urchins three silvers. They caught each coin with quick fingers and even quicker bows. Silver changed hands and she stuck her own in her pocket. Before her very eyes, they vanished on scampering feet, their dirty cheeks tight with smiles. It had been so long since Valine was hard up for money, so she wasn't quite sure how much a silver got one today, but when she first left her home, a single silver was food and board, with water and fresh linens for three days. It was also just food and board for a week. And she could stretch a single silver longer if she starved.

"That was a little obvious," Sarim hissed, fingers biting into her upper arm as she easily glided towards the healer's shop.

"Was it?" she asked innocently, so pure that Sarim instantly had his hackles up. It took him a few moments before he deflated and his grip slackened.

"You two literally have everything planned out."

"And several back-up plans." She held up a silver pin of the moon cycles that the urchins had slipped her. Taking it out of its clay imprint, she pinned it to Sarim's breast. "Like I said— expectations."

The road here widened around to accommodate a series of businesses lining up in an arc; from the left was a squat butcher shop, then a sapphire-signed tailor, a bakery with large windows, a narrow bookshop, a cozy café offering chai, and an apothecary. They entered the apothecary.

The brass bell above them announced their entry. They bypassed the greeting area and welcomed themselves to the back and only a step into the room had her nose assaulted with the scent of herbs; of star anise and lemongrass, rosemary and bergamot. The room was rough wood, the floor polished by footsteps alone, warm light spilled from gas light in an amber fixture, shelves full of books and drying herbs, anatomical models and posters scattered across tables and walls. At the center was a contraption of blown glass with bubbling liquid, and a mess of ingredients before it, lumped into indistinct piles. But what truly captured Valine's attention was the presence of noctis root, blackwort, and vervain.

Saints and daemons.

Valine stumbled back a step, urging Sarim back towards the open door and fresh air.

"She's making godsbreath. Stay away from that table." Valine's voice was low, but strained. She pointed at the red mush, black powder, and dried flower. It wasn't combined or distilled yet, but when it was, it would be deadly.

Godsbreath was one of the most dangerous poisons in Enneive, its properties reacted poorly with moisture and oxygen, and when breathed into the lungs it caused the blood vessels to swell and the lungs themselves to explode, leading to the victim drowning and suffocating in their own chests.

Sarim's fear flared in his eyes. "What about you?"

"I'm immune."

"*What?*"

"I'll explain later. Please just do what I say."

His lips tightened; she could tell from the slight pucker of the linen. "Please be careful. Malik will have my head if anything happens to you."

"I'd like to see someone try."

"*Valine.*"

"Trust me." She kept her eyes wide, pleading. She was skilled in the art of seduction, but she also knew parts of seduction that people didn't like to talk about, and it involved groundwork, and groundwork was calculated. It was this calculation Valine used to her advantage, using the softest parts of her features to persuade him to do what she wanted.

He was silent for a long moment before he finally huffed a breath and put his hand to his head.

"Fuck, you'll be the death of me."

Suddenly, the curtain of glass beads tinkled from the other room, and a woman of about forty years appeared. Her hair was graying but mostly still brown, her light skin was creamy, her cheekbones high and round, eyes of chocolate with thin lines just whispering against the edges. She was slender with curves where every man wanted them, hands calloused, and fingertips stained. She stopped short and gasped before them, then immediately bowed.

"Your Highness."

Because this woman thought she was in the presence of the Crown Princess of Luneth.

CHAPTER TEN

Sarim immediately played his part. For this impersonation to be successful, Valine would need to speak as little as possible, because she may have resembled Crown Princess Larysa Olympias, and she might be wearing her stolen jewelry, but she did not sound like her. It wasn't just the accent that was wrong, but Valine's voice was noticeably refined against the princess's light consonants and rounded, rolling vowels. Which was why the "bodyguard" was so essential.

The woman bowed deeply, and Valine waved her hand carelessly, allowing her to stand. Sarim donned an impetuous air, while Valine rediscovered the regal arrogance, she'd buried years ago. It was an effective ruse if one did not look too hard.

Valine's ink-stained locks tumbled from beneath the wrap, and the ostentatious orange earrings hung like chandeliers from her lobes. The makeup added an extra effect, enhancing the night-dark eyes both the assassin and princess possessed.

"My name is Delphinia. How might I service you, My Princess?"

She was looking at Valine, but with a sanctimonious tilt of her head in Sarim's direction, he stepped forward with a domineering presence that sent thrills of intimidation throughout the room.

"I will speak on behalf of the princess during this venture." He had deepened his voice to a sinister rumble, the normally gravelly tones were now mountains brushing mountains.

Delphinia's gaze whipped to him, and she took in his tall frame, the navy blue of his garb that was one of the official colors of Luneth, the silver moon cycle pin that was Luneth's crest, the scimitar at his hip displaying Luneth's weapon of choice, the entire ensemble that marked him as a palace guard. They'd left nothing to chance.

"Of course. How might I be of service?" she repeated.

Sarim glanced around the shop, tucking his arms behind his back as he crossed in front of Valine. His gaze snagged on a shelf of jars, multi-colored hues of green or blue or brown powders and herbs. Valine recognized many of the fragrances, many of them illegal in Runell, but looser restrictions in many of the other kingdoms. She watched him with a reproachful stare. He hovered in front of labelled jars, and though they were written in the Stygian language, she could decipher it—Stygian was one of the four languages she'd mastered, even if it was nearly a dead tongue.

All over Enneive, Ennveian was spoken—or the Common Tongue—but each kingdom did have its own language, among others. Most people could speak two languages. Valine knew five fluently—Ennevian, Adraalian, Runish, Xatho, Stygian, and enough Thyccan to get her by.

Monkshood, used for aches in the joints. Belladonna, used for ails of the stomach. Hemlock, used for agues of the lungs. In insignificant doses such poisons had healing properties. But their true doses? A seed of hemlock, the berries of belladonna, the touch of monkshood; all spelled death.

"The crown requires a very specific poison."

Delphinia sobered instantly, eyes nervously flickering to Valine while she turned the lamps down low, casting deepening shadows into the oppressive aura of the room. "You are in the presence of a great many poisons. Which do you desire?"

"We do not want the godsbreath you are brewing," Sarim declared, silencing the anxiety on Delphinia's face. She deflated in relief. "We come to you for fleur de mort."

The relief Delphinia expelled immediately evaporated, and a burst of horror gleamed in her eyes. It was unthinkable when she thought they wanted godsbreath, it was unforgivable when they asked for fleur de mort.

Fleur de mort, or daemon's blood, could only be found in Luneth. It bloomed when the first necromancer, Mrithun, was slain and his life blood nourished the roots of the rose garden he'd fallen in. He then became a patron, and in a patron's near deity, undying death he was named a daemon. Ever since, the garden in which he'd slipped from this mortal coil was cursed to bear the continent's deadliest poison. None had been able to replicate it, or its untraceable effects and none had ever survived the daemon's post-mortem curse. As a result, every rose in that garden bloomed ebony and its stem bled scarlet. The daemon cursed fleur de mort in every fiber of its composition.

"Realistically, we are not asking, madame," Sarim told her evenly. "I think it unwise to deny the discretion of the crown."

"It may take me a while to procure the ingredient," Delphinia delayed, wringing her wrists.

Valine gave her a piercing glare, one so powerful, it could be seen despite the majority facial covering. She decided to risk speaking. She could don a passable imitation, but only for so long.

"Do not insult us by pretending you do not possess it already."

Delphinia jerked, and fear skittered across her frame. Valine hedged a guess that the apothecary had never had dealings with the royal family; someone who regularly dealt with illegal merchandise and expensed poisons was not as skittish as this.

"*Now,*" Valine commanded with all the authority of Crown Princess Larysa Olympias of Luneth.

"How many doses?"

This time Sarim interjected. "One, with room for error."

Nodding once, sharply, Delphinia darted beyond the glass-beaded curtain. Sarim and Valine did not move, they shared a loaded glance and simply waited. A moment passed, then two, and then Delphinia returned, and in her newly violet gloved hand was a glass vial with murky black and red flora. It was no longer than her littlest finger with crushed petals and stem fluttering at the bottom. One dose was a pinch.

Valine, with gloves in hand plucked the vial while Sarim exchanged a pouch of gold. Feeling a miniscule twinge of shame, Valine pocketed the vial because with that purchase of poison, Delphinia had spelled more than one death. It was up to fate's hands if she would be included in that web.

"*Sankta vu,*" Valine thanked Delphinia in Stygian.

"*Vusa Ishkae,*" she responded in kind.

And without a second glance, Sarim escorted Valine out of the apothecary and into the blinding Luneth sunshine.

Once Valine and Sarim had collected Olivander and the other guard, they retrieved their horses, and returned to camp. Their hunt for the flute had been unsuccessful, yet they did not know that. They'd returned with a flute, but it was a trick. Something played on unsuspecting and foolish men by an opportunistic vendor. Valine falsely commended them—they needed not know that a flute against sand serpents did not exist. However, the soldiers back at camp had successfully erected their tents, and were now gathering up a meager amount of wood for a fire. It was sweltering during the day, but the nights plunged close to freezing.

Valine feigned a headache and retired to her tent, but truthfully, she just wanted to be alone with her thoughts—to compartmentalize her plans, and enact Malik's wishes. She stared up at the roof of her tent, made from a water-resistant, treated linen, and let one of her many facades fall. She had layers upon layers of falsehoods and trickery, doffing the guise of Larysa Olympias was a balm of relief. She dared not shed another mask.

Before they'd rejoined their group, they had stopped in an opium den, and discarded of their conspicuous linens—Sarim had traded navy for burgundy, and Valine had switched the white for taupe. Into her satchel the jewels and pin had gone, and tossed to the addicts their clothing went. They ensured they were not noticed upon arrival, and their departure was as equally inconspicuous. Thus far, everything had gone relatively smoothly, it was just that the next step risked all their lives, and Valine loathed to admit it, but she was terrified.

After some time, Valine's racing thoughts had softened edges and their shouts became a low hum as she fell asleep. She tossed and she turned, ink staining her thin pillow. It was not a restful slumber, but for a moment it was enough.

Sarim woke her for dinner with a bowl of stew. The rich scent of beef, broth, and vegetables had her immediately scrambling to sit up. She took the proffered bowl with a smile of thanks, and he handed her a hard crust of bread. She was surprised when she took a bite that the insides were warm and chewy. Sarim took a seat across from her on his own cot, digging into his own bowl.

"You and I are on watch in two hours, but I figured you wanted some time to eat first," Sarim told her between bites.

Valine swallowed a bite of carrot and potato. "I wouldn't be able to sleep anyway."

Sarim paused while dunking his bread in the broth. "Why is that?"

"Because," Valine started, stirring her stew aimlessly, anxiety making her fingers shake. She stopped. "We're all not making it to Talloh."

"Valine." Sarim's tone had her eyes shooting to his. "Malik would not have sent us through the Twilight Sands if he didn't think you had it under control. You are capable and there's something about you that he can't help but want for himself. He wouldn't risk you if he didn't think you'd make it out alive. I'd like to think he wouldn't risk me either. He's been my closest friend for the better part of my life."

"And the guards? Olivander and the others?"

Sarim hesitated glancing away. "Malik makes difficult choices, many of them ones I would not make myself. But he has a kingdom to run, and he must think of the gain versus the loss. I believe he hopes we'll all remain unscathed, but he's willing to risk soldiers if that's what it takes."

"You know this, yet you still remain loyal to him?" Valine questioned, but her reasons were not accusation, they were curiosity. If someone like Malik with a darkening soul was worthy of the faith that Sarim displayed, could Valine be revered with similar belief?

"Those he cares about, he puts above all else. That's the only reassurance I have and I choose to believe in him."

"And you're fine with that?"

"No one has ever given me more."

Valine's heart sank and before she could reply, Sarim stood, pulling up to his full 6'4" frame. There was a sad acceptance in his dark honey eyes when she caught his gaze, and she couldn't help but imagine what sort of existence quantified such softened desolation. He'd been sold, him and his family separated because of loss and greed, and while none of it had been his own choice, he'd suffered greatly for it. That was the glaring difference between their pasts. Valine had been distanced from her family by death and envy, but she had chosen it. She had been the one to wield the scythe.

"I'll see you at watch." And with that he ducked out of the tent, his dark hair slipping forward with the movement.

Valine was once again left alone, as she had originally wanted, but she found that she no longer desired her own company. Something about Sarim's grief triggered a pang in her heart, something so reminiscent of guilt and camaraderie. Perhaps because their youth glided along similar lines, perhaps it was because the way he saw his loss was likely the same way her brothers had interpreted theirs.

And it was her fault.

CHAPTER ELEVEN

Two hours later, after finishing her stew and scrubbing her face clear of any lingering dust and cosmetics, Valine donned her black riding cloak and adjusted her many knives and sheaths. She'd changed once again, as her taupe linens were not durable enough for the icy desert nights. Instead, she wore high-waisted leather leggings and a storm blue, sleeved shirt with silver chains crossing the cleavage.

As Valine stepped into the night, she noticed Olivander and the other guards had already retired for bed, the quiet sounds of blankets rustling and clothes changing mixed with the snap and crackle of the fire Sarim sat before. Leaving the barrier of the tent behind, Valine crossed the sand to the Valmotti Warrior. The night scent of cooling dunes and the faint breeze pulling from the Lazuli brought a chill as it stirred her hair. For now, the ground was golden brown, but tomorrow—too soon—the grains beneath their feet would darken to a deep plum, and the tenuous balance of their lives would shift underfoot.

As she took a seat next to Sarim, she said nothing at first, staring heavenward. Stars dotted the violet sky. White fire bursts, drawing constellations of the saints and daemons. Valine recognized several. There was Nafiza, the saint of the mind, who was once three sisters—she held a mirror. Vitus and Mrithun, the star-crossed saint and daemon lovers, forever reaching. Barak and Stymir, the conjoined twins of lightning and storm, pierced with a bolt. But the entire sky was Charna, daemon of darkness, and her daughter needed no constellation because Nylantia was every star.

"Are you in love with him?" Valine asked bluntly.

Sarim turned to her slowly, eyes slightly widened, brows ever so lifted. "Who? Malik?"

"Yes. Are you in love with the king?"

Sarim cracked a small, crooked smile, showing off a slightly more than normal pointed incisor. "No, I am not. Though once I thought I was." His eyes turned distant in remembrance. "I prefer both females and males, but when I was training as a Valmotti, I wasn't allowed to pursue either. When Malik bought my contract and ripped it up before me, I believed myself in love.

"He told me that I was free, but he would be honored if I chose to serve him—with pay, mind you. At the time, I was a freshly turned eighteen-year-old man who had never been shown a whisper of consideration, but suddenly, I had every possibility at my fingertips, offered by a crown prince, no less. Of course, I thought the barest of human decency was the prerequisite for love. So, I agreed and was given everything I'd needed and never got. I had my own chambers, clothing, coin. I had food I didn't need to fight for, I had servants—who were treated well—tending to me. I felt like the king." He scoffed to himself. "I couldn't comprehend the things I'd been given were without strings. So, I propositioned him."

Sarim met her eyes, and she realized what she'd seen earlier in his gaze. They were the same. Once upon a time, Sarim had been her—new to the palace, given every wonder the kingdom could offer, services purchased for never wanting. Both finding themselves with hearts pining for the king.

"Did he accept your pursual?" she asked, surprising herself with the knot in her chest. The king was surely no virgin, and neither was she—so why did her throat turn so thick?

"He did not."

Valine felt the jealous anxiety bleed out of her.

"He knew I was not in a healthy headspace. I'd just come from years of abuse and maltreatment, and he did not want to take advantage of me. He told me that I saw him on a pedestal he did not deserve. That a savior complex was not what he wanted to give someone so they'd bed him. He told me perhaps if, once I had worked through the damage the Valmotti had done to my psyche, he would consider it again if I found myself still seeking him."

"Have you worked through it?" Valine questioned, twisting her fingers, staring into the embers.

"I believe I have."

"And?"

The question hung in the air.

"I do not find myself yearning for him. He has become my best friend, and I owe my life to him, but no, I do not wish to be with him. For a moment," Sarim hesitated. "I thought I felt a spark…with you."

Valine's heart thundered. She could deal with romance when it was a weapon—when it was faked to serve her means. She could have sex to get to a mark when it was false to do the job. But when someone showed her their heart, and she could not give the responses they wished, she wanted to run.

"I—I…" Valine swallowed.

"It's all right, Valine." He patted her knee, resting his hand there. "I said I thought, not that I do. I think it's that I felt a kinship. A connection because I've been in your shoes."

Valine cracked a smile and a hoarse laugh. "Somehow, I can't picture you in these boots." She lifted her foot for effect, and the black leather slid up over her knee. The laces threaded were through elaborate silver eyelets, and buckles of silver serpents crossed her calves.

"You've never seen me outside of uniform, assassin. How do you know I don't wear lace blouses and velvet pants in my free time? I feel like they'd pair quite nicely with those."

"It would certainly turn heads."

"And that you do," Sarim started and turned serious. "You know there's something starting between you and Malik, don't you?"

Valine inhaled sharply, fingers reaching for his, the ones resting on her booted knee. "I feel…something for him, but I fear what it means. He is a king, he must marry a princess. He must have his queen."

"And that can't be you?"

"I—"

"As someone who was deprived of everything his entire life, consider it. Even if you lose him in the end, isn't that worth the moments you do get? Even if you do get hurt, you can say, for a time at least, you got what you wanted?"

For a moment, the world disappeared out from under her, the darkness blotting out the stars, the flames withering while Valine contemplated. She wanted, oh, she *wanted*. She was always wanting and yearning. She'd always been selfish, even when she was a precious lady in the Desdemon household. There was always more to be had. She was like a basilisk with its hoard—because everything she acquired, she kept. Even if the newer, shinier bauble was within reach, she took both.

She wondered if she had Malik, the King of Adraali, if she kept him, would he always give her more? He could take the world, and she would be part of it. She would be the hand at his side, but could she be lucky enough to be the hand on his heart?

"Are you so sure that Malik is what I want?"

"I think he's what you need."

Valine was floored. "How so?"

"You both possess a brutality and goodness in equal measure that few do. You are a matched pair and are both desperate to be understood. How could you not be drawn to such harmony?"

"You presume to know a lot about me."

"I was trained to read body language, and I have the unique perspective of once being in your position and deciphering the differences in him from ten years ago and now." Sarim sighed. "Look, I'm not trying to force you into something that you don't want. I just don't want you pining after someone you could have had before if you'd just opened your eyes."

There was a personal note to Sarim's words, and Valine cocked her head.

"I thought you didn't—?"

"Someone else."

Valine was instantly intrigued. She turned more eagerly toward him, mouth set in a toothy grin. "Who? Have I met them? Is it someone at the palace?"

Sarim glanced at her askance, opening his mouth as if he were about to speak, but instead shook his head and scoffed. "Now, why should I divulge that to you?"

"Okay, well, first of all, you pried into my love life with all the grace of a bull, and second, are we not friends? Shouldn't friends tell each other these things?"

Sarim rolled his eyes to the sky but smiled. It was a warm, genuine smile, and it lit up his handsome face. He was truly striking: dark hair, a short, groomed beard, bronzed and golden skin, eyes like amber and honey. Anyone would be blessed to see that face every morning.

"I think you should go to bed."

"Oh, my saints, I *do* know who it is!" Valine gasped. "You wouldn't be telling me to fuck off if I didn't."

"I didn't tell you to fuck—"

"Is it Freyja or Alastair?"

Sarim's lips thinned, and he stared pointedly into the fire as if his non-answer could will her away, and one of them would evaporate on the spot. Surely, Sarim wanted to combust in that moment.

Valine grinned, and clutched his shoulder excitedly. "So, when are you going to make your move?"

Sarim sighed. "I think I can handle the first watch without you. Go to sleep."

She pouted. "You're no fun."

But instead of arguing, she wrapped herself in her riding cloak, and laid down before the fire, basking in its bone-permeating heat. As she shut her eyes, flames danced behind her lids, and she wondered with whom Sarim's heart lay, and dreamed that Malik's belonged to her.

CHAPTER TWELVE

Valine's gift was death, and she was certain that it was coming that day. It wasn't that she could tell if someone sick was about to die with any more accuracy than the average person, but there was a tenebrous tension in the air. She knew their company had been touched by Mrithun.

Upon waking that morning the guards had everything packed and loaded onto the horses. That morning Valine did not reveal she did not sleep. She had listened to the sounds of Sarim's breathing, the crackle of the fire, the rustle of the wind on the tents. Sarim had not been any wiser to her careful evening of breaths and so when she arose with a yawn, he smiled and bid her good morning. She returned the smile with mirth she did not feel.

Excusing herself to the Lazuli, she relieved her bladder behind some bushes and gave herself a whore's bath with the cold river water. Splashing her face was no match for caffeine to energize, but it certainly helped dispel the dredges of sloth that pervaded her.

She was afraid and unwilling to take the next step. No one in their right mind crossed the Twilight Sands, not when the Muravo Mountain Pass existed. Even the kraken-infested seas were a safer bet. It didn't matter that the mountain pass was home to the arachne, the carriage-sized spiders did not bother travelers. They were fair and just creatures, symbols of justice and vengeance. They only sought to equal the scales of the native law of the land. Highwaymen were hesitant to thieve in the pass, fearful to stoke the arachne's wrath and be devoured. But the *plan*. That was the problem.

Sarim found her sitting on the edge of the river, watching the rushing current ripple beneath her feet. He took a seat next to her silently as she plucked reeds and shredded them in her anxious fingertips.

"You really think something is going to go wrong, don't you?" Sarim asked her quietly.

She tore the papyrus apart. "I *know* something is going to happen."

"Are you…are you a divinamancer? Malik figured you were a mage, but we didn't know what. I suspected aethermancer from the Luneth assignment."

"No, I'm no clairvoyant nor a wind wielder."

"So, what are you?"

"What a curt thing to ask a lady," Valine deflected.

Sarim smiled, exasperated. "I thought we were friends. Shouldn't friends tell each other these things?"

Valine narrowed her eyes at the echoed sentiment. Tossing her remaining handful of reeds into the river, she got to her feet. "Tell you what; if we survive, I'll tell you."

"Oh, come on!" Sarim complained to her retreating back as he scrambled to his feet. "This friendship is beginning to feel awfully one-sided."

She laughed despite the fear and saddled her horse.

From astride her horse, she surveyed their encampment, all evidence of their stay removed and buried. The ashes had been doused in sand, the flat squares where the tents had been were already disturbed by the wind, new ripples forming, every scrap of their belongings accounted for. It was as if they'd never been there, and no one in Luneth would remember them.

"Everyone ready?" Sarim called out, pulling up on his palomino quarter horse. Its sandy coat was gilded beneath the morning sun.

Valine's chestnut stallion cantered from side to side, picking up on her nervous energy. She wondered why everyone else wasn't as terrified as she was. The others' horses content beneath their riders. Did the legends of the sand snakes fall to myth in Adraali? In Runell they were nightmare bedtime stories. Survivors of the sands wove elaborate tales in taverns and at parties. Valine had heard their horror growing up, and as someone who'd lived near basilisk territory, where the kingdom's male royals were riders, she dared not underestimate the other creatures in Enneive.

"Let's do this," she said in a quick breath, pulling linen up over her face.

And with that, they took off, traversing the sands, the hooves eating up the miles between Luneth and Talloh. Turning the hourglass on death's watch. The hoofbeats were a low rumble, like steady thunder from Styrmir's own mages. Sarim and Valine took the lead, three guards flanking each of them, their party of eight stirring up sand and golden clouds.

Valine's thighs ached with every clench and bounce in the saddle, her dark eyes burned with the bite of dust, her teeth twinged in her jaw. Leaning forward, she forced her breathing to steady, pulling ahead to get out of the cloud of dust they were tossing up. Valine and her steed crested the top of a dune, and she stopped dead in her tracks. The others quickly caught up and they too, paused.

Her heart hammered as she saw the sand below the steep curve of the dune turn dusky. The muted purple shade of the Twilight Sands was a massive expanse before them, the darkness more present by the looming mountains to the west. Valine looked wistfully at the Muravo Mountain Pass, the semblance of safety. She knew they couldn't risk nearing it. The sand serpents were drawn to the constant vibration of travel through the pass but could not penetrate the rock. It was also wise to avoid the east, where the ocean lapped against the shore and pounded like a heartbeat upon the earth. A heartbeat the serpents wanted to consume. In all the insanity of the sands, the safest route through the most dangerous crossing was directly through the middle of it.

What was the saying?

The eye of the storm.

Valine knew without looking up that they were crossing the border into Talloh. Even though she need not look, she gazed upwards, and there, she saw two of Talloh's three moons hanging in the sky.

Without a word, Valine began to descend the dune. With every second they drew closer to those dark sands, the dread in her gut gained weight, from a cannonball to an anvil. With every hoofbeat, the knot in her throat transformed from a walnut to an apple. She could not speak; she could scarcely breathe. Her hands shook on the pommel as her stallion chuffed, and when his hoof finally touched upon the Twilight Sands, a bolt of terror pierced her.

It was real. It was truly happening, and it was happening now.

The rest of the group continued behind her, a little more reserved now that the shadows loomed upon them. Valine's horse became increasingly agitated as her anxiety threaded around her like a noose. He chuffed and whinnied, pulled on the reins, and pulled off course.

"He's normally much better behaved," Sarim said, suddenly coming up beside her.

She jumped, and her horse startled, quickly tapping his forelegs on the sand. Sarim exclaimed a *woah* and immediately flashed a hand out, rubbing her horse's neck in reassurance. Valine's nerves were shattered, but Sarim kept calming her horse, murmuring soft praise and gentle pats, all while seated on his own.

She suddenly felt very silly, like a stupid little girl playing pretend. He made her furious. It was that fury that began to burn off some of the stress she was pouring out.

"It's not him," she told him, the hindrance of her emotions abating. "It's me. Horses are natural empaths, and I am far too on edge right now. He's picking up on that."

"It seems all is going well, though."

"You knock on wood right now!" she gasped.

Sarim searched comically, suddenly a light in his eyes as he made a fist and motioned to his crotch. "Will this do?"

A laugh burst out of her. "You're impossible."

His laugh joined hers, and her horse settled significantly. "It's okay, Valine, I'll keep you safe."

Touched by his words, Valine carefully twirled her fingers, her necromancy swirling tentatively about him but hitting a wall. She slowly prodded along the edges of his aura, trying to find a weak spot with no luck.

"Are you wearing a Veritasium Medallion?"

He startled. "Yes, why?" he asked, brows narrowing.

"Do you trust me?"

He paused, taking her in, and she didn't take it for a hesitation but rather a contemplation. "Not entirely, but enough."

"Take it off. Put it in your bag for now."

Sarim kept his brows lowered but slowly reached into the neckline of his tunic and pulled forth a silver chain with a silver labyrinth medallion hanging from it. Pulling it over his head, he watched her and then tucked it into the front pocket of his satchel.

"Now what?"

"I'm taking precautionary measures." And with that, she allowed her necromancy to creep into him, sinking her hooks in and keeping him tethered to the earthly plane.

A little-known fact about necromancers was that a person could be resurrected "wrong," and of that wrong way, there were two possible results. The first wrong was when the necromancer's magic was not tied to the deceased, and they could only be brought back as a mindless slave—an automaton cursed to the commands of their mage. The second wrong was also when the magic was not connected to the dead first, but instead of being brought back as a shell, the necromancer could sacrifice a piece of their soul and return the living to their body without repercussions. The only catch was the previously deceased were now tied to the lifespan of the necromancer who'd resurrected them.

The "right" way involved the necromancer keeping their "hooks" into the victim and killing them while tied to the magic. Under those conditions, the mage could bring the dead back to life as many times as the magic user wished without the risk of turning them into husks. When doing so, they could reanimate with a command tied to their lifeline that would kill them if they broke the oath. Of course, there was the risk of the mind shattering over successive resurrections, but the insanity was irrelevant to the current situation.

Sarim massaged his chest directly where her invisible smoky magic pierced him. It wasn't painful, but there was a touch of pressure. She was only ensuring that if he somehow were to come to pass on this journey, she could bring him back easily.

"What did you do?" he asked.

"I hope you never have to find out."

The rest of the day passed in tense silence, the temperature ratcheting up to uncomfortable levels. The guards around them were whispering sharply between themselves while Valine and Sarim kept pace at the lead of the pack. Valine still had her hooks in Sarim, and every now and then, the Valmotti warrior rubbed his sternum with a disconcerted look on his face.

When the sun was high in the sky, a temporary shelter was erected, and the horses were rubbed down and given water. Valine felt guilty and fed her stallion half the apple that was part of her rations. He took it gratefully, and she patted him supportively. One of the guards cared for the horse next to hers. She recognized him as the one who'd ventured into the city with Olivander. He smiled at her, his light eyes against his dark skin reminded her strikingly of Malik, and she found herself longing.

Nearby, Sarim lounged on a closely woven blanket, his head on a tent roll as he popped dried cranberries into his mouth. She found herself seated at the end of the blanket by his feet, legs drawn up, wrapping her arms around them, and resting her cheek against the tops of her knees. She was making herself as small as possible while she looked at him.

Sarim glanced over, raising a brow. He was so at ease and she didn't understand it.

"You're still worried," he stated simply.

Her eyes flickered around their camp, nothing but violet sand and violent sun for miles. The sky was clear and cloudless, the sun white-hot. For all intents and purposes, it was a beautiful day, the sun and moons high in the sky. But they were in the middle of the fucking desert, and she knew with every fiber of her being that there were sand serpents beneath them.

"Sarim, I'm terrified," she bit out. "There's a reason no one has crossed the sands in a quarter of a century."

"And that's exactly why we'll be fine. The serpents are drawn to the mountains and the coast—we are near neither."

"Except for at the end of the sands. We have to meet up with Malik at the break in the pass."

At the final curve towards Talloh of the Muravo Mountain Pass, a gap in the mountains opened to the Twilight Sands. It was narrow but enough for their company to get through. She prayed that it was too small for a serpent to breach.

He assessed her carefully. "You really want to leave, don't you?"

"I'd prefer not to stay in one spot longer than necessary, so yes."

He cast his eyes around and found the men still standing. "Tell them then."

Valine nodded quickly, got to her feet, and crossed over to the soldiers. "We need to pack up and leave."

One of the soldiers, a man with light hair and a patchy beard, stared at her uncomprehendingly. His brown eyes were small, but there was a vacant light in them. Valine recognized it as stupidity.

"Are you serious?" he asked, scoffing and incredulous. He turned to the dark-skinned soldier with the light eyes and rubbed elbows with him. "You hear that, Athan? The lady says we need to leave." He laughed, and so did the others who'd caught the comment.

"I'm serious. We can't stay here."

Athan looked at her pityingly, and rage swirled in her. She loathed pity. "With all due respect, Lady Hardgrave, the horses need to rest, and we're hungry."

"Well, we're all certainly going to rest when the sand serpents kill us, won't we?"

This time, Athan laughed. "You seriously believe in sand serpents? You really think giant snakes are hiding in the ground?"

Valine gritted her teeth, fury and fear creating a violent maelstrom in her chest. "Yes, I do. I'm surprised you don't believe me. We live in a world with kraken and basilisks and fucking giant spiders and flaming birds, yet you don't think the barren deserts are home to monsters?" Valine threw her hands up. "Mrithun and Vitus help me. You are fucking useless."

Valine turned on her heel and found Sarim already packing up his necessary supplies, his horse once again saddled and ready. The other men ceased to think it was so funny.

"She said we need to leave," Sarim said, low and deadly. "I suggest you take heed."

The soldiers nodded and set to work, embarrassed flushes burning on their cheeks, but Valine was too anxious to enjoy their shame. She had hardly unpacked herself, and it was seconds more, and she was ready. Four of the men made quick work of the tent, and within moments, it was collapsed, taken apart, and stowed away. Within another few moments, the men were saddled, and the horses were ready. Valine spared one final glance, tugging at her shoulder bag, and took off—the rest of the riders following behind.

Suddenly, a geyser of sand erupted behind them in a violet explosion, scattering wide and high against the white-hot sun. A reptilian roar sounded, piercing in its pitch, and their horses screeched in response, rearing up.

Valine's steed, already so high-strung from her nerves, reacted the most violently. It threw her from its back and then took off across the sands alone. She landed on the plum-colored sand hard, her shoulder throbbing, a blade digging into her hip, and a bright bolt of pain in her knee. Looking up through her dusty lashes, she caught sight of her worst nightmare.

Exactly where their temporary camp had been set was a titanic sand serpent.

CHAPTER THIRTEEN

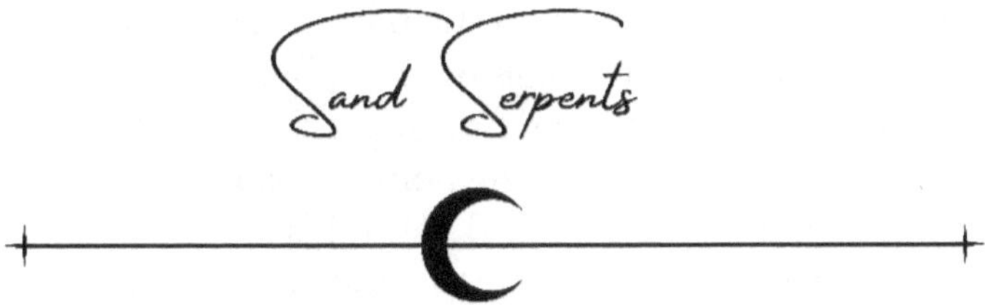

The sand serpent was easily seventy feet long, its scales the dusky purple of the sands. It roared, its mouth spread five feet wide, four sets of fangs dripping venom while its secondary maw began rotating with a hundred razor teeth. It was eyeless and depended on the wide frill that spread ten feet beyond its head to detect vibrations in the air and sand to seek prey. It rattled its frill with a screech that rivaled any Valine had ever heard, the spasmodic wavering of it spraying sand wide. It pushed up on its two wiry arms, its three claws dragging furrows in the earth, and began encroaching.

Valine scrambled to her feet, meeting the terrified gazes of her company. She'd never wanted to be wrong so badly in her life. "What the fuck are you doing? *RUN!*" she screamed.

The six guards wasted no time taking off, with fearful yells and screams of terror, they kicked their horses into a race for their lives. Olivander had unearthed the flute from his pack and was producing sharp and unmelodic notes that pierced the ears. Sarim, the bold and brave idiot, raced towards the serpent. Towards *her*. The look on his face was pure conviction, his honey eyes determined, his jaw set.

"Give me your hand!" he yelled, reaching down.

Valine did, and in the most impressive maneuver she'd ever witnessed, Sarim grasped her roughly by the forearm and hauled her up onto his horse, landing astride his lap and facing him as he whipped the three of them in an arc and shot after the other riders. Pain shot through her arm, but she ignored it—the adrenaline surge blinding her. She gripped Sarim about the middle, trembling in utter terror, the pommel digging into her rear.

She couldn't believe he'd risked his life for her.

Looking back behind them, Valine watched as the sand serpent shrieked and dove across the sand, propelling itself along with its two scythe-like limbs, tearing into the dark sand beneath it. Towards them.

"Fuck, Sarim! It's coming!"

"I know! Fuck, fuck, fuck. I'm so sorry, Valine, you were right."

"This is not the time for 'I told you so'. We just need to get out alive. Do not travel in a straight line. You need to zig-zag and confuse it. I know it'll take longer, but please trust me."

"I will never doubt you again."

Sarim listened to her and began zig-zagging across the desert, their soldiers so far ahead of them, Valine didn't dare tell him that they were clearly the first prey. She just held her breath and stared behind them as the nightmare that came true launched itself across the sands in leaping arcs and sinuous propulsions. As the beast drew closer, her heart hitched higher. Their horse was fast but the serpent was faster. And it was ravenous.

"I don't think we're—"

"Don't fucking say it!" Sarim commanded.

Valine felt helpless. With human monsters, she had her necromancy to aid her. She was an assassin and a death mage. She was the monster in human eyes. But on animals, her magic was useless. She could no more part a horse's spirit from its form than she could fly. It wasn't possible, the magic did not work on pure and natural beings. She couldn't kill a plant, and she couldn't kill the serpent.

They were fucked.

Ahead of them, Valine heard the sounds of screams and an abrupt squeal from the flute. She whipped her head to the side. Their zig-zagging journey had taken them perpendicular to their company, and there, in the middle of the men and horses, was another sand serpent. Four of the horses reared and threw their riders. In another purple burst, a third serpent emerged. Three enormous sand serpents surrounded them.

Now they were absolutely fucked.

"Fucking saints!" Sarim shouted, urging their racing horse faster, a steady lather working itself on the horse's beautiful champagne coat. "Valine, please, if you have any saints-damned magic, please try it. Otherwise, we are absolutely going to die."

Valine watched in horror as the second sand serpent lunged and took a rider from its steed, blood spraying from its maw as the rotating teeth shredded and pulped blood and bone and flesh and sinew. The third beast whipped its thick tail, and the other mounted rider was flung to the sand, his face crushed and destroyed, his chest crumpled and inverted. His horse fared little better. There was hardly any time to process the quick deaths before one of the serpents slithered across the sand and reared up. It lunged forward, catching Olivander in its fore-jaws, and succinctly snapped him in half. Olivander's lower body fell aside, intestines and organs spilling across the Twilight Sands, staining the violet scarlet. The serpent crunched Olivander's upper half, blood spurting from its maw and erupting into a crimson mist—the useless flute with it. The beast then lunged for Olivander's horse.

Feeling her stomach roil and vomit surge in her throat, Valine grounded herself by clutching onto Sarim tighter. His muscles flexed beneath her hands, and sweat from their bodies dampened their clothes. Her spine was arched painfully from the saddle, and her thighs burned from trying to stay astride.

The serpent chasing them wavered between the contingency and them, uncertain where the most bountiful prey lay.

"Please, if there's anything you can do," Sarim prayed.

She was helpless and vulnerable. They continued to zig and zag. The other two nameless soldiers were dead in quick succession of the other, one caught beneath the vicious claws, and the other pulped in that horrible rotating maw. It was just Athan, Sarim, and Valine left.

With a last desperate hope, Valine tightened her hooks on Sarim and separated them from the rest, tying them to herself. With one arm wrapped around his torso, she lifted her hand high. Drawing from the depths of her necromancy, she screamed through the pain in her shoulder and the pain in her soul as she pulled from the dregs of her magic. Black smoke wreathed her, coiling up her arm and twining between her fingers. She gathered the tendrils, wrapping them into a globe of onyx. When the sphere was the size of a man, she reared her hand back and shot it forward with a throwing motion, spreading her fingers wide. The compressed ball exploded out of her and expanded into a massive haze of smoke, wrapping around their pursuing serpent. The necromancy clung to the sand serpent—coiling, restraining, tightening.

Valine's eyes widened in shock, but she spared no hesitation as she twisted her fingers one by one in a rotation and *pulled*. The magic roped around the serpent's throat, just behind its frill like a lasso. It tightened, and as she snapped her fingers closed into a fist, the black smoke severed the titanic sand serpent's head. It landed with a momentous crash, the earth quaking beneath it. Scarlet flooded the sand like a river, washing through a dam. The head laid several paces from its body, the rotating maw slowing as the final nerves and synapses ceased.

"*Holy fucking saints,*" Valine managed, vertigo trickling through her.

Sarim glanced behind them and gasped. "Fucking Mrithun and Bela, *what did you do?*"

She looked up at him, her hopeful dark eyes meeting his amber ones. "You asked what I am." She wrapped the magic around her fist again, and gathered it into another sphere, pulling more necromancy from the death surrounding them. "I'm a necromancer." And she shot the magic at one of the remaining serpents.

Before the beast could snap at Athan's fleeing form, Valine scythed her magic down, and like a blow from a broadsword, it cut the serpent in half. It thumped to the ground, and blood steadily pumped from the sand serpent's sinuous body, spouting like a faucet turned on full.

The scent of blood was thick in the air, cloying in her lungs. The Twilight Sands were turning red with a wash of violence. For a moment, the sands were a crimson plain, littered with serpent corpses and human viscera and offal.

Fatigue began to fringe on Valine's consciousness, spots of black dotting her vision. She leaned into Sarim for more support as they rode on, pushing for the final survivor of their entourage. For a final time, Valine evoked the power within herself, drawing from the deceased serpents around them to fuel her magic. She twisted the sphere of smoke in her hand, working it quickly as the final sand serpent began striking at Athan.

The violet-scaled beast shrieked at Athan, pushing up on its clawed legs, and lashed its long tail. Athan miraculously managed to leap over the sweeping tail, and the enraged roar that erupted from the beast sent terror skittering down her spine.

With a haze across her vision, Valine shot her magic at the sand serpent, funneling the necromancy into a spiked pillar. With a twist of her wrist and closing of her fingers, she drove her hand and magic down, the black smoke piercing through the serpent's skull just as a fang tore through Athan's midsection. It fell, crushing his horse, with Athan in its jaws. The final survivor of their guards passed the veil as the venom lanced through his blood.

She was too late to even consider saving him. Sand serpent venom was virtually instantaneous, as the seizing of his limbs proved and the foam at his mouth identified. Had she been quicker, she still would have failed. She already had her protective hooks in Sarim, and she was tired—so, so tired.

Valine wavered; her necromancy never exhausted her like this. Her magic drew from death, from the decay of the forest floor and the fallen in battle. It was charged by bones and blood and fragments of death. But in destroying these beasts, she had to draw from herself, as well as the dead. She had to pull from the dregs of her soul to kill those daemon-damned—

Daemons.

Sand serpents were created by the saints and daemons. Was that why she could kill them at such a cost? She could not harm animals because they were pure and untouched by the saints and daemons. But the beasts, they were *created* by them. Humans, meanwhile, were not pure and virtuous. Even the most devout of individuals had some sort of wickedness about them. Even so, every human in some way was touched by the saints and daemons.

She'd never understood why she had the limitations in her necromancy that she did, and even still, it was mostly theory. It had always plagued her why pyromancers could set a sheep's wool alight, but she could not use her magic for a merciful death. Or how hydromancers could drown a bird midflight, but she could not quiet its gurgles and invoke her necromancy. Even how aethermancers could steal the air from the lungs of a mountain cat, but Valine could not end its gasping breaths with her ebony smoke. Her only understanding was that the elements were already present, and they only focused on them. The animals were directly affected by their indirect actions. Valine's magic, however, was always direct, and that was the difference.

"You're a fucking necromancer *and* an assassin?" Sarim exclaimed, casting his gaze around the destruction around them. "And Malik knew this?"

Valine wobbled, the scent of copper—of blood—potent in her nostrils. "I only just told him." Her voice was breathy and thin.

Sarim stopped their horse, and gazed down at Valine, clutching her cheeks in both of his hands, lifting her face to his. She felt a tickle in her nose and wetness spilled down her lips, past her chin. Blood. "Did you know your magic worked on the serpents?"

She shook her head weakly. "It's not supposed to work on animals. It's why I didn't try until I thought we were going to die."

"Does this normally happen when you use necromancy?"

Again, Valine shook her head.

"Shit," Sarim muttered and began readjusting her. "We need to get you on this saddle properly and get the fuck out of here."

Sarim's strong and capable hands had her seated before him on the saddle, her hips bracketed by his thighs, her body caged by his arms, her head lolled against his chest. She was fighting tooth and nail to stay conscious, but the fog across her mind was potent.

"Valine, I need you to stay awake. If there's another one, you have to get rid of it or we're definitely not making it through. Do you understand?"

This time, Valine nodded.

With that, Sarim kicked off, and they sped across the Twilight Sands, leaving desolation and Valine's failure behind them.

CHAPTER FOURTEEN

It was nightfall when they reached the edge of the Muravo Mountain Pass, a journey that was supposed to have taken two and a half days cut to one. Having encountered only one more sand serpent that Valine sent to its grave immediately upon its emergence kept their pace quick. She felt more ill after the feat and Sarim grew more panicked.

Black scattered her vision, her nose was steadily bleeding, a slow leak, and her taupe linens were ruined by the rust and claret stains. She hadn't told Sarim, but blood had begun to seep from her ears and eyes, too. The rolling movement of the horse was simultaneously soothing and nausea-inducing. All she wanted was for it to be stopped and for her to be lulled to slumber, but too often, Sarim checked on her, and too often, her responses were less than satisfactory. Those replies caused the gallop to increase.

"I'm going to tell you a secret only because I hope it's the only thing that'll keep you awake with me." Sarim's voice was a rumble through her chest and mind. She was drawn to the sound, like a moth to the light. "I do love someone, but I fear revealing it. If I tell them the truth, they can use that to hurt me. And I don't mean deliberately, I mean simply that if they do not feel the same and they know I yearn for them, it would kill me inside. I couldn't imagine that truth hanging between us at all times while we have to operate within the court daily. To wish and want and hurt. It's better to stay quiet, playing with the fantasies where I never have to worry."

There was silence, but Valine mumbled, urging him to continue.

"I think I pushed at your feelings for Malik harder because I was too afraid to act on my own. It was easier to take myself out of the equation. Saints, it's such a double standard." He snorted. "It feels stupid now, those feelings, especially since we almost died. That was fear unlike any other, and my hesitation towards revealing my feelings feels so insignificant in the grand scheme of it all. I don't know why I waited so long…and now I think I might chance it. Because if I die without even having tried…I think that's almost worse than any other response."

Finally, they stopped. Sarim jumped off the horse, reaching up for her as she virtually tumbled from the saddle. Scooping her up in a carry like one would handle a newborn babe, Sarim held her against his chest, his heart thundering beneath her ear. She began to close her eyes for the thousandth time, and this time Sarim let her. She had the sensation of darkness gliding above them as they crossed into the alcove carved into the mountain. Sarim deposited her on the rocky ground, but she couldn't find it in herself to care.

Time must have passed because she awoke to the sound of Sarim's quarter horse nickering nearby, chuffing happily at the moment's rest.

Through the sliver of rock they were wedged in, Valine could see the star-flecked night sky, Talloh's third moon replacing the burning sun. It was stunning to see the three white spheres glowing in the sky, arcing over the Twilight Sands. It had always been a wonder to her why Talloh was the only kingdom that possessed a triad of moons. Why not Ixaitha? Ixaitha was just as northern as Talloh was, just on the eastern side of the continent. She didn't know what pull Talloh had over those orbs among the stars, but she thought it unlikely she'd figure it out.

Sarim touched her hand and gently set a canteen into it. Valine shakily brought it to her lips, cool water running over her chin. She took a small mouthful and swished before she spat, removing the taste of the blood that had leaked down her throat and past her parted lips. Returning the tinny metal to her lips, she drank slowly, steadily. She'd expended herself too far, first with her magic, then with the first touches of dehydration. She knew she was in perilous danger if she did not see a healer or vitamancer soon.

She set the water down beside her, the echoing slosh bouncing around their hiding place. She mumbled to herself incoherently, and she heard Sarim's boots send rocks skittering. Strange, she must have closed her eyes again.

She was hardly lucid when Sarim lifted her and settled her in his lap, draping a blanket over them. He took her discarded canteen and took a pull from it, carefully sipping. It was the only sound around her now. Her vision was unreliable, and all she could smell was blood. Touch was only Sarim and the blanket. Taste was still blood. She wondered why she suddenly felt so cold. But she didn't bother pondering it because Sarim's voice abruptly sounded so distant, and why did he sound so frightened?

Valine thought it didn't matter and then suddenly nothing did.

When she woke next, she felt like death warmed over. She felt like she'd been torn right from Mrithun's doorstep by Vitus himself. Valine wondered if she really had died and something brought her back. She didn't move, but slowly she collected herself, carefully orienting her body.

Valine lay on her side on rocky ground, her face pressed into her hand, a rough blanket cast over her prone form. Her face and fingertips were cold, but everything else was warm. More blood had leaked from her nose in slumber and crusted there, but it had stopped some time ago. It had slipped down her throat and thickened her breathing. It's when she took stock of her hearing that she heard Sarim's voice.

"Alastair! Quickly, Valine needs you."

She heard the distinct sound of hurrying steps, and suddenly, the scent of sunshine, blackberries, and cedar washed over her. The scent of Runell, of Alastair, and his lower notes of mint and tobacco brushed her senses. She tried to smile but failed. She tried to open her eyes but found herself unable to.

Valine felt panic lace her blood.

"What happened?" Alastair's sonorous voice demanded, and she could've wept from the relief of hearing such familiar cadences.

"We were attacked by sand serpents and she killed them."

"She *what?* How?"

"She's a necromancer, that's how," Sarim snapped.

"She told you?"

Valine swore her heart stopped at that voice—that dark, rumbling voice that carried notes of formality and casual air. She knew the king's voice already, the tone and flow of how he spoke, and she recognized that royal Adraalian accent by the soft slip of the letter S.

Suddenly, she heard the sound of flesh meeting fabric-covered flesh—a shove. Who was shoving who?

"You sent us on a fucking suicide mission!" Sarim.

There was a second sound, a sharper noise. This time it was flesh on flesh—a punch. Was Sarim fighting the king? Surely not. Surely, he wasn't punching his best friend over her.

Valine managed to open her eyes, and everything was hazed with pink. She found Alastair's blurry form directly in front of her, bright red hair wild and sky-blue eyes filled with worry. Beyond him, she saw Sarim and Malik facing off, the latter with a red mark on his jaw. Sarim *had* hit him.

"What are you talking about? She can kill without a touch; the sand serpents shouldn't have even got near you."

Valine noticed Alastair stiffen and turn slowly. "Mal," he started softly, pityingly. The king whipped his gaze to the Runellian. "Life and death mages can't touch animals."

"What?" Malik asked, shocked and hollow.

Alastair shook his head. "We can't affect animals with our magic. The fact that she did…she's more lethal than any necromancer I've known."

"She almost died doing it. I don't think she'll be trying it again any time soon," Sarim bit out harshly, glaring daggers at Malik.

"That's not possible, she—but she'll be okay, right?" Malik questioned softly, dangerously. There was an unnamable emotion overlapping his words—it was something akin to fear.

"I don't know. Vitamancers and necromancers can nulli-fy each other. I've never heard of them keeping a symbiotic bond, but I'll try."

Did they not notice that her eyes were already open? Or were they so bloody they couldn't tell the difference?

Alastair's hands hovered over her body, sapphire light glowing from between his fingers and trickling into her chest. The sensation was warm and buzzing, she felt it from the roots of her hair to the tips of her toes. Alastair continued to cast his hands slowly over her, grazing her clothing, and he stopped directly over the center of her sternum.

"Holy saints," Alastair cursed.

"What is it?" Malik asked, moving closer. She could make out that the dark clothing he was wearing was viridian and gold—Adraali colors.

"She made a tether." He turned his head to Sarim as if following the line from her to him. "Her necromancy is attached to you right now. It's quite literally the only thing keeping her alive."

"Why would she do that?" Malik asked. "What does that mean?"

"A precautionary measure," Sarim echoed her earlier words. "She told me she did something. She asked me to take off my medallion and to hope I never find out why."

"I've heard of it, but I've never seen it done," Alastair marveled as his hand hovered between her breasts. "If you had died for whatever reason, she could pull you back immediately, and whatever fatal wounds you would have had would disappear once she broke the tether. Had you died, you would have come back as *you* and not a mindless servant to her."

"And because she did that, my being alive is keeping *her* alive."

"Correct."

"Fucking hells," Sarim exclaimed softly, fisting his hands in his hair. "So, what do we do?"

Alastair paused, thinking, and it was when Valine saw a light in his eyes that she gained hope. He turned away from her, drawing his vitamancery back into his core. Gazing at Sarim, he smiled.

"I'm going to heal her through you."

Malik paced nearby, stress and anxiety a steady rhythm to the king's steps. Alastair was crouched before her, rolling up his white sleeves, displaying marble-white arms, with tattoos winding flora and fauna across his skin. Sarim had moved next to Valine, clutching her hand in his, and saints his skin was hot. Was he running a fever? Or was Valine turning into a corpse already?

"I really fucking hope this works," Alastair muttered as he pressed a hand to Sarim's chest and the other to Valine's. As he did so, he let his sapphire light leech into them.

Suddenly, that light that had felt so warm and buzzing before was hot and electrifying. Valine felt her spine arch up from the floor, a gasp releasing from her blood-crusted lips. The pain was exquisite. It was the worst agony she'd ever endured. She felt as if she were being flayed alive, that someone was peeling her skin back, layer by layer. She felt as if someone was carving her fingertips with a scalpel, over and over, quick and precise. Her blood was charged, like fire and starlight were racing through her, burning her out.

Sarim let out a low grunt, breath hissing through his teeth. Valine's mouth opened in a silent scream, her heels digging into the dirt, her chest still arching to the heavens. She wondered if this would kill her, if dying were better than this torment. For a moment, she felt so weightless, and the euphoria struck her as odd, but before she could contemplate it further, the feeling of weight returned, and she slammed onto the ground. She felt as if thousand-pound chains were bearing her down. She didn't think she could move.

And then she took a breath and it was fire and pain, but it was life.

Valine blinked rapidly; her breathing hitched. Sarim's hand was still in hers, and she clutched it desperately. It was sweet relief when he squeezed her hand back. She wanted to laugh, and so she did.

"Valine?"

That voice. That daemons-damned voice. Valine turned her bloody gaze over to the king—her king—and found herself not filled with wrath as she should be but yearning.

"Hello, Your Majesty." Her voice was wrecked, but her humor was not.

A delighted, wicked smile crossed Malik's face, and he dropped to his knees before her, capturing her jaw in both hands, cupping it, and pressing his forehead to hers. He was safety, hope, and her future, and he didn't care that she was covered in blood.

"I am so sorry, Valine. I didn't know. I thought your magic would protect you. I was wrong, and I am so incredibly, deeply sorry for everything I put you through."

Valine couldn't believe what she was hearing, but the scent of black orchid and tobacco and cinnamon was so potent in her lungs, so heady in her mind, so hypnotizing to her soul, that she couldn't fathom anything beyond the man—the king—kneeling before her.

"What happened to what you said about—"

"Fuck what I said," he growled. "I was wrong, and next time you tell me an idea is mad, I will listen to you. This I vow."

Her heart lodged in her throat. "Okay."

Malik nodded and released her. Next, he turned to Sarim and took his forearm in his hand and brought Sarim into a hug. The embrace was emotion-filled and tension-wrought.

"I am so sorry, my friend," Malik murmured into his shoulder. "I made an error, and I apologize. I never wanted to risk your life. I thought wrong, and the fault is mine. Do you forgive me?"

Sarim hesitated, pulling back, but he nodded, clapping Malik on the shoulder. "I forgive you, but I swear on all the saints and daemons, on Mrithun and Vitus themselves, that I will not forgive you if there is a next time. If you ever send us in blind with half a plan again—we are finished."

Malik ducked his head. "I can accept that. And I thank you for keeping her alive, and for everything you did."

Sarim nodded. It seemed words were beyond him, and 'you're welcome' wasn't enough.

"Alastair, can you tell Freyja to escort the prisoners this way?"

Alastair nodded and did, and suddenly, Freyja appeared with two death row prisoners being prodded before them. One was a pale-skinned, dark-eyed, and dark-haired female. The other was a tall, bearded man with bronze skin, brown eyes, and black hair. At a glance, they resembled both Sarim and Valine. Valine recognized them from their venture to the dungeons where they'd begun to plan the Luneth-Talloh plot.

Sarim and Valine were needed in Luneth but could not be spotted there as anyone but the crown princess and her bodyguard. It was why Malik had offered a form of freedom to the two prisoners. To be decoys, body doubles for Valine and Sarim in the carriage through the pass. That way, the two of them would be accounted for in Malik's retinue at the checkpoint when they were not truly present. These two prisoners were their alibis.

Presented before the king, they both raised their chins in deference. Malik made a grand gesture to the gap in the pass. "There is your escape. If you wish for freedom, you must brave the Twilight Sands. If you survive it, you earn your life. If you don't, you receive your sentence." Malik's voice was hard, his eyes cool. "I thank you for assisting your kingdom. May the saints and daemons give you the justice you deserve."

And with that, Freyja pushed the two forward, out and into the Twilight Sands. Two more victims for the sand serpents to devour. Once they were two paces out, the two prisoners looked back, and Freyja waved with her fingers, before she twirled them and brought down the stone between them. Sealing up the gap in the Muravo Mountain Pass for good.

CHAPTER FIFTEEN

Inside the carriage, Malik had a death grip on Valine. The rocking motion and the aforementioned hold were much preferable to Valine than another second in the Twilight Sands. It was a luxurious coach, no doubt, a smooth ride with wheels carefully negotiating the rocky terrain. It was done up in slick black wood, polished to an impossible shine, gilded with gold accents of flowers and snakes. The irony was not lost on her.

Upon the hunter green velvet seat, Malik stretched out, Valine's still weak form pulled across his lap, her head resting in the crook of his arm. The aroma of his scent was a spell on her senses; it was divine and wicked. Steadily, he brushed her hair back with his beringed fingers, delicate and sure, running through her dark tresses. The sensation was enough to lull her to dreams.

At some point, Sarim checked in on her, and Malik flinched, a possessive air rushing around them before he seemed to realize and relax. Neither Valine nor Sarim missed it, even in her semi-conscious state. She wondered what it meant and if she should be worried.

The few times Valine roused herself, too drained to do much else, she glanced out the curtained window. The drapes were drawn back enough to display the dark granite of the mountain walls and the stubborn beams of sunlight that managed to peek through the ceiling of the pass.

The Muravo Mountain Pass was created some hundreds of years ago by a ruinmancer, when he came to the conclusion that too many people were dying while crossing the Twilight Sands and too many ships were being wrecked by kraken. Unfortunately, at the time, the sea or sands were the only way to Talloh, and Talloh was rich in resources of jewels and fruit and exotic vices. From a logistic viewpoint, cutting them from trade was impossible. So, the ruinmancer, Ilyas Muravo, decided to create a pass through the mountains that bordered Talloh and Pravo—the majority of which belonged to the latter, who engaged in battle whenever approached. Using controlled detonations and slave labor, Ilyas Muravo became the father of the Mountain Pass, for which he'd given his namesake.

Despite the incalculable number of lives Ilyas saved, he had no regard for mortal life, and the arachne who lived in the mountains he so recklessly exploded through knew this. Countless slaves perished in the pursuit of his project, and the arachne watched and waited. Biding their time. Once the pass was completed, the carriage-sized spiders descended on the man to mete out the justice for every life lost by his hand and mind in their mountains. A single lance from their bladed legs per death. It had been said that he was unidentifiable by the end of his sentencing.

From what little Valine could gather, she understood they should reach Talloh by the next morning. Traveling the entirety of the pass, starting from the entrance at the border of Luneth, took four days. It followed the shape of the mountains, with a sharp turn that added an extra day that the sands did not.

"You owe me three silver!" Freyja shouted in triumph.

Valine turned over at the outburst, rotating in Malik's lap to face the others. He lifted his hand from her head and re-settled it once she was comfortable, his fingertips brushing at her temple. His other hand was resting on the ledge of the carriage's side, fingers pressing to his jaw in a thinker's pose.

She wondered what the others thought of the positioning. If the king were treating her as a pet or something more. She didn't dare think on it for hope or for shame and pulled herself up, pushing herself as far from Malik as possible. Malik didn't react.

Valine and Malik were cramped in their spacious carriage with Freyja and Sarim playing cards, and Alastair wedged into a corner reading a book from a Melusdan author. There was a small table between them that folded down from the carriage wall and currently an array of cards, coins, and baubles were spread across its shiny surface. The majority of which were on Freyja's side.

"I only owe you two. You cheat!" Sarim tossed back, flicking two coins at her.

She caught them in a fist, and her hazel eyes flickered with a jubilant gleam. She examined them carefully, spinning them towards the light in the carriage supplied by a luxmancer riding outside their transportation. Aside from their group inside, there was a contingency outside made up of an assortment of mages and magic-less foot soldiers. Most of which, should be unrequired to visit a friendly kingdom, but on journeys, one could never be too careful.

"Are you sure these grays are real?" Freyja used the slang for fake silver, the counterfeit coins known to be made from various gray materials either dipped in silver or polished temporarily in clear fluid that lent the signifying color.

Sarim leaned back, crossing his muscular forearms across his built chest. "Frey, I was nearly devoured by sand serpents. Cut me a break here. You really think I would've had time to make grays? And if I did, do you really think they would be what I saved when we were trying to outrun them?"

"All right, that's fair," she allowed, holding up her hands in surrender, the silver pinched between two fingers.

Freyja smiled as she chucked her bounty into the pot at her side, her white teeth even and Valine noticed that her canines were slightly sharper than a regular person's—nothing like Ishaq's demonic ones. Definitely nothing from the Ixaithan Empire's reign. It reminded Valine of those in myth whispered about—the blood drinkers that prowled in the Black Arbors.

Something niggled at Valine's mind, and she noticed Sarim's smile, his pointed incisors. She remembered hearing something about how people were drawn to those who shared similar qualities to one another, and in a burst of realization, Valine knew who Sarim had fallen for.

"So, were we all hired by Malik? Or what is everyone's story?" Valine asked suddenly, startling the others.

Alastair lowered his book to his lap. His elaborate marigold and caramel clothing was simultaneously an eyesore and the most fashionable outfit she'd ever seen. The pants were brown velvet, speckled with stars, and his corseted waistcoat was caramel, rotations of the moon gilded across it, while his shirt beneath was bold yellow, billowing sleeves. And then his cloak. A beautiful monstrosity, pinned with his topaz sun, was a wild floral pattern of mustard and cinnamon, hand-sized daffodils, marigolds, roses, sunflowers, and dandelions scattered across it with browning greenery.

"I inadvertently was," Alastair said airily with a candid smile. "I was sent away by my parents because they were so scandalized to have a gay son. The alcohol, drugs, and debauchery were fine, but the moment they saw me kissing another man? Virtually sold off." He lifted his hand and examined his nails, remaining an unaffected air, but Valine knew he was hurt.

"My mother said I'd make a pretty whore," Freyja told her, lounging back and smoothing the beige blouse she wore. "I brought down the house with her trapped in the cellar for that comment. I only let her out and restored the house once she apologized. She never said it again, but I know that I damaged something irreparably that day because she flinched every time she looked at me." Freyja pursed her lips. "So, to answer your question, yes. I sold myself to him at fifteen, offering my services as a ruinmancer to Adraali. And thank Bela, he was in need of one."

Valine had heard of parents selling their children to brothels as teens, but younger than fifteen? Valine could only think of Captain Ishaq and the young girls he raped, of Lord Bayliss and the youth he craved, of her father whose tastes ran close to children.

"You were fifteen, and your mother wanted you to become a whore?" Valine asked.

"No, I was actually thirteen, but I lasted another two years in that hovel before I ran off to the palace. I figured if my mother were afraid of me, others would be too, and at least I could get paid for it."

"Saints," Valine cursed. "I'm not condoning her actions, but why didn't she try to sell you to mercenaries instead?"

"I wish I knew."

"You already know my story, so yes," Sarim answered last.

"Well fuck, do all of us have shitty parents?"

Valine glanced around, and everyone had raised a hand. Including the king. But it was clear that he was not going to be sharing. Valine bit her tongue to keep from asking because all she'd ever heard was that King Saalim Halil Amir was a benevolent ruler, devoted to restoring his kingdom. But just because he was a great king, did not mean that he was a good father.

Camping out inside the Muravo Mountain Pass was not something Valine had ever imagined herself doing, but that night, upon the fall of the sun, the entourage was propping tents at their stop. Malik and current company were meant to remain in the carriage until the labor work was done, but Valine found herself jittery, ejected herself from the door, and stepped out into the cool air of the pass. The three moons did wonders to illuminate the mountains, cutting blades of white against the unforgiving rock. Men were busy affixing torches to holsters in the walls, and Valine realized that this was a common stopping point for travelers. In addition to the holders for the torches, there were rings to thread rope for privacy curtains or attaching tent poles.

She'd practically died earlier in the day, and despite the brush with her element, the necromancer found herself eager to move. She was drained, but she was alive and wanted to feel every moment of it. Even the horrible pain that languished in her limbs. It was also posturing if she were honest with herself. She didn't want others to think her weak. To find her vulnerable. She'd clawed her own in this life, and just because she was born to noble roots didn't mean she had its advantages now.

Slowly sauntering over to the campfire that had flickered to life, Valine warmed her hands and made sure she was seen. It wasn't just for her ego's purposes but to solidify her alibi.

She silently thanked the saints and daemons that her favorite outfit had survived the catastrophe with the sand serpents. She had her tall black boots with skin-tight black leather pants, and tucked into the extremely high waist was a white silk blouse, low cut, crossed with silver chains like her lost blue one. On her shoulders was a welcome addition, a viridian riding cloak with a nearly invisible tableau of all the original mages. There was the original death mage, Mrithun, with his eternal lover, the original life mage, Vitus. The union between the mage of darkness and light, Charna and Lucius, and their resulting daughter, Nylantia. There was the war of the base elements of water, fire, earth, and air—Aenon, Seraphina, Dunia, and Anvindr, respectively. All the mages were represented, with their feats that sent them to sainthood and daemonhood alike.

"You are such a remarkable creature," a voice whispered at her side.

She turned to him, the heavy tail of her hair swishing the scent of the night up between them. Malik stood next to her, a small smile just for her brushing his lips. She could feel his presence acutely, like her own personal flame, and she was the moth caught by his light. She knew he was dangerous, and yet she couldn't stop herself. But what she had to remind herself was, she was no mere moth, she was a monster, too.

"Oh, do elaborate. I would love my feats of awe painted before us."

"Well, we can begin with the largest, that you managed to kill not just one, but four sand serpents."

Valine admired her nails, feigning bashfulness. "All in a day's work."

"And you successfully masqueraded," he whispered, suddenly leaning close to her, his intoxicating breath on her throat, the shell of her ear. "Which, I may add, I am thinking of holding as a theme for Nyxia's annual ball."

"You want to see me in a mask, do you?"

She suddenly felt his hot palm on the small of her back, beneath the cloak. "I certainly do. A mask and nothing else."

His hand slipped lower, just gracing her ass, and in response, wet heat pooled between her legs. She shifted towards him, letting her fingers drift over his hipbone.

Filthy thoughts invaded her mind. Fantasies of her and Malik, sprawled on dark sheets, so much skin revealed—the cream of hers, the bronze of his. She imagined what it would be like, the two of them clad only in extravagant domino masks, Malik's face between her thighs. His wicked smile and an even more wicked tongue.

Suddenly, overhead, there was the sound of clicking, and Valine was broken from her explicit trance and looked up. And promptly wished she hadn't.

Above them was one of the arachne. She was the size of the carriage they'd ridden in, her sleek, black carapace reflecting flame and luxmancery. Her eight legs were razor-sharp spindles and her two large eyes were like the petals of lilacs. She watched them, surveying with a sentience that unnerved her.

Arachne were weavers of dreams and desires and deliverers of justice. They sought to right untold wrongs, particularly those to which they'd borne witness. But in seeing the wants and yearning of individuals, they saw the horrible and wondrous deeds that had been done. They balanced the scales and weighed the crimes. They punished their own personal slights and the most irrevocable harms.

Only the most terrible of people experienced a visit.

Valine held her breath, her lungs burning with the effort.

Daughter of Mrithun, the otherworldly spider greeted within Valine's mind. It was wondrous and dreamlike, the voice so feminine and yet so daemonic. *I see inside your twisted soul. You are a blade and an auge. You are poison in tea and a weapon in finery.*

Valine felt her insides turn watery, fear coursing through her like an icy river. The arachne was measuring her, and she feared she wasn't up to par. It was the first time Valine truly feared the spiders. It was the first time she'd encountered one since she began dealing death that wasn't warranted by more than coin.

The arachne slowly descended, and shouts went up around them. Malik caught her about the waist, tightening his grip. The spider watched the interaction with oddly human understanding. Soldiers and mages were backing up. It was never wise to intervene between an arachne and her justice. One must step back and allow the scales to be tried. Opposition spelled demise.

Breaths were held, and Valine heard the distinct sound of a carriage opening, and a violent curse. It was Sarim's voice. Alastair's swearing soon followed, and the sound of Freyja's footsteps cut the tension before they were abruptly stopped, presumably by one of the entourage grabbing her.

The arachne stayed silent, watching, her purple eyes blinking only once. She cocked her head at them, and Valine shivered. They hadn't accounted for her own horrible deeds to be the plan's undoing.

Valine slipped a hand behind her back and began gathering her necromancy. The magic was depleted, slow in its restoration and languid in its movements, sleepily winding through her fingers. It was the speed of molasses in the Frost Season, but she kept calling the black smoke in her palm.

"We want no trouble with you, Dream Weaver," Valine informed her.

The arachne tsked, her pincers clicking together sharply. Valine's heart raced, pounding in her ears. Malik's surely sped, for he clutched her protectively, subtly pushing her ever so behind him. He couldn't hear what the spider was telling her telepathically, but it took no scholar to figure it out.

That necromancy you are gathering tells another tale, Death Dealer.

Valine wavered.

The arachne can see what horror lies in hearts, and yours is rotten, the arachne hissed, and Valine whimpered. *You have killed innocents, and you are determined to set in motion a chain of events, of which has consequences you will suffer greatly for.*

In that moment, Valine knew she was guilty. She had known on a deep level, but to have her crimes and sins laid bare between them, Valine *knew.* And despite knowing, she did not feel remorse.

She lifted her chin. Not in defiance, but in acceptance.

The arachne should find your cursed soul guilty, but even the wretched are capable of good and vengeance. The spider bowed. *You avenged my sisters when you slew our mortal enemies.*

Valine nearly staggered and blinked wildly. "I—I what?"

You were capable of destroying the beasts that devoured my kin when none other could. For that, I thank you and offer you absolution for the wrongs you've committed. This leniency is offered only to few, and if I couldn't read your desires, your tyrant king would be tried tonight. But you have chosen, and the arachne will allow you life, and the boon of your heart—just this once.

The spider began to crawl back up the wall.

"Thank you, Dream Weaver," Valine acknowledged hoarsely, ducking her face to the flames.

You are welcome this time, Death Dealer.

CHAPTER SIXTEEN

Great Flame

Overhead, phoenixes soared.

It wasn't yet daybreak, but they were already on the road once again. Valine hadn't minded the abrupt departure from the night's camp.

After the visit from the arachne, Valine had torn away from Malik and rushed to the tent set aside for her. She had barricaded herself within and refused to let anyone inside. Malik and Sarim were the most determined of sympathies, but Valine was locked in the cage of her mind, and her mind was snarled.

Death had come for her a second time, and it was only through a twist of fate she'd survived the most recent attempt.

She had been tried by the arachne, and she had been found guilty. Yet still, she lived. And if not for her, then Malik, too, would have been the subject of their justice. Valine didn't dare contemplate how damning that pronouncement was. Instead, she clutched a pillow to her chest and bit down on it, suffocating the tearless sobs that threatened to be unleashed. She stared at the four walls of the canvas, dark eyes wide, watching shadows and the light of flame play outside the tiny sanctuary.

She had slept fitfully, and when she woke, she was equally shocked and unsurprised to find Sarim sleeping outside her tent, Malik pacing nearby. There were circles under his eyes, but he had a coffee in hand, and he smiled.

Sarim had woken and took leave to relieve his bladder, and Valine had made her way to Malik. The king passed her his half-full mug, and she gratefully took a sip. She smiled when she tasted the cinnamon. She should have known. When he took it back, he didn't say anything but pressed his mouth to where hers had been only moments prior. Her heart flipped.

"Do you want to talk about it?" He hadn't needed to elaborate on what he meant by *it*. There was only one *it* he could be referring to, and Valine wasn't ready to face it.

"Not yet."

"Okay," he whispered and offered her the coffee once more.

Now, by the light of the moons and the flames of the firebirds, Valine looked skyward. Two phoenixes blazed across the sky like shooting stars, the horse-sized birds of prey shooting sparks. Their elegant tail feathers were long lashes of flame, leaving smoke in their wake. They were feathered in orange and red fire, their forms were streamlined and virtually weightless, with incredible wings spanning two men with arms outstretched.

"Did you know phoenixes are only native to Talloh?" Alastair announced from beside her.

She was startled to find someone else awake in the carriage. To her right, Malik was asleep, head against the jostling wall. Across from her, Freyja was propped on an arm, her legs in Sarim's lap, while the Valmotti warrior himself was outstretched, feet between her own.

"I did. I've just never seen one before."

Alastair leaned back his fiery head. "They are majestic creatures. Loyal only to other phoenixes and their patrons. It has never been known for one firebird to attack another."

"Truly?"

"Truly," Alastair confirmed. "That doesn't mean they are non-violent, though. Phoenixes will pluck out your eyes and burn you alive if you attack or encroach on their territory. And if you manage to kill them, they remember what you've done once they're reborn from their ashes."

Valine was aware, and even so, she humored him. "Remind me never to piss off a phoenix."

Alastair gave her an endearing, patient smile. "I know you're just being kind. You already know all this, but have you heard the tale of how Mrithun and Seraphina came to be the bearers of the phoenix?"

This time, Valine was intrigued. Despite having Mrithun to thank for her necromancy, this was not a story she'd heard before.

Alastair laughed before resettling his face into a grim air, becoming deadly serious.

"Before Mrithun earned daemon status, and before Seraphina was beloved as a saint, they were the first mages of their patron magics. Mrithun was lord over death, and Seraphina was wielder of flame. And they were as close as kin. As children they fancied playing with their magics, heretics of the Old Faith blaspheming against them and the new power they possessed. They cursed at them and stoned them in the streets. They were outcasts, as the rest of the patrons were.

"When Seraphina was nearly blinded by a volley of rocks, the fury that erupted from her was untold horror. From her rage and fear and rejection was a production of Great Flame, a winged beast not formed of this earth. She lost control of her creation, and it ravaged the village Seraphina was birthed into, reaping destruction everywhere it went.

"It took Mrithun's intervention to quell the Great Flame. He tethered her fire, binding it to the laws of death, giving it earthly form. Once he wrapped the Great Flame in his dark magic, he doused its flames, and it smoldered into coals.

"Seraphina grieved her loss, but after a week and a day, her creation rose. Born in an avian body, feathered in shades of flame. It was no longer the ethereal creature formed from hate, but rather a terrene being invoked by loyalty. Because Mrithun stood by Seraphina, so did her flame, and with that, the bond between them was sown."

Valine screwed her brows into a frown. "If Seraphina massacred a village, and Mrithun saved it—why is she heralded as a saint, and he a daemon?"

"Why indeed?" Alastair smirked wryly. "People like order. They like when things make sense. They do not appreciate when something is not the black and white that they like. What they believe is that fire can be cleansing, but forget the destruction. That death is bad, and life is good. But one is a painful truth, and the other blissful ignorance." He leaned forward. "It's why Vitus is a saint, and Mrithun is a daemon, despite Vitus wronging the death lord many times over. Anything that doesn't fit in their predetermined boxes sparks doubt, and doubt has the same ramifications as hope. It's a threat to order, so we keep our mouths closed and nod when we're supposed to."

"That's not true."

"Isn't it?"

"I refused to be part of the machine that Runell designed me for, and I took parts of it when I left," she hissed, wrath firing in her veins.

"So, you are a threat to the way things are."

Valine's hackles rose, her mouth thinning. "If questioning things that don't make sense makes me dangerous, then so be it."

Alastair was silent, but slowly, a smile crept across his handsome face. "I think you'll fit in quite nicely."

A rush of air escaped from Valine's parted lips. She hadn't expected Alastair to virtually welcome her disregard for the way things are.

Evening her breathing, she looked out the window once again, catching a hint of sparks dancing on the horizon. Seraphina and Mrithun were an unlikely duo but forever bound by the phoenixes their combined power created. It was a wild thought, but she found herself pondering the unpredictable group they had assembled in the carriage. A king, a warrior, a dignitary, a mage, and an assassin. A colorful assemblage that was painted with strokes of red.

It was midday when Valine caught sight of the oasis. It was glittering blue, a radiant sapphire in the velvet darkness of the Twilight Sands. Slowly, the Muravo Pass opened its arms, the ominous mountains pulling apart from its impenetrable embrace, allowing more and more sunlight and moonlight to burn across the sky. It widened above them until the ceiling of the pass was gleaming blue.

Valine craned her neck to see more beyond the window. The place and the coast were past the oasis—paradise. She wondered if everyone had the same thought after days of traveling through the tenebrous air of the pass—if everyone thought that the grand white palace ahead was such an idyllic dream.

Light from both the moons and the sun reflected off the golden spires and domes of the tops of the palace, the entirety of the majestic structure done up in blinding white, arched doorways and gilt balconies dotted the entirety. Three minarets soared into the sky, and Valine knew, from the placement of two of the orbs, that upon the Tri-Moon Festival, each moon crowned the towers like pedestals of the gods.

Tallohians did not follow the faith of saints and daemons. The royals brought with them, from an unknown continent, the religion of the Stygian. Of three moon gods: He, She, and They. The people of Talloh agreed the patrons existed, but not that they had ascended to godly rankings. They believed there were higher powers beyond and before them.

Further, the ocean glimmered turquoise as it crashed against violet surf. The palace was raised upon a crest of the earth, the city of Selyndyr below teeming from the gates of the palace to the edge of the shore. Markets were bustling at the ocean's edge, churches reaching through the throng of buildings designed low and elaborate. Nothing was higher than the Crown and the Gods.

The pass turned into flat rock that curved around the oasis and led directly to the city. Around the far edge of the oasis itself were dwellings and shacks, used more for temporary shelter than living because, despite the closeness of the palace, they were still on the sands, and it was still very possible that sand serpents could attack. It was why there were guards stationed at regular intervals upon the road.

Bearing arms, each soldier had a pistol holstered and a long-barrel firearm in hand. Paired with them was a mage; evenly arranged were pyromancers, hydromancers, aethermancers, and terramancers. The four basic magics were common but powerful, and their presence made the most sense in a battle against a sand serpent. A luxmancer would be useless, as their affinity for blinding would be hardly effective against an already blind beast. Fire, water, air, and earth were their best fight if they could not find mages of lightning, storm, or destruction.

"Valine, I want to ask you to do something very difficult for me," Malik began carefully, calculating. Valine turned to him and could see in his eyes that he had weighed this decision heavily. The knowledge of it sitting behind his eyes.

"As we discussed, I will hear it, but if I doubt the merit of it, I will refuse."

Malik hesitated but nodded once. "I don't want you to use a pseudonym. I want you to be represented as you are, *who* you are. If you arrive with Adraali with a Runellian name, it will aid in the dissolution of Runell's grip on the west."

Valine inclined her head, measuring the king's request. It was simple, and it was true. She did possess a Runellian name— a powerful one at that—and that fact would not go unnoticed in Talloh. A Runellian lady allied to a near enemy? It would cast doubt.

Talloh was most closely allied with Luneth—Pravo amicable with both kingdoms—but Runell possessed only a tentative alliance with the three. She knew that Runell was trying to conquer the realm, just as Malik was. Their reach was spreading across the continent, slowly like a disease. Valencya and Thycca were caught in the middle, and the problem was that only one could be won. The two were enemies, sworn to hate. They would choose the other side for spite, but they were the center and firmly divided both Runell and Adraali. Especially since Valencya had ties with Dubon and Thycca with Luneth. It was only their indecision that had thus halted war. Once one declared Adraalian or Runellian alliance, things would move quickly.

Valine met Malik's blue-gold, gold-blue eyes and nodded once. "I will bear the Desdemon name."

CHAPTER SEVENTEEN

They arrived at the gleaming palace within the hour. The golden gates were opened, and their retinue found themselves in a beautiful courtyard. The ground was pristine and displayed a masterpiece of a mosaic in shades of ivory and violet, gilt with a talented hand. It depicted the Tallohian gods, each clasping a moon above their heads, glimmering stars surrounding them.

A man dressed in pale livery opened the carriage door, bowing as he did so. In order, they filed out, Sarim taking the head while Valine tailed behind Malik at the rear.

For a moment, she was unsteady on her feet, surrounded by so many people, so many enemies. She deduced quickly that the walls were fortified with double the usual measure of guards and that every exit was closely watched. They may have been invited with a friendly hand, but the other held a blade— just in case. All the Tallohian soldiers were garbed in white, while Adraali's own stood solid in black. The only connecting features were the hints of gold that adorned both.

"Welcome to Talloh, Your Majesty," a dark-skinned, softly-spoken man announced, bowing grandly to Malik. "The city of Selyndyr awaits you. Pleasures and celebration abound."

The air was scented with a bouquet of flora, the exotic scent of jasmine, and the cerulean ocean carried on the wind, mingled with the undertones of boiled leather and oiled metal. Around them, pampas grass swayed gently from glass vases while bronze-skinned servants waved large white feathers. The tinkling sound of fountains sang from beyond the ivory archways, soaring palm trees ghosting beyond the tenements.

"Many thanks," Malik answered politely, dispensing with the formalities of a herald himself. "I look forward to enjoying the splendor of your divine kingdom."

"May I announce the honored presence of the Gods-Blessed. King Jericho Aku Mayar, Queen Amaris Elara Mayar, and their daughter, the Crown Princess Jacira Lusin Mayar."

Behind the soft-voiced man were the three named royals, grand in poise, style, and air. The royals of Talloh were so very unlike their people. The three rulers had moon-pale skin, unheard of in the northern kingdoms and the unforgiving sun. They believed it was a sign of their status and virtue by the gods that they so resembled the three moons they'd been *hand-chosen* by. Therefore, they went to great lengths to preserve the integrity of their moon flesh.

"It is a gift to be within your presence," Malik said, dipping his head in deference. Even after days of travel by carriage, the Adraalian King was as beautiful and put together as ever.

Valine and the others sank to a knee until the king waved artlessly for them to rise.

The king was a tall man, well-built without the paunch his fifty-four years expected. His hair was the silver of graceful aging, carefully styled beneath the golden spikes and glass orbs of his crown. A crown that was studded with as many diamonds as there were stars in the sky.

"An honor few are bestowed, for certain, we do not deign to give our proximity to just anyone. Such sights are for the worthy. Whether they be our chosen foe is as equally possible as the selected friend."

Valine's lips tightened at the thinly veiled insult from King Jericho, but Malik was unruffled and retained that silky smile that made her heart squirm.

"I do not doubt that is the truth. We are as equally certain we extend the same platitudes," Malik continued seamlessly as he swept his arm towards our group. "And may I so humbly introduce my closest of confidantes. Freyja Nahara, Alastair Whitechurch, Sarim Kahlil, and Valine Desdemon."

Two Runellian names, the presence of which were not lost on the royals.

Queen Amaris stepped forward, soft shock igniting behind her jade eyes. She placed a hand on the bodice of her satin gown, the sun reflecting the metallic material in a blinding way. "It is our utmost pleasure to have you all present for our sacred Tri-Moon Festival. Perhaps it will open your eyes to the magnificence of the Stygian Ones."

"Perhaps, Your Majesty. I would love to learn the glory of Talloh's mighty crown."

"A mighty crown it may be, but the gods are all-knowing and good, so it is their halo I prize." With a flick of her fingers, stars bloomed above her delicate diamond tiara, tiny white fires that circled and burned around the queen's brow.

A stellaemancer.

The Queen of Talloh was blessed by Nylantia, the patron daemon of the night and stars. But Valine knew better than to comment as such because the people of Talloh did not believe Nylantia and the other patrons were regarded as the legacy they were elsewhere. They believed all the gifts came from their three gods, and a gift of the cosmos upon their star-touched queen only further cemented that delusion.

"Truly an astonishing feat, Queen Amaris. One I am certain you are worthy of."

"The gods would not have chosen me for my husband-king if that were not the case."

"Oh, certainly," Malik said with such grace Valine wondered if he wasn't mocking her. "The gifts you possess are awe-inspiring. The stars aligned for this joyous occurrence. For if not for them we would not have gathered for such a glorious celebration. I'm sure this will be a festival one cannot forget."

"Yes," Jericho interjected, "a celebration made for appreciating our sacred gods and not another's wife."

"I agree. While such matters are lovely, I do not presume to know the dreams of gods and plights they encounter when creating such heavenly hosts for their gifts and seek only to offer reverence where it is deserved. Others kneel at the altar of their devotion, mayhap I will find myself there as well."

Valine smirked at the careful navigation of Malik's statement. The negotiating of respecting the queen and insulting the king with a final barb inflecting infidelity. She wondered if Malik would make plain a threat to seduce the beautiful queen or if he would let the infection of uncertainty fester, permitting it to disease in his thoughts.

Color bloomed high on the king's cheeks, fury kept on a short leash, but the same color rose on the queen's apples for an entirely different reason.

Valine felt jealousy stir ruinously in her chest. She quelled the riot; she had a mission here, and thoughts of where Malik's cock might go would not derail the subterfuge and political acrobatics she must deploy.

"I can have Sylvan guide you to the appropriate houses of worship should you find yourself seeking the need to kneel at a temple," the Tallohian King bit out.

"Oh, that would be appreciated. Though, I must admit to scholarly intrigue, as I believe I've found the temple I wish to worship," Malik informed the other king and Valine's heart jolted when she realized this was directed at *her*. His words were aimed towards her at the tail end of his sentence, the insinuation clear. He discreetly perused her, his tongue flicking against his teeth. His fingers curled, and Valine burned.

Lightheadedness quickly pulsed through Valine, and she had to blink past the momentary lapse. The mixture of heat and travel was the likely culprit—though she couldn't entirely rule out her recent near-death.

King Jericho blinked once, not enough to be visibly off-put, but enough for the man to wonder if he'd read the signs wrong and he was at fault. He straightened, and a newfound smile plastered itself across his face.

"Well, my fellow king, I would quite enjoy sharing tales of your travels and the delights you shared along the way. I'll instruct Sylvan to get you situated, and we shall meet at third bell for refreshments on the Izar Balcony?" Jericho beamed.

Valine struggled to understand the sudden change. Was the inference of Malik's interest in Valine and not his wife enough for Jericho to switch so suddenly?

"I would love nothing more; I look forward to scintillating conversation."

The three royals tilted their heads in acknowledgment before turning on their heels, and departing through one of the many arches with a contingency of guards. Malik and Valine were left with their company, surrounded by their own soldiers, and circled by Talloh's.

Sylvan—the dark-skinned man—greeted them with a warm smile. "If you will, please follow me to the Vesper Wing, and I will direct you to your assigned rooms. Your people will be assigned to the nearby guest barracks."

"Well, I will certainly be drinking in the garden, and I need vivacious company to join me," Alastair announced. His bold yellow outfit was like a ripe citrus or a preening bird—eye-catching.

Some of the younger courtiers freckled throughout the space tittered excitedly, and Valine knew Alastair already had them on a hook. Here, the Runellian was fostering the beginnings of false friendship, the pretense to discover the secrets of Talloh and bring about its downfall. She smiled, and with that, they followed.

Valine's room was azure. It had beautiful papered walls patterned with large peacock feathers with white marble floors. There were doors opened to a balcony that faced the ocean, the cerulean and turquoise waters lapping at the plum shore. On the far side of the room, a plush bed lay upon a gilt-edge dais beside an attached restroom with hydromancer-powered plumbing promising a rainfall shower. A quaint sitting area in the center of the suite drew it together, and on the south-facing wall was a white door with a six-pointed star for a handle.

Curiously, she tried the door and found it unlocked, the door swinging inward. Valine peered through and found it to be an adjoining suite. She narrowed her eyes at the similarly decorated room. Only this one was grander in scale and decor.

Stepping through, Valine found herself face to face with Malik.

"Hello, Little Liar, how serendipitous this has become."

Valine swallowed and cast a nervous glance around the room. She had an adjoining suite to the King of Adraali in the palace of Talloh. She was unsure how her life had become so complicated and how her intangible lines had dissolved.

"Did you arrange this?"

"I did. I thought it would be easier to pass information, and if they think we're lovers, then so be it."

"Right, well…" Valine trailed off. "I suppose I should inform you of the events in Bastia."

Malik sobered, plucking at his cuffs. "Yes, of course. Please enter and close the door behind you."

Valine did so, and found the king in just his shirtsleeves, the neckline displaying sharp collarbones, and the glimpse of a tattoo peeked out from the edge over his heart. Her mouth went dry at the sight of his gleaming chest, the powerful column of his throat. She followed the lines of his body and found his hands busied upon a pair of crystal glasses, pouring water over sugared irises and glazed orange peels. Saints and daemons, his hands were beautiful. His fingers were long and elegantly tapered, his nails short and painted gold and a tracery of veins were prominent, casting up his arms. Those were hands that she wanted on her—in her.

She was so focused on his hands that she didn't realize he was offering her a drink. She shook her head and took a sip of the sweetened water and stopped him before he took a drink of his own. Taking his hand gently, she pried the glass from his grip and gave him her own.

"You never can be too careful," she told him, with her not-poisoned beverage in his hand. She took a drink of his. Also, not poisoned. "Both safe."

Malik cocked his head and smiled. "Thank you."

"Don't mention it."

Valine circled to a nearby chair and lounged in it, draping her legs over the arm. "So, most things in Luneth went according to plan, but as I expected, some things along the way went awry."

"Do tell," Malik encouraged, taking a seat on the edge of his own chair.

"Well, for starters, I had to kill the dealer by stabbing, so that was unfortunate. And also, I lost nearly all of my belongings on the sands." She sent him a dark look. "Thanks for that by the way, a death by sand serpents is low on the list of desires."

"That is my fault." He paused, panic flickering in his eyes. "Do you still have—?"

"Yes, don't worry. I still have the fleur de mort and everything else."

"Good, good. And you were properly seen?"

"Everyone thought they were walking in the presence of Larysa Olympias. Trust me, I know what I'm doing. This isn't my first assassination."

"Right, yes." Malik drank deeply from his flavored water. She could see the slight tremble in his fingers as the ice clinked. He was nervous. "I should leave you to it, shouldn't I?"

"Most assuredly," she responded, sucking on a candied peel. "Tonight, I'll return, and we'll share what we've learned. Does that sound acceptable?"

"It does."

"Delightful," Valine pronounced, finished her drink, and stood. "Then I will see you tonight."

CHAPTER EIGHTEEN

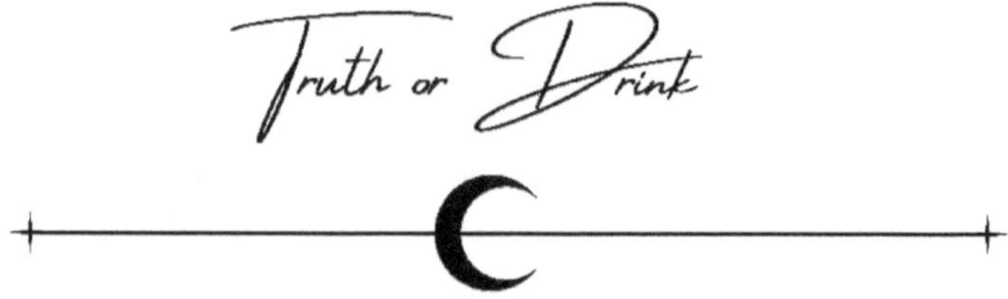

Valine redressed in clothing more forgiving to Talloh's heat. Many of her possessions had been safely ensconced in Malik's carriage on its voyage across Enneive, and what was lost on the Twilight Sands was minor. The pants she wore were virtually sheer and billowing red, the high waist circled by a golden chain belt. The equally thin top was cropped with sleeves that were little more than decorative.

She was meeting Sarim, Freyja, and Alastair in the garden of the Vesper Wing, beginning the basics of politicking. The three of them were already present, seated upon plush cushions and woven furniture, and dressed similarly to her. They were eating a plate of cold meats with cheese, and vegetables with hummus, in addition to several dishes of honey-roasted dates. Pitchers of flavored water perched on the low table, and a bowl of grapes sat nearby. Valine plucked a grape and sat next to Alastair.

"So, tell me about this festival. I must admit, I've never been to it," Valine started, pulling the bowl of grapes in front of her.

"You know that Talloh is the only kingdom to have three moons, right?" Freyja began, sipping a cucumber and mint water. "Once a year a giant violet star burns behind the three aligned moons, and bathes the kingdom in violet. It is said that Talloh was the birthplace of the Stygian gods, and this event is the anniversary of their sacred arrival.

"The celebration begins with prayer, a gift, and then dancing. What happens after is up to the attendees and their proclivities," Freyja scoffed and nibbled on a piece of hard cheese. "I've heard in years past there were orgies among the nobility."

"Say it isn't so!" Alastair rocked back in mock scorn. "Orgies and debauchery, I would never have guessed."

Valine knocked shoulders with Alastair, his jewel-bright eyes filled with mirth. "Why do I have the feeling you are the instigator of these salacious events?"

"Like a blade to the heart, you are, Desdemon! I'll have you know, I've participated in one and incited none."

"Somehow, I don't believe you."

"It's true! It was the last time I was with a woman! She was a radiant thing, but unfortunately, the delights of the female form are not for the likes of me."

"We, as a female species, grieve the loss."

"It's too bad, really. Imagine the damage I would do if I preferred both sexes, thank the saints."

"Oh, shush," Valine teased, tossing a grape. Alastair caught it in his mouth, tumbling to the ground. They collapsed in a fit of laughter just as new figures entered the garden.

Just as they'd timed it.

The girl at the center of the group was Crown Princess Jacira. Her golden hair long and waving behind her, jewels spun in her tresses, lavender silks upon her. She was petite and slender, with soft sloping features, and large doe eyes that were a startling shade of lilac. Behind her was a man with chestnut hair and a slight tan, and to her other side was a soft-looking individual with blue eyes and light brown hair.

Jacira held aloft a crystalline bottle—spirits. "By royal decree, I demand you allow us to drink with you." It was said with a smile, and clearly meant as a joke, but there was no possibility of refusal—which was not a problem, as this was exactly what they'd wanted to happen.

"We would love nothing more," Alastair said grandly from his post on the ground, spreading his arms wide. "Best seat in the house is right here." He patted his lap.

The princess tossed her head in a laugh and handed off her bottle to one of her waiting guards. She crossed the space between them on dainty feet and dropped herself onto Alastair's leg, lounging back and draping her arms behind her. One brushed Valine's shoulder. The two who accompanied Jacira found spots on cushions among them.

"I do hope we learn some refreshing facts about these unfamiliar faces today," Jacira said, stroking up Valine's arm. "And perhaps inclinations may be revealed."

"They may be," Alastair rescued, sensing Valine's unease. "And may I be so bold as to wonder who your delightful friends are?"

Jacira simpered. "This is Tallulah, heir to the Illise Mines—" she indicated the other individual, "and this is Balchon, heir to Raziche's Den." Slavers, crooks, and drug lords then.

"A pleasure to meet you both," Alastair offered, kissing their proffered fingers.

Jacira snapped her fingers, and one of the guards poured the spirits into a thin stemmed glass. A summoned servant appeared, barefoot and dressed in worn linen. The servant dropped to a knee and sipped carefully from the glass—a poison tester.

"Gods, it is unacceptably hot out here!" Jacira complained, her voice like an arrow to the mages. "The aethermancers are not performing their duties as they should. If we paid them, I'd be garnishing their wages right now."

Jacira's nose turned up at the same moment that a breeze casted over the group. Valine looked over, and saw a tired-looking wind wielder moving his hands with the new flow of air.

"I think there's more that could be done about this heat, is there not?" the princess continued, looking at the poison tester.

Something nagged at Valine, a sense of unease, and as she studied the ochre-skinned poison tester, and air mage. The tester's eyes flickered to hers, full of resentment—just for a pause. She saw the unnatural darkness gather around him, before he pulled his hands apart, and shade casted over the garden.

He was an umbramancer—a mage of darkness.

It was then that it clicked. The exhaustion, the ire. Valine realized that things had changed in Talloh and that mages—if not stars-blessed like the queen—were slaves.

Valine had mentally excused herself, busying her mouth and hands with food and drink so as not to answer while her mind whirred. Magic wielders were in servitude, and Valine wondered how far that extended. Was it a punishment for criminals? Were they all unpaid? Was it forced bondage? These questions were rampant as she assessed the space and caught sight of a pair of mages working in tandem—a hydromancer and an aethermancer—cooling, humidifying, and circulating the air.

"Is it true that abortifacients are illegal in Runell?" Jacira asked suddenly, snapping Valine from her reverie. Valine realized the princess was asking *her.*

She took a sip of her plum wine to disguise her startle. "That is true. Contraceptive tonics and herbs are also outlawed."

Jacira screwed up her pretty face in disgust. "So, what do Runellians do to prevent?"

"Pull out and pray," Alastair quipped darkly.

Many disagreed with Runell's laws regarding bodily autonomy and access to protection. Unfortunately, the king had the final say, and his word was law in the name of tradition—a tradition that Valencya fervently echoed and Adraali adamantly opposed. Their sentiments on same-sex relationships were similarly viewed.

Despite the fact that such restrictive proposals directly conflicted against the constitutions of the patrons, Runell persevered their archaic views. Their religion was that of the Old Faith. Of a god and his consort-wife, whose power was all, and his wife's was subservience to him. They were the image in which Runellians were forced to uphold as the epitome of piety. Failure to follow in their steps and participation in sin ended with a punishment of eternal nothingness and madness. And in regards to the Old Faith, everything was a sin. Sex before marriage, alcohol that was not ceremonial wine, homosexual relationships, gender identities that did not align with those of birth, magic, adultery, blaspheming, treason, murder, theft, infidelity, infertility, abortion, contraceptives, disobeying one's husband, being born a woman, aiding sinners. Valine knew she would have burned on nearly every account if she had believed. But, of course, the rules never applied to the men.

"Truly?"

"That, and tracking one's cycle," Valine supplied. "But that isn't always reliable, so unfortunately, there are many bastards running amok."

"I cannot imagine Runell participates in many orgies then. Us Tallohians must show you how a proper festival is celebrated. Contraceptives are freely offered and encouraged during such rites."

"Oh, you'd be surprised," Alastair muttered into his drink, and Valine fell into a bout of laughter. "And if your solution to this problem is homosexual relations, I would agree, but such practices are also deemed criminal."

Jacira's mouth curled in horror, and Valine wondered how sheltered this princess was. She was raised on the backs of commoners and the blood of slaves. Surely, she understood the world was cruel and unfathomable?

"I must dissuade my father from adopting similar practices."

"Why would he in the first place?" Valine questioned.

"It's possible it may be conditional, but I assure you, I will not stand for such heinous censoring of a person."

"I would think so, Jac, or you would be in mighty trouble if that were to pass," Balchon commented, showing off painfully white teeth. Jacira stuck her tongue out, and Balchon continued. "It's not like we haven't all dabbled, and what is life without the flavor of curiosity to be sated?"

"I concur," Alastair toasted, raising his glass.

Freyja and Sarim were distinctly quiet, nestled together with heads bowed, whispered conversation flowing between them. Alastair was being an esteemed conversationalist, while Valine was constantly examining every word. She should have been searching for secrets, but it was the Valmotti and ruinmancer that had Valine inspired. She could use them and whatever was budding between them to further their goals. She made a mental note to speak with them.

"This talk is so dreary!" Jacira lamented. "I propose a game!"

"Fantastic idea. What does Your Royal Highness suggest?" Alastair was truly carrying on the charade they needed, but the fact that the Runellian lordling was so fond of parties and debauchery—and an orgy or two—helped enhance his natural element.

"Truth or Drink. We ask each other a question, and you must answer or elect to drink. No topic is off limits!"

A chorus of enthusiasm spread through their group, agreements and eagerness threading behind devious eyes and devilish smiles. Even Sarim and Freyja seemed hooked on the idea. As a Tallohian custom, it was poor luck to use magic for amusement a fortnight prior to the festival, so in spirit of that, typical hired—or, in the case here, indentured—entertainments in the form of hydromancers and other mages had been halted.

Valine smiled from behind her drink. Mentally, she categorized how she was going to play the game; she would lie through her pearly whites, bits of truth stuck between the teeth of her falsifications. She would don the façade the Desdemon name provided, casting a smokescreen of frivolity and caustic loveliness over her sharp edges. But the best lies came from the most honest truths, and Valine was prepared to lay herself bare.

"Freyja!" Jacira announced. "What is your favorite position?"

"No hesitation before getting into the sexual questions, hmm?" Freyja pondered, eyes quick as a flicker, glancing at Sarim. "I think I'll have to say on top. I like being in control."

"Excellent choice, now you ask someone else anything!" And Jacira actually clapped from her Runellian perch.

"Balchon, what is the hardest drug you've used?"

"Curious one, aren't you? While it may come as a shock, I revere my body and consume only alcohol as a recreational substance…but I also smoke grass and dabble in opium and psilocybin. Ah fuck, I've also tried a little of everything." He laughed at his proverbial list of drugs.

"A better question would have been what you haven't tried," Tallulah teased, leaning into the brunet.

"Valine," Balchon bellowed, gunmetal gray eyes boring bullet holes into her. "How many people have you slept with?"

Valine smiled, a small, lethal thing. There was no need to lie when the truth would do. This was a harmless answer, and it would only do better to damage Runell's image. "Thirty-six." Balchon raised a brow and curled his lip in appreciation—she ignored him. Skewering a look across the garden, freesia and jasmine scenting the air, she met amber eyes. "Sarim, have you ever been in love?"

The Valmotti warrior hesitated, and Valine knew he was forcefully keeping his eyes trained on her, and not the woman at his side. The woman he so desperately wanted to look at when he wanted to answer. But instead, he drank.

Around the circle, the questions were asked, truths were spilled, and drinks were swallowed. Valine drank when she was asked about first loves, and lied when she was questioned about magic. She was careful with her questions, ensuring she wasn't targeting the Tallohians unjustly, but cataloging their every answer.

"Jacira," Alastair began drunkenly, "who gave you the best orgasm of your life?"

Jacira, equally drunk, leaned back against the vivacious redhead, her eyes glittering with drink. "Oh, definitely, Pandora. Gods, she does this thing with her tongue—" the princess visibly shivered in remembrance, "absolutely her."

"Oh, you can't just leave it at that!" Valine protested, the first fingers of alcohol grasping her. "What is this tongue maneuver that you speak of?"

Jacira grinned and downed the last of her drink. "I shall keep the secrets of oral sorcery to me and mine."

Valine quirked a brow. "Is that an invitation?"

The crown princess pursued the assassin with liquid eyes, wet with alcohol and desire. "As delectable as you are, darling, I fear I must refuse and confess my monogamy. Pandora continues to be my partner to this day."

Valine hummed in mock disappointment. "Please inform me should that change."

She had never been with a woman when she wasn't sharing a man. She had never pursued nor particularly desired one. It was astounding, truly, that she'd been an assassin for as long as she had and used sex to get to a male mark, yet sex hadn't been a tool for the fairer sex. It was with Jacira she wondered if she had to employ such tactics, but in the same thought, Malik came to mind. Their argument on the bridge, his belief in her capabilities, the tender way he'd held her in the carriage. A knife twisted in her gut at the prospect of romantic and sexual pursuits—even should they be false—with anyone else.

"I will be sure to," Jacira demurred, hiding a smile behind her suddenly refilled glass.

From the heart of the palace archway came a servant in ecru linen and a violet sash. He stopped before the assembled group, taking in the vices of alcohol and the spirals of smoke coming from the end of Balchon's joint as he bowed quickly.

"A message from the king, Your Highness, Lordships, and Ladyships. Dinner will be served in the Zodiac Hall at seven o'clock sharp. Semi-formal attire is requested, and the meal will consist of three courses, a round of pre-dinner drinks, and dessert, which a bevy of post-meal drinks will be served."

"Thank you, Radja. You are dismissed."

"Good day, Your Highness." Then, with another dip, the servant scurried off.

"Well," Jacira began with a clap. "If we are due in just over an hour, then we must wrap this up and prepare. I do not believe in being tardy, as we should always respect the clock that the gods have set forth."

"Yes, you are very much correct," Alastair agreed, not daring to roll his eyes like Valine knew he wanted to. Both of them had been indoctrinated into a self-flagellating religion in Runell. It was no surprise they shared disdain over this one, too.

Quick farewells were bid, and the Tallohians departed in a flash of purple, gold, and white. The remainder were the Adraali crew, surrounding guards, and servants, including the enslaved mages. Valine caught their eyes, the tiredness that ringed them, the fatigue in the waver of their stances. They were burning themselves out, risking draining all for the comfort of cooled air for arrogant, pious royals.

Alastair offered Valine his arm as the group set out for the Vesper Wing.

"That was quite illuminating, wasn't it, dear Valine?" Alastair murmured into her dark hair.

"More than you know," she whispered as the set off, information tucked away like a list in her pocket. A list that was soon to rapidly grow.

CHAPTER NINETEEN

Discreet and Commendable

Valine excused herself to freshen up, and as she did so, she used it as an excuse to check the adjoining door between hers and Malik's suites in case he had any pertinent information to pass along before dining. Alas, his rooms were empty, and Valine sighed, readying herself to rely on the information she already possessed, and that which she would glean at the table. Gossiping and gloating were two things that were always present at dinner parties, and no matter how secretive or humble the person, pride and desire won out.

As she donned a fresh coat of claret lipstick, Valine touched up her cosmetics, adding a swish of gold liner to her lids and added bits of crushed gold to the apples of her cheeks. She still wore red, but instead of the gauzy pants, she had swapped it for a gown that was little more than sheer panels stitched together. The plunging neckline, in addition to the high slits, left little to the imagination. If the light hit it just right, one could just see her nipples. She added a finely woven gold chain bralette in order to encourage some imagination. It was provocative and elegant, and the heavy ruby earrings she added only enhanced this effect. She kept her rings—deadly ones included—she did not keep her undergarments.

When she exited the room, Alastair was there, holding out an arm, bedecked in Adraali viridian. He was wearing copious gold chains in lieu of a shirt beneath a vibrant jacket—she noticed absently that they matched. His pants were high-waisted with fabulous gold buttons embossed with starbursts, and he wore strappy metallic sandals.

"Don't you look ravishing," Valine commended, admiring Alastair up and down.

"Me? Do you own a mirror, darling?" Alastair was awed, spinning Valine with a hand. She twirled for him, showing off the non-existent back of her dress, and the long creamy length of her legs. "Everyone will be tight in the pants at the sight of you."

"Mm, I do love an excuse to make loins stir."

"You are an unrepentant tease."

"And don't you forget it."

They laughed as the two of them escorted the other to the Zodiac Hall. She was taking in the grandeur of polished white walls, gilt-edged apses framing them, columns the only walls offered against the Twilight Sands and the sea beyond. Their shoes clicked against the pale stone, and Valine's dress made a whisper against the floor. Guards stood at regular intervals, more than one startling at the bold dress she wore, and in response, Valine smiled and lifted her chin.

The Zodiac Hall was done up in more than just Talloh's signature colors. In addition to all the bleached stone, yellow metal, and plum shades, the hall was awash with a variation of hues. The curtains which fluttered in the wind were magenta and the carpet beneath the mahogany table was lemon with a pattern of exotic birds. The high-backed chairs were upholstered in a riot of fuchsia, emerald, orange, and canary. The loud fabric depicting either flora or mythos, Valine couldn't tell from the distance. The table was set with goldware, chalices encrusted with jewels, and a flourish of greenery ran the length of the wood.

Perched and lounging in their chairs were important people festooned in rainbow hues, most donning the signature Talloh flavor, while others—such as Valine and Alastair—elected for something new. Jacira, Balchon, and Tallulah were already seated, the three of them in flamingo, tangerine, and coral, respectively. The princess was the only one with a rose quartz crown. Next to the crown princess was a slender woman with a sheet of platinum hair. Her gown was a secret of colors, flashing in the light from green to lilac, to citrus to powder. She was serene, and despite her beauty, Valine noticed her rough hands—she was no royal.

Handwritten papyrus name cards were folded on each plate, and Valine found hers directly in front of the woman in the shimmering dress. Alastair's on her right. She swallowed when she noticed Malik's name at one head of the table—a place of honor. Only Sarim's and Alastair's names separated them. Freyja's was across from the princess herself. They took their seats, and Jacira quickly introduced them.

"Valine, Alastair. I'd like to introduce you to Pandora."

Alastair cocked a brow. "The infamous Pandora. Pleased to make your acquaintance."

"Infamous?" Pandora asked, her melodic voice light with teasing. "Jaci, what filthy lies have you told them?"

"Oh, only the filthiest of truths, my love." Jacira grinned like a fiend, and heat rose on Pandora's lovely cheeks.

"Is that a hint of a Lunethian accent, I hear?" Valine inquired, delicately sipping water as she eyed the allegedly tongue-talented woman.

"It is!" Pandora glowed. "My father was a travelling merchant from Bastia, and my mother a midwife here in Selyndyr, though she was originally from Valencya."

"A woman from two capitals, a rare find!"

"Yes, despite their different views, I value both sides of my heritage. I hope to continue to blend my two cultures and perhaps share them with a particular crown."

"Your open-mindedness is admirable."

Pandora blushed again prettily.

As more guests filtered in and drinks were poured, Valine made small talk with the princess and her friends, watching each new individual take their seat. There was a duchess from Luneth and her bumbling idiot of a husband, a drunken lord, and a pinched-faced lady hailing from the border of Runell, a countess from Valencya, several Tallohian nobility, and a council member from Pravo—the only country in Enneive that did not follow a monarchy. But then a figure appeared, and Valine's stomach bottomed out and filled with wings.

Malik entered, dressed in a shade of light blue that brought out the tone of his eyes. Copper accouterments glittered on his person, from his buttons to the fine stitching on his jacket. His shirt was more substantial than Alastair's, but that wasn't much of a feat at current. It was ivory lace, the first few pearl buttons undone to show off his chiseled chest and smooth brown skin. She realized that his tattoo was covered with makeup, and it only confirmed what she thought it was.

As he scanned the room his eyes fell on her, and heat instantly gathered in his eyes. She turned liquid under his gaze. She could see his thoughts in his eyes, the slow, languid way he devoured her that only showed how much he wanted to put his own hands on her. She imagined what it would be like to be splayed out on this table among the gold chalices and monstera leaves, of Malik sweeping the dinnerware with a powerful arm and pinning her down as he—

Valine forcibly tore her mind from the fantasy, but she knew it showed on her face, and it showed on his that he knew all the filthy dreams she'd summoned.

The King of Adraali crossed the room, and took his seat at one head of the table. It did not miss notice that upon his effortlessly styled hair was a small bronze crown. Spiked and studded with pearls. Valine wondered distantly how many he owned.

When Malik had entered, so had the King of Talloh. He, too, was crowned, but only his was starlight and Starfire—a matching pair to the one which sat upon his own queen's brow. King Jericho gestured grandly to the room and the feast being delivered to them.

"Is this not proof that the gods have chosen us? That we, of the Mayar line, are the true prophets of their Word? We are devout and so have we been rewarded thus." Jericho's voice was powerful, near fanatical in its belief. "The moons shine upon us, the glow of the orbs pouring from our very flesh. Evidence that we are divine."

Valine stifled a snort into her wine. Malik's eyes zeroed in on her, amusement flashing. She marveled at how the Tallohians were eating up the nonsense the king was spouting, and she was internally grateful to the other royals' forced composure. A lord was particularly struggling, and the duchess was coughing to cover up her slip.

Unfortunately, a countess—Magdalena something or other—of Valencya was absolutely enamored. Likely because her own complexion was exactly the color that Talloh valued. It infuriated Valine to no end that this delusion was so active in an otherwise forward-thinking kingdom. Aside from the slavery, Talloh's beliefs and laws were a far cry from the restrictive traditionalism of Runell and Valencya. How was it that these royals were "divine" simply because they were fair-skinned? They had usurped the original natives from the land when they'd crossed eldritch seas and set foot on violet shores. It wasn't just that they'd stolen their land, culture, and heritage, but to add insult to this theft, the people were enslaved and continued to be so.

Thinking such dark truths sparked an anger in Valine. Did this palace originally belong to the first natives? Or was it built anew on the bones of its predecessor? Were the portraits torn from the walls and murals painted over? Or were tapestries burned and buried beneath rubble? The more she thought about it, the more furious she became and the more she wanted to see the kingdom burn.

Hatred festered in her eyes as she stared down the Usurper King. His silver and white visage branding against her psyche like a hot iron poker. She adjusted her brow—softened it—and righted her jaw—unclenched it. With more imperceptible changes, she'd thus altered loathing into adoration, and when the king met it, he believed it.

Jericho licked his lips when he saw Valine's heavy gaze, pools of darkness a seductive lure that only coaxed with a slow drop of lashes. An encouragement to follow their path to her decolletage. And follow they did. She was careful not to let her looks linger too long—for fear of getting caught out. She used servants passing courses—a savory broth soup and a mixed greens salad topped with goat cheese and dried fruit—and topping wines to weave the labyrinth of deception through the feast. Valine watched and waited, eager for him to slip-up in his body language.

And slip he did.

His eyes flickered guiltily to his daughter when he heard a feminine laugh—he was being a sleazy father. His hand tightened on his wife's placid fingers as his brow lowered with internal thought—he was being an unfaithful husband. His gaze shot skyward—he was sinning against his gods. But the fourth slip up had Valine gasping behind her water glass—horrible, wicked triumph utterly burning through her.

Malik noticed, questioning her with a raised brow. She smirked, her tongue skirting her molar as she shrugged. Malik let loose a sweet, sharp smile. A crooked little thing that would have buckled her had she been standing. Her king dipped his head to hide his pride—not from her, but from everyone else. Valine decided in that moment she would tear asunder the entire Tallohian monarchy to see that smile grace his lips again, and that's when the assassin realized she had it bad.

Pandora came when the main course was being served. It was quiet enough, but it was hard to miss Princess Jacira's fingers working between the girl's legs when they were seated directly across from her.

Valine pretended not to notice the girl shuddering in her seat, the way she subtly rolled her hips against Jacira's hand. She was good at hiding it. Biting into the bread roll to disguise her moan was clever. The assassin was under the impression that she was the only one who noticed, because while she wasn't the only one looking for ulterior motives, she was the only one who noticed the subtle cues that could bring down the Mayar name.

Jericho's face was red with drink, and his voice was increasing with every drop. Valine wouldn't have been surprised if he suddenly broke out in sermon, professing undying loyalty to the Stygian Ones, and the unequivocable promise he solely possessed.

"A toast!" the king declared, liquor bright. "I want to thank everyone for coming tonight." Valine bit down on an unladylike sound as he continued. "It is a pleasure to share the wonders of this kingdom. To new friends and longstanding allies, may our faith in each other and the gods be unwavering."

He just had to add that last part in there, didn't he?

Valine joined the toast as she caught the flare of embarrassment that was blooming on Pandora's face—or maybe that was the lingering effects of her orgasm. Valine wasn't sure.

Alastair leaned into her, the scent of blackberries and sunshine more potent with the deluge of alcohol the redhead was imbibing in. "I didn't hallucinate that, right?"

"What?" Valine questioned low, popping a mint leaf from her flavored water in her mouth. "That pathetic toast or Jacira fingerbanging Pandora right across from us?"

Alastair choked on his drink. "Come again?"

"I'd rather she didn't."

He continued to splutter. "When did that happen?"

"Mm, right when we were getting our lamb courses. She reached completion right before the toast."

Alastair glanced in dismay at the recently pleasured woman, noticing her still rosy cheeks and the fine sheen of perspiration at her temples.

"And I didn't notice this, how?"

"She was very discreet. It was quite commendable, really."

"Saints, and I thought this dinner was becoming a bore."

"Alastair, dear, it's only just beginning."

The scents of roasted lamb and herbed potatoes were drifting off as the empty—or near empty—plates were whisked away by attentive servants. Valine slipped her attending a ruby, one she had stolen from the Desdemon vault twelve years ago. The servant's eyes widened at the weight and worth of the stone. Valine smiled as he enthusiastically poured her another glass of plum wine. Unbeknownst to everyone else, but her wine was severely watered down, and she was not nearly as tipsy as she'd played. Inhibitions lowered together were foundations for tête-à-têtes including salacious secrets, which Valine was greatly anticipating. Only dessert remained before she could lay her traps.

As her attending servant placed before her a decadent cake of chocolate and rum, she slipped him a note, tucking it into his sleeve as she reached for her water. His eyes widened only an increment before he stepped away against the wall once more. Unruffled, she returned to her cake, forking a rich mouthful with a slight moan. Jericho noticed the sound. So did Malik.

"So, Jacira, as a crown princess, have you any advice for a companion attending for prospective brides?" Valine inquired, drawing the blonde into conversation.

Jacira blinked in surprise, and her brows furrowed as her eyes flickered between Valine and Malik. "I thought—that is, I had assumed—that you and King Malik were perhaps involved."

"No, but even so, has that stopped a man from taking a bride before?" she joked and immediately bit her tongue. Her saints-damned father was a king, and she just implied rake-like behavior.

"A comment in poor taste, but you are not wrong."
Valine exhaled slowly.

"I suppose you will have to make it clear to these women that you are not after the king yourself and that they can trust you with secrets that they may need relief from. However, they will feel threatened by your status; you are a Desdemon, and as such, you have just as much potential to be queen as they do."

Valine swallowed her water sharply and took a long pull from her plum wine. She hadn't wanted to think such thoughts. When she was a common assassin and necromancer, she was powerful and dangerous, yes, but when she donned the Desdemon name, it was a badge that brought a different level of reverence. One that could turn that pin into a crown. Should she enter into anything with Malik, it would be little more than a dalliance, and she wasn't sure she had the strength to break away from him should that come to pass. His marriage would always be a political one, and she owned no sway with Runell any longer. She may have the title, but she did not have the connections.

"I doubt they will think that when I am but a lady amongst princesses," Valine demurred.

"I would not be so quick to dismiss the power you hold. Do not forget it because they will not."

Jacira had no idea how true that was.

Before she departed, she twisted her fingers beneath the table and slowly let her necromancy trail below the tablecloth and up silk. Carefully, Valine let her magic seep into a chest, and tentatively, she sank in her hooks, tying the knot quickly. She busied her recently magicked hand with a glass of cucumber-mint water, watching her mark rub their chest ever so slightly—she hoped they dismissed it as heartburn.

CHAPTER TWENTY

The hallways were cool, and the chill had Valine's nipples standing at points as she sought out her clandestine meeting. At midnight, she was to ascertain information within the Lunar Meadow, a stretch of lush grass interspersed with white flowers strewn like stars below a sacred view of the triad of moons glowing high above. The meadow was false, tended by mages to allow its continued prosperity and vitality, located upon one of the many towers where a minaret should have surely gone. Instead of the religious tower, the flowers and sky-filled arcade took up its residence.

Valine was still in her flimsy crimson gown, and the night air brushed her as she crossed to a shadowy alcove, courtesy of the veritable wall of arches crowning the space. There, she waited with a ruby-encrusted dagger strapped to her thigh and a vial of silvered viper venom tucked into her hair. In the darkness, she summoned her necromancy, unwinding the magic from her core and threading it through her fingers and across her black-painted nails.

She had gone out on a limb, employing a servant she hadn't known where their loyalty lay, but she guessed by the treatment of the ones around them that it was likely they weren't content with the cards they'd been dealt. The fact that she'd slipped the man a gem probably hadn't hurt her odds. Even so, she wasn't one to risk unnecessarily. Which was why she continued to pull her necromancy to the surface.

It was only minutes later when the servant who'd been attending her scurried into the moonlight, a harried look on his face as he cast frequent glances about. He was in his early thirties with a head of dark hair that had the beginnings of silver at his temples and a soft build from lack of exercise but plenty of standing. There, he stood in the center of the light. In the very middle of the grass, and unseeing of her in the dark. When she stepped out, he startled.

"If I promised you immunity from any fallout, would you believe me?" Valine began, walking out of the dark, and she imagined just what she looked like. Blood and smoke, and night and stars. She was mysterious with her dark, long-lashed eyes, and she was seductive in her provocative dress. But more so, she was dangerous in so many forms, and it became more and more evident as the curiosity in his eyes slowly seeped into fear. She could see the instinctive part in his brain telling him this was a predator, despite the way other parts of his brain were warring with such a fact.

"That depends on why it would happen," he answered, clearing his throat of the gruffness that belied his anxiety.

"That's fair. How about I start somewhere else." She paused, bringing up her non-tangible smoke-wreathed hand by her face, examining the lethal magic. "How are servants treated in Talloh?"

He swallowed once. Twice. "We…we are paid."

"All of you?"

"No."

She cocked a brow. "Paid, credited, or indentured?"

"We are glorified slaves," he admitted. "We are given pennies while they eat the finest foods, sip the most expensive wines, and sit on the most luxurious velvet while wearing the softest of silk."

"I have seen that. And mages?"

"Pardon?" He seemed taken aback.

"Mages, magic users, wielders, the like. How do they fair?"

Sweat began to bead on the man's brow, and Valine had a realization.

"You are a magic user."

He inhaled sharply, animal panic alighting in his eyes. "No, no, I am a lowly servant. I—I am nothing."

She advanced; he stumbled back. She continued; he went defensive. His nostrils flared, and his gray eyes turned steely as his jaw tightened. She could practically hear the teeth grinding behind his thinned mouth.

It was then she sensed the change in the air. It was charged. A soft cracking sound permeating the night as she felt the hair on her head lift, and a buzzing overtake her skin. Valine didn't think, she just acted. Lashing out with her necromancy, and anchoring the servant to her, she created a tether in the blink of an eye, and squeezed. He gasped, and staggered. Clutching his chest, he looked at her in abject horror.

"You are a fulgurmancer," she announced, poorly restrained fear widening her eyes at the lightning and storm mage. Had she not been prepared, the servant could have killed her in a flash, and it would be coined an unfortunate, tragic accident.

She would've been dead in a red dress beneath three moons in a false garden.

"What did you do to me?" he choked, opening the buttons on his shirt to search his bare chest. Nothing was there but a sparse scattering of hair.

"I created a tether, and it will remain there for the duration of this conversation. Should you threaten to bring down the heavens on me, your living will allow my survival. For now, you cannot kill me, and I forewarn you now not to attempt again in the future."

"You're a necromancer."

"Yes, now that these pleasantries are out of the way, what can I call you? Servant is demeaning, fulgurmancer is so indifferent, and Gifted-One-of-Barak-and-Styrmir is a bit of a mouthful, don't you think?

"Hanish," he introduced curtly with a lowering of his black brows.

"Lovely to make your acquaintance," she said placidly as she twisted her fingers. She crossed her index and middle and then touched her littlest finger to her thumb, securely knotting the tether, and lowered her hand. "I'm Valine."

He scowled; this was information he already knew.

"So, I'm assuming from the hidden nature of your magic that mages are not well revered here."

"No," he bit out, practically spitting. "Unless you are a stellaemancer, you are forced into servitude without pay. They justify this slavery by telling them that the Stygian Ones have blessed them with these gifts to better serve the gods and the rulers. You saw all the mages on the front line. The four elemental types along the mountain pass and vitamancers there to heal the wounds they may sustain. Fulgurmancers guard from the minarets, warding off sand serpents and striking down fleeing prisoners, as well as anyone else that manages to get across the Sands. Luxmancers keep the palace lighted like an eternal sun when the whim takes the king. Umbramancers give the gardens shade or are forced to discipline misbehaving servants and prisoners by shrouding them in darkness so thick and impenetrable to drive them near to insanity. Hydromancers and aethermancers are forced to cool the palace, draining their magic for twelve hours until they collapse from exhaustion. All so the king and queen can wear their heavy fashions and protect their bloody white skin."

Valine had seen this, and it was what had tipped her off to the poor care of the people. The swaying on the feet, the empty eyes. And while the breeze was nice, it was not required for all time all days. Continuous use of this magic would surely kill the mages. Didn't the king know this? She asked just that.

"Of course, but they don't care. They just outsource more mages from beyond the Sands as far as Luneth and Runell."

Valine stiffened at that. People with magic in Runell kept their mouths shut because the Old Faith deemed magic a sin, and it could be punished to the greatest degree. She knew that Runell hid its depravity below a sheen of grace and traditionalism. The beautiful structures and lace-like towers built on blood and bones. But to know they were knowingly and willingly sending mages to their death for *cool air* in Talloh…was reprehensible.

"And the rest of the mages? The clairvoyants, empaths, telepaths, and vision wielders?"

Of all the mind mages, vision wielders—or psychomancers—were the rarest, able to alter all perception to those around them with varying degrees of effectiveness and potency.

"The mind mages are kept in camps for 'safety'. Their abilities are deemed too dangerous to the public to be unsanctioned and unsupervised." Hanish snorted. "They pose a threat to their rule and the actual will of the gods—should they truly exist."

"And the last ones?" What she and Freyja were.

Hanish's light eyes were like stone as they met her dark depths. "They are killed on sight and without hesitation."

Valine's nostrils flared as she breathed sharply.

"I don't imagine you're threatening to turn me over?" she asked, tightening the tether—not enough to hurt, but enough for him to notice.

"Not if we can make a deal."

"I'm listening."

It was there, on a faux rooftop garden, that Hanish and Valine laid out the agreement and the plan. Valine would help Hanish and his wife and children escape the oppression of mages in Talloh—his second daughter was already showing signs of inheriting his lightning—while he would feed her intel and gossip the other servants passed along. She hammered in the stipulation that she was not to be named nor revealed to secure the information and that her necromancy be kept secret. She warned should anyone discover her identity from his mouth, she would kill him. They both agreed and went their separate ways, with Valine carefully untying and removing the tether from Hanish's person after leaving him with two directives.

Valine, evasive of guards, and light on her feet, followed the necromantic tether she'd made earlier, letting it pull her along in the maze of corridors. As she realized exactly where she was, she donned a new guise. One of drunkenness, as she staggered around the corner. She found herself facing four guards, standing armed to the teeth before the King of Talloh's golden arched doors.

"My apologies!" Valine slurred, stumbling in her heels. "I left my rooms for some air—I think…I think I had too much wine—and I must have gotten turned around, and now I am so lost." She turned heavy-lidded, glossy eyes on a guard a few years younger than her—likely the newest recruit. "Would you be so kind as to tell me where I am? Or perhaps guide me back?"

"Sure," he agreed, his voice rough but in a forced way. "It would be my pleasure to guide you back. Do you perchance know which room in the Vesper Wing is yours?"

"It's—"

A shriek filled the air, and Valine startled at the sound. Immediately, her gaze flew to that grand door and the crown and moons embossed on the top of the lintel. She understood exactly what kind of outburst she'd just heard and ducked her head to hide her grin. Faking embarrassment. "Oh, dear me, I really am in the wrong place. And to think I could have stumbled in on someone!"

Pretending to fall against the wall, she twisted her fingers and undid the tether, letting the black, smoky magic spiral out from under the door, and back into her person. The guard seemed very concerned, and stepped away from his post, and held her elbow as she babbled nonsense and thanks.

Obediently, she followed the guard and played up her intoxication as he "saved" her from falling with a quick steadying of her shoulders—very politely, she may add. As he guided her to the peacock room, she thanked him in the hallway and made her way back to her rooms. Behind the door, she sagged against it. With her head against the wood, she slipped off the heels, casting them aside while she sighed.

"Who was the lucky soul who had you all alone dressed like that?"

Valine started at the voice, eyes zeroing in on Malik who was lounging on one of her armchairs, facing the door with a whiskey in hand. His shirt was unbuttoned scandalously low now, and his hair tousled as if he'd been running his hands through it. He was backlighted by the moons, and Valine's heart flip-flopped at the stunning image he cut. His feet were planted, knees wide, and his arms relaxed on the chair's edge. The drink dangled carelessly from his fingertips.

"Hanish, a servant hiding his fulgurmancery. We struck a deal. And a guard who was so chivalrous to guide a lost, drunken maiden back to her room."

"Really?" He seemed impressed. "Not even a day has passed."

"I'm good at what I do." She shrugged.

"Yes, I can see that."

His gold-blue gaze turned hot, and he licked his lips. She had the overwhelming urge to bite his lip, to kiss him, and the space between her legs throbbed as she took him in. Watching him tilt his head, toying the glass with long fingers, had filthy thoughts racing through her. She composed herself to the best of her ability and crossed the room, standing before him with heavy, dark eyes. Keeping his gaze pinned with hers, she reached for his glass. He let her take it, and she took a small sip.

"Just in case," she whispered past the burn.

"Your commitment is invaluable."

"Thank you."

"So, your meeting with Hanish, how did it go?" the king asked placidly as she returned his drink.

"Well, he nearly brought Barak's wrath down upon me, but after I tethered him, he seemed to come to his senses, and we vowed to help each other out."

"I'll kill him," Malik declared evenly. Despite his tone being so careful and guarded, the stiffness that bled through him and the anger a conflagration behind his eyes, belied the truth.

"That's not necessary. He'll be our in if we can get him out."

There was a question on Malik's face, so Valine filled him in on the treatment of the mages and the supremacy in Talloh, adding that she had promised to help Hanish and his family flee the forced subjugation.

It was ludicrous that the Mayar family had come to power, and even more mind-boggling was the fact that they were holding onto it. Their ancestors had arrived by sea from a strange continent, fleeing unknown peril or punishment, and had declared Talloh sacred, gods-blessed land. Within three years—their self-professed sacred number—they had conquered the land, ruling one of the most northern kingdoms of Enneive for more than three centuries. How they battled or won over the people were lost to texts and word, the winners having written the history as they perceived it—or wanted it believed. Still, Valine wondered, because the Mayars were some of the only fair-skinned people from the mysterious land north actually living in Talloh, it wouldn't have been overtly difficult for the native people of the first Talloh to rise up and crush them. So, the question was, why didn't they?

"They won't be able to leave with us, but I'll arrange it," Malik finally told her after she explained the full case of her meeting with Hanish. "Is there anything else you learned?"

"Perhaps."

Valine hid her smile as she slid away, digging through a chest of drawers. Offering the king an excellent view of her backside as she let him see the back of her gown and how it exposed the entirety of her spine and the dimples in the small of her back. Valine felt the heat of his gaze and sensed it warmer as he moved toward her, the soft pad of his footfalls alerting her. There was a light clink as he set his drink down on a passing table. She shifted her beaming smile into a sly smirk as she set her sleep clothes atop the dresser and turned to face the King of Adraali.

He was before her. Tall and imposing, and utterly intoxicating her. His scent was all heady tobacco and black orchid, the spice of cinnamon enhancing the aura of him. They stayed locked like that for a moment. Her breathing him in, him taking her in from her parted ruby lips, to peaked nipples, down her shapely legs, and surely to the liquid desire aching in her center.

Malik's eyes flickered to the small pile of ivory silk she'd deposited atop the mahogany, and he reached for her—past her.

She held her breath as he plucked up the small pieces of fabric, holding them out for his own personal perusal. The ivory silk was a skimpy pair of shorts, lace-edged, and a short-sleeved blouse with mother-of-pearl buttons—this, too, scandalously short on its hem.

"May I?" he asked, extending the pieces towards her.

She didn't think she could manage words in that moment. She just nodded.

Malik went down on a knee and looked up at her from underneath a lock of black hair. She thought that she would come undone right then and there. The potent look in his eyes held a promise as he slowly reached for her ankle. Propping her foot on his knee, he skimmed his fingers delicately on her calf.

"You were saying?" he asked politely as his fingers made circles on her ankle—it had her thinking very *not* polite things.

"The king is having an affair," she managed, her voice breathy.

"Is he now?" Malik inquired as he threaded her foot through the leg hole of the shorts.

"Mmhmm," she confirmed, quite distractedly as he set her right foot down and exchanged it for the left, doing the same thing.

"Interesting."

His fingers were doing *interesting* things all over her legs. She fought back a moan as he slowly began lifting her shorts up her legs, beneath her lusty dress, featherlight on her knees, before he reached her thighs. He watched her breaths quicken, and surely, he knew how slick her core was with desire. His fingers were so tantalizingly close, and she felt the lack of his presence there like a physical ache, her empty center begging for him to fill it. Those fingertips turned to palms as he dragged the silk over her ass, thumbs grazing the crease of her thighs. The silk immediately soaked as he settled the shorts into place. His fingers were tucked into the waistband, pausing before pulling away and standing in front of her once again.

She swore she wore imprints of his fingerprints.

"With who?"

Wordlessly, he took her hand and slipped it through the sleeve of the top, and then caught her wrist and gently nipped at her fingertips before he let it fall back to her side. He repeated this—minus the nip—on the other side, but only this time he kissed her knuckles, his tongue darting out to flick between her fingers.

Her knees nearly buckled from the erotic threat it held.

"With his daughter's lover, Pandora."

Malik quirked a brow. "How scandalously messy."

"I was thinking borderline incestuous."

"Yes, I suppose you have a point there." He paused regarding her, and she couldn't tell if he was calculating the next move in their plan or how to ravish her. She hoped it was the latter. "How did you discover this?"

"The way he looked at her at dinner, and then I tethered her and followed it to the king's bedroom where I heard her climax—that's the second one I was present for, just tonight."

"You also saw Jacira pleasuring her during dinner?"

"I did."

"She's insatiable, apparently."

"Apparently," she echoed.

So, there she stood, the silk shorts damp with her arousal beneath a scarlet dress with a silk sleep shirt unbuttoned over it. But with gazes locked, Malik slid his fingers behind Valine's neck, found the tiny clasp there and the entire dress fell in a crimson puddle on the floor. He quickly found the catch for the bralette, and that, too, fell.

"I think Pandora is the key to unravelling this royal line. She must have a good reason for fucking both the king and the princess. Perhaps she is eager for the throne?"

Valine shivered as Malik's hands found the buttons on her blouse, his knuckles grazing her sternum. The skin between her breasts electrifying. It was embarrassing how hard her nipples were, and it was only more apparent as his hands brushed against one. She bit her lip to keep the low sound from escaping her throat as he passed the buttons through their holes. He was on the third of her five buttons, and all she wanted was for him to tear the fucking shirt off her, but instead, for some unknown reason, she allowed him to do quite the opposite. And it was one of the most erotic things she'd ever experienced. On the last button, his hands were on the smooth skin of her abdomen, taking his time as he appraised her and her restrained reactions.

"You don't think just plain fucking is her motivation?" Malik questioned as he threaded the last button and let his hands wander to her silk-clad hips. "Incredible sex can make even the most level-headed of people do the utmost questionable of things."

"Would you possibly know this from experience?" Was that *her* voice that was so thready? And her brain that was so addled?

"Mmhmm," he murmured in answer, pulling her in close, and she felt her eyes roll back in her head when she felt his insistent length, hard and hot on her belly through the pants he still wore. "One day, I think I'd like to show you—if you'll have me." And with that, he reached between them and cupped her over her shorts, the heel of his hand pressing right on her clit.

She couldn't help it. She cried out as a bolt of pleasure fissured through her, her tightly wound nerves begging to explode. He groaned in satisfaction, and immediately, her dampness seeped through the shorts and onto his fingers.

"Little Liar, you're so wet already," he murmured. His voice was so husky, so sexy. She wondered how she'd survive the encounter. His one hand tightened on her hip while the other languidly circled, and she found herself clutching at him, feeling the hot and hard feel of his chest and abdomen rippling beneath. Her breaths were coming in short, and thoughts were beyond her. Words non-existent.

Slowly he dragged his hand up, rubbing that bundle of nerves with his hand, as he brought his finger to his mouth and slowly sucked it. Tasting a hint of her through silk on his skin, and Valine felt everything in her go hot and liquid.

"Well, I think this meeting has been most revelational. I look forward to tomorrow's visit."

With that, he detached from her and stepped away, leaving her in a lusty haze so thick it took her several moments to navigate the fog and understand what he'd just done. He wasn't going to sleep with her? He wasn't even going to kiss her? He was just going to tease her and leave? Her sexual frustration must have shown on her face because Malik smiled—still clearly aroused, himself—and walked slowly back to the adjoining door.

"Goodnight. Sweet dreams, Little Liar."

"Goodnight, cruel man."

He laughed softly as he slipped through the door, and Valine stayed stood in the center of a discarded red dress, hot and bothered and alone. She couldn't think past the arousal turning her blood hot and thrumming potently at her core.

Angrily, she stomped over to her bed and got on it, pushing down her soaked silk shorts, and bared herself to the moonlight. Reaching between her legs to circle that little nub that Malik had so callously teased, she thought of the king and his skillful fingers. Imagined it was him dipping his fingers into her wet sex. Him stroking her pussy before coming up again to circle.

Minutes later, she was panting, a sheen of sweat on her skin, a hand fisted in her sheets as she used the other to fuck herself. Valine sensed she was on the brink of that peak, and as she reached it, it shattered through her, and she bit down on her hand to muffle the cries. Her hips rolled against her right hand, still working herself as she came down from the climax. It was several minutes later when she began to ponder what Malik's goal in getting her so riled up had been.

But it was several moments after that—after she'd pulled her shorts back on, and settled into bed, mostly sated— she realized that, while she'd told Malik all that she'd learned that day, he had divulged nothing, despite his promise to do so.

CHAPTER TWENTY-ONE

Valine was invited to the immaculately maintained back lawn late in the morning the next day. She arrived on scene, surrounded by palm trees and crescent-shaped gardens filled with golden and violet flowers and a scattering of shades propped on the edges of the area delegated for games. The scent of jasmine, gardenia, and fresh fruit was ripe in the air, interspersed with the bite of liquor. People milled about with drinks and food in hand, and Valine was disgusted to note that aside from the servants and guards, the darkest-skinned people present were Malik and Sarim—and they were hardly that compared to many people she'd encountered.

Jacira was nearby, wearing a sheer gown in powder blue that had strategically placed gold swirls over her breasts and matching bangles that clinked together whenever she moved. There was a high slit in the side that exposed her light skin and a row of golden anklets that danced up her calf. She grinned when she noticed Valine approaching, dropping Pandora's hand with a quick kiss to the knuckles. The gesture had Valine's face flaming at last night's memories, and she had to forcibly cool herself as Jacira flung her arms around Valine happily.

"Val, my sweet, you must be my partner for the three-legged race!" Valine resisted the urge to snap at the nickname. "There is something utterly athletic about you!" Jacira simpered, leaning into her, and Valine wondered what number of mimosas the princess was on.

"I would be honored, but wouldn't you rather have Pandora?"

Jacira groaned and threw her head back, arms still wrapped around Valine—it wasn't even noon yet, and Jacira was already well imbibed. "My father's rule; no teaming up with romantic partners. We're encouraged to seek out guests in the spirit of fostering a friendship." Jacira's glassy eyes turned sly—or at least, that's what Valine guessed she tried to do. "But we are already friends, so we don't even have to try, right?"

Valine sucked on the inside of her cheek, considering and hiding a smirk. "Right. But you must tell me who the incorrigible cheaters are, so I am on the lookout for them."

Jacira squealed with delight and disentangled from her. Looping her arm through Valine's, she guided her on while her ever-present and near-forgettable guards followed them. "Balchon is a horrible cheat, and Cersei denies it, but one time I saw her pull the tie of Tallulah's dress, and the entire thing unraveled! Of course, it was all fine since Tallulah used it as an opportunity for an improvised orgy. My goodness, what a rush it was! Have you been to an unplanned orgy? Oh, Valine, there is so much more passion in it—albeit, it goes by much faster as the stimulants aren't provided in advance—but gods, what a time it is."

"Aren't you and Pandora monogamous?" Valine questioned.

Jacira seemed taken aback, shocked that Valine had not only called her out but refused to play into the fantasy the princess was surely going to try to bring to fruition. Valine wondered if she'd overstepped too far. She was trying to ascertain what, and if Jacira knew about the affair. Not that Valine was one hundred percent certain there *was* an affair, but she was sure enough to tell Malik. But it seemed her worries were for naught because, in a blink, Jacira had resumed her blissful expression, slapping a languid smile in place.

"We are, but…" She cast her gaze around furtively. "I happen to like watching."

"Everyone has things that get them off. There is no shame in that matter," Valine reassured her as they joined the rest of the group. Jacira made hasty introductions, and Valine only processed a handful of them, managing only to remember one fact about each of them and not the three she'd mentally trained herself to.

Cersei, a voluptuous woman with long honey hair and tawny skin, tanned from the sun with a scattering of freckles across her pert nose, grinned at Valine with perfect little teeth. The ferocity in her amber eyes had Valine immediately thinking of a lioness. She was likely Valine's age, as was nearly everyone present. She wondered if there was anyone over the age of thirty on the lawn.

"Has Jacira laid claim to you, hon?" Cersei, her voice a smoky growl, asked her as she puffed on a phoenix-shaped pipe. Gray coils dissipated in the air.

"She has. Apparently, I'm an athletic choice."

Cersei surveyed her, seeing past her coral silk and the gold rings that held it all together to the muscles and curves beneath it. It was true, Valine did have somewhat of an athletic build to her. However, no matter how hard she tried, there was a stubborn amount of weight that refused to leave her thighs, hips, and rear, giving her a perpetually shapely form. She knew this was desirable in many parts of Enneive. However, it greatly impeded her ability to pose as a man when need warranted it.

"I think she just wanted to see firsthand any jealousy you may have."

Valine narrowed her brows. "I don't understand."

"Ah, she has paired her darling Pandora with your king for the race. If you did not know, Pandora is a charming creature, and an unabashed flirt. Shame she had such a terrible headache last night and sought a dark room and her own bed, hmm?"

Valine had to physically bite her tongue to keep her face neutral.

"Quite the pity," Jacira responded airily, "but I assure you a good night's rest and quiet seems to have rejuvenated her greatly."

She directed attention to her lover. Across the space, stretched out beneath a linen tent, was Pandora, with Malik standing nearby, conversing carefully. The blonde did seem to be lively, though Valine knew it had less to do with rest and more to do with at least two orgasms. She laughed, and the sound was like tinkling bells. Valine narrowed her eyes and fought the ire that rose. She had no right to feel jealous. However, she had every right to feel betrayed by him reneging on their deal. She ignored the small voice in her head reminding her that she was a lowly assassin and he was the king. She then squandered it by telling it she was a lady with the Desdemon name and a necromancer, and he was just a man.

"I may not be able to partner with her for the tournament, but I assure you I will use every opportunity to keep her nearby. Like now, we will go around and ensure everyone has a partner for today!" Jacira nodded towards the two of them.

"Lovely speaking with you. Valine, I will seek you out at the noon bell. That's when we begin."

Without waiting for a response, Jacira sauntered across the grass, plucking another mimosa up on a passing tray. On her way, she gathered Pandora, plundering her with a wild kiss as she brought her up to height.

"I thought it was a race," Valine queried Cersei, confusion written across her face.

"Oh no, that's only the first part of it. There is also a scavenger hunt, a game with an ice cube, another with an orange, and, of course, tug-of-war."

"Fuck, how did I get tricked into this?"

"Don't be so quick to dismiss it," Cersei chided. "There is endless food and equally endless refreshments."

Valine sighed. "Who is your partner?"

"That very tall warrior whom you travelled with—Sarim." Cersei's eyes turned feral, and Valine recognized the intent there. It was a hunt, and that look was attraction. "Do you know if he is Valmotti?"

"He is," Valine confirmed.

Cersei side-eyed her and licked her lips. "That is very good news, indeed. I suppose I should get to know my partner for the day, should I not?"

"It would be wise, I think."

"Well," Cersei declared, standing up gracefully, her coral gown sticking to her like a second skin, "I shall be on my way, may the best team win, hmm?" She good-naturedly jostled Valine's shoulder, and the assassin offered her a sharp smile.

"May the best team win."

Valine was left alone again, and as a server passed, she secured her first mimosa of the day and found an empty tent behind a tree. Her drink was perfectly balanced, with just the right amount of champagne, and fresh-squeezed orange juice—they'd even added a decorative slice dipped in sugar.

"Care to test mine as well?" Malik asked from her right.

"It would be quite daring to poison all these mimosas, would it not?"

"This is true. However, imagine how chaotic it would be if only one were poisoned—left to chance."

"Mm, you're right. We shouldn't tempt fate."

She handed Malik her own mimosa—sipped once—and traded it for his. Valine took a healthy swallow—not poisoned—and crossed her arms over her chest, the mimosa dangling from her fingers. Malik turned to face her, his eyes playful, a hint of smile curling up the edges. He was dressed in black, a loose shirt whose buttons were half undone, and sleeves rolled up to display wonderful arms. They were brown and traced with veins. A gold ink athame with a wickedly curved blade was tattooed on his left forearm, as well as a black ink tattoo of script—though he moved too quickly for Valine to read it.

"How did you sleep last night?" he inquired blandly.

"Fine. And yourself?"

"Great, made even better knowing what I know."

Valine felt blood rush to her cheeks. "And what is it you think you know?"

Malik leaned down to her, whispering in her ear, and his daemons-damned scent enveloped her. "Did you think of me when you did it?"

"Did what?" she asked, voice strained.

He softly chuckled in her ear, and the places she'd touched last night came alive again. "When you pleasured yourself. Did you imagine it was me? That it was my fingers inside you and not your own?"

"I'm sorry, you're mistaken."

"Am I?"

"Yes."

"Hmm, so you neglected your needs and left yourself untouched all night with all that wet silk? You didn't let that pussy come on your fingers?"

"No," Valine lied, her throat thick.

"Do you know what I think?" he asked, catching her earlobe between his teeth. He was really doing this, in front of everyone—granted, they were shielded beneath a tent behind a palm tree. She wasn't even sure his silent and near invisible guards were privy to this encounter.

"What?" Her voice was embarrassingly thready.

"That you are still a pretty little liar."

The wildest desire slammed into her, and in that moment, Valine wanted nothing more than to throw Malik down onto the lounge chair in this one-walled tent, kiss him, and fuck him into oblivion. She wanted to tear his clothes off and feel his fingers between her legs like she imagined last night. She wanted to feel even more than that. She wanted to feel him beneath her while she rode him or to feel him roll her over and pin her to the grass, thrusting into her. Making her scream.

Valine met Malik's eyes, and she knew he saw what she wanted. He opened his mouth and shifted towards her, but just then, Jacira whistled.

"It's time! Find your partners and follow Hanish. He will explain the rules!"

And so, they parted, having not said anything, but having said almost everything between gold-blue and night-dark eyes. They wanted each other, and she didn't know how she was going to keep her hands off him with only a single door separating their suites.

CHAPTER TWENTY-TWO

Jacira was one of the most competitive people Valine had ever met in her life, and it was only solidified by the fact that they were on the third and final round of the three-legged race. The two of them were competing against Sarim and Cersei, Freyja and Tallulah, and Malik and Pandora. Alastair and Balchon had long ago bowed out in favor of drinking wine and being pampered. Despite Alastair's careful politicking and countenance surrounding the Tallohian's, he kept a distance between himself and the delicacies and debauchery offered. Still, Valine knew a part of him secretly loved it. Surely, he missed the life he'd had until he was shunned?

Hanish was on the sidelines, dressed in the same white linen—or a duplicate of—as he'd worn last night. He raised his arm in the air, a formal golden pistol in his grip, and pulled the trigger. The eight competitors took off with the shot, and it was clear that this round was much more physical than the previous two had been.

Valine was shouldering against Cersei, digging sharp elbows into ribs, and small hisses of exclamations lit the air. In the nick of time, she remembered Jacira's recollection of previous events, and Cersei's probable cheating, as the lioness in question reached to grab Valine—a move strictly off-limits. Jacira and Valine found a good rhythm in the first race and continued with it, understanding that Valine had to slow ever so while Jacira had to push herself a little harder to keep even. They wrested other competitors on their run, Valine managing to trip Cersei with a well-placed kick to the ankle—all was fair among liars and cheats. She began to tumble to the ground, but Sarim—the hulking mass of muscle and strength he was—managed to pull up the honey-blonde woman. Freyja and Tallulah overtook Sarim and Cersei, laughing as they sped past, while the former had to build up their own once again.

The green lawn was plush under Valine's bare feet, but her foot still smarted from the kicking, and she bit out a curse. As it was, Valine and Jacira were in first place. Cheers and toasts were going up, and inhibitions declined. Drinks were sloshed over rims, and smiles turned to touches and turned to kisses. On the sidelines, there was more than one couple with their tongues dancing, hands groping in such a way that would beg a lashing in Runell. Just behind the princess and the assassin were Malik and Pandora, and it became quickly evident that the King of Adraali wanted to win.

Like the rest of them, Malik was barefoot, the hems of his black pants rolled up. Valine was startled to see a serpent tattoo on the top of his foot. His nails were painted gold and finely manicured. Unfortunately, those finely pampered nails were becoming grass-stained and embedded with dirt. And it became abundantly clear as Valine was admiring the king that he and Pandora had significantly gained on them.

Pandora was ecstatic, her face rosy and her grin jubilant as her arm was wound around the king with the ground rapidly passing beneath her. Valine could see from the girl's mannerisms that she was no royal, and she wondered how she'd climbed to the upper echelon of society she was entrenched in. Was it all sex? Was it all devious? How did she come to meet and become lovers with Jacira and Jericho? How long had it all been going on? Valine didn't know, however none of it mattered as Jacira was yelling in her ear.

"We're almost there!"

Just as the princess announced this, Valine was knocked off kilter by Malik. His shoulder checked into hers, his hip following in quick succession in such a manner that Valine had no hope of recovering. She went down, Jacira with her, and the only consolation was that Jacira's momentum had effectively tripped Malik and Pandora. The four of them effectively rolled across the lawn. The princess was tossed over Valine as she hit the grass, tasting dirt and taking the brunt of it on her chest. She rolled to her back, trying to breathe, urged by Jacira's flight, and felt a second impact. They landed, all four of them together in a tangled heap. Malik on top of Valine, his chest on her pelvis, and Pandora sprawled across Jacira, her face somewhere near Valine's ribs.

"*Fucking hell,*" Malik hissed, pain in his voice.

Cheers went up as Freyja and Tallulah hopped past them, crossing the white banner of the finish line. Cersei and Sarim were close on their heels and in perilous danger of ending up in a similar situation to Valine.

For a moment, Valine couldn't breathe. The impact had knocked the wind out of her, and she was certain in all the commotion that she'd taken a knee or an elbow to the head. As she tried to climb out from underneath the mass, she realized that Pandora and Jacira were sharing a moment. Giggling and touching each other. Valine was horrified to imagine an orgy erupting right then; when she was legitimately tied to the princess. Her panic-filled eyes met Malik's, and he had seemed to come to the realization at the same time as her. The two of them scrambled to get up, helping each other despite the virtually dead weight attached to them.

Somehow, they managed to get to their feet before an orgy broke out, but even so, Valine wasn't eager to stay attached to Jacira just in case. She bent low, her head throbbing, as she worked through the knots on the rope holding them together. She did it quickly and with proficiency, thanks to her assassin's training and other extracurricular activities. Malik watched this all with a brow raised.

"Don't even ask me to help you. You attacked me," Valine warned as she crossed the finish line. Malik followed.

"I can't believe you'd accuse me of something so heinous."

"I'll accuse you of worse—perhaps battery of women. I'm sure you were the one to whack me in the head."

"You're a malicious thing."

"You wouldn't change it," she threw back, tossing up a middle finger for good measure.

It struck Valine as scandalized expressions crossed those around them, that Valine and Malik did not behave like king and subject, but rather the way friends did. The way people who are comfortable with each other interact. Were they friends? She didn't think so. Friends didn't comment on friend's masturbation habits or touch them like Malik had touched her. They certainly didn't help each other dress, especially in such a sensual manner. They also didn't keep secrets and withhold information like Malik had. And so, Valine was angry again.

A gorgeous woman dressed in servant's attire stalked up beside Hanish with a large black slate, marking down points in white chalk. Her long ebony hair swung freely, though one side was pinned with an opal barrette. The top four spots were taken up by the four teams that had recently raced, in the order in which they'd won—placing Freyja and Tallulah in first. Malik and Pandora were in third—as Pandora crossed the line after Jacira—therefore, Valine and Jacira were placed last at the top.

The female servant announced a refreshment break, and servers went around with newly loaded trays. Hanish caught Valine's eye, signaling with two fingers by his knee. She nodded. As everyone became distracted by the food and drink, Hanish locked the gun into a velvet-lined box, depositing it into a waiting guard's hands. He then took up a tray and strode towards Valine. As Hanish swept low to offer her the assortment of pastries and other baked goods, she plucked up a square of baklava as he tucked a note into her opposite hand. She thanked him, and he bowed, skirting the other guests and dipping in offering.

Valine bit into the dessert, tasting honey and walnuts in the flaky pastry. Covering her mouth with a hand under the guise of politeness, she read the note tucked into it.

1) *Unclear*

2) *Complicated*

Midnight, same place.

Valine hid a smirk by stuffing the rest of the square in her mouth and tucked the note within her lace brassiere. During the brief break between events, Valine opted to use the toilets tucked near the palace. It was a small building of white stone and climbing bougainvillea. Before emptying her bladder, Valine reproduced the note, shredded it carefully between her fingers, and flushed all evidence of it behind. Had modern plumbing not been available, she would have had to risk disposing throughout the gardens or swallowing it—something she'd rather not do if it could be avoided.

When Valine returned to the masses, it became painfully evident that in her absence, liquor had been passed much too freely. Everyone was kissing, smoking, or drinking, or participating in other acts of debauchery. Valine surveyed the lawn, finding familiar faces; Malik was smiling a sleek and dangerous smile at some royals, Valine knew the barest of blackmail about. Jacira was straddling Pandora on a lounge chair, the top of her dress hardly covering much of anything anymore. Cersei and Sarim were cheering as Freyja displayed her phenomenal limbo skills with a drink in her hand—her flowing orange pants allowed her plenty of flexibility—while Balchon and Alastair held the ornamental staff she crossed beneath. All of them in various degrees of intoxication—Malik the least, and Balchon the most. But all the while, Tallulah was conversing quietly with the queen who had just made an appearance with King Jericho.

The king was clearly searching for his shared lover, and Valine watched his expression change the moment he found her. It was for a moment, but a dark look passed over his face. The beginnings of a scowl furrowing his brow, his lips down-turning and thinning, a clear look of anger and jealousy. But it flashed away just as fast. He was then clapping a lord on the back with a hearty grin. Valine saw it all, even if no one else did.

Steadying herself, Valine began crossing the lawn towards the queen, nabbing a flute of champagne from one tray and a vial of plum syrup from another. She kept walking as she added the sweetened extract to her drink and deposited the empty glass on another tray. She was sipping the burgundy-tinted bubbles as she came upon the queen and Tallulah. Valine dipped in a polite curtsy, meeting the hard jade of Queen Amaris's gaze. Her lips turned into a mockery of a smile while Valine vowed to act her ass off.

"Queen Amaris, it is an absolute pleasure to be welcomed so warmly to Talloh. And to such a delightful tournament before the festival has even begun. I feel so truly blessed and honored to be present. The Stygian Ones must shine their light down upon you fondly."

The weight in Amaris's gaze lifted ever so, the jade softening as a true smile broke across her countenance. She was garbed in dazzling silver-shot satin, the wavering lines of which sparkled like storm-tossed waters. She was still wearing that magnificent star diadem.

"The pleasure is all mine, Lady Desdemon," Amaris declared, taking Valine's hand in hers. Valine tried to hide the jolt that went through her from use of her family name and the touch from the monarch. "The stars spoke to me last night, you see."

"Did they?" Valine feigned interest as she sipped daintily. "Would you be willing to reveal the wisdom they shared?"

"They divined a great many things will come to this nation. Our ascension to god-hood is tied to such prophecy." Amaris looked from side to side furtively, squeezing her hand more. "I do not like to put such stock in gossip, but I have been told that upon your journey here, you were tried by arachne, and were found worthy, is this true?"

Valine swallowed, and Tallulah's gray eyes widened as they leaned forward. "That is true. I was tested. It was a truly terrifying experience, Your Majesty. In that moment, I felt as if my entire life had been pulled from my soul and read by a being with greatness I cannot comprehend."

"Gracious. I'd heard it, but to have it so clearly painted…you must be a truly remarkable person." Valine couldn't put into words how treacherous she truly was. "It was foretold our savior would find ancient creatures, and those creatures would bow to their will. I believe this is you. I believe you are known to the stars and that they have crowned you in destiny."

Valine didn't put much stock in destiny, but it would be insulting to the queen who was virtually extolling Valine's virtues, to point this out. She wondered how much of Amaris's star-seeing was drug-induced, and how much was wishful thinking. As wondrous as stellaemancers were, they could see very little of the future beyond large, vague events. It was well known that divinamancers were the only true sources of prophecy, and as Hanish had educated, they were hidden away for the danger they posed. Valine wondered if the queen was not lying entirely if she had sought a divinamancer herself, who spouted the same prophetic bullshit she was serving Valine. She didn't like to linger on the thought because what if Valine was on a path she did not choose, and rather a saint or a daemon had set her on it?

"I cannot express to you how privileged I am that you think of me so highly. I will cherish your words forevermore."

Amaris clutched her hand even tighter. "Lady Valine, do you think a royal wedding may be in your future?"

Valine blinked and tried not to choke on her plum champagne. "Um, I do not imagine so, Your Majesty. I have no prospects or suitors, and to be quite honest, I'm above the ideal age for a royal marriage."

Amaris scoffed and patted Valine's hand, finally letting it go. "I'm not worried about your age. I'm more concerned about a certain secret dalliance."

"Oh?"

"Yes, I have heard—not that I search for this sort of talk—that you and King Malik are...friendly. And I will not lie. I've seen with my own eyes some of this admiration."

"Yes, we speak fondly because, as you see, I am to be a companion to his prospective brides come the Blooming Season. I was welcomed along to learn the ways in which a court operates and how to best support his future wife." Valine refused to pinpoint why this statement pained her.

"Valine, you are meant to be much more than just a companion."

Valine inhaled. What the queen didn't know was that she was so much more than that already. Necromancer. Assassin. A Desdemon. Falling for the King of Adraali.

CHAPTER TWENTY-THREE

The rest of the afternoon devolved into a swath of depravity and disposed inhibitions. The tournament was loosely played and won. Sarim and Cersei found themselves with 97 points, with Freyja and Tallulah coming in shortly after with 92, while Malik and Valine scored in the low 60s courtesy of their partners' inability to tear away from each other. When the orange that must be passed without hands was between Jacira and Pandora, the two found mysterious ways for the orange to slip, and for their lips to find the other's. Valine wondered how much Jacira truly cared for the girl or if it was just the whirlwind of a new romance that had her so unfettered in her public affections.

Sore and tired, Valine opted out of the rest of the night's events, claiming a headache. In response, Amaris directed the beautiful female servant—Hafsa—to guide Valine to the Head Healer and instruct him to prepare a tonic for her. She thanked the queen, and let Hafsa lead the way. Meanwhile, the assassin documented every turn and potential secret hallway, noting suspicious tapestries, regularly shifted furniture, and discreet breezes.

They found themselves in an archaic lab, not unlike the apothecary's shop in Luneth. Colored glass was a mural on the wall, holding all manner of elixirs and potions, while a wooden table was laden with various mortar and pestle sets and chopping blocks with wickedly sharp knives. It was there in the lab, surrounded by aging and yellowed books, that Valine met the Head Healer.

"Healer Das, this is Valine Desdemon. Queen Amaris has requested a headache tonic for the lady," Hafsa said, her dulcet tones chiming through the room in ripples and rolls. "During the race today, she sustained a blow to the head, and I fear it may have led to an ailment of some sort."

Healer Das appeared days shy of seventy, with olive skin, pale from lack of sunshine, and wispy white hair that stuck to his head in airy tufts. His eyes were granite and earth, solid and immovable as they took her in behind his owlish glasses, finding her clothing grass-stained and missing threads. He was dressed in indigo robes layered with lilac silk, a chain of golden medallions hanging low and swinging against his portly belly. He cracked a smile, displaying a missing tooth near his molars and papery lips in dire need of balm.

"A wondrous event to meet a Desdemon," Healer Das exclaimed, setting down a pouch half-filled with coin. Sitting up on creaking joints, eliciting a wince, he hobbled over to the women. "Are you perchance Dáinn Desdemon's daughter?"

Valine fought back bile. "I am."

"Oh, I knew your father well once upon a time, dear! Next time you see him, would you tell him Mareek Das still owes him a favor?"

"I…" Valine morphed her sick delight into a farce of dismay and sorrow. "I apologize, Healer Das. He passed away several years ago."

Mareek Das's face fell, Valine's words falling like a physical blow, and the healer had to physically sit down. He was forced to seek a seat that Hafsa was all too quick to provide. She had moved soundlessly and quickly—Valine filed that information away for later.

"Was it a peaceful passing?" he asked, sorrowful.

Valine weighed her response carefully. She wanted to tell him the truth—that it certainly wasn't—but that wasn't the portrait she wanted to paint of herself. She wanted to be seen as the still grieving daughter, the child who missed her beloved father. Not the murderess who grinned like a cat who got the canary when she thought about his demise.

"I hope so," she finally managed. "It was an assassin, and unfortunately, the culprit was never caught." Yes, very unfortunate.

Healer Das shook his head mournfully, whispering a prayer to the Stygian Ones. Slowly, he returned to his feet and shuffled over to the wall of multicolored glass, perusing the bottles. He tsked as he hobbled to a chest of drawers, pulling open one and peering in before he selected. It was cerulean, the liquid inside sloshing viscously. Cradling the tonic, he crossed the room and presented it to Valine. Tentatively, she picked it up, examining it for herself.

"This is one of Queen Amaris's own. She has famously expounded on its success—she suffers from migraines, you see. A tonic like this is only the best for Dáinn's daughter."

Valine forced a smile. "Thank you, Healer Das. Your generosity will not be forgotten."

"Anything for you, dear." His tone shifted, and Valine's hackles went up. "Your father and I got into much mischief back in the day, and might I add, festivals were never quite the same after he married your mother. But of course, had that not happened, you would not have been born, and what a shame that would have been." A lascivious glint sparkled in the healer's eyes, and Valine wanted to stab out his eyes just for that look. She knew what it was. She'd seen it. She abhorred it.

Gritting her teeth, Valine managed another round of thanks and escaped with Hafsa, feeling the old man's lewd eyes burning on her backside. It took everything in her to rein in her fury, the fury that she'd inherited from the horrible man who'd spawned her. As they returned to the Vesper Wing, Valine sensed Hafsa's eyes flickering to her warily but said nothing on the matter as she deposited Valine at her doorstep.

Immediately, she locked the doors and windows, setting a trip wire at each threshold when she pulled the curtains tight. Once all was completed, she stripped herself of the ruined clothing, and took a brief shower before collapsing in her bed, wrapped in a robe, tonic untaken.

Valine awoke when it was true darkness and dressed quietly. She pulled on a black silk negligee and a lace robe, then piled her hair in a messy bun atop her head before securing it with a clawed clip hiding a spike of silvered viper venom. Her rings were still in place, garrote included, and for good measure, she added a thigh sheath beneath the small dress, hiding the dagger on the opposite side from the slit.

She slid on her wrapped sandals and slipped into the night beyond the Vesper Wing. She avoided all the guards on the way to the Lunar Meadow, skirting the moonlight, and weaving between the shadows. When she arrived, Hanish was already there, pacing.

"What is your update?" Valine asked, stepping from the darkness.

Hanish leaped, instinctively reaching for lightning. Valine responded with a lash of her necromancy.

"Gods! Do you have to do that every time?"

"No," she returned, smiling. "But it's fun."

He sighed and shook his head, exasperated. "You were right about the Illise Mines. They are using divinamancers to navigate the tunnels. I just don't know how much Tallulah is aware of." Unclear was clarified.

"And Raziche's Den?" Valine prodded.

"Has fingers in everyone's pockets. At least half of Talloh's nobility is in varying degrees of monetary or favor-based debt with the gambling den." He handed her a rolled coil of parchment. "Here is a list of names who are in the deepest."

Valine took the list, exchanging the information for coin she'd pocketed during the tournament—it was astounding how many people kept loose coin in their pockets, and it wasn't Valine's fault they thought it fell to the grass, never to be seen again.

"Malik is arranging your departure, but I need you to keep looking into Balchon and Tallulah. And in addition, I need to know more about Cersei."

"Is that all?" Hanish cocked a dark brow.

"No, actually. What do you know about Hafsa?"

Hanish cleared his throat, discomfort clear on his face. "She is my wife."

Valine was blown away. "*She* is your *wife?*" She blinked several times. She hadn't deduced an intimate relationship between them. They'd hardly looked at each other, and she hadn't sensed any tension—sexual or otherwise.

"Yes, why are you so surprised?"

"You did not act like it."

Hardness entered Hanish's eyes. "We are not allowed to. Showing bonds or relationships between servants is grounds for lashing. Hafsa and I have been taken to the whip many times for the slightest of infractions."

"That is barbaric."

"Do you wonder why we wish to leave?"

"No." Valine shook her head. "I certainly do not." She hesitated, meeting his eyes carefully. "I want to ask you something, but I do not want you to lie to me."

Hanish motioned for her to continue.

"Your wife's background is no mere servant. Is she part of the Ōrdinem?"

Hanish blanched, but he did not move. His breathing turned tighter, and his eyes flared ever so slightly.

"How did you guess?"

Valine held his gaze, no joking present. "The moonstone. She's also too graceful and quick. It's easy to spot when you know what to look for."

"Do you think anyone else has figured it out?" Anxiety rang in Hanish's voice.

Valine considered. "No, I don't think so. She would have been killed or extorted for it by now if so. Please tell her to be careful. I can't promise no one else will discover this."

"I will."

"I have to ask…if she's part of the Ōrdinem, why are you stuck here? Can't they help you?"

"She has refused to complete her last assignment since becoming a mother, and her views on killing have changed. So, until she does, they will not answer our pleas."

Valine wavered with a decision, finally biting the bullet. "What is the assignment?"

He told her.

"I'll take care of it."

"What?" He was aghast.

"If she disappears and her assignment is not finished, they will hunt her down. I don't fuck around with the Ōrdinem for that very reason."

"How will you—?"

"Don't worry about it," she interrupted. "You help me, I'll help you. Investigate that shit for me, and I'll have this handled."

"Thank you, Valine."

"Don't thank me yet, I haven't done anything."

"It's more than anyone else has done for me…so thank you."

Valine squashed the warm feelings that bubbled to the surface of her soul, forcibly resisting the urge to rub the sensation rising in her chest right around her heart. Was she going soft? No, no, this was tit for tat. This was an exchange. You did not make allies by making demands. You made them by making deals. You had to lead the bees with honey. Vinegar only served to piss them off.

"Find that information for me," she commanded and turned on her heel, leaving Hanish in the moonlit meadow.

Valine was scouting the halls, searching for mysterious passages and emergency exits from the way of the aviary, when Malik found her. She had just finished penning three letters which she sent by falcon, though only once was necessary. The other two were a charade. Valine pretended not to see him, and it was all the more satisfying that he didn't know this when he attempted to accost her in an alcove, and she was the one who had him pinned instead.

Malik blinked those blue-gold eyes, stunned to find himself with stone at his back when it had been his intention to have her in that very position. A smile crept across his face, sexy and cool, as he took her in, the clinging silk and exposed throat. Heat built between them, only furthered by the press of their bodies against each other. Valine's arms were shoved against his shoulders and chest, sprawling out while their knees locked together, legs tangled. Instead of being dismayed, he was turned on and showed this by circling her waist.

Panic flooded Valine. This was not what she had anticipated, and truly at this point, what was stopping them from fucking right then and there? Her lines and rules? Both were becoming horribly flimsy and they both knew it. She had stated her boundaries, yet invited him to flirt, virtually giving him every reason to chase her—because she secretly wanted it. She was letting him pursue her, she was not stopping him when he was touching her. The sexual tension between them was ramping up, pulling tighter, the taut thread between them a breath from snapping. All she wanted was—

No.

No, she was angry at him. He used her. He used her to get information and then fucked off to bed. That did not a deal make.

"You lied to me," she fired quietly.

Surprise laced Malik's features, but still, he did not yield in his hold. He actually began circling her lower back with his thumbs—it felt divine. "About?" he said with such calm, fingers still working knots from her.

"We had a deal, information exchange, and you reneged on it. I gave you what I knew, and then you left."

"I left," Malik breathed, leaning forward, his mouth brushing the shell of her ear. "Because if I didn't leave, I didn't know how I wasn't going to fuck you had I spent another minute in your presence." He bit her ear gently, and she gasped.

"Do you want me to tell you the numbers in which Talloh's taxes differ from Adraali's? How I convinced Jericho to counter an agricultural deal with Pravo that will only make Pravo richer by the supply-demand that I have promising investments in? What of the alliance that Jericho seeks to form with the Desdemons of Runell, an alliance that I assure you is shot with your presence here?

"Is that what you wanted to know? That your mere existence has resulted in the questioning of a powerful monarch?"

Valine knew that he wasn't just talking about Jericho's political ambition but his own feelings, and Valine did not have the capacity to sort it out. Not when she had Malik's breath on her throat, his lips parted on her skin, her pulse against his teeth. She had rules, she reminded herself, but all she could think about was: Why stop? Why didn't they tumble to bed together? They were adults. It was just sex. All these times Malik put his hands on her, Valine had resisted the urge to do the same, but finally, the dam against her will broke, and her hands found themselves beneath his shirt, skimming his hot golden skin. She felt his abs ripple with his increased breathing, and she felt his cock harden against her belly.

"Malik…" she whispered, tilting her face up to him. She wanted him so badly it hurt. She could feel the desire aching in the apex of her thighs.

Malik's hands roamed lower, grazing the bare skin of her thighs, hitching up her dress to cup her rear against him. He ground his hips into her, his fingertips pressing on her bare skin, and she hoped he left bruises.

"Valine…" he moaned back, tipping his face down.

As they began to reach for each other, their lips a breath away, loud footsteps thundered down the hall, a belligerent yell emphasizing them. Valine and Malik broke apart in shock, peering out of the alcove to watch a very uniformly white figure dash up the hall towards them. Illuminated in the moonlight, it became painfully evident the person was wholly naked, the member between his legs flopping comically about. Sweat and other bodily fluids stuck to his skin. His eyes glassy, pupils blown wide.

"Get back!" he screeched, and Valine realized with shock that the naked, running man was Balchon. "Quit chasing me daemons, you can't have my cock!"

Valine stood still, processing his words as Balchon ran past, heedless of their presence. His bare feet continued to slap the stone floor. Whether the event was induced by drugs or a dare—Valine suspected the former—Balchon was utterly unaware of the near kiss he'd interrupted. Seconds later, the jangle of armor and weapons came upon them while Valine and Malik were still caught in a compromising position. Four guards rounded the corner, clearly chasing Balchon.

They slowed, and she knew what they would see soon—Valine's black negligee hitched on her thigh, Malik's hands covering his prominent erection, both their faces flushed with lust and embarrassment—and she held her breath. But it was for naught, because they raced past, unknowing of the king and the assassin hiding in the shadows. Unaware they were harboring tension that could've been cut with a knife.

As they disappeared, Valine deflated, palming her forehead, and immediately dragged Malik inside her room. Once safely away from potential prying eyes, Valine pulled the vial and clip from her hair and tossed them on the entry table.

"We can't get caught like that."

"Like what?" Malik asked, crossing the space between them, caging her against the wall. "Explain it to me."

"No, we can't do this." She reaffirmed the dam that so nearly shattered. "I do not sleep with people that pay me. I don't like mixing money and sex. It complicates things."

"Is that what you want?"

He was so close, Valine couldn't get a breath that wasn't scented with black orchid and tobacco. "What I want is irrelevant. This is business, and I haven't yet told you what I've learned."

Malik stepped back, realizing the spell was broken and respecting the clear shutdown of the situation—a situation it was all too clear neither of them actually wanted to prevent. Even so, he moved to her fainting couch, and she filled him in on everything Hanish had told her, from his wife to Balchon and Tallulah, in addition to the treatment of romantic entanglements between servants and the resulting consequence of showing it. She also revealed Hafsa's connection to the Ōrdinem and her unfilled assignment.

"Are you planning to complete her assignment?" Malik asked levelly. She couldn't deduce how he felt about it in that moment, and his response was going to sway her answer. But unfortunately, he was stone.

"If it does not jeopardize the mission here, yes."

"You *cannot* get caught."

"I haven't yet."

"That's not true—we got you."

"That's different," she dismissed, a furious flush rising in her cheeks. "That was a setup."

"And are you sure this isn't?" Malik questioned; eyes flinty.

Valine bit her lip, glancing away. She had considered that Hanish was lying to her, and even if he wasn't, she wondered if he would immediately blame her for the crime upon its commencement. She had to weigh the risks, and she knew that the only way to get Hanish and his family safely out of Talloh, was to finish the job. She could, of course, refuse to help them escape, but what was stopping Hanish from turning her in at that point? It was too messy to contemplate, she'd gotten herself in too far. Betraying Hanish would only result in his death or hers. But she had a contingency.

"No, but I have to do this," she told him determinedly. "I need to instill his trust with this."

"I can't lose you," Malik bit out.

"I'll be careful. Trust me."

Malik laughed, a harsh sound. "I shouldn't, but I do."

"Have I given you reason not to?"

"No."

"And I won't." She crossed the room, standing before him, taking his hand and placing it over her heart. "I am a liar and a cheater. I am a murderess and a traitor. But I will not betray *you*. I swear it."

Malik swallowed once, and nodded. Valine dropped his hand, and for a moment, they were still and silent, staring into each other's eyes, leaving so much left unsaid before he left the room.

CHAPTER TWENTY-FOUR

Valine had influenced Balchon's thought patterns in order to get an open invitation into Raziche's Den. It took little work—suggestions and light complaints, queries and compliments, and then he was hooked. Like clay in her hand, Balchon invited her to accompany him to a night of gambling, and he was only too pleased when she accepted. Even more so when she suggested Freyja accompany them on his other arm.

She could practically see the fantasies coming alive in his mind.

After leaving a discreet note for Malik, Valine visited Freyja in her suite. Hers, unlike Valine's, was magenta and violet; bursts of flowers papered the walls, and gold-framed furniture scattered the room. It was upon fuchsia chairs that Valine and Freyja sipped flavored water and discussed.

"I need you to come with me to Raziche's Den tonight. I already promised Balchon," Valine revealed.

Freyja raised a made-up brow. "And I have a feeling this isn't a visit just to have a fun night of gambling, is it?"

"It certainly is not," Valine confirmed.

Freyja smirked. "What do you need me to do?"

Valine grinned and told her.

Later that night, Valine and Freyja were waiting in a courtyard after getting ready together. The blonde clad in a stunning dress of azalea pink, sheer except for the tiny teardrop-shaped crystals that covered her modesty, while Valine wore a skin-tight dress with her signature thigh-high slit in a shade of sapphire. They were standing with two guards appointed by Balchon, the man himself arriving in a loud tunic of bloodred damask and a golden brooch with the den's crest—a lion with a spade in its mouth.

A breeze brought the scent of night, jasmine, and ocean, lightly touched with Balchon's cologne—a musky blend of patchouli, liquor, and salt. He smiled, displaying a wide, white grin. His brown hair was pushed back with product, a few strands blowing in the breeze. Valine had left her hair entirely unbound save for a jeweled barrette—a weapon, of course—combing back the hair that hung over her shoulder. Freyja wore hers in a high half updo, parts of it hanging around her face to curtain it softly, while the pale waves were pulled into ornate twists.

Balchon opened the ostentatious carriage and bowed out the door, the sight of his red attire so stark against the ivory and gilt-edged vehicle. The horses were outfitted in a ridiculous amount of gold, their harnesses liberally showing the lion's crest of Raziche's Den.

"Don't you two look delicious," Balchon announced, leering. Valine preened, even though her fingers itched for one of the many blades hidden on her person.

It wasn't that the Raziche heir was unattractive, but there was something to him that was incredibly off-putting. The intensity of his eyes, the feckless adoration he had for drugs, and the general carelessness he owned as a person that had her ill at ease. He seemed harmless enough, but Valine had seen enough men extol the virtues of their wives only to abuse the power they held over servants and maids. She did not trust men.

"You do like to flirt, don't you?" Valine teased back, revealing none of her internal ire.

Balchon cocked his head to the side, aiming for charm. "It's in my nature. Especially when two beautiful women are attending me for the evening."

Valine smiled through a baring of her teeth, imagining popping two fingers into his eyes. She was not a kind person and she was rash. Malik saw that, and he even liked it. She pushed that thought out of her mind immediately.

Freyja and Valine entered the carriage with Balchon, their guards hopping on the bench atop. Balchon regaled them with tales of the grandeur they'd experienced in the den. It was the most luxurious of any establishment in Talloh. In addition to being a gambling hall, it also boasted a gentleman's club, brothel, and opium den. Truly, it was a mystery how the Raziches had earned such a monopoly over the debauched resources when it seemed new card dens, and whorehouses popped up every month. She wondered how they all stayed in business.

The travel to Raziche's Den was a quick one, carried over smooth pavers, the night sky grasping at hints of lilac, the stars painfully white. As they trundled, Valine felt excitement brew, and it shot skyward when Balchon declared them at their destination. He escorted them out of the carriage, Valine gazing up to see a grand building of obsidian. Luxmancer lamps glowed against its shining façade, pumping music escaped the confines of the den. A giant lion's head perched above the entrance, rendered in gold, and displayed in its jaw was a ludicrously large ruby shaped like a spade. The thing was nearly the size of her head.

"Remarkable, isn't it?" Balchon asked as he sidled up to Valine, wrapping an arm around her waist while he did the same to Freyja on his other side. Valine wanted to snap his wrist. "The ruby was a gift from Illise Mines. I believe it was Tallulah's great-grandfather who'd given it to mine."

A *gift*.

A ruby the size of a basilisk egg was a *gift*.

How fucking rich were the Illises and Raziches?

"It's truly spectacular," Freyja marveled with false awe. The ruinmancer was just stroking his ego, but it worked—it always did on simple men like him. Flattery gets you far and all that nonsense.

"Come," Balchon urged. "I would love to show a few games."

The girls smiled and let Balchon drag them into the lion's den. They didn't look twice at Balchon, letting the heir pass uninterrupted. Inside, the den was red. Everything from the floor to the walls to the ceiling. It was all red velvet and smoke. Golden lights glowed from everything, gas-powered and luxmancer alike, tiers of seating and games lay ahead of them. Servers clad in gold domino masks and black satin graced the establishment, patrons burning cigarillos in fingers and from stems, the thick scent obscuring the bitter smell of body odor and sour breath. There was a wide variety of people present, but everyone dressed in the best of finery, jewels dripping off them—and in some cases, onto tables. Above was a mezzanine that led to a hallway covered by two guards, the lighting there dimmer, meant to discourage curious eyes.

That was where she needed to go.

Balchon plucked up three masks, and three champagne flutes from a passing server, passing them to Valine and Freyja. She forced herself not to think of what Malik told her about a mask and nothing else. Smiling, Valine donned the mask and sipped daintily, watching the gold flakes swirl against the bubbles. It was light and crisp with the tiniest hint of florals. She downed her glass and deposited it on a passing tray.

It was time.

Valine placed a hand on Balchon's forearm. "Before you show us around, would you mind if Freyja and I were to freshen up?"

Balchon gave her a disarming smile, sipping his flute. "Of course." He pointed to the left. "Through those golden arches, you'll find the restrooms. I'll wait by the bar." He indicated further to the left, a single booth standing between the two locations. Not ideal, but she'd make it work.

Valine and Freyja made their way to the toilets. Once inside, Valine checked each of the stalls—empty. She locked the door behind them, her eyes zeroing in on Freyja.

"I need you to buy me some time. Can you dim the lights out there?"

Freyja considered. "The gas-powered, yes, the luxmancer, no. They'd sense me messing with their magic."

"I can work with that. Give me ten minutes."

Freyja stepped out of the door and slowly lifted her hand, letting the gas lights dim, and Valine darted out while everyone else was distracted by the sudden lack of light. Using the shadows, she made her way up the stairs, approaching the first guard. She pulled on her necromancy, not enough to kill, but enough to toy with his brain, enough for him to see stars. He closed his eyes and reached out a hand to the rail to steady himself. Valine slipped by him, releasing her magic.

She was out of eyesight after that point, the lights in the den brightening once again. Valine startled. That was *not* ten minutes. Traveling down the hall on silent feet in a blue dress and a gold mask, Valine met the second guard. Before he set eyes on her, she reached out with her necromancy—

And found nothing.

She startled at the lack of magic. She searched within her, feeling for that dark smoky magic to find nothing in its place. Panic threaded through Valine just as a prick of nausea loosed through her, and with that, awful realization took over.

Fucking mage shade.

It was highly effective but highly unethical. A poison used sparingly, as it more often than not became lethal—even more so with consecutive doses. Most times, it was due to dosing, as most people didn't realize how potent it was. One petal from mage shade was enough to nix a mage for a night. It was one of the very few substances that her necromancy was no match for—it operated outside the bounds of magic. It was the antithesis of magery.

No. No, how did this happen? How was she dosed?

Valine realized just as the guard caught sight of her.

The *fucking* champagne.

"Hey, what are you doing up here?" the guard demanded.

Valine panicked—but she wasn't an assassin for nothing. She rushed him, flicking the cover off one of her rings, and ducked his grasp as she spun up to his side and punched him in the side of his head. The spiked ring with silvered viper venom struck inside his ear. He went down with a cry as the venom quickly took effect, and Valine glanced around, searching for a hiding place. She left the man slumped on the floor and opened the closest doors. On the third one, she found a utility closet.

Dragging the man from the floor, she stuffed him in the closet to deal with later. She knew he couldn't live after seeing her up here, but it had to look like an accident.

After locking up the soon-to-be-dead guard, Valine hurried to the end of the hallway, where a gold-inlaid door presented itself. Valine plucked the jeweled clip from hair, deconstructed it into a set of lockpicks, and set to work. The door opened for her like it *wanted* her to discover its secrets.

The room was empty, and she felt true fear flitter through her. She was doing this entirely without magic, the mage shade still working through her system. Creeping into the room, Valine made her way to the heavy mahogany desk, rummaging through the drawers until she found what she was truly looking for. The second drawer had a false bottom, and she found the debt ledgers inside.

Flipping through, she went looking for specific names and specific sums. She scanned the papers while keeping an eye on the door, anxiously waiting for it to fling open and reveal her and all her foolish plans. Finally, she found the name she was looking for, and grinned. She memorized the sum. Because she wasn't stealing anything physical, she just needed numbers.

Valine stuffed everything back together and then went to one of the matching cabinets, and found a metal box. It was unlocked. Valine opened it, and inside were satchels. She opened one and saw white powder. Perfect.

Snatching the satchel, she stuffed it in the bodice of her dress and slipped from the room once more, ensuring she hadn't left any clues to her presence. Satisfied, she left and returned to the closet. Pulling the oaf from storage, she yanked and pulled, sweating as she hauled him to the first door she'd tried—a parlor. Inside was a lounge and a glass table. She hoisted the guard onto the lounge. Once in position, she checked his pulse. It was fleeting already. He had minutes left.

Valine worked quickly, spreading the white powder on a silver tray with the accompanying glass tube, pushing it into uniform lines. A drug overdose was always believable. Dipping the glass rim in the fate stealer, Valine traced the guard's nostrils, leaving residue. She tilted his head back for good measure and deposited a fine layer of it inside.

It was done, and moments later, the paralyzed guard died. Valine frowned at the turn of events, but shrugged it off, depositing the glass tube on the floor as if it had rolled from the guard's hand, the other resting on his chest. It was unfortunate, but it was necessary.

She dipped her hands in a basin of water as she left the room, closing it up behind her and heading for the stairs.

"*Fuck*," she muttered, remembering the first guard. She didn't have her necromancy, nor Freyja's ruinmancy to help her this time. She could always kill him, too, but that seemed excessive and messy. Not to mention unexplainable. No, killing him wouldn't work. Could she jump the rail? Surely, she could find a way down unseen?

Valine scanned the gold rail, and noticed at the very end was a red velvet curtain. She glanced up at the rod holding it up—it was not promising, but without magic, it was her only option. Sighing, she backtracked and made her way to the curtain. She gave it an experimental tug and gritted her teeth. Tying her shoes together behind her neck, she climbed over the rail, barefooted, and slid behind the drapes. Quickly, she lowered herself, the tension in the velvet fabric causing her immeasurable anxiety. She was sliding down the curtain when she gauged the landing and just let go, dropping onto the red carpet on bare feet. A blonde, curvaceous woman startled at her sudden appearance from the curtain but returned to her drink, unbothered.

Shoes donned once again, she slunk around the edges of the den, eyeing anyone up who looked too closely at her. She managed to return to Freyja once again, a thin sheen of sweat on her brow as Freyja stared at her incredulously.

"What the fuck happened?" Freyja hissed.

"I'm pretty sure the drinks were laced with mage shade. I lost my magic after the first guard."

It was a shady practice, but not unheard of. The use of mage shade made it so that players couldn't unfairly use their magic to cheat, and because the doses were so miniscule, they considered it low risk. Even so, it explained why Raziche's Den was frequented by more non-magic folk than mages. The playing field was evened.

"Yeah, I did, too," Freyja admitted angrily. "What the fuck did you do?"

Valine sighed. "Trust me. You really don't want to know. Let's just give Balchon a good night and forget the rest."

Freyja gave her a side-eyed look. "You killed someone, didn't you?"

"Sure did."

They gave Balchon a fun and carefree night. Allowing his thoughts and eyes to linger on Valine and Freyja, allowing fantasies of the three of them to bloom—but never come to fruition. Valine and Freyja played up the sexual energy Balchon so clearly wanted to see, urging more touches, and flirtations, and laughs, and tempting scenarios. His vision was clearly compromised by the fate stealer he was liberally snorting—though he was kind enough to offer some to Valine and Freyja despite their refusals.

He truly was so easy to manipulate.

Valine felt the magic-cancelling drug exit her system as they were leaving the den, her necromancy coiling as if it were a snake groggily waking from sleep. And it was pissed. She was able to keep her mind off of things when she returned to her suite and began penning letters and forging documents.

Still clad in her sapphire dress, she pulled out the clay mold from her belongings and made a shoddy job of casting some grays into a seal. Once the weak sigil was created, Valine dripped some wax on the forgery and stamped it with a false Lunethian seal.

CHAPTER TWENTY-FIVE

The letter arrived seven days later. Days which Valine had filled with navigating the secrets of the palace, and deducing which one was best to infiltrate, categorizing which to leave to back-ups. She had found herself winding her way up the narrow spiral staircase to the aviary, the sounds of feathers rustling and caws cutting through the midseason air. It was a lush, vibrant day filled with warm breezes and the scent of seawater. Most of the royals had just recovered from their hangovers from the tour-nament day and the following private celebrations, so Valine had been left to her own devices while they languished in their rooms and attended less exciting activities. She'd hardly seen Malik the last few days, the king having been ensconced in polit-ical meetings regarding trades, taxes, alliances, and all manner of bureaucratic nonsense.

Valine crept across the hay-laden stone floor. Walls of perches and cages encircled her, bins of seed and chests of raw meat surrounding her. The scents of the sunny day intermingled with the sour stench of venison and bird shit, with hints of moldering underlying the hay and dirty linen.

The falcon she'd sent in the direction of Adraali had returned, viridian string tied in a neat bow around his ankle, a crisp scroll tucked into the sheath. Valine stuck her hand into the wooden chest of raw meat and held it out to the falcon. He fluttered his wings excitedly and hopped closer. His beak darted for her hand and broke the skin. She bit out a curse as pain ripped through her palm. She dislodged the scroll and unfurled it, blood smearing across the back of it.

Valine thought back to what she'd written.

Dear Diana,

After having spent only days in Talloh, I am in awe of the royal shade, and I write to you to inquire about the procurement of garments in such a vibrant color—perhaps a gown? It would surely pair well with opal or moonstone, don't you think? I've seen such combinations here, and I must say, I'm surprised I never thought of it before! Are you familiar with it?

I'd like to express greetings from the house of Raziche. I've learned that your family is familiar with the lineage. Would you like to confirm if this is true? I'm sure your household would be grateful to hear news of their current status.

Your friendship is invaluable, and I am eager for our reunion after the Tri-Moon Festival.

With Regards,

Valine

She had to be careful with her wording, should the letter be intercepted in any way. To a layman, it was a woman writing a friend or servant, inquiring about frivolous things like dresses and sending pleasantries to family friends. Of course, the other two letters were penned similarly—frivolously—and she knew those letters would not return in the same haste as Diana's. The Ōrdinem wanted their missions completed, and the expediency of this letter would make it come to fruition.

Dearest Valine,

I am certain I can procure garments in the shades of violet and plum. I am familiar with the pairing you described, and I can confirm that the light stone is more complimentary than amber. To the best of my knowledge, I've never heard of the two together.

It has been six years since I've heard from the Raziche family, and word from their station has been difficult to come by. I do confirm that we extend our approval, and eagerly wish to thank you for helping us reconnect.

Upon the commencement of the festival, I wish to gift you with a family heirloom if you would so accept it.

Yours in Faithful Service,

Diana

So, the Ōrdinem did send Hafsa to kill the mark Hanish identified. Valine wasn't going to trust the word of a man who had less to lose than her—she had to be certain. And how serendipitous was it that she had a lady's maid who happened to be in that very same order? Valine also appreciated the clarification that only the assassin was present and not a healer, too. Not to mention the fact that Valine was being offered a membership into the Ōrdinem once the kill was carried out. The only question she still had was why Hafsa wouldn't finalize the assignment.

She dismissed the thought. The why was no longer important. It was the how, now. Ideas unfurled in Valine's mind. She needed to pull this off without fingers pointing in her direction. This needed to be regarded as an accident. This death was just one of many hurdles required to secure Talloh's servitude to Adraali, and while Valine didn't particularly care, it did help that it truly was for the greater good.

As much as she favored her garrote, it would never do. Perhaps failed autoerotic asphyxiation? Of course, that still left her as a potential suspect, should it not be ruled an accident, and she couldn't afford any suspicion since she was sent to kill the King of Talloh. She settled on poison. It was tried and true, and she knew how to get away with it.

Smiling to herself, Valine descended the staircase, depositing the scroll in a brazier as she left, seeking out Hanish.

It was the evening; shades of blush and lavender painted the sky from the view of the parlor in the Zephyr wing of the palace. They were all propped up on cushions, Valine having manipulated Jacira into summoning her friends, and cronies, and allies for tea. It was the perfect ruse. An informal tea hosted by the princess? The blame could not fall to Valine, and she had ensured that Hanish was the servant who would be bringing in the tea. Valine would make sure she was the one to serve it.

Across the low table was an assortment of small sandwiches, pastries, and samosas, with tureens of hot dips, and bowls cold spreads, offered by a wide variety of crackers and bread, dressed intricately with artfully placed flowers. Currently, they were sipping on flavored waters while the tea brewed, Valine having added a particular blend of nightshade to a particular teapot from the hand of Hanish.

As an assassin, Valine always kept a small store of poisons and blades hidden in the velvet lining of her trousseau and a specific set of items hidden in a locked chest. Both of these items were currently in Hanish's possession. It took Valine much confidence to entrust Hanish with so much that could indict her, but of course, the threat of necromancy can do wonders for motivation.

Jacira was draped over Pandora, while the other girl ran her fingers through the princess's hair, a serene smile playing on her lips. Her eyes were sparkling with a cleverness that Valine wondered how no one else saw. Tallulah and Freyja were engaged in a lively discussion regarding the overrated stance of diamonds, bringing up the grandeur of rubies and emeralds, while Sarim watched Freyja quietly from beside Valine. On Valine's other side was Balchon, chatting amiably with Alastair, telling him of the terrible trip some mushrooms had taken him on days past and how the daemon patrons wanted to eat his dick. Valine knew about that much too well. And then, there was Malik. The king she had not seen in days was flirting with Cersei. Bright, hot, jealous rage flooded Valine, and she quaked to think about what her territorial reaction meant. What it hinted towards, and all the truths it hardly kept at bay.

Palm fronds waved gently in the breeze generated by nearby aethermancers, the need for hydromancers unnecessary as the air was already full of expectant rain. The use of mages only infuriated and reaffirmed her duty. The scent of jasmine and freesia spiced the air as Valine's stress colored it just as potently—if only to her. The anxiety was only slightly diluted by the carefully formulated plan, contingencies upon backups at her fingertips. She was giving the air of languid relaxation when, in reality, every string of her nerves was pulled taut.

Cersei's vivacious laugh had arrows shooting out of Valine's eyes, and she only tempered her reaction by leaning into Sarim and whispering to him.

Valine slowly unfurled her necromancy, allowing it to seep into her target, and letting it fester. She smiled when her victim rubbed their head as if an ache were beginning.

"Do you think Balchon knows everyone saw his dick and balls when he went screaming past our rooms about the daemons?" Valine asked.

Sarim guffawed, tilting back his head, his shoulder-length hair hanging behind him. "You missed when he initially stripped. He began raving about the true heir to the firebird, and that sand serpents were going to breed in the throne room."

"Oh my, I'm sad to have missed it. But I'm curious as to why he had to be naked."

Sarim cracked a crooked smile. "Something about becoming closer to the gods' creations. That was until the patrons turned on him."

"Oh, so he thought he was speaking prophecy?"

"I'll have you know," Balchon interjected playfully, "that I stand by my statement. The tincture I consumed opened up my third eye and led me to the path of the gods, and the valley of their wisdom."

"I suppose we'll never know," Valine said, faux solemnity coloring her tone.

"Perhaps. But, since you brought it up…" a lewd smile graced his lips. "What did you think of my equipment? As you so proudly admitted, you are familiar with the appendages."

Valine chuckled. "I've seen better, but I've seen worse. It's a fine specimen to be sure, but alas, it is not one for me."

"What a shame. I was hoping to make your top ten."

"I hate to disappoint."

"Well, if you ever decide to try it out, surely keep a good rating in mind."

Valine laughed, a happy sound that she was sad to say was false. "A sound plan."

"Honestly, this low-energy event is much needed, things have gone tits up with the business." Balchon turned to Valine conspiratorially. "Can you believe one of our guards was stupid enough to steal from us and overdosed on fate stealer? Fuck, what shit irony."

"No! Oh saints, that's unfortunate."

Just then, a bell tinkled, and servants arrived, carrying an assortment of teapots in porcelain, silver, clay, and glass. Valine met Hanish's eye, watching him bring over the pot, the façade of which was Vitus beholding a staff, only to hide Mrithun holding his blade inside.

Getting to her feet, Valine brushed her silver skirt free of wrinkles. "If I may, Your Highness," she began, addressing Jacira. "I've heard that it is a sign of respect as a guest to pour the tea, and it would be my honor to be the first to do this if you will allow it."

Jacira beamed. "By all means, please begin." She gestured grandly, and Valine dipped before carefully taking up the teapot Hanish held on a tray.

Deliberately, Valine stoppered a hole with her finger and went around the circle starting with Alastair, coming around, not stopping to meet eyes with Malik even though he tried to catch hers. She poured for Sarim, and then she moved her finger to a separate hole, pouring for Balchon. The cup filled with amber tea, and Valine's hands did not shake. Finally, she poured her own and then returned the now empty pot to Hanish, who lightly bowed and disappeared to replace the teapot.

"Care to test the tea for me, Valine?" Malik's voice cut Valine like a blade, and she froze. The King of Adraali was holding out his gilt-edge teacup, a challenge in his eyes.

Valine curled her lips in a facsimile of a smile. "Why of course, My King."

"Why is she testing his tea?" Tallulah asked in confusion, their narrow brows pulled together.

Alastair rolled his eyes. "It's their weird foreplay. Call it fucked up flirting."

"Oh, they're sleeping together?" Balchon asked as if neither Valine nor Malik were present in the room.

Valine couldn't help the flush that burned in her cheeks as she crossed the center of the space, skirting the table of appetizers. Cersei watched her calculatedly, her lioness gaze hinging on territorial. Valine wanted to snarl back.

"No," Sarim corrected, "but they may as well be. They're obsessed with each other."

"*Sarim.*"

Malik's sharp admonishment was like a sword. It fell heavy, and with conviction—one simple swing, and the air in the room flattened out under the word of a king. For a moment, it seemed as if everyone realized that, while they were among royalty with Jacira, they were in the presence of a king with Malik. They had forgotten.

Sarim cut his gaze askance, his jaw gritted under the verbal lashing. He wasn't wrong, but the problem was that he called them out on it in public when Malik was supposed to select a bride next year. Surely, this would fuel gossip. If not for what was going to happen next.

Valine delicately took the teacup, and blew across the steaming surface, sipping prettily before returning the not poisoned tea to the king.

"Delightful."

She returned to her seat beside Balchon and Sarim, taking her teacup from the table and sipping it. Bitterness exploded across her tongue, and she fought to keep it from her face. It was what she expected from an actually poisoned cup of tea.

"Valine, if you would, I'd be ever so grateful if you cared to taste my tea," Balchon said suggestively. "I would be so very appreciative of the gesture."

Valine smiled, and she had to keep the malicious glee from it. Oh, this was too perfect. To be witnessed drinking from his cup was the most divine sign from Mrithun she could have imagined.

"I suppose I can entertain this taste for you."

And so, Valine did.

She tasted the bitter poison in his tea, and showed the venom on her teeth. "Lovely brew."

Balchon grinned. "I can die a happy man. Do you reckon you know what it is?"

"I believe it's a chai masala."

"That's exactly what it is!" Jacira clapped delightedly.

Balchon physically recoiled. "Oh, I hate chai."

He hated chai?

Chai?

Chai, the national tea of Talloh was this plan's fucking downfall? How could Valine have had such a massive oversight as to the flavor of *tea* that Balchon would consume?

Immediately, dark, hot rage filled Valine, and it took everything in her not to take the fucking cup, and dump it down Balchon's throat herself. But of course, that would be a little too obvious. Even still, Valine found her fingers curling, her necromancy eager to lash out, crawling from the edges of her person like a storm cloud on the horizon.

"Lucky for you, chai is my favorite," Cersei purred. "Would you be a doll and pass me your cup?"

"My pleasure." Balchon practically jumped to his feet.

No.

No.

No this could not be happening.

It was as if everything slowed in motion, as if movement was caught in stasis, each of Balchon's footsteps steeped in molasses in the Cold Season. She watched as a cat-like grin crept across Cersei's mouth, the poisoned cup of tea drawing ever nearer. Valine's thoughts were a rampage, horror clouding her judgement, fury pushing her to irrationality.

With panic fueling her, Valine lashed out with her magic, her dark tendrils of necromancy diving for Balchon's back, spearing through his chest. She twisted her fingers into a fist, and with those blades of magic morphed, Valine turned them into a vice, and squeezed. She could feel the frantic beat of his heart beneath the absolute power of her magic, and the reaction was instantaneous.

Balchon gasped and staggered. The fine porcelain cup shattered on the gold-veined marble, poisoned tea splashing wide and glaring like an amber eye. Balchon dropped to a knee, clutching his chest, eyes straining, mouth gaping. Valine could see the blood rushing to his face, saliva dribbling out of his mouth, his eyes turning an alarming shade of cerise.

Shouts of surprise and fear went up about the room, guards startling from their posts, aethermancers faltering in their manipulation of the air. Cups clattered in saucers, and feet hit the floor.

Valine held Balchon's heart a moment longer, the gambling den heir making ugly choking noises, spit flying from his struggling breaths. He was turning blue, his eyes shot, vessels burst. Another struggled breath later, and Valine let go, her magic withdrawing back into her with force that belied her outraged emotions.

Everyone was surrounding the heir, crouching by him, concerned hands upon any bit of arm or shoulder available. Everyone but Malik, whose livid stare speared through her, the wrath radiating from him was a palpable thing, those not-quite eyes burning a furious gold. His full lips were set in a thin line, and even though she'd beckoned her magic back, it too, recoiled from the fury that beheld her.

She'd fucked up.

"Are you all right?" Pandora queried, her jade eyes soft, dismay coloring her features.

Balchon lay on the floor, breaths ragged, patting his chest. Sweat dotted his brow and set his normally impeccable hair into disarray. "I think so. That was…I thought I was dying."

"What happened?" Sarim asked, and though his voice held just the right amount of concern, Valine felt the tension the Valmotti held by not looking at her. He knew what she'd done.

"It felt like my heart stopped. Like something was crushing it."

"Has this happened before?" Valine asked hesitantly.

"Not like this. Not this bad."

Valine was thrown for a loop, and recollected herself with a couple blinks. "What do you mean?"

"I'm no stranger to drugs, we all know this, and sometimes it has an adverse effect. It's not usually this delayed though. But I suppose I've never taken such potent vices before the other night. It's bound to have greater consequences."

"Are you sure you're well?" Pandora pressed.

"Yes, and I would much rather everyone forgot about this terrible incident. May we return to tea? I'm eager to try out the lavender and lemon-grass blend I smelled earlier."

Balchon got to his feet, rubbing his chest as he returned to his seat next to Valine again. The assassin asked a gentle assurance for appearances sake and was reassured. A servant was summoned to clean up the broken cup and poisoned tea and moments later all evidence of Valine's attempt was wiped away. Hanish returned with the replacement teapot—a replica of her assassin's pot, only this one had one compartment, and not two. It was a contingency in case they elected to examine all the pots for signs of artifice. Unfortunately, his rush was unrequired. Hanish sketched a curious brow, and Valine shook her head indiscernibly.

Nearby, Pandora steepled her fingers against her temple, staring into her cup, overwhelmed with the event. They all returned to their teas, and Valine, in a sullen mood, bitterly drank every last drop of her poisoned tea while Malik stared her down, promising words she didn't want to hear.

CHAPTER TWENTY-SIX

"What the fuck did you think you were doing?" Malik shouted at Valine from within his suite. "I mean honestly, Valine, were you really going to kill the heir to Raziche's Den in the middle of a fucking tea party?"

Valine pinned her eyes on the soundproofed azure wall, studying a turquoise fresco which depicted the mind mages when they combined into one. The three sisters, in order to save one, had to join as one being, sacrificing all individuality. Valine wondered how it felt to love or be loved that much.

"You know, I am speaking to you," Malik bit out, anger lacing every word.

She pulled her eyes from the artwork. "It rather felt like you were shouting at me."

"Oh, don't be pedantic, it's beyond you."

"Is it? Because according to you I'm an imbecile."

"Are you serious right now? You're bitter because I'm pissed you tried to kill gambling royalty? What did you think was going to happen, huh? The fucking Tri-Moon Festival is the day after tomorrow, do you think the princess will want to celebrate if one of her closest friends suddenly died? You kill Balchon and all our plans go to shit."

"He needs to die if we're to get Hanish and Hafsa out!" Valine fired back.

"I don't give a flying fuck how many people need to die to keep them working for us, but they cannot die until *after* the saints-damned festival, Valine!"

"Oh, I'm sorry I wasn't given a fucking itinerary of the murder list, did you want me to pencil in Balchon before or after the king?" She pretended to search. "Give me a second, I'll write it all down."

"Fuck off with that. You know damn well I'm right and you don't want to admit it because you're ashamed of yourself."

"I'm ashamed of nothing," Valine hissed, fingers turning to claws. "You knew I was going to kill him—I told you this!"

"I didn't think you were going to do it in front of everyone! I thought you'd be more discreet, maybe an overdose, alone in his bed, an unfortunate accident! Maybe he decided to get drunk and fall in the sea. You could have arranged a fucking kraken attack and I wouldn't have minded! But at a princess's tea party? Are you serious?" He paced angrily. "We need this festival to happen!"

"You said you trusted my instincts on this!" Valine yelled, wanting to hit something. "Don't turn this around because you don't like my methods, I was given explicit permission to do things my way. If you don't like it, then you can find some other assassin for your plan of world domination."

"You don't even understand!"

"Enlighten me then!"

Suddenly, like a tidal wave, Malik was in her face, shoving her against the wall. "I am trying to protect you!" Heat flared in his eyes, the scent of cinnamon washing over her. "And you seem to think this is all a saints-damned joke!"

It was then that Valine realized what she didn't see before. Malik was angry, yes, but beneath that veneer of hostility was fear. The king was afraid, and she realized with a start that it was fear *for* her. Some of Valine's fire banked beneath that look.

"I'm sorry," she whispered, pushing down that hot-temper gifted from her father.

Malik was taken aback, surprise flaring in his eyes before something new lit them. "Sorry isn't enough."

Before Valine could process his words, Malik had both of Valine's wrists captured in his hand, pinning them above her against the wall. The position had her stretched, her midriff bare, her breasts heaving with angry breaths. Malik pressed himself closer, a knee between her legs, finding the slit in her skirt and staying there. She could feel his length hardening against her hip, his own chest against hers fluttering with aroused and furious breaths. Instinctively, Valine's leg hitched on Malik's hip, wrapping around the back of his knee, pulling him close, the grinding eliciting a moan from her as zings of pleasure rushed from between her legs. Malik's other hand found the small of her back and pulled her even tighter to him, fingertips digging in, and she hoped they left more bruises.

Trailing his lips across her jaw, he allowed the slightest of pressure, the barest of kisses before he nipped the sharp edge of her chin. "You have your rules, but I told you to break them. You want me, why hold back?"

"Because," she breathed, writhing against him, eager for that friction. "If I don't have my lines, I am lost."

"Then perhaps you need to be found."

A whimper escaped her, and she couldn't help it. Her lips sought his. But when she tried, she met only air. Malik's cheek rubbed against her as he whispered in her ear, his short start of a beard scratching her face.

"I won't kiss you," he whispered seductively. "That would be too much like a reward. I want to torture you, to have you crying out for the pleasure I'm withholding."

"You want to punish me?" she gasped, incredibly turned on and shocked.

"I do," he breathed, grinding his thigh against her apex. She was sure he was feeling wet heat swell within her. "I want to get you close to your peak, and when you're about to come…I won't let you."

She moaned in response.

He splayed his hand on the small of her back, fingers on her backside as he pushed harder, the friction exquisite. Valine tossed back her head and moaned, and when she bared her throat, Malik latched onto it, his mouth hot on her skin. His teeth grazed and sank, suckling and leaving trails of lust along her collarbone. She knew he was leaving love bites and she didn't care. Everyone already thought they were fucking, what was stopping them? Her rules? She was already working for a royal, she may as well sleep with him too while she was at it.

Valine rolled her hips against his hard thigh, the motion rubbing that little bundle of nerves that he so neglected. She wanted him, she wanted him so badly she burned with it. She'd fantasized about him daily, in quiet moments and in busy ones, when he was close and when he was away. He consumed her, and she wanted to consume him. She wanted to feel him inside her, driving into her, fucking her into oblivion.

His scent was all over her, that daemons-damned black orchid and tobacco mixture. It was heady and intoxicating, and it was her complete undoing.

As if he were gracing her with a gift, the hand that was at the small of her back slid down to her knee, sliding along her thigh. His fingers crept under the slit in her gown—and she thanked whoever designed that specific feature—and found the lace edge of her underwear. She thrashed against him, eager for his touch, but his other hand still had her wrists pinned. He was toying with her, tracing the edge, a fingertip slipping beneath and gone again. She groaned, his mouth busy on her chest, his tongue gliding along the top of her bodice, dipping between the swell of her breasts. Still, she was grinding against his leg, his erection still prominent against her thigh. Her breaths were coming as pants, little sounds of moans and whimpers escaping her.

Malik groaned against her skin, his hips surging. "Were these the sounds you made when you finger-fucked yourself?" Malik paused as she gasped. "Tell me, and maybe I'll let you come."

"Yes," she gasped wildly.

"Did you think of me as you played with this sweet little pussy?" Malik's voice was low and husky, and Valine could feel an orgasm creeping up on her, the temptation of this man alone was enough to drive her over the edge.

She rode against his leg and let his fingertip slip beneath her panties, the lightest brush against her clit. She cried out in pleasure, feeling her climax drawing closer.

"Did you, Little Liar?"

"I did."

"Do you think you deserve to come?"

"Yes," she practically begged. She was not above it, not when she was so close.

"No, I don't think so."

And Malik pulled away.

Valine cried out from the loss and the frustration that filled her. He still kept her wrists in his hands. Her knees wobbled and she was aching for release. She knew she was a mess, her hair was askew, her eyes lust-addled.

"I told you this was no prize, this was a penalty."

Valine licked her lips. "Please, Malik. Make me come for you." Her breath was raspy, full of desire.

Something flared in Malik's eyes and he pressed close once more. "Beg again," he commanded.

"Please, touch me. Let me come."

Malik released her wrists and grabbed her by the hips, opening to him as he shoved her against the wall, rougher. His hard cock through his pants perfectly positioned against her clit—saints she was close.

"I want to watch you shatter into pieces on me. I want to know I'm the one doing it to you."

"Then take me," she pushed.

"Not today. Today is not a day for rewards. This is a gift."

And then he was rolling his hips against hers, the hard line of his cock rubbing her sensitive clit. She could feel her wetness dripping down her thighs, soaking her panties, and he kept the delicious friction going. Valine thrust her hands in his hair, feeling the silky soft strands against her hands as she tipped her head back. The king's hands were rough on her ass, pushing and grinding. She felt the orgasm building within her, her nerves coming alive as it grew and grew, soaring within her. Her moans were getting louder and she sank her teeth against his shoulder to keep from screaming.

"Come for me, Valine."

The orgasm shattered through her, and she *would* have screamed if not for her teeth buried into Malik's shoulder. Malik helped her ride through the waves of her climax, her hips surging and he met her for each one.

Slowly, she came down from the high, and Malik let her slide down his front. She had to steady herself against the wall to keep from falling over. Her knees were weak, her body deliciously heavy.

"Let this serve as a warning to what my punishments entail." Malik's voice was steady, but she knew he was anything but. His erection strained painfully against his pants, a wet spot over the hard ridge of it and Valine knew it was from her. "Do you think this will happen again?"

It was a threat, and a promise, and an invitation, and a request.

"I think it will."

"I think it should."

With that, Valine left Malik's suite, the echoes of her orgasm between them.

CHAPTER TWENTY-SEVEN

Lincoln Dagger

Valine had ventured into the city with Jacira, Pandora, Tallulah, Cersei, and Freyja, the crown princess having demanded a visit to a dressmaker for the finest attire for the Tri-Moon Festival. It hadn't mattered to the princess if they already had garb for it. That wasn't the point. The point was gossip. Valine anguished over the fact that she was missing out on a day of sleuthing and trading information with the servants, but she reminded herself that she'd gone out early that morning with Desdemon jewels and Amir gold to bribe. Thus far, she'd learned more about the mines and den, as well as an unsettling secret of Cersei's. Even so, it wasn't enough. Valine knew she was missing something big, what it was, she didn't know. Even then, she took this opportunity to wend her necromancy to further another plan.

"Have you ever had gooseberries from Cuuevota before, Valine?" Jacira asked as she plucked up a round purple-blue berry and examined it against the light.

Valine cocked a brow. "Fruit from the black market island? I cannot say I have."

"Hmm," Jacira hummed. "It's funny. The exact shade seems to match the love bites on your neck. Just here." Jacira tapped the side of Valine's throat. "And here." She continued, indicating her collarbone. "And even here." She tapped the swell of her left breast. "Curious that, isn't it?"

Heat burned on Valine's cheeks. She'd applied cosmetics, but evidently not very well. "Very."

Jacira giggled and popped the berry in her mouth, taking a bushel and tossing a silver coin in payment, thanking the seller by name. She offered the berries to the rest of them, and Jacira looped her arm with hers. "I must ask, how was he?"

Valine's tongue felt thick. "We actually didn't...we didn't have sex."

"You didn't fuck, and yet you look like that?" Jacira was equal parts shocked and impressed. "Gods, the day you two do… I don't know if I want to watch or be as far as possible."

Valine laughed nervously and popped a gooseberry in her mouth, letting the sweet flavor explode across her tongue. The sounds of the city around Valine were different than the messy streets of Luneth; the streets of Talloh were paved in white stone, mosaics of golden moons and suns demarcating intersections and forks. Tapestries of the Stygian Ones hanging from high walls and buildings, everything light and airy and gilded. Servants scurried about, scrubbing walls and sweeping sand from the stone. Mages moved and cooled the air, tending to palm trees deposited in pots, and flowers growing in painted, wooden boxes. Gold domes topped many businesses, sheer curtains flittering from balconies in natural and aethermancer breezes, and fountains bubbling upon walls and in the city square. The scent of the sea was so potent Valine could taste it on her tongue. It tasted clean and pure. Compared to Bastia, Selyndyr was paradise.

"So, if you didn't sleep together, what *did* you do?" Pandora pressed from Jacira's other side, smiling brightly. She was wearing a floppy white hat to protect from the sun, and the lace on it cast shadows across her delicate face.

"We had an argument."

Pandora blinked her pretty green eyes, her white blonde hair slipping from its coil in the oppressive heat. "You…you fought with the King of Adraali, and you're still here?"

"Oh, it's not as if it were a physical match. We simply raised our voices," Valine dismissed.

"No," Freyja intruded, and Valine startled, turning toward the platinum blonde's hazel eyes. "That's just it, no one fights with Malik and escapes the encounter without chastisement, injury, or banishment—unless it is truly and properly well deserved. Not even Sarim or Alastair."

Valine's mouth dropped open, and in that moment all thoughts left her except for the stupid fact that she was the only one present that did not have some shade of blonde hair. Pandora's the lightest, Cersei's the deepest. From snow to honey. It was this ridiculous thought that kept her from breaking apart.

"Well, if that's the way the king fights, I'd love to see how he fucks," Cersei said airily, grinning that ludicrous cat grin.

"Oh, Cersei," Jacira chided. "Come now. It's clear the king fancies Val. Why are you trying to chase a man who has his eyes elsewhere?"

"That is not confirmed, is it, *Val?*" Cersei hit the nickname hard and Valine knew she realized Valine didn't care for it.

"The king has stated certain intentions—like finding a bride next year—so I would not encourage any pursuit," Valine hedged carefully.

"Don't want a little challenge, hmm?"

Valine noticed that as usual Tallulah was remaining auspiciously silent, and the assassin realized how often she forgot their presence. She wondered if that was deliberate.

"I don't mind. You and he are free to do what you will."

Cersei laughed. "Gods, you are so easy to rile up. Do you truly think I am so interested in your king?"

Valine startled. "You're not?"

"No, if anything I am intrigued by Sarim, but I have a feeling he is also taken." Cersei's eyes flittered to Freyja, and whether the ruinmancer didn't hear or pretended not to, Valine didn't know. "Besides, I'd never want to be queen. That's much too hard. Perhaps I'd pursue a lord, but I enjoy my independence if we're being completely honest here."

Had Valine read all the situations wrong? Was the look she thought territorial actually something else? Perplexed? Curious? And what of the flirting? Was that just flippant? And the use of the nickname, was it just her attempting camaraderie and Valine was already soured against it? Was Valine's head really so far gone that any woman who got close to Malik sent threatening energy through her? She paled when she realized this was likely true.

"For someone that has had many lovers, you seem shy to admit what was done," Jacira prodded none too discreetly.

"We..." Valine sighed. "Okay, well, he pushed me against the wall, and he spoke of punishments and rewards and..." Valine's face heated. "I reached pleasure, but I will reveal no more."

"Val!" Cersei groaned. "You cannot leave it at that."

"Oh, but I must." The thoughts alone had her turning wet again, and she'd rather not peruse the wares in the street while aroused.

Valine twisted the thread on her necromancy and was saved from having to answer more when Pandora groaned.

"Gods," Pandora cursed. "I've been having terrible headaches lately; I think I need to sit down."

"Perhaps you have imbibed too much wine and not nearly enough water," Tallulah suggested.

"Actually," Valine said, digging through her bag. "I have a tonic for that. Healer Das gave me one of Queen Amaris's mixtures after I received a knock to the head during the three-legged race, but I fell asleep before taking it. Would you like it?"

"Oh, would you mind?" Pandora asked gratefully.

"All yours." Valine handed over the vial, and the woman drank the entire thing. As she did, Valine began to slowly unwind her necromancy surrounding Pandora's brain.

Pandora blinked as she pulled the now-empty vial from her lips. "It's already fading," she said, astounded.

"Then I definitely encourage you to seek out the healer. I'm sure he can make you more should the headache return." Because tomorrow it would.

A few minutes later, Pandora drifted away from their group into a jewelry seller, Freyja, following with several of their guards. The princess's lover was fingering the gems on a multi-hued choker, want written plain across her face. Jacira made a sudden sharp turn, and Valine turned to the princess to see if she'd noticed the longing, but in Valine's distraction of the lover, she hadn't realized where they'd ended up.

Why was Jacira visiting a blacksmith? The princess had no need for steel or weaponry. She glanced at Tallulah and Cersei who still lingered with this portion of the fractured group. Cersei's face was twisted up in distaste, her sun-kissed skin turning red with—what was that, anger?—some dark emotion, while Tallulah simply pressed their lips in a thin line, their gray eyes casting about the city core.

"Hello, Lincoln," Jacira practically purred.

Valine's brow rose almost to her hairline. Well, this was interesting.

A handsome, flushed-faced man appeared in Valine's line of sight. He was built like a bear, strong and tall with large, rough hands and a sweaty mass of dark hair plastered to his forehead. His eyes were brown, but there was a secret warmth in them that spoke of humble beginnings and graciousness. Beneath the layer of dust and sweat, Valine deduced his skin was perhaps a shade or two darker than Cersei's, lending the suspicion that he was mixed race, further affirmed by his features that held hints of typical characteristics from specific regions. His lips were full, his brows straight, with an oval and mostly symmetrical face.

The man was shyly cleaning his hands with an equally dirty rag, a new flush deepening the red that burned already from the heat. "Hello, Princess Jacira." His voice was a pleasant rumble. "How might I help you today?"

"I am in the market for a decorative dagger, and I am infatuated with the craftsmanship I've observed in previous blades. I thought a symbolic equivalent would be appropriate."

"About what size, Your Highness?"

Jacira hummed, and Valine would have been blind not to notice the way the princess's eyes sank to the area between Lincoln's legs. Valine bit her cheek to keep from reacting, turning her eyes to Cersei. Fire burned in her gaze. She *was* angry, but Valine gathered—after compartmentalizing her own emotions—that it was due to the disregard Jacira clearly held for other people's emotions.

Because it was very clear in that moment that Jacira was anything but monogamous.

Jacira continued her thinly veiled flirting, describing the size of a dagger she wanted—the length of a forearm seemed excessive—and settled once Lincoln—blushingly—explained the weight versus aesthetic feature of the blade. Apparently, Valine wasn't following along properly because she realized with a start it was going to be a hair accessory running parallel to her spine.

The business concluded and coin exchanged hands, the contact lingering much too long for polite encounters, and Jacira set off, towards her other lover. The fast clip the princess placed set her apart from the rest of the group and Cersei sidled up to Valine, popping the gooseberries Jacira bought in her mouth.

"She wasn't even trying to hide it, was she?" Cersei muttered darkly.

"How long has it been going on?" Valine inquired, taking a berry Cersei offered.

"At least four months, she's been seeing him since the Blooming Season."

"Why does she go on about monogamy then?"

Tallulah cackled from Valine's other side. "Power. Admiration. Moral superiority. Take your pick," Tallulah told her, evidently fed up. "I love her, but she is sloven with her lovers."

"This is a habit now?"

"It started with Cesaire—a merchant from Luneth—and then it was Esmeralda, and then Pandora was everything, but now she's losing interest, so here is Lincoln." Tallulah shrugged elegant shoulders. "She tires of people easily and I worry she keeps me around only because I complete her triad that reflects the Stygian Ones."

Valine stiffened, realizing that Cersei represented She, Balchon He, and Tallulah They. Or was Jacira She and Cersei an interloper? Was Jacira placing herself as queen of these gods? Was the princess so full of herself she was trying to manifest godhood?

She realized from what Jericho was raving about all those days ago indicated she could be.

Valine looked to where Jacira was sticking her tongue down Pandora's throat, the other woman moaning and fusing her hands in the princess's hair. If that was losing interest, Valine did not want to see what infatuated was.

The rest of the outing passed uneventfully. Their group arrived at the dressmaker's shop and within seconds they had been measured and Jacira gave them free reign to do with the dresses as they wanted. The only stipulation was that they had to be stunning and completed by tomorrow evening. Even Valine paled under the command. Jacira clearly thought money could buy her everything with no regard for time. The dressmaker and their assistants shared panic, and when Jacira wasn't looking, Valine went up to the dressmaker.

"If it's any easier, use as little fabric on mine as possible."

The dressmaker deflated with relief. "Anything else?" they asked.

Valine considered. "I enjoy slit skirts,"

The dressmaker smiled, their white teeth shining on their golden face. "I can work with that, thank you."

Valine's network of spies and servants was growing, and by the time she received an invitation from the queen, she'd already had knowledge of the request an hour prior. Valine had waited in her suite, nursing one of Talloh's signature flavored waters. Upon the knock on her door, she stood regally and took the invitation, following the messenger to the queen's chambers.

The king and queen kept separate chambers, not even adjoining ones at that, but suites that faced off from across the narrow hall of the Heaven Wing. Valine had been in this wing only once, and it was by pure chance when she'd followed Pandora's tether to the king's door. Like King Jericho's door,

Queen Amaris's door was golden and crowned, though this one by a diadem of stars.

Two guards at their posts opened the doors with a flourish, both swinging open to reveal a foyer of gold and white. Wisteria climbed the ceiling and wrapped pillars, and a sun embossed table held a vase of hyacinths, lavender, and peonies—all in complementary shades of purple. The messenger bowed and swept from the chambers, the guards closing the doors behind her.

The sound of squealing hinges was a final tone as Valine entered deeper into the queen's rooms. Only when she arrived in her drawing room, it was not Amaris who greeted her.

It was Jericho.

CHAPTER TWENTY-EIGHT

Valine stopped dead in her tracks when Jericho rose from Amaris's lilac couch, the king's fine gold and silver robe shimmering atop his black leather breeches and open-collared white shirt. His silver hair was perfectly coiffed, his steel gray eyes were hard and unflinching. A hint of a smile twisted his smug lips beneath his short, trimmed beard.

"Lady Desdemon, it's a pleasure to speak to you in such an intimate setting," Jericho said, folding his hands behind his back. "I hear you've made quite the impression on my queen."

Valine composed herself. "You are too kind to say that, Your Majesty."

"But it's the truth," he stated. "My wife thinks you are our chosen one. She tells me you have been prophesized in the stars."

Valine held her breath, realizing the treacherous waters she was wading into.

"Is it true you have encountered arachne and phoenixes on your journey here?"

She nodded. "Yes, this is true."

"Three is the sacred number of the Stygian Ones. Perhaps we can send you to the sands to face the serpents? Three beasts. Three trials. Three times, you will have been deemed worthy."

He need not know she'd already fought sand serpents and survived.

Valine's heart began to sink as Jericho took three deliberate steps towards her. His gaze was intense, the steel of his eyes cutting through her. She inclined her head to meet his domineering height and could smell the scent of citrus and musk on him. It wasn't an unpleasant smell, but its foreboding was repulsive. The king drew ever closer, and Valine's alarm flared. She could kill him, but she would be caught.

She had to endure.

"Your praise is too high, Your Majesty. I was simply lucky."

"And who grants luck if not the gods and stars?"

Under the guise of blushing at the attention of a king, Valine looked away. Eyes trained on the white curtains that fluttered in the wind, revealing a slice of marble balcony and turquoise sea. The walls were austere, tall with blinding marble and pillars painted gold. Purple and its array of hues was the only reprieve of the stark shade.

"I'm hardly anyone special. I'm the fourth child of a lord, and I hold no lands or remarkable title."

"But you could."

Jericho's voice was directly before Valine and she spun to face him. He was so much closer than before, close enough to touch. His chest was level with her eyes, and she noticed the distinct lack of a Veritasium Medallion. He however, did have a Robursium Medallion. That was a non-issue. Valine steeled herself, inhaling sharply.

"What would you think of being my queen?" His fingers grazed between her breasts, his palm splaying out—a digit hooked in the neckline of her bodice.

She stared at him open-mouthed. "Your Majesty, I cannot. You already have a queen."

"I could have her dealt with, should you choose me."

Valine blinked, at a loss. Frozen, she couldn't figure out how to pull away from his unwanted touch. "What are you saying?" she asked dumbly.

Jericho reached out and cupped her jaw, his thumb skimming her lips. "I will make you queen once Amaris is deposed. All you have to say is the word."

"Your Majesty, I am flattered, but this is treason, and…neither you nor I are available."

"So, the rumors are true?" Jericho's hand tightened on Valine's jaw to the point of pain, and unlike with Malik, she did not trust this king. "You're fucking him?"

Valine swallowed, stared at the King of Talloh, and lied. "Yes, and I don't think he would take too kindly to you touching what is his."

It seemed it was then that the silver chains Valine had wound around her throat gaped enough for Jericho to notice the marks that marred it. "It seems I was mistaken. I imagined you would be better than a bastard king's whore."

Valine gritted her teeth and tore herself away from Jericho's punishing grip.

"You are meant for so much more than a plaything. You are prophesized by the gods. You should be my queen." Jericho's voice became zealous, an unhinged light in his gaze. He advanced on her, backing her to the wall. "By right of the gods, you are mine, and I could take you if I wished."

Jericho reached for her, and Valine leaped back, hitting solid stone. She felt like a caged animal, and she didn't know if she could close her eyes and endure or fight it out. She'd used her body to get to a mark before, but now there was something cheap to it, and Valine refused to let this man touch her. She would kill the king here if she had to. Screw the plan. If the king was found dead in the queen's chambers, who is to say it wasn't the queen who did it?

But she couldn't.

His hand went to the slit in her dress, foreign fingers brushing the skin of her thigh. He was pulling it up despite Valine's own hands shoving back down and away. He resumed his pursuit, and Valine readied to retreat into herself so as not to ruin Malik's carefully forged plans. His fingers brushed the lace of her underwear, and she began vanishing away.

"I'll fuck you right. I will make you forget his name and bring you to nirvana."

"I would caution you to stop."

It wasn't Valine's voice that broke the tension of the room. It was Amaris's. The queen entered the room, splendid in gold, her shoulders covered by a short cape of white. Her hair was piled in springy coils atop her head, her star diadem perched there.

"I think it is time you left my chambers, *husband*," Amaris said the last word like an insult, the venom on it stinging in the air.

Amaris was like a radiant savior, composed and determined, glowing in the afternoon light while stars winked around her aura. She held her chin high, and her green eyes turned hard as gems, her defiance a beacon of hope.

It reminded Valine eerily of the mythos of Nylantia when she crowned Bela, patroness of destruction and ruin, as her consort, cloaking her in stars for all of eternity so that all would know the love she had for the daemon.

Jericho backed up and pinned Valine with a glare. "No one will believe you," he whispered as he passed her, shouldering against the queen. "*Cunt*," he hissed as he left the room, slamming the door behind him.

If she hadn't already planned to kill the king, she would've on this encounter alone.

"I'm so sorry, Your Majesty," Valine breathed. "I received an invitation. I thought I was meeting you."

Amaris sighed. "You are correct, I did send for you. However, I didn't realize Jer would accost you, and for that I apologize."

"He…"

"He propositioned you and offered to have me killed, correct? And then when you turned him down, he was going to force himself on you?" the queen guessed. Valine nodded, and the queen sighed. "I knew this day would come. I should have known when he discovered the stars spoke of you."

"I don't understand. How are you so calm?"

"I am a queen, Valine. And one day, you will be, too. Just not to this kingdom."

"How are you so certain of this?" she inquired, worrying her fingers.

"Because I have seen it. It is foretold."

"What are you going to do?" Valine asked, switching topics, suddenly uncomfortable with the line of conversation.

"As I have always done. I will continue to rule and hope to foster better relations between our kingdoms. Jealous kings seek war, but powerful queens endure." Amaris paused. "And you will endure."

It was an echo of what Valine had thought during Jericho's advance.

"I don't mean to be discourteous, Your Majesty, but why was I summoned?"

Amaris sat on the lilac sofa Jericho had vacated, and she motioned for Valine to take a seat. She did, perching on the edge of a matching ottoman. "I summoned you," she said regally, "for tea."

And with that, she rang a bell and a servant arrived, carrying a silver teapot, steam curling from the spout.

"Do you take milk? Or sugar?"

Valine had stayed for two cups of chai before departing. Amaris and Valine had spoken of pleasantries and expressed excitement for the festival, and Valine was grateful Amaris reminded her that part of the festival was to give a gift to the person you cared for most. It was with this that she realized the dagger from Lincoln was Jacira's gift.

She was in her azure chamber when she locked the door and tore off her chains, tossing them to the floor with a rattle before scrubbing her face from Jericho's touch. Her leg, her thigh. She sank to the floor beside the gold pedestal that held the washbasin and cloth she'd used, her face between her knees, pushing back tears.

It was stupid. Valine was not unused to unwanted advances. She knew terrible men held power, and they used sex and rape to wield it. If not for Amaris, Valine didn't know what would have happened, but she expected she would have endured. She ground her teeth together, her throat thick as she struggled for a breath that didn't burn with anxiety.

The sound of a soft click alerted Valine to the adjoining door opening, and it was a second before Malik's hurried steps crossed the room and he was crouching beside her, his hands on her arms. She stiffened before the security of him registered. His touch was warm, comforting, wanted. With tentative trust, she eased with Malik. The floodgates opened when she felt his secure presence, and Valine cried. It was not ugly, heaving sobs that she wanted to let out, but the tears were running down her face freely.

"What happened?" Malik demanded, his fingers sliding from her bare arms to cup her face. She flinched when he touched her chin. He noticed.

Valine lifted her head. Tears dripped from her dark eyes when she met Malik's light ones, and they burned. He took her in, her lip that quivered, the way she held herself.

"What happened?" he repeated.

"I was supposed to meet with the queen," she managed. "But the king was there instead."

Unadulterated rage flared in Malik's eyes. "Did he touch you?" The question was flat, Malik's voice modulated into careful calm.

Her jaw worked. "A little. He tried."

"I'll fucking kill him."

"That's my job," she said hollowly.

"I don't care, I'll rip his fucking head off."

"No, Malik, please don't. It's okay. I have it under control. I just needed a moment."

Malik was silent for a moment, his hand on her arm, the other caressing her jaw. It was a comforting blanket to the touch Jericho had given her, and she felt like Malik's was erasing the memory.

"Can I hold you?" he asked so softly she wasn't sure she heard right.

She nodded anyway and suddenly Malik was moving beside her, leaning his back against the wall and wrapping his arms around her. She leaned her head on his shoulder and he tightened his grip before he scooped up her legs, cradling her in his lap, her face now nestled into his chest. She stayed like that, breathing in her favorite scent in the world while he rubbed comforting circles on her back, his head pressed against hers. They were silent, but their touch was everything. It said everything and her heart swelled with the enormity of it all.

This touch was nothing like the orgasm-inducing one he'd given her last night, but it was just as desperate. She could feel the pull between them, like the tether she used for her necromancy. It was piercing her heart, the thing between them, and it grew painfully. As if it were a rose sprouting its thorns, wrapping them in an anguished embrace.

Later, Valine returned to the healer for a headache tonic. She didn't need it, but she did need the excuse. As she descended the steps to the room, the scents of herbs overcame her, the sounds of bubbling and flame crackling reaching her ears. Healer Das was in the center of the room, pouring honey into a flask, combining it with lemon. Valine figured it was the beginnings of a remedy for sore throats. It was then that she noticed Pandora was there too.

"Valine!" Pandora said, surprised. "Hello there, what brings you down here?"

"Um," she stalled, realizing a headache tonic would not do, but she did have another idea. "I'm actually looking for a contraceptive tonic."

"Oh!" Pandora gasped, blushing. "Of course. I shouldn't have asked."

"It's all right," Valine reassured. "It's not like everyone doesn't already know."

Healer Das set the tincture down and spun to Valine, that lewd look still present in his eyes. "And do you need the male or female contraception?"

"Both, if you have it, please."

Healer Das nodded and went over to a set of drawers painted a chipping indigo and riffled through the contents, pushing aside labels and bottles. Clinking followed before he turned around, two bottles in hand, one murky green, the other light brown.

"Do you know how to take it?" he asked, and Valine ignored the disgust that roiled within her. She could just imagine him telling her he could show her how, and she'd rather not murder him—at least until after the festival.

"I do, thank you. Two silvers?"

Money exchanged hands, and Valine left with two tonics in hand. Blood rushed to her face at what it meant to her and then to the rest of the world. Mostly, she wondered what Malik would think of the purchase, and heat swirled within her.

Valine made a detour into the city, seeking specifically, and purchased what she needed. She traded substance and information with Hanish and then returned to her room, ate a dinner of appetizers, and immediately fell asleep, thoughts of Malik plaguing her in dreams.

CHAPTER TWENTY-NINE

Brave

The afternoon of the Tri-Moon Festival was filled with the busy movement of servants carrying trays and decorations—everything from floral arrangements to metal banners of the moon cycles and statues of the Stygian Ones. Valine was to meet with Jacira and the others, the crown princess having commanded that they all get ready together. The way there was a tide of servants, Valine having to skirt more than one dangerously leaning object or decoration.

In Jacira's lavender suite, five dress boxes were tied with twine, sealed with a gold wax stamp, and tagged with a name in golden script. Those from the outing were scattered about the room, drinking flavored waters in preparation for the alcohol for the night and picking at a fruit tray. Valine was last to arrive and when she did Jacira let out a cheer. "Now that you're here we can take a look at all the dresses!"

Valine prayed that they passed Jacira's inspection.

Jacira herself went first, uncovering a gorgeous creation of royal violet silk, both the back and neckline dropping to deep Vs, a thin chain holding a crescent moon at the apex. Fluttering drop sleeves had tiny crystals dangling from them, giving the appearance of dew drops. More crystals and diamonds dotted the bodice and trickled down the skirt and if the princess were touched by rainfall. Or starfall, Valine realized.

It was beautiful.

Jacira was clearly pleased and Valine breathed a sigh of relief as she encouraged the others to open theirs.

Tallulah's dress was thistle, a subdued off the shoulder dress with a collar grazing neckline and a cowled back, brushing mid-spine. And though the cut was simple the dress entirely encrusted with pearls was anything but. Freyja was next, hers amethyst, the garment held up by the skinniest of straps, and if not for the color, and amethyst stones studding it, it would give the illusion of skin. Because it was utterly skintight, meant to hug every curve and cup each breast. Cersei's was completely sleeveless, the neckline sweetheart, and the slit thigh high. Unlike the other dresses, Cersei's wasn't truly purple. It was mulberry, a much closer to pink shade. Then there was Pandora's, so pale lavender it was near white, in a wrapped style akin to the chiton dresses of Luneth, threaded with gold and silver. Valine realized that these dresses were not made yesterday, they were taken by other women who had commissioned them and taken in or out as needed.

Valine held her breath as she opened hers and she instantly recognized the color. It was blackberry. Blackberry for the Desdemons. Gently, Valine pulled out the garment and found that it sparkled intensely. The skirt that had two hip high slits was attached only by the barest stretch of material before it met with the neckline that plunged past her sternum. It was off the shoulder with long sleeves and glittering with stardust. The back was open, but the entirety of the spine was drawn with a chain of the moon's cycle.

"Oh my, Valine…" Jacira said softly. "King Malik is going to tear that thing right off of you."

It was perfect. Maybe even made for her.

The Tri-Moon festival bathed the entirety of the palace in purple light, the gardens and lawns aglow, the burning star behind the moons beckoning and casting the night in so many levels of heat. It was the lawn where the tournament was held that had been transformed. The trees were strung with silver and gold banners and chains of the moon cycles, statues of the Stygian Ones, He, She, and They were on a raised pedestal, They holding a sphere of violet quartz, She and He holding crescents turned in opposite directions. Ivory chaise lounges faced a stage, a clearing before it meant for dancing, while servants wove through the growing crowd.

Valine sipped plum-flavored water leaving an imprint of black lip stain on the rim. Her makeup was a mix of smoke and glitter, her lids dark with gold wings and her cheeks dusted with crushed goldleaf. Gold hoops dangled from her ears, and rings circled nearly every one of her fingers, the nails of which were painted the same metal tone as her eyes.

Freyja was beside her in her skintight amethyst gown, her hair curled and falling over one shoulder to reveal the ear dripping in jewels, from the curve to the lobe. Her makeup was subtle, brown liner, crushed pearl on her cheeks, light pink lips.

"Is there something between you and Sarim?" Valine asked point-blank.

Freyja turned to her, an arched brow raised. "Is there something between you and Malik?"

Valine flushed. "If I tell you the truth, will you answer me?"

"Maybe."

Valine sighed, licking her lips. "There's something…and there would be more if I let it."

"Elaborate," Freyja demanded.

"I have rules. You know who I am—what I am. I do not sleep with those who employ me."

"That's what's stopping you? *Money?*"

"I don't want it to cheapen anything."

"Valine," Freyja admonished. "You can't cheapen what you have. It's just up to you if you want to lose him when he has to marry next year." Freyja paused. "Or *you* can marry him."

"I can't," Valine wheezed.

"Why?"

"I don't have the right name or connections. He needs to make alliances with a marriage. I can't give him that."

"You're a Desdemon. You don't need any other name," Freyja smirked. "Besides, with what you're doing, I doubt he needs alliances from marriage. You can manipulate anyone with your chosen one status."

"I am not the chosen one," Valine argued.

"Tell that to everyone in Talloh, then. Because they think you are."

Valine hid the anxiety that swelled with that revelation, of how many people were thinking of her, especially as a prophesized one. "You still haven't answered me."

Freyja groaned, throwing her head back. "I love him."

Valine was surprised that Freyja came out with it so clearly, but the absolute truth in the blonde's eyes was undeniable. She could see the hazel depths growing with unease at the pronouncement, the regret of speaking it into existence.

"Then tell him," Valine urged quietly.

"I can't. What if he doesn't feel the same?"

"Freyja, I travelled across the Twilight Sands with him and when someone thinks they're about to die, they let their secrets out. Trust me, he loves you too."

Shock lit up Freyja and the ruinmancer pulled her spine straight. "I should go find him."

Valine's smile was moonlight-blinding. "Then get out of here and do that."

Freyja departed from Valine with a vixen's smile, and Valine knew that look was promising Sarim a night he would never forget. Internally, Valine cheered, but on the outside, she remained cool and composed, watching the milling crowd in varying shades of purple. Near the edge of the crowd Valine found an empty chaise and took a seat, resting her feet. The heels she wore did wonders for her long legs but there was only so much pain a girl could take.

Jericho took to the stage and everyone quieted, the king of Talloh regal in vibrant purple, gold lace trimming his elaborate jacket. "I would like to begin the Tri-Moon festival by opening with a prayer." Everyone ducked their heads and Jericho was suddenly rapt, his eyes casting heavenward. "We are gathered here to honor the great gods of the Stygian skies. To commemorate the divine right they have blessed us earthbound beings with. He, She, and They are law, their word divine guidance. We celebrate them here tonight, at the altar of their moons, the star shining their sight upon us to deem us worthy.

"Please join me with an offering tonight. Offer a sacrifice of self or object to three this night to prove your godliness and faith. Please ask Them to protect us and guide our unwavering hand. Please ask Him to give us strength to follow their grace. Please ask Her to offer mercy and compassion for our mistakes."

The sentiments were echoed, Valine ducking her head in false reverence, staring down to the bottom of her water glass, watching the ice melt against the plum slices and apple blossoms.

Jericho raised his hands to the moons and from the vantage, he was cupping the greatest one in his hands. "Blessed be our Stygian Ones, blessed be their followers." The prayer was repeated and Jericho slowly lowered his hands. "Now, I urge you to find a view and enjoy the following performance."

Jericho gestured to the orchestra who crossed the platform before descending from the stage. Valine caught him looking at her and she dashed her eyes away. But she could feel his fire burning her, she knew he was leering. He wanted her—not her soul—but what she offered him; power, status, reverence, and she knew he would try to take it against her will.

Valine gritted her teeth, suddenly wishing the king was just a simple man she was allowed to kill with a flick of her fingers. But he wasn't, and she wasn't willing to risk the plan because the king was as despicable as Captain Ishaq had been.

Music started up, a gentle plucking of harp strings and delicate violins, a low cello vibrated through the chords while a bell chimed with a sound like magic. It was a rendition of *Prize and Treasure*, a ballad composed by a warlord hundreds of years ago when a leader stole a bride and fell in love.

"You look beautiful," Malik said, sliding onto the chaise beside her, holding her gaze as he slowly trailed his eyes down. Devouring her form.

She looked at her king with gratefulness and an aching desire. In response, she leaned back against the arm of the lounge, allowing him a greater view of everything she had to offer. His eyes followed. "Almost good enough to eat."

"Maybe I'll give you a taste," she said, settling her foot on the seat, coyly parting her knees, and closing them.

"Tease," he chastised, shifting in his near black clothing.

"It's not teasing if you're following through," she told him boldly, lifting her drink.

"And are you?"

"Perhaps I am."

"What of your rules?"

Valine shrugged. "I've broken them before for less. I think I can manage breaking another for you."

A devilish gleam touched Malik's eyes. "Dance with me," he proposed.

Valine cocked a brow. "How do I know you won't trample my feet?"

"I am a king. I have been trained in every manner of dance you can imagine."

"Sounds like blackmail."

Malik laughed. "Dance with me," he repeated.

"Okay," she accepted, holding out her hand. Malik took it and guided her to the dancefloor before the stage. Several other couples and even a triad or two joined.

Wrapping an arm around her waist, Malik splayed his hand on her lower back, pressing the cool metal of the moon cycles into her spine. She shivered in a mixture of chill and delight. Malik's front was deliciously warm and she could feel every one of those golden buttons pressing into her skin through the thin material of the dress. He guided her effortlessly through the movements, spinning her when the notes hit, picking her up when others soared.

"You may not know this," he began and she knew a smile colored his voice. "But you are a delightfully talented dancer."

"It may have escaped your notice, Dear King, but I too was trained in the art of dance."

"And death," he whispered in her ear.

"And that, yes," she confirmed.

"I would love to hear the story of how that all came to pass."

Valine's heart dropped. "It is a long and terrible story."

"It is still one I wish to hear."

Valine sighed. "You will think differently of me after I tell you."

"Try me," he pressed, bringing them to the edge of the crowd.

They swayed, hardly following the movements anymore and Valine put on a brave face. She was baring the worst of her inner turmoil to this king, the king who held her in his arms and looked at her like she hung the stars. But the hands he held were soaked in blood and stained black with death.

"I had a lover when I was eighteen," she began, her voice wavered. "I fancied myself in love with him, but I was not ready to settle. Apparently, my father decided I *should* settle, whether I wanted to or not. I had contraceptive tonics illegally imported as Runell has outlawed all forms of contraception, and though I'd kept it secret, my father found out anyway.

"He tampered with the tonics my lover and I used to *prevent*," she said the word with weight and understanding dawned on Malik. "And only once I took the tonic after I'd lain with him, did I realize what the difference in taste meant."

"He laced it with liberwort, didn't he?" Malik asked.

Liberwort was an herb and the only effective agent that cancelled out the effects of the contraceptive tonic. It also helped aid male fertility. With Valine's necromancy, she'd detected the poison-like herb immediately, but because she'd already consumed the mixture, and because it wasn't a true poison, it was too late. It was meant to instantly absorb into the blood, so not even forcing her to vomit would prevent it—though she tried.

"I explained to my lover what I understood of the change in tonic and he admitted he had a part in it." Valine closed her eyes against the betrayal. Against the shame. "My father had paid him to trap me with a child."

The past surged within her.

"We can have a baby, Val. We'll marry. You'll be my wife. I knew you wouldn't agree if I asked, so I figured this would be a better alternative. You wouldn't have to choose."

She shut her eyes against the unwanted memories.

"That's why you have your rule," Malik breathed. They had stopped dancing, but he still held her.

Valine lifted her face and gazed at the king. "When I found out I was so enraged that I killed my lover and ran." She gritted her teeth. "My father covered up the murder, of course. He couldn't have his first daughter sullying his name by being revealed as a murderess." She smiled sadly. "I was due to bleed two weeks past, but my cycle did not come, and I knew that my lover and father had succeeded."

Malik drew his brows together in concern, his hands tightening on her. She swallowed and continued. "I travelled to Thycca on foot and stolen horseback."

Thycca neighbored against Adraali, the centermost kingdom in all of Enneive, and it was well known for its diversity, and welcoming of all people. Thycca did not discriminate between sexuality, gender, race, status, or power. They were notoriously progressive and inclusive, pushing for equal rights of all peoples and access to every form of wellness, including contraceptives and abortifacients.

"When I crossed the border, I demanded the location of the first apothecary I could find. When I did, I asked for abortifacients. I was given the herbs without question and I paid for the elixir the apothecary made." Valine looked away, angrily. "I do not know if I was truly with child, but I was not taking the risk. Regardless, that night I bled and I vowed to kill my father the next time I saw him."

Malik was silent for a minute. When he finally spoke, Valine felt like she could breathe for the first time. "I think you're incredibly brave for going through that, and even braver for telling me."

Valine had never shared this information with anyone. No one knew of the worst weeks of her life. The betrayal, the fear, the deception. It had eaten her alive, and she knew with all that rage brewing inside of her she would not have been a fit parent. Not then.

Malik wrapped her tightly and Valine settled into him.

She realized with horror that she was truly in love with him.

CHAPTER THIRTY

Malik and Valine returned to the chaise lounge they'd vacated to dance, plucking up two flutes of champagne, each drinking deeply. The bubbles tickled Valine's lip as she drank and she watched the king. He too, was drinking and watching her. Music swirled behind them, a more upbeat song playing, Valine thought she recognized the tempo as something reminiscent of *The Orchard*, but she wasn't certain.

Valine was leaning on the lounge chair, a bare foot in the grass, the other behind the king. Desire swirled in Malik's eyes, the gold being taken over by the blue as he drank in the expanse of creamy skin she displayed. He licked his lips, his hand reaching out. She let him draw circles on her bare leg, his eyes never leaving her. They coasted up to her knee and she held her breath as he slipped higher and descended again. Him teasing her.

"I have a gift for you," he whispered shyly.

Valine smiled softly. "I have a gift for you as well."

"You do?" he asked gently.

Valine slipped a finger up a sleeve and produced an item wrapped in paper. It was the width of a finger and tied with twine. Malik unfurled the paper, and read the writing inside. She knew what it said, she'd penned it herself.

1) ~~Do not work for royals.~~

2) ~~Do not fuck those who pay you.~~

Malik's gaze snapped up to hers, heat roiling in his eyes. The same heat that was coiling low in her belly, aching between her thighs.

"You're breaking your rules," he breathed.

"I am, and that is not your only gift."

He glanced down at the vial that the writing hid, twisting it in the light.

"Is this—?" Malik began.

"It's a contraceptive tonic. I wasn't sure if you were already taking one," Valine interrupted. "That is…if it is needed."

There were several different contraceptive tonics, catered to each sex. One was monthly—which was very expensive—another was weekly—moderately affordable—and a third was daily—low priced and easily accessible, though with larger room for error. These were the weekly sort.

Malik grinned. "I take one regularly, but this is perhaps the best gift I've been given."

"Truly?" she asked shyly, a smile blooming.

"Absolutely." He slipped his hand into his pocket and produced a ring. Valine's eyes flew to his face and Malik laughed ruefully. "It's not what you think. Not quite."

Jericho's voice announced another performance behind them, but Valine ignored it, too enraptured with the ring Malik held out to her. Valine examined it closer and she discovered the ring was a golden serpent, meant to coil around a finger with an emerald in its mouth and blind opal eyes. The tiny fangs were wrought as claps, holding the marquis gem in its miniscule jaws. It was stunning and it was so much like Malik.

"This ring makes known you are under my protection. It makes known that an attack on you, is an attack on me. With it, you are announcing that you belong to me."

"Malik…this is a consort ring."

"It is," he confirmed.

"Are…are you asking me to be your consort?"

"How you wear the ring will define to others what we are." Malik took her left hand, taking her index finger. "With this one, you are trusted. You are known as a confidante." He moved to her middle. "With this one, you are mine. You are known as my lover." Then he moved to her ring finger. "And with this one, you are my equal. You will be known as my wife and queen…if that is what you want one day."

Valine held her breath at the enormity of what Malik was offering her. He was offering her marriage if that was what she desired, but he was also offering her whatever she was comfortable taking. Valine felt emotion swell within her, her heart bursting at the seams. She looked into Malik's gaze and beheld what poured from him. She could read this king like a book, written in a language just for her.

Thoughts of his future brides plagued her. What would they think of the king keeping her as a lover? Could she handle watching the man she loved court other women? He couldn't be hers, not truly, could he? He was offering everything if she was willing to take it, and though her heart was, her revenge was not. He needed to marry a royal to burn Runell to the ground. After that kingdom was destroyed though, could she have him then?

"You are free to choose which finger you shall wear it on, if at all," Malik told her, his voice bearing so much weight. The tenderness in his tone buried itself in her heart. "But I would love nothing more than for you to wear it with pride."

She swallowed. "The middle," she whispered.

Malik grinned and slid it onto the finger she indicated. It slipped perfectly into place, and Valine wondered if the ring itself was charmed or crafted by the saints.

"So, this is official?" she asked.

"As official as you want it."

"I must say," she said sultry. "I've never believed in waiting until marriage. Don't you think it's a little premature to deem us lovers before we've fucked?"

"We could always change that," Malik teased. "Do you want to find somewhere private?"

"Please," Valine responded, rising to her feet.

Suddenly, Valine heard the sounds of moaning and skin slapping. She turned to the stage in confusion, only to find her eyes greeted with the sight of a live display of coitus. A bronze skinned man was thrusting into a red-haired woman, her legs on his shoulders, her back arched, her hair cascading over the edge of the bench that was brought onto the stage.

"Oh! Oh my," Valine gasped, rounding on the king. On her lover. "That is quite the surprise."

Malik chuckled low in his throat, his hand finding her lower back. "You deal with blood and death all the time, but acts of sex turn you into a skittish colt?" he whispered.

"No!" she hissed. "But a little warning would have been nice."

"Oh, there was plenty of warning. You were just too busy to notice."

"My apologies, I was practically getting engaged. I'm sure you can see why I may have been otherwise preoccupied."

"I consider that a lovely compliment."

Quietly, Valine and Malik slipped away while people watched the sexual act being played out on the stage in various positions, many of the watchers copying the acts or engaging in new ones on their chaise lounges. As they departed, Valine caught sight of Pandora with her face between Jacira's thighs.

Valine cast her gaze away when Malik took her hand, leading her past servants who delivered her knowing looks, and up a flight of stairs. On the marble floors their heels clicked and Malik guided them back to the Vesper Wing, confidently striding to their rooms and opening his door heedless of the guards still posted there. Within moments of stepping into his suite, Malik had the door locked and his hands were all over her.

With a gasp, Valine was picked up, her legs wrapping around Malik's waist as he crushed her lips with his. The kiss was rough, his tongue slipping between her lips to meet hers. Sliding against and tasting of plums and cinnamon. She wrapped her arms around his neck, hands fisting in his hair as his hands cupped her ass, kneading her supple flesh. His teeth caught her lip, pulling lightly, and she moaned into his mouth. His lips returned to hers, kissing fiercely, passionately, his hips grinding into her with vigor that promised pleasure.

Valine pulled from Malik's mouth, kissing up his neck, pulling his head back by his hair, and meeting his blue-gold eyes. "What have you done to me?" she whispered.

"Not nearly enough yet," he responded, carrying her over to the bed.

Malik dropped her onto the plush mattress, her skirts a mess around her legs, and the exposure of her hipbones showed that, just like the red dress, she was not wearing any undergarments. She went up on her elbows, giving him a sultry look with dark *fuck me* eyes, and parted her legs, thin blackberry fabric the only thing hiding her wet core from his eyes.

"*Fuck*," Malik whispered reverentially as he took her in.

"I did offer you a taste," she told him, shaking out her long dark hair.

"I need more than that," he growled, prowling over her.

He captured her lips once again, his hand coming up to her throat to squeeze ever so slightly. Valine moaned, and she felt Malik's smile on her lips. "I see that's something you like." He kissed her jaw. "Noted."

He began kissing further down, her collarbones being doted on as his hand sprawled over her neck. His nose skimmed down the center of her chest, following the line of her sternum before he pulled back the shimmering fabric covering her left breast. Her exposed nipple was hard and peaked, and Malik smiled before he took that little pink bud in his mouth and nipped it. She mewled in response, arching her back to allow him more access while her core throbbed in response. She was so wet, and she needed him. He pulled the fabric away from the other breast, baring this one too, and he performed the same action while rubbing the other with his thumb, his hand cupping it.

Valine couldn't help it; her hips moved of their own volition, and her hands searched for him, finding the buttons on his black shirt and tearing them open. His chest was sculpted, his abs ridged and golden, fine black hair spotted his chest and below his navel, following a trail below the waistband of his pants. And beneath those pants, his arousal was clear, the hardening length pushing painfully against the constraints of the trousers. Valine palmed him through the material and Malik groaned, catching her nipple with his mouth again while his hand drifted lower, slipping between those wonderful slits in the skirt and finding her wet core.

"Fuck, Valine," he moaned as his fingertips brushed the apex of her thighs, swirling against her clit. Her breaths came rough as she circled with her hips, eager to feel his fingers inside her. As if he sensed her impatience, he slipped a finger inside her, finding her dripping wet. She bucked against his hand as his thumb pressed down on her clit, circling with exquisite pressure while his finger was buried inside her. He plunged in and out of it and continued circling while she kept palming him, her other hand in his hair.

"Don't stop, Malik," she breathed, arching.

"I need to taste this pussy before you come again," he growled against her breast. "But trust me, I will get you there."

She dropped her head against the pillows in anticipation. "Okay."

Malik kissed his way down her body, pushing aside the shimmering fabric of her dress and baring her soaking-wet sex. He kissed the inside of her thigh and then the other, his nose brushing right where she wanted it. He teased her again, kissing a third time, looking up at her. And then suddenly, his mouth was on her.

His tongue laved the very center of her, stopping at that little bundle of nerves and circling it with his tongue. Malik flicked it with the tip of his tongue before pressing his mouth wholly against her pussy, his stubble scratching her thighs as his tongue buried itself inside her. Valine moaned at the excellent technique. He returned once again to that sensitive nub and sucked it into his mouth, biting gently, and Valine swore she saw stars. Never had anyone bit her clit, but she wanted him to do it again.

"Whatever you're doing, don't stop," she gasped.

"As you wish," he murmured against her.

Malik flicked and suckled at her clit, bringing her close to the edge, his mouth knowing exactly what her body wanted. Her hands were buried in his hair, her hips thrusting against him, and he had to cross an arm over her hips to pin her down. She could feel her orgasm building, and when he bit her clit again, she shattered. Valine cried out, Malik continuing his endless, perfect movements, his tongue carrying her through the waves of her climax. Valine had never felt such a powerful rush before, never had a partner continued pleasuring her through her orgasm before Malik.

Valine was languid, weak in the knees, her legs trembling as she looked down at him with lust-soaked eyes. His mouth was wet with her arousal, his lips shimmering as he licked the taste of her. He held her eyes as he kissed her inner thigh.

"You are my favorite flavor," he told her, crawling up her, his hand coming between them and cupping her oversensitive sex. "And I plan to have it again."

"It's yours," she breathed.

Just as she began reaching for Malik, a sudden banging erupted from their door, and before they could react, the door burst open, revealing four guards, Alastair and Cersei. Valine scrambled to cover herself, Malik moving protectively in front of her.

"Do you fucking mind?" he demanded, eyes shooting daggers.

Alastair's hair was sex-tousled, but his eyes were grave. "I'm really sorry to interrupt, Mal, but there's an emergency."

"What kind of emergency dictates disturbing us when we are obviously preoccupied?"

Alastair's next words fell like a blade.

"There have been three murders."

CHAPTER THIRTY-ONE

They were being interrogated in Malik's chamber about their whereabouts during the coitus act of the Tri-Moon Festival, but many eyewitnesses testified to seeing the King of Adraali and the necromancer disappear together. The guards outside Malik's suite confirmed seeing them enter shortly thereafter and admitted they were very certain they had not left the chamber during that time. Valine and Malik sat side by side on the bed, the four guards still standing in the room, Alastair and Cersei sitting on the blue velvet chairs, heads in hands.

Balchon, Tallulah, and Countess Magdalena were dead, and upon their corpses were corresponding notes.

My offer to He.

My offer to They.

My offer to She.

Valine felt herself blanch.

Jacira and Pandora were ensconced in the princess's chambers under heavy guard, lock, and key. The queen was sequestered in her own, while King Jericho ordered interrogations and searches of rooms.

Valine was not stupid enough to leave her chest of weapons and poisons in her room. She had found a nearby secret alcove, a boarded-up entrance covered with a thick layer of dust and cobwebs, and had tucked it safely in there. And even should it be found, it did not bear her name, initials, or any other identifying features. It was a simple box with an iron padlock. The only weapons she kept on her person or in her room were those easily explained. Like her Desdemon blade and Malik's gifted dagger. One was a family heirloom, and she used it as a letter opener; therefore, it was not ridiculous to see it on her writing desk. The dagger was for self-defense.

Besides, the murder weapons were not a dagger; it was an overdose, poison, and a bullet. Three different deaths for three different bodies.

One thing Talloh practiced that made it difficult for royals to get away with crime was the guardia. A force that was organized by the people of the kingdom. They were appointed by nomination and election, paid by a combination of the crown and additional taxes the people pooled together. With this organization, it made it difficult for nobility to hide their misdeeds and bribe when they worked in pairs and sought justice. To further discourage taking bribes, the investigators were tried yearly by the arachne, to discover if any ill intent or falsifications were made during their search. It was brutal, but it was effective, as those who handled the law must be upstanding citizens in all forms. Otherwise, the arachne would stake their wrath.

The guardia were conducting a full investigation into the deaths, but they confirmed it would be a difficult case due to the festival. There were too many coming and going, too many unaccounted for, too many motives. For every motive, there was an alibi. For every opportunity, there was a hindrance. The fact that it appeared sacrificial was more alarming to Valine than anything else.

It was clear from the investigating team that Valine and Malik were not involved in the crime and they wrapped up their interrogation with a nod of urging caution and a departing wink.

Alastair and Cersei departed with a somber look, the redheaded Runellian supporting the blonde who'd just lost two friends. Once they too left the room, Malik turned to Valine.

"It was you, wasn't it?"

Valine stayed silent, her eyes flinty.

"Valine…" Malik's eyes softened as he realized. "You didn't mean to."

"No, it's not that. I killed Balchon. I poisoned his drugs so it would look like an overdose." she admitted. "I bought some opium and laced it, then gave it to Hanish to slip into Balchon's stash. He would've never known." She paused fearfully. "But the notes and the others weren't me."

She didn't know who could have placed the notes and done away with Tallulah and Countess Magdalena, or how they had prepared them. She assumed that Balchon had been found in relative seclusion and the first person to happen upon him was inspired. They used his death to appease their false gods, then decided to go for the full trio. But who?

Valine felt genuinely guilty for being a catalyst for Tallulah and the countess's deaths. She'd liked Tallulah and she felt even worse when she considered Cersei—for having lost two of her friends. And while she didn't know the countess well, she still felt bad. Because of some zealot, two people that shouldn't have died had the candles of their lives snuffed out. And it was Valine's fault.

"Do you think someone took advantage of the situation?"

"I don't know for certain, but that's exactly what I think," Valine whispered. "But I can't help feeling like this is going to come back around one day."

"Then we'll be ready for it. Sacrifices must be made, Valine," Malik told her, cupping her face. His eyes held hers intently. "We will get through this."

She nodded, and Malik placed a chaste kiss on her lips.

"Come to bed with me," Malik whispered. "You need to sleep, and I don't want you alone tonight."

Valine agreed, slipping into her room to grab a silk negligee. She returned to find Malik in the bed, a pair of black satin pants replacing the formal attire from the festival. Valine climbed in beside him, settling her head on the turquoise pillow, the silk sheets like cool fingertips on her skin. She was facing Malik, and the king smiled at her. Sweetly. Disarmingly. Despite the fact that she'd revealed to him her greatest shame, her first betrayal, he still looked at her like this. Like she was the most beautiful and fearsome creature he'd seen, and she was his.

He touched the golden ring he'd placed on her finger, tracing it and threading their fingers together.

"I like seeing this on you," he admitted.

"I like wearing it."

Malik leaned into her, placing a tender kiss on her. It was slow, sultry and languid. Their tongues slowly glided against each other, a spark leaping between them, and their fingertips turned to kindling as their touches stoked the fire of their desire. He cupped her cheek, brushing her cheekbone with a thumb as he pulled back, the lavender moonlight illuminating the handsome king's face.

"Goodnight, Little Liar."

"Goodnight, My King."

Breakfast was a somber affair. There was heavy silence where Valine and Malik dined in the Vesper Wing garden with Alastair, Freyja, and Sarim. The guards and aethermancers stationed around were all a part of the lack of sound. Valine added two slices of kiwi to her paltry plate, and though she was starving, under the funereal silence she thought it would be in poor taste to consume so much when they were respecting the crown princess's mourning.

Valine hadn't meant for it to be like this. She'd anticipated Balchon taking his drugs somewhere in the garden, passing out, and succumbing to the drugs, and that would be the end of it. Opium overdoses weren't uncommon, and Balchon was too open with his recreational activities. But the fact remained that both the heir to a gambling empire and a blood-soaked mine were dead. Even if inadvertent and not by her own means. She was frustrated that the plan had gone awry and even more frustrated with herself.

This was why she didn't work for royalty. It was complicated and messy.

No one spoke. They sat together quietly, pushing food around their plate. The Adraalian circle knew what was coming and so they had to play a part. None of them were truly that devastated, perhaps a touch of unease, but no desolation.

They were set to leave Talloh the next afternoon. The Adraali group was invited to the university graduation of Liesl Ryniel, second princess to the Thyccan Kingdom. One of Malik's prospective brides. Valine couldn't help the savage surge of jealousy that rushed through her blood. But she couldn't think that way, and she was not done in Talloh like the rest of them.

It was a promise they could not break, even in light of three deaths. Valine knew missing the funerals was in poor taste but they had a previous obligation. With that being said, they weren't the only group departing that day.

After the scene of breakfast was completed, the day passed somberly and quietly, and they all returned to their rooms, packing their belongings. The next day, Valine dressed for travel in black leather pants and an equally dark blouse. She paired it with a light travelling cloak of gray wool and her favorite thigh-high boots. Her hair was in a long tail atop her head, and when the servants arrived to take her belongings, she let them.

It was a mirror of the previous fortnight as they stood in the courtyard, facing the Tallohian royals, the king and queen stone-faced for entirely different reasons, while their daughter stood weakly, leaning on Pandora with red-rimmed eyes. Valine banished the pang of guilt that wormed through her. She was an assassin and a necromancer. She should be unaffected by death she wrought. Jericho stared at Malik with poorly concealed rage. The queen kept her gaze on Valine. On the woman the insanity-touched queen deemed a future ruler.

"I wish we were departing under happier circumstances," Malik began, clasping his hands. He wore funeral gray in respect for the deaths. "We thank you for sharing your sacred festival with us and for introducing us so fondly to the Stygian Ones. I wish you nothing but what you so rightly deserve and that justice shall be meted."

Jericho inclined his head, and Valine fidgeted, twisting her consort ring. The gold of her ring caught the sunlight, and Jericho's eyes fixed on it. His nostrils immediately flared in anger. She was officially taken by the King of Adraali. His *chosen one* was chosen by another king.

"May I offer you the same salutations with equal intent," Jericho sneered. "Your stay here has been completely eye-opening, and perhaps in time, we may repeat this event with different results."

Malik held silent, his face unmoving. "I am sorry for your grief. The deaths of Balchon Raziche, Tallulah Illise, and Countess Magdalena were tragic losses, and they will not soon be forgotten," Malik said as he curled his fingers in his clasped hands.

Valine felt lightheaded just as Jericho's face transformed, rage overtaking him in a wild tantrum. *"How dare you?"* he spit venomously. "You worthless little bastard! You say anything like that ever again, and I'll have your tongue cut from your whoring mouth!"

Everyone present startled. Queen Amaris took a step back, her summoned stars trembling, belying her fear. Malik reacted too, balking and stiffening his broad shoulders. But it was delayed. Valine narrowed her eyes at her king, assessing. She watched his form, every part of him, sensing something remiss.

"Jericho," Malik said, cautioning. "What has come over you? Are you quite all right?"

"Do not presume to know me," Jericho raged. "I am chosen by the gods, and you are nothing but a simpering bastard your mother spat out of her harlot cunt."

"I would advise you to stop this line of transgression," Malik commanded, regal calm covering the true fury that burned beneath the surface. His fingers twisted in rage, and he moved them behind his back.

It was then, as another wave of vertigo struck her, Valine realized she was wrong.

Jericho rushed at Malik, and the reaction was instantaneous. Sarim stepped in front of Malik, drawing a broadsword from his back. He stood tall and imposing as guards shifted and stepped uncomfortably around them. Freyja leaped forward, shattering the fountain with a sharp screech, her hands moving the shards of rock into a rotating cage around the King of Talloh. The blades of stone spun in a ritual-like dance as if Jericho were a fire primal witches spun naked around. Jericho stopped only feet from the edge of Sarim's sword. The spinning rock the only thing keeping him at bay. Freyja's brows drew together in concentration, keeping up the movement. It was showy, and it was precise, and it was more than effective.

"I believe we should now take our leave," Malik offered. "I am regretful to discover that we could not find kinder terms to part on. My thoughts are with you and yours."

"Fuck you," Jericho snarled.

Malik smiled sadly, but Valine saw the smug truth beneath the façade. As Malik clasped his hands together once more, she watched his index finger slip inside the hold of his hands, his thumbs altering position.

Malik was not fidgeting in rage.

He was performing magic.

The King of Adraali was a psychomancer.

Psychomancers were rare. They were one of the three mind mages, their patroness Nafiza, was the being who was once three sisters. Psychomancers were originally gifted by Aaseayah, the middle sister, the abilities ranging from telepathy to vision and memory alteration. It was clear from Malik's performance that his gift was the latter. Whatever he was making Jericho see, it was not what everyone else was observing. Whatever it was, it was enough for a king to lose all royal composure and lash out with rage.

Valine stared out the window of the carriage, seething. Malik withheld incredibly pertinent information from her. That was twice now. It wasn't lying, but deliberately withholding was just as bad. She was sure the rage showed on her face, because her jaw ached with the pressure of keeping it still.

When they stopped in the Muravo Pass, Valine got out and strode off. Malik quickly caught up to her, reading her body language. He grabbed her by the arm and whirled her around. Ire flashed in her eyes. She felt her lip curl without her volition, and Malik froze, taking her in.

"You figured it out," he said flatly. He did not release her.

"What?" she hissed, rage flooding her face. "That you're a fucking psychomancer and didn't fucking tell me?"

Malik covered her mouth and glanced around sharply. No one had seemed to notice. "Do not say that again," he admonished her softly. "No one knows."

Valine felt some of her anger evaporate. "No one?"

"No one," he confirmed.

"Have you ever used it on me?" she asked, her voice steady, her eyes hard. Wrath simmering beneath the surface of her skin.

Malik held her gaze, and without hesitation, he told her. "No. But I have used it around you." He sighed and ran a hand through his hair. "I don't use it very often because the false memories create a ripple in the air and anyone nearby will feel it. If they know what to look for and are sensitive to it, it's obvious."

"The vertigo."

"Yes. Which is why I usually reserve it for high emotion situations and generally expose it only in circumstances that a bout of lightheadedness would go unnoticed."

Valine realized he'd used it when they first arrived in Talloh. The sudden change in the king hadn't been from a change in attitude. It was from a change in memory. And Valine's fatigue was not from travel, it was from exposure to Malik's magic. He'd also used it when she'd first revealed she was a necromancer.

"You cannot tell anyone," he implored her, capturing both her hands. "Please."

"I won't say anything," she replied automatically. Then realization struck her. "That's how. You're going to make everyone think I haven't left the group."

Malik smiled, it was part relief, part anxiety. "Clever little liar."

Struck with emotion, Valine clutched Malik's face and brought his lips to hers in a furious kiss. She parted his lips with her tongue, and the glide of his against hers had her moaning into his mouth. Their lips caught between teeth and were traced by tongues, a rough battle of wills and emotion. She broke from him and pressed her brow to his.

"Never use it one me."

"Never."

"I have to go," she whispered.

"I know," he said softly. "Please be careful."

"I will, I'll see you soon."

He kissed her harshly and she responded in kind. When they broke apart again, Valine stepped back, unclasping her cloak, and handing it to him before slipping against the rock.

"Be careful," Malik told her again, wanting to say something else, longing burning in his gaze.

"I will."

She turned and slipped into the shadows. Although she didn't say it, she was leaving her heart behind.

PART TWO

CHAPTER THIRTY-TWO

To the Ground and Sea

Valine bided her time, waiting on the edge of the Muravo Mountain Pass, watching the sun slip below the horizon, anticipating the guard rotation changing. She waited for the mages to return to the palace, to relinquish their posts along the last stretch of road before entrance to the palace. As the rotation at dusk commenced, Valine bolted from the pass, materializing her necromancy into a smoky shield and darting behind the shelters that bordered the oasis. A repeated dance of running and hiding before she got to the last one. The mages were facing the yawning expanse of the Twilight Sands, the threat of sand serpents a far cry from the immediacy of the danger that skirted behind them.

Finally, she bolted across the last stretch of sand, her boots shushing against the sand, the small puffs of disturbed air masquerading in the twilight as she wreathed herself in necromantic smoke. She reached the cliff face that Selyndyr was raised upon, and from within her satchel, Valine produced spikes that she added to her boot and a set of pitons. Dusting her hands in the sand, Valine took up her gear and began to climb.

It was arduous and technical, rocks crumbling beneath her feet and fingers. Her hands were aching with the feat of supporting her weight, blood and blisters screaming against her palms. She knew her fingertips were stripped raw by the halfway point, like points of fire. Sweat streamed in her eyes and slipped down the nape of her neck as she continued to haul herself up the cliffside.

Talloh had little in the way of guards aside from the ones posted along the pass. Valine had watched their rotations over the past few days under the guise of enjoying tea on the balconies, learning even more from Hanish's helpful intel. The risk of a takeover from the mountainside was a ludicrous number, and the possibility was next to none. The ocean was hardly ventured due to the risk of kraken, therefore the need to guard from the sea was only monitored by the most skeleton of crews on the North Point lighthouse. She was sure there were guard posts on the other seaside, but they were not close enough to the north-western seaboard for it to matter.

Valine's climb had her limbs trembling, her lungs begging to burst, but still she climbed. The cool air was the smallest reprieve, the wind however, was an obstacle Valine could do without. It tossed her hair about her face and strands stuck to her sweaty forehead as she blinked past the burning moisture.

She chanced a look up. Thirty more feet. She could do it.

Hauling herself up by cramping muscles, Valine ascended.

Fifteen feet.
Ten.
Five left.

When Valine pulled herself over the top, she lay upon the sharp shale, lungs heaving, limbs shuddering and spasming. Sweat coated her entire body and her lips were dry, drier still was her throat. Valine stared up at the stars that Amaris communed with, finding the constellation of Nafiza, of Malik's patroness. She strained for breath, pulling her hands up to the three moons.

Her skin was shredded, the fingertips bloody and torn, dozens of blisters erupting over her hands, filling with fluid. She groaned, but she had expected this. She just trusted that her necromancy would help heal her quickly.

"You look like hell," Hanish stated dryly.

Valine shot her eyes to the fulgurmancer standing over her, the man holding a flask of water. Valine took it greedily, gulping down the cool liquid and spilling much of it on herself. It was empty before she was ready for it to be finished. Hanish wordlessly handed her a second one. She finished this one, too, and got up on shaky legs.

"I'm going to be honest," Hanish said, embarrassed, "I didn't think you were going to survive that climb."

Valine shrugged. "It was the only way."

Hanish pulled out a salve from his pocket and helped her cover her hands with it, hissing quietly in pain as he did so. The numbing agents in the cream helped immensely, and Valine dumped a third flask over her head. If her clothing wasn't stuck to her before, it certainly was now.

"You'll come back for us?" Hanish asked.

"I swore I would," Valine told him efficiently as she counted the items in her satchel, donning fingerless leather gloves. "But you need to be here when the body is found. You cannot escape the same night as an assassination."

Hanish guided Valine to the secret passage at the base of the palace. "This one leads you to the servant's wing. Take two lefts and then a right, and after that it's a straight stretch up. I left a candle burning in the storage room. Once you get there, push the second shelf in, and it'll take you to the Nova Wing. From there, you'll recognize the Vesper Wing. I'm sure you can find your way from there."

"Thank you, Hanish. Truly," Valine told the mage, clapping him on the shoulder.

"Just follow through, all right?"

Valine knew Hanish meant on both her promises, and she nodded, disappearing as Hanish disappeared up a trail, a woven basket slung over his arm.

The passage was dark but surprisingly dry, dust and cobwebs littering every wall and the floor. Insects scuttled along with her steps, and Valine felt her way for the turns. After she'd followed two lefts and a right, she carried on a straight stretch and found the slightest sliver of light—the storage room. Valine blew out the candle and pushed the shelf. Recently oiled hinges allowed no sounds and Valine smiled.

Quietly, she crept, blending into shadows. During her stay, she'd learned so many hiding place. She'd traversed these halls day and night, constantly watching. Valine counted breaths and footsteps, darting away or around when needed. Finally, Valine recognized the artwork of the Vesper Wing, the elaborately painted floors of stars and mandalas running like a scroll across the expanse.

Valine had left her chest of weapons in the secret alcove hidden behind a long tapestry and fainting couch. She slipped into it, opening the chest by feel alone, grabbing everything she needed to frame the people for the perfect crime. She had the earrings, the poison, the tonic, and the list.

Armed with her instruments of falsity, Valine descended to the healer's lab. She tentatively stretched out her necromancy, feeling for life. She found the slow heartbeat of the healer sleeping. Quietly, Valine entered the lab, dropped the earrings into a box, and tucked the fleur de mort into the indigo drawers the healer kept the contraceptive tonics in. Valine smiled when her suspicions were rewarded, seeing a vial with Jacira's name on it. She ensured that it was clearly in sight before she slipped the forged document about debt ownership into a thin drawer and swept from the room.

From the Vesper Wing it was a short trip to the Heaven Wing. Valine traipsed through the halls before she paused in an alcove before the king's door. Four guards were stationed outside of his room, with no possibility of entry without sight. But that was just fine, Valine did not need to enter.

No man had been able to recreate the effects of fleur de mort, but Valine was no man. As a necromancer, she held within her the ability to kill in any manner. She could mimic asphyxiation. She could copy blunt force trauma. What she couldn't recreate was some of the evidence. She could not put feathers in lungs from a pillow suffocation. She could not leave splinters from a spear. This was why she favored poison. So little of poison left residue.

Valine's bloodied and blistered hand reached out. She let her magic unfurl and watched that intangible smoke seep from her fingertips. She watched as it slid across the floor, sinuous like a snake, past the unwitting guards and under the door.

The magic was a part of her, therefore she felt with it. There were two people present in the king's chambers, and Valine probed gently. One was certainly a man, the other a woman. She continued searching and discovered the woman to be Pandora. As she pulled away from Pandora, Valine searched against the man more firmly. She recognized the predatory form of King Jericho.

Still pressed against a shadowy alcove, Valine curled her fingers into claws, letting her necromancy take root. His Robursium Medallion stood no chance. She let it spill down Jericho's throat, roiling the acid in his belly until it burned through the lining, put pressure inside his blood vessels until they burst, seized his muscles, boiled his brain. Valine closed his airway and lanced his eyes, letting blood pour down his cheeks like crimson tears. She turned his lips blue and she felt him suffer. Jericho's death was agony, Valine knew. She'd studied fleur de mort. She knew it was one of the most painful poisons and its rarity made it obvious when it was used. Its signature was unique.

During the final step of the king's death, Valine drew it out, slipping into the king's consciousness. She could see his suffering through his soul, it was anguish and Valine delighted. She smiled a daemon's grin and she let Jericho see it. He raged beneath the pain of his death and she let her magic speak.

"I wanted you to know it was me that brought your kingdom to the ground," she whispered in his head. *"And that I was happy doing it."*

Jericho struggled and gurgled. She let the death hover for a moment, and then she razed through his skin, and pulled his heart through his chest. It sat there, its last feeble pumps suffering, before it stopped and the last trails of blood leaked out of Jericho's mouth.

King Jericho Mayar of Talloh was dead.

Valine wound the magic back into her, the guards none the wiser, a sleeping Pandora due for a violent surprise. She smiled as she exited the halls, weaving her way back to the storage room and through a new tunnel.

The new tunnel led her down past the empty dungeons, under the heart of the castle and through ancient pathways used by builders and mistresses. Valine wove her way through, counting the steps until she reached four-hundred-and-four. At four-hundred-and-five Valine pushed against the wall until it clicked. When it did, she found herself in a room, dusty and draped in white cloth. It was living quarters, long abandoned. Valine speculated it was a mistress's space, as it faced the ocean and had a wonderful view of the coast.

Throwing open the plate glass doors, Valine felt the icy whip of ocean air throw her hair from her face, tangling the dark strands about her like fingers of seaweed. Another thing about this room was that it faced directly off of a cliffside. She gazed down at the shore, watching the surf crash against dusky sand. She swallowed.

Unwinding a length of rope from a corner of the room, she pocketed the pistol she'd hidden with it, and went back to the rail. Valine wrapped the rope over the wrought iron railing as an anchor, and grasped it in her hand, praying it held. She tied the other end around her waist, taking a deep breath as she lowered herself over the side of the balcony, she braced her legs and began to descend. It was slow and arduous, her salve, sweat, and blood covered hands slick inside her gloves. She couldn't use gloves while climbing because it severely impacted her ability to grip, but sliding down a rope was essential.

She was dropping slowly when she heard the first groan. Her eyes shot skyward toward the fence that held her. The metal was leaning precariously, bending against her weight. She swore, sliding as fast as she could without snapping her spine or wrenching her shoulders on the stopping impact. The iron groaned again, and she sped up.

"Fuck, fuck, fuck," she muttered, careening down the cliff face, the chill night air biting her cheeks, her hair following her descent like a cyclone above her head. She counted the remaining feet. One hundred. Ninety. Seventy-five.

The balcony began to screech in earnest and nervous sweat beaded up on her forehead, panic swallowing her in its hold. The beach was fast approaching. Fifty feet. The ocean lapped greedily. Thirty-five. She was so close. Twenty-five.

At fifteen, the balcony gave, and Valine plummeted. She swallowed a scream in her throat, preparing to tuck and roll, being mindful of the rope. She crashed against the ground, hitting her shoulder on the sand and rolling, letting momentum carry her into the ocean. It hurt—*fuck*, it hurt. But she was alive. The balcony rail slammed into the ground where she'd made impact, landing with a solid thud and a puff of sand.

Valine laid on the shore, ocean water crashing against her like a cool caress. Her hair was soaked, she was sore, but she'd done it. She pulled herself to her feet, finding a tender ankle and dragged the evidence of the broken balcony further into the ocean, calculating the distance of low tide, and depositing it into the darkness of the sea. Because two of Talloh's moons were stationary like two orbs hung in the sky, they had little more effect on the tides aside from a near constant high tide and the "low tide" being not all that low. After, ankle barking, she limped her way to the harbor.

The harbor stank of fish and more salt-tanged air. The men were grizzled and burly, missing limbs and eyes, but they did not question the woman dressed in black when she asked for a cloak while holding out gold coin. They also did not question when she asked to depart for the border of Valencya and Luneth immediately.

Within fifteen minutes she was boarding a ship, sitting next to barrels of silver-scaled fish, drinking deeply from a flask of whiskey, a flagon of water beside her.

The ship was called *The Elegance*, a Valencyan vessel that transported basic cargo and illegal imports, everything from drugs to girls. Valine kept this in mind for a later assassination. The captain was a lecherous man twice Valine's age with a frosty gray beard and salt spray hair. A scar bisected his face, cutting across the bridge of his bulbous nose. His name was Wallace Yarl, but the men on the ship just called to him as Captain.

The assassin must have cut a dangerous figure, because not even Captain Yarl dared to come close to her as they sailed from the harbor. She began cleaning her dirty nails with one of her many blades, sighing at their cracked and broken state.

The screaming began before she was finished.

Valine smiled as bells rang and shouts went up.

"The king is dead!" She heard from land, and the captain's gaze lurched to her, paling so that his scar stood out stark white. His mouth dropped open, his gray eyes flaring with genuine fear. Valine kept cleaning her nails, a smile on her lips that curled from her teeth. He knew what she'd done. He didn't know how, but he knew. Valine did not deny it. It didn't matter what he knew. He was going to die soon.

He stepped toward her.

She pulled out her gun and aimed it at him. She didn't even bother looking at the captain as she examined her nails.

"Don't return to port," she said flatly, the toll of bells punctuating her words. "Turn around, and I'll kill you too."

The captain just nodded and commanded the men to sail. It could have been her imagination, but she thought that they put on an additional burst of speed.

When she asked for quarters at daybreak, she was given the captain's with a key. She found a beautiful gold pistol, emblazoned with the sun and a crescent moon, filigree dancing across the barrel. She took it as well—for security. For extra reassurance, she bound the captain to her with a tether in case anyone tried to murder her in her sleep. They didn't, and she slept soundly. The ship followed the coast as closely as possible, avoiding kraken in the deeper waters and reefs closer to shore. Any captain worth his salt knew the safest routes to take around the horseshoe-shaped waters within Enneive.

Valine monitored their progress, and when they were in the deepest stretch of the ocean, a day from reaching the port of Valencya, she killed the entire crew and sank the ship. She'd heard enough to know they regularly stole girls and sold them, trafficked them into prostitution and other flesh trade. They didn't have any qualms about ruining those girls' lives, so she had no hesitations taking theirs. She sarcastically apologized to the captain for the necessary evil and escaped in a dinghy with pockets full of gems and coin.

She kept the gun.

CHAPTER THIRTY-THREE

News had reached Valencya when Valine reached the harbor. On foot from where she'd stashed the dinghy in a cave system, enough time had passed that other travel had made word known. Her hands were raw and her muscles stiff and fatigued. She climbed up from the beach on tremulous nerves, taking the stairs deliberately, one at a time, listening amongst the gossiping sailors.

"Killed in his bed and caught with his daughter's lover, can you believe it?" a man crowed as he hauled crates towards a tavern flanking the harbor. "Apparently it was this big plot with Luneth. They even supplied the poison to do it!"

"The lover was in on it?" another man, this one with reddish hair asked as he fileted fish. His mastery over the blade as he gutted, cut, and portioned was astounding.

"Yeah! And get this! Apparently, she blackmailed the head healer about his gambling debts and paid them with jewels from Princess Larysa to get him to help because she was fucking her too."

"You're shitting me," the fishmonger gasped.

"No, deadly serious, my man! There were documents about the princess offering to pay off his debts to the Raziches if he did it, too. And the healer was even caught with more of the poison in his rooms! No doubt ready to kill the rest of the royal family."

"So why did the lover do it?"

"Apparently, she wanted the throne and King-fucking-Jericho wouldn't give it to her, so she fucked her way through the other royals till one offered a crown to her." The crate carrying man dropped the wooden boxes on the step of the tavern. "How she managed to get Princesses Jacira and Larysa, I'd like to know. I'd like to find myself a royal pussy, too."

"Well, if they're inclined to only women, you sir, are shit out of luck."

The other man harumphed and made a sound about changing their minds with his cock, but Valine tuned them out by that point. She'd heard what she'd needed to.

Larysa Olympias was in no way involved with the Talloh coup, but they needed to strain the relations between Luneth and Talloh, and an assassination framing Luneth monarchy was the way to do it. Malik couldn't have the west allying into an empire, Runell was already taking powerful strides in that direction, and Valine would rather die than see that to fruition. Larysa couldn't deny the stolen jewels, and she had no alibi for the procurement of the fleur de mort, Valine had made sure of it. She'd killed Larysa's drug lord to do it, and then she'd falsified the princess's signature and seal to finish it off. The princess meanwhile, had no one to corroborate her locating in the seedy part of town.

Valine's job was done. She'd successfully put Jericho's murder on everyone but her. No eyes would look to Malik. No eyes would look towards her. Smiling, she left the docks behind, hid beneath her cloak, and traversed towards the Whitefinn Inn.

By the time Valine made her way to the inn, rain had begun coming down in gray sheets. The panels of rain had the cloak slicked against her head, the water-resistant coating beginning to fail as rain trickled through and down her neck. She could hardly see through the deluge, her eyes narrowed in the gloom, the scent of petrichor heady in her nose.

She opened the heavy door of the white stone building, the wet draft causing the patrons to stir, glaring openly at her as she crossed the recently—and pointlessly—swept floor. Valine kept her head bowed, nothing but the pointed curve of her pale jaw and supple swell of her lower lip visible. She did not hesitate as she graced across the floor, immediately heading towards the large figure in the corner.

She took a seat across from the man, the brown cloak he wore dotted with rain, nothing but his lower jaw visible as well. Had she not known any better she would have thought this Sarim. But she did know better, and she would recognize that black orchid and tobacco scent anywhere. She knew he would assure the patrons they saw a Valmotti warrior and not the King of Adraali.

There had been moments Valine wondered how the king had ventured without his bodyguards so often in such questionable places, but now, knowing his pyschomancy, she understood.

As she slid into place, a steaming bowl of stew was set in front of her. She cupped it immediately with her ruined hands, luxuriating in the heat it seeped into her cold and aching bones.

"Is it done?" Malik asked lowly.

"It is done," she confirmed.

"Are you well?"

She shrugged; the movement painful on her exhausted body. "I'm a little worse for wear, but nothing extensive."

"Your hands," he whispered, reaching over the tabletop and pulling one from her bowl.

They were still a mess, healing blisters a wet and angry red, dried blood caked in her cuticles, her nails torn and jagged. For the first time, Malik was seeing them without all her rings on them. She'd pulled them all off—consort ring included—and tucked them into a velvet, cotton-lined, and waterproof pouch for safe keeping. Even so, she hadn't been able to help herself, constantly reassuring herself they were still there.

"They'll heal," she said nonchalantly.

"I know," he replied, slowly bringing her ruin of a hand to his lips. The kiss stung her palm but it was chaste and so intimate, the king's mouth on her filthy, blood-soaked hands. For a breath, she felt like she was gripping the entire power of the world in some intangible hold. She immediately batted the thought away.

Pulling back, she tucked into her stew, tasting rosemary, thyme, and bay leaf, enhancing the broth of the lamb and potatoes. There was something green in it too, some dark leafy vegetable she couldn't pinpoint. She didn't dwell on it, she simply ate, scooping the wooden bowl until her spoon scraped the empty bottom.

"I assume it wasn't poisoned," Malik chided.

Valine swallowed. "Even if it was, I would have eaten it."

"Does it not even make you ill?" he questioned.

"No. I can taste it, but it doesn't bother me in any way. Alcohol hardly affects me because it's similar to a poison, but not wholly part of Mrithun's Apothecary so I can still feel some degree of inebriation."

"I've never heard poison referred to as Mrithun's Apothecary," Malik commented lightly. "You never did tell me—where did you train?"

Valine chewed on her lip, hesitant. "I'll tell you another time." She cast her gaze around. "Should we be on the road?"

The moment held for a moment, neither of them meeting the other's eyes from beneath their cloaks. It was bated breath and charged air. Valine couldn't help but remember only nights ago when she'd felt Malik's mouth between her legs, his tongue swirling cleverly over that little spot of hers. She remembered the climax he'd coaxed from her, the growl he'd let out when she did. She wanted nothing more than to drag this man up the stairs to a room and have her way with him. She could see in his eyes that he was having the very same thoughts. His mouth was parted and she could see that silky and talented tongue just behind the white of his teeth. She thought about it, she truly did.

"We should go."

Malik sighed. "Yes, we should, Sarim is waiting at a warehouse."

They left together, keeping a careful distance even while sparks zinged between them. A light feeling of vertigo stole over her and Malik met her eyes meaningfully, he was letting her know that he was using his magic and she appreciated the communication. They crossed the threshold, and all she could think was leaving was the last thing they wanted to do. But they had carefully laid plans and carefully laid plans were not to be derailed by desires of *getting* laid.

The rain continued, the gray slog made worse by the thunderous downpour. Statues of white marble were being painted anew, clouds of dust from travelers running off the curves and edges of togas and shifts, aquiline and hooked noses, crowns of laurels and harps. White marble beneath their feet was slick and filthy, and arches and pillars towering above them offered little but aesthetic reprieve.

Malik led them to an unmarked shop and pushed Valine inside. It was empty of everything but dusty boxes and a Valmotti warrior. Sarim stood, a viridian cloak slung over his shoulders, a look of apprehension on his face. That look quickly morphed into relief when he saw Valine.

"Glad to see you're alive."

Valine noticed something new. "Glad to see a hickey on your neck."

Sarim immediately blushed, his face filled with pleased guilt. She was happy that Freyja and Sarim had finally made something happen. She would have to ask one of them for details later.

Wordlessly, the men exchanged cloaks and offered Valine a new one. She donned it, disposing of her ruined one in a decrepit box before the three of them escaped through another door and into the waiting carriage. Within minutes they were loaded and heading towards the rest of the retinue.

Inside the carriage, it was warm and she exchanged an even warmer look with Freyja when she saw a matching love bite on her neck. The interior was fraught with tension, everyone inside it wanting to know how the plot in Talloh had panned out. Only those present—and Hanish—knew what had truly transpired.

Malik's hand was hot and heavy on her thigh, a comforting and steadying weight that brought her back down to reality. Her body was sore and exhausted, and she wanted nothing more than to sink into a hot bath and soak. She hadn't let her guard down in days, and she felt the tension in her shoulders. The present moment was the most she'd relaxed.

But relax she finally did and fell into unconsciousness.

It took three days of travel to reach the palace of Valos, the capital city of Thycca. In regards to architecture it was startlingly similar to Valencya, following the same lines of marble statues and pillars, carved frescoes and plinths and stages and daises scattered among streets and parks, deciduous trees, thickly needled and dark green, the scent of pine and rain oppressive. The buildings were steeply gabled and accented with timber and stone, with windows of diamond panes. Every doorway had a grand archway of stone that contrasted against the rest of the structure while the doors varied in a riot of color, reminding Valine of stained glass.

That was where the similarities ended. Thycca was richly blessed with plentiful lakes and vast mountain ranges, rivers cutting through the kingdom with tireless abandon. Thycca was also cursed with a prevalence of quakes, floods, landslides, and hurricanes. There was also the ominous border of the Black Arbors at the southernmost point, a shadowy line of trees that was rumored to be the veil between the saints and daemons. The border crossed the ocean on both sides, extending like a final determining line, a stark warning to go no further.

No one had entered the Black Arbors and lived.

Valine hadn't put much weight in the superstition, but she also had never dared go near the shadow border. She knew enough magic and magical beasts existed; she didn't need to piss off the patrons too.

Rather than stay in the palace like they'd done in Talloh, they had heavily guarded room at the highest revered establishment, the *Blue Blood Prince*. Valine thought it was fitting that they were being kept at arm's reach within Thycca, this mission was a formality and cover, whereas Talloh was thinly veiled negotiations—and firmly veiled assassinations. What Valine wasn't ready to face though, was the proof of a woman who was supposed to be her lover's potential bride, and soon she would have to befriend her.

The inn was luxuriously decorated, dressed in heavy woods and rich fabrics of velvet and jewel tones, chandeliers dripped elegance and light, cushions were tufted and patterned, rugs were opulent and busy.

They were shown their rooms and they all made quick work of changing and freshening up. Their stay in Thycca was only for a night, only for the graduation ceremony.

The five of them, dressed in reserved but colorful formality, were escorted to the university's ceremony and guided to a specific area predetermined for royals and their entourage. For the first time since they'd departed for Talloh, they were surrounded by guards, circled by tall men and women dressed in black, viridian, and gold.

Valine found it stifling, and she couldn't help but pull on the collar of her white silk blouse, unbuttoning and rebuttoning the top pearl before settling on two undone, exposing just the first teasing of her cleavage. She thought she felt Malik's eyes on her breasts but she didn't look up to confirm it, there was something so tempting and satisfying about not letting him know that she knew. She wore a sculpted corset of viridian, gilded with filigree, the shape of it enhancing her curves, while the lines were cut elegantly above her hips, the clasps holding it together fashioned out of gold chain and sunburst eyelets.

The rings were back on her fingers.

Malik was dressed similarly, his leather pants not quite as tightly fitted as hers, but his corset was identical in everything but style and vibrancy—his bolder. He wore the typical male version, the filigree stitched rather than sculpted, the shape similar to a waistcoat. Instead of a white blouse he wore black, and atop his head was a subdued gold crown.

They took their seats, Alastair next to her in his very loud citrus-toned outfit, and both Sarim and Freyja in matching black and gray. Their seats were elevated above a stage, a dark blue curtain separating the graduates from the rest of the viewers. Valine prepared to hunker down, stifling her possessiveness that was sure to rise.

The ceremony commenced beautifully, the students and their majors declared as they crossed the stage, and when Liesl Ryniel was called, Valine was shocked to see such a petite creature cross.

Princess Liesl Ryniel was bird-like in thinness and grace, her stature short and her frame delicate. Valine thought she could snap the girl's bones between two fingers. She had dark brown, nearly black hair, and small features set in an oval face that only made the darkness of her eyes quiet, rather than fearsome. She held herself with a silent solace and scholarly air, someone Valine imagined would much rather tend to one of the many overflowing greenhouses scattered throughout Thycca rather than rule it.

Valine clapped politely when Liesel crossed the stage and so did Malik, but he very impolitely stopped and reached his hand between Valine's legs in the darkness.

She smiled and kept smiling throughout the rest of the ceremony.

CHAPTER THIRTY-FOUR

The letter arrived for Malik during the drinks and congratulatory speeches. A servant had swept up to them with an envelope sealed with violet wax. It was a request for aid from Queen Amaris of Talloh, seeking allyship and support during the kingdom's upheaval following the assassination of the king. Malik immediately penned a letter offering troops and compassion, conveying that they would return to Selyndyr the following day.

Just as they had hoped.

Malik had been careful and precise with his interactions with Amaris and Jericho. He had ensured that the queen knew that their aid would be freely given, while letting the king feel it would be conditional. This was further enhanced by his psychomancy. Leaving false memories and statements when necessary, fueling a fire and unease and jealousy where it was needed. Malik's machinations also further drove a wedge between the husband and wife, souring what little amicable air they may have shared.

The plan was moving along swiftly, and as soon as deemed acceptable, they departed from the ceremony and back to their rooms. They all hardly spoke, knowing that their responses were going to be watched by the rest of Talloh. It took a week of travel to once again reach Selyndyr, the weather holding up, raining only sporadically, allowing them to camp comfortably on the heavily guarded roads and once again within the Muravo Mountain Pass.

Valine had held her breath for the duration of that portion of the journey, convinced that the arachne would come to weigh her again. They did not.

She had sparred with Sarim each morning. Pulling away from the group far enough to comfortably hone their skills away from prying eyes, and enough to pressure Sarim for info on him and Freyja. They bartered wins for secrets, and many battles were lost on his end. Valine pressed for the truth of their encounters. And it was encounters, *plural.* Apparently, Freyja had desired him for much longer than he'd thought. Now the two of them were fucking like rabbits, punctuated by suspicious sounds coming from tents and from shared horsebacks.

As much as Valine wanted to have her way with Malik, she could not. It was one thing to suspect the king's favor for her; it was a whole other to flaunt it.

The mages stationed along the pass nodded solemnly at their retinue, garbed in funeral gray. It was the absence of color, the absence of life. It was the presence of loss. The mages had shadows under their eyes, purple rings that only enhanced the withdrawn pallor of their skin. Valine realized they were being overworked. She vowed to make reparations.

A serpent's cry took up the sky and Valine's gaze whipped to the sound as her stomach dropped. Gasps and sounds of dismay rose up around her.

From one of the balconies a basilisk and rider ascended. The basilisk bore white scales and gray feathered wings with the face of a snake but the hooked beak of a vulture, lined with serrated teeth. Its four legs ended in four talons and each were as long as her forearm. The beast was several times the size of their carriage.

Valine could see little more of the rider than a banner of pale hair and dark flight leathers. She froze, staring at the rider high above as they flew southward to Runell.

A basilisk rider spelled bad news.

She continued staring until they disappeared over the mountains and horizon. When it was gone she turned to Malik and he was stone-faced. Even so, she saw the worries and thoughts eddying behind his eyes.

Was Talloh allying with Runell? Were they offering aid just as Adraali was? What was Amaris's intention?

She didn't know, and it made her uneasy.

The carriage trundled along, despite the basilisk's recent presence. Their entire crew was bedecked in gray or violet in respect and reverence to Talloh and their plight for aid. Black was meant for the day after a loss, gray for the following weeks. Valine felt the moments slip by faster and faster as they approached the palace, recognizing the entrance to the courtyard upon them. Once they stopped, Valine stepped out with Malik, greeting Amaris and Jacira.

The queen and princess were pale—paler than usual—with red-rimmed and dark-circled eyes. Their hair, despite being elegantly styled, appeared lank and lifeless. There was something about all the loss they'd endured, the travesty that was thrust upon their kingdom that had sunk their souls to trying degrees. Amaris, star-touched, was now ruler of an entire queendom, and Jacira, impetuous, was now once removed from the throne.

Jacira would be queen upon her twenty-fifth year.

Valine noticed the distinct lack of Pandora. The princess's lover was likely being locked in a dungeon somewhere far below the palace, and she couldn't help but wonder what had come of her affair with Lincoln.

Amaris visibly deflated at the sight of them, her relief palpable in the air. Before Valine had time to think, the queen was rushing towards them, arms outstretched. To Valine's greater shock, Amaris wrapped her arms around *her*. Valine startled but quickly responded, holding the queen in mourning gray to her breast. The queen was heaving silent, tearless sobs against her husband's killer, unwitting of the bloodstained hands that soothed her back.

Valine could see Jacira over the queen's shoulder. The vivacious princess had a face of stone, and Valine could see that something integral had fractured inside the girl. She didn't know if she would ever resurface. She had lost her father, two of her friends, and her lover was soon to join them. Valine felt guilt, but she squandered it. She signed up for this. She knew this.

"I am so glad you have returned," Amaris whispered. "The stars told me Mrithun was the cause of my queendom's descent."

Because now it *was* a queendom.

The queen's words had ice sliding down Valine's spine. Was she perhaps not as insanity touched as she'd believed? Did the stars really speak to Amaris as often as she was quoted? Worry began to worm its way through Valine in sick coils.

The queen released Valine and Alastair swept the princess up in an embrace. She'd forgotten that Alastair was well-versed in political pleasantries and immediately he'd dived into reassuring and manipulating. Valine couldn't catch the words but she knew the tone. It was coercive and compelling, drawing threads of hope through the throng of despair. Slowly, she saw the girl crack her shell.

Malik was silent nearby, hands clasped and offering consolations and apologies. Valine had tuned out the repetitive falsehoods. They were not sorry; they had done this.

Sylvan, the servant who'd announced them the first time was directed to show them to their suites again. They were given the same rooms in the Vesper Wing, Valine's was still joined with Malik's. She was sure the rooms had been cleaned, but the echoes of the past still lingered. Memories of the walls she was pressed against, the armchairs the king had waited for her on, and the bed Malik had nearly fucked her on.

Valine had been in her room for all of ten minutes when a knock sounded. She answered and was surprised to find it was Hanish, his sharp features eerily familiar to her by now.

"Hello, Valine," he greeted.

"Hanish, lovely to see you."

"The queen has requested your presence in the war room. She claims that you will be a queen one day and therefore your input is invaluable." He paused, a smirk on his lips. "I couldn't help but notice a certain king blushing when this was announced. Is there any merit to this?" he teased and Valine realized that he was joking with her. She wondered how much he'd held back prior to the assassination; she wondered if he realized how integral he'd become in her journey.

Valine sighed and held up the consort ring on her middle finger. "Does this answer your question?"

Hanish looked at her approvingly and lowered his voice. "You have a fascinating way with kings."

"Oh, hush."

"Mm," he hummed halfheartedly. "I'm to show you the way if you are prepared."

"I am," she replied, following him. "Do you know anything about this basilisk and rider?"

Hanish glanced over his shoulder. "It was Prince Sildruil and the queen refused him—whatever he was offering."

Prince Sildruil was the second prince of Gallae and one of the most talented basilisk riders on the continent. Valine had met him once in her youth and a memory niggled—was there talk of a betrothal between them? Dáinn Desdemon had tried to arrange a marriage for her more than once, so it was possible.

"Hmm. Keep an ear out for anything more?" she requested.

"Of course." Hanish cleared his throat. "I must say, in all the uproar of the change in monarchy, the storm that raged over Selyndyr the following day has caused a stir of gossip. People have believed it was the wrath of the gods. Quite unfortunate that a strike of lighting sheared the balcony off of a suite. The whole thing fell into the sea, what a shame the damage was caused before a proper investigation of the palace could be brought to attention."

Valine caught the wink.

"Thank you, Hanish."

"Thank *you*," he whispered.

"I told you I'd come back."

"And so you did."

CHAPTER THIRTY-FIVE

The door of the war room was gold with an emblem of a crown, bisected by a sword, and three moons around the hilt, with a burning star in the pommel. Elements were repeated over the door, triads of moons, swords crossed, supernova stars, and broken crowns. The gilded doors were swept open and Valine entered to find the queen leaning over a table strewn with documents, Malik on the opposite side, pointing at writing in another while Alastair was sitting at the open window with Jacira, offering her a cup of tea.

It was a dark room, heavy stone and rich wood, the masculine lines a vicious reminder that Talloh had never been a queendom. The little light that shone through was from the window Jacira was haloed against, the dangling lantern over the carved map of Enneive cast shadows in the valleys of the world, deepest around the Muravo Mountain Pass, the Laskava Mountains and Valencya's Triad. Rivers were wrought in lapis lazuli, lakes were sapphires, the sea was crushed pearl and turquoise.

"Before we begin, I want to make clear that Runell's presence here was unwanted," Amaris said. "I sent away the prince and told him I needed time to consider an alliance but truthfully, it is unlikely that I will accept."

Malik inclined his head. "I appreciate your honestly, Queen Amaris."

Amaris nodded back and Valine remained silent.

Malik had turned from the table with documents to trace a line on the map, tracing it from Adraali and through the pass to Selyndyr. He traced a second along the shoreline.

"These are the two routes my soldiers will take," Malik was saying. "It will be a show of support on all fronts that matter, and everyone in the west will know that Adraali is with Talloh. Seeing your queendom fortified will dissuade any others from trying to usurp your throne while you reclaim your power. It will send a clear message that Luneth's coup will not bring you to your knees and that Runell's influence northward is, in no uncertain terms, unwelcome."

"What is in it for you?" Amaris questioned, eyes hard. She was staring at Malik's gold-painted nail hovering over her queendom. A queendom he could squash beneath that very hand.

"Power, influence, justice. It is the ability to right a grievous wrong before it's committed," Malik answered honestly, sprawling his hand over the whole of Talloh. "I have spies, as nearly every monarch does, and mine speak of rumblings in Gallae. Of works designed to take away rights founded in the very values of this queendom. They seek to control bodies under the guise of protecting life, seeking only more soldiers and more pieces in their machine to serve them. They seek to abolish marriages made from love simply because they do not fit the constraints of their customs.

"Queen Amaris," Malik said soberly. "If this would come to pass, marriages of triads and same-sex would be outlawed in addition to those between couples of different skins. Gender identities aside from biological sex would not be acknowledged. Contraceptives and abortifacients would be illegal. Sex would be relegated only to the marriage bed and it would become a punishment and a duty. If I may be so bold to say, it would be the undoing of many countries' freedoms." Malik's gaze turned hot. "I will not see our world turn back centuries on the whims of bored old men."

"You have to understand my hesitation," Amaris said, contrite. "You are asking me to open my halls to people who, according to my late husband were enemies. Adraali's presence here will send a message, that a queen is so weak to need a foreign man's help."

"I do understand, Your Majesty, which is why I am offering two contingencies. My soldiers will travel two separate journeys and if you wish it, I can command them to don civilian garb. We can keep this quiet should you want to see the response from other kingdoms. Consider it a test of allegiance. With this you will understand who you're up against."

Amaris glanced at the map and her daughter, seeing the damage wrought in such a short time. From her understanding, it was a crown that had destroyed everything, that Pandora's desire for a royal title stole her security and complacency. The queen bit her lip and cast her hard jade eyes heavenward. Valine bit back a gasp when she saw white mist across her eyes.

A tracery of stars flitted about Amaris's head, bobbing in an orbit around her crown, carefully circling the golden queen. Her eyes remained white and glassy, open to the heavens. The eerie ability sent shivers of true fear down Valine's spine.

She caught Malik's shocked expression, one he hastily composed as he set his jaw and waited for Amaris to finish convening. His hands curled into claws over Talloh. He wanted the queendom, and he was doing everything in his power to take it by anything but force, but Valine knew that Selyndyr was vulnerable, and he would use force if he needed.

Amaris blinked and cleared the haze from her vision, eyes once again green. She steadied her gaze on Malik, levelling him with a powerful look. A look passed down from Nylantia.

"The stars have verified the whispers you have heard, but they could tell me little more. They have told me that Mrithun is blocking their ability to speak clearly."

Valine felt a jolt of white-hot fear spear her. The queen was truly a powerful stellaemancer after all. She was not star-touched by insanity, she was star-touched by the patrons.

"Talloh accepts your offer, King Malik Jirani Amir of Adraali. I accept your offer of aid," Amaris declared, inclining her chin regally. "Please begin the proper preparations."

"At once, Your Majesty," Malik conceded.

"I require you to stay until the morrow," Amaris expressed flatly. "We will have public executions tomorrow and I wish for you to be present for them."

"Of course. We will stand by you," Malik proclaimed.

"In addition, I have another favor to request." Her eyes darted to Valine. "The stars wish to speak to you. *Alone.*"

Valine froze in place, ice flooding through her. She glanced around at the others in the room, they too, were still. Amaris waved a hand and everyone moved for the door, departing the room. Malik paused by Valine brushing her hand with his own.

"I'll be just outside," he whispered, and then he too was gone.

The door fell shut and Valine turned to face the queen. Already her eyes were cast above, that milky glaze over the jade, eerie and ominous in the beautiful royal face. Suddenly, a voice spoke and it was not the queen's.

"Daughter of Mrithun," the Not-Queen began, slowly bringing Amaris's face to Valine's. The smile that took over the queen was positively daemonic. "You have been an infuriating creature for us patrons."

"*Nylantia*," Valine breathed.

"In the flesh," Nylantia confirmed, a vision overtaking Amaris.

Nylantia appeared as a woman of night black skin, moon white hair, and nebulous, multi-hued eyes like two dying stars that stared out from beneath a brow of silver galaxies. She was shapely beneath a gown of darkness, her presence like that of the vastness of the heavens. She was overpowering, immense, and spectacular.

"Why did you want to speak to me?" Valine asked, her voice tremulous. She was truly and utterly afraid. She was in the presence of a daemon, the Patroness of Night and Stars, the child of Light and Darkness. She was the product of a saint and a daemon, the love between soulmates eclipsing all laws of the world. Charna and Lucian had disobeyed the restrictions of the universe, restrictions that Mrithun and Vitus—for all the love they shared—had never been able to bridge.

"Mrithun declared you under his protection, and we cannot whisper of your plots to our chosen ones. All we can do is warn them with promises of an undying queen and a deathless empire. But this is taken for prophecy and salvation, not the annihilation you represent. If we cannot take you, we will command you."

"I don't understand," Valine quavered. "I am no queen."

"Oh, do not play stupid with me, girl," Nylantia spit, her visage flickering over Amaris's. "Do you truly not see where your destiny is heading? Are you truly so blind to that ring on your finger? You will be queen one day. The king has already fallen for you."

"That's not true," Valine managed, the consort ring heavy on her finger.

"Isn't it? Did he not already offer you the option? And you did not take it?" Nylantia snipped.

"I cannot. He must choose a bride. He cannot overpower Runell without an ally's aid."

Nylantia stepped forward and leaned in, her cosmic eyes riveting. She tilted Valine's chin with a frozen finger. "Your quest for vengeance is blinding you. He will invite the brides under a guise just like the one you have accomplished here in Talloh. He is not calling them for marriage, he is calling them for a scheme. Where is the continent's tension meant to shatter Enneive apart next?"

Valine held the daemon's eyes for a moment. "Valencya and Thycca," she whispered.

"You are clever, daughter of Mrithun. Once the kingdoms are fully divided, he will make you his queen. It will be the only time you will accept him. If you said the word, he would do it tomorrow, but I have read the fates you have tied and you will not allow it. Even with my interception."

Valine chose to ignore the queen's proclamation; she did not believe the daemon. She had not signed up for ruling. She was an assassin and a necromancer. She was no queen. And Malik did not love her.

The thoughts soured in her gut.

"You have only two options now, and that window is closing. You can choose to leave your mage king behind and return to a life of dealing death for coin and doom your world, or you continue on your selected path to the throne. But once you find the Call of the Phoenix and claim it, it will be too late to choose—for it will choose for you. But be aware that when you do, you will experience indescribable loss."

"The what? Doom? What are you talking about? What if I don't want to play this stupid game? What if I choose my death instead?" Valine bit out, frustrated, that famous Desdemon temper flaring.

"That avenue may be more difficult to come by than you might imagine." Nylantia patted Valine's face. "Choose your fate and know that you are deciding the fate of more than just Enneive."

"I didn't ask for this."

"That does not matter," she replied, backing away. "Decide. We are watching."

"Why do you care? And why does Mrithun care for that matter?" Valine pushed.

Nylantia clicked her tongue. "If you cannot figure that out yourself, I cannot help you."

Nylantia flickered, those burning eyes capturing her. "Mrithun is stalling fate, but should you wait too long, certain threads may be cut. Other patrons do not have the power he does."

Valine felt a gasp catch in her throat, and before her eyes, Nylantia disappeared, and the haze departed from Amaris's eyes. The queen blinked several times and took in Valine. Her mouth opened in a small O, and Valine needed no mirror to know her face was a sketch of horror. She was shocked still, numb, and empty.

Amaris tapped Valine on the shoulders and still she remained still. She called her name. She did not respond. Amaris called for Malik and the king burst into the room. Valine sensed, in some distant part of her, the king's presence and his dismay.

"The stars wished to speak with her alone," Amaris explained. "I was not privy to the details. I allowed them to use me as a vessel to speak, and when I awoke, she was like this."

"*Valine.* Valine, can you hear me?" Malik demanded, hands cupping her face. She felt the touch on the surface, and she struggled to meet it. Inside she was screaming, drowning within herself. "Valine, come back to me. Wake up."

She clawed at her consciousness, dragged herself to her nerves. She felt a stirring and latched onto it, forcing herself out. Her hands tingled, her skin felt clammy, her eyes burned with pricks of tears, her jaw ached. But she could feel.

She inhaled sharply and sagged. Malik caught her around the middle and she clutched at him desperately. She found herself staring at him, at the King of Adraali. She was looking at the man that the patroness had claimed loved her. Did he?

Malik held her, hope and desperation burning in those gold-blue eyes, relief swelling from beneath those wondrous depths.

"It was Nylantia," she whispered.

And then she fainted.

CHAPTER THIRTY-SIX

She awoke in her bed, nerves frayed, with Malik and an unfamiliar healer at her side, both of them peering down at her curiously. This healer was a woman, but she wore the same rich robes as Healer Das. Though unlike him, she did not have that discomfiting leering light in her eyes.

"Drink this, dear. It'll settle your stomach," she said softly, handing her a warm mug. "You've been out for a couple hours."

Valine scented peppermint, ginger, and chamomile so without hesitation she sipped it. It was exactly what she had smelled and she smiled timidly at the healer.

"What happened?" Malik asked uncharacteristically softly. His hand moved towards her, but he seemed to think better of it before he made contact. She stifled the wave of disappointment that washed through her.

"I…I don't remember," she lied, eyes flickering over to the healer. The healer, not being an idiot, noticed this and stood without offense.

"I will leave you two alone, but please call for me if you feel unwell. This heat gets to people. I will call for an aethermancer to circulate more air in your suite."

"Thank you," Valine said, shamefaced.

The kindly healer left with a small smile and a nod. On slippered feet, she disappeared from the room.

Malik searched her eyes the moment the door shut with a final click. "What happened?"

Valine sighed and leaned back against the pillows, exhausted but telling him everything—apart from the revelation that she was going to be his queen and that he'd already fallen for her. She refused to acknowledge that as truth. By the end of her explanation, her mug was empty, and her nerves had settled. She was peering down into the blue glaze of the pottery mug she held, trying to stare through it so that Malik wouldn't detect the little untruths she'd peppered in the tale.

"You truly believe this was Nylantia?" Malik asked from his newly standing position beside her, running his hands through his hair.

"I told you—I *saw* her, Malik. It was really her."

"Fucking Vitus and Mrithun, shit, and fuck," he spit, pacing around the room, pulling at his hair. "Valine, this is not good."

"You think I don't know this?" she groused from her nest of blankets. The room was fairly warm, but she was chilled to the bone, no doubt from an encounter from the patroness. "And what is Call of the Phoenix supposed to mean?"

Malik froze and looked up at her slowly. "What did she say about that?"

Valine narrowed her brows. "I told you—she said that I needed to find it."

"You did not," he said flatly. "You said once you found the call. You didn't say what call you referred to. Did you leave anything else out?"

Valine swallowed. "Yes."

"What," he said curtly. A muscle feathered in his jaw.

Valine set her teeth, looking askance. "It was personal."

"So, you don't want to tell me."

"Not yet," she whispered.

The air was charged, and the tension in the room was palpable. She refused to meet his eyes, but she could see him in her periphery, his frame seemingly held up by stress and ambition.

"Okay," he said softly.

Valine startled, watching him draw nearer. She was even more shocked when he sat on the end of her bed, staring at the turquoise bedspread. His fingers traced a line of gold thread, gliding over her covered ankle, and there he began to swirl patterns on her calf.

"So, you don't know what the Call of the Phoenix is?" Malik asked lowly.

"No, should I?"

"I'm surprised you don't. It is a tool or a spell to summon a firebird to you, to make it your familiar. I was wondering why it was coming up in conversation more often."

"That's impossible," Valine sputtered. "Phoenixes are only loyal to their own. They do not answer to anyone."

"Not impossible, but incredibly rare." Malik continued his swirls. "Phoenixes will only answer to the blood of Seraphina or Mrithun."

"How does that help us?"

Malik slowly lifted his head, his gold-blue eyes held a wild gleam. "What did Nylantia call you?"

Daughter of Mrithun.

It wasn't the first time she'd been referred to as such. The arachne that judged her had also called her that.

"You don't think…" Valine breathed, panic lacing through her blood.

"I think exactly that," Malik said slowly—cautiously. "I think you are truly a daughter of Mrithun. Not just in the sense of your necromantic abilities but in blood. It would make sense. Why you were able to kill the sand serpents with your magic, a feat no one else has replicated. You are an undiluted line of Mrithun. You are as potent as it gets."

Valine felt anxiety sliding through her.

"The patrons years past had visited humans and sired heirs. It is not as commonplace now, but surely not impossible. Are there any other necromancers in your family?" he asked, reaching for her hand. He took it as she shook her head. "Did you ever wonder?"

"No," she breathed. "I've always been told I look like my father, that I inherited his temper."

The more she thought about it, the more she questioned it. Did she truly look like the man who'd half-assed raised her? He had dark eyes like her, yes, but who's to say that Mrithun didn't also have dark eyes? And of her temper, surely the lord of death stoked rage now and then? But maybe that fury was all hers since she lived in a kingdom oppressive towards women, designed for the benefit of men. Was it true? Was she truly not the daughter of Dáinn Desdemon?

"I need to get air," she gasped, leaping from the bed and grabbing a cloak as well as her satchel of menstrual pads. She slipped on a pair of boots—not her thigh-high ones—and made for the door.

"Wait!" Malik grabbed her by her upper arm. They met eyes, and she didn't see anger there, she saw understanding and conviction. "Please be safe and come back to me."

"I will," she said, a sense of déjà vu taking over her. Before she could change her mind, she swept from the room and made for a destination and distraction. She knew what she was going to do—the question was if it would work.

The dungeons were low-lit, the hood of her cloak casting her deeper into shadows. In Talloh, the dungeons were unguarded, and the risk of escape was virtually impossible. And should they manage? Where were they to go? The sands and the serpents? The sea and the kraken? It had taken everything for her, a necromancer, an assassin, a lady to pull it off, and even then, she'd needed inside help and the backing of a completely different kingdom to do so. So, while not easy, the risk was negligible.

Valine was graceful as she floated across the stone, carrying with her the knowledge of higher beings and the magic that coursed through her veins. She was a dangerous creature, and she would imbue every part of herself with it. It was an intimidation tactic, but it was generally effective.

She found the cell she was looking for and stood before it, twisting her beringed fingers in front of her. The magic tethered to her mark, seeping in and settling like hooks in flesh. Her mark awoke with a gasp, startling up from the rough, moldy pallet that had been provided. The acrid stink of piss was in the air from the bucket in the furthest corner of the cell. Valine wondered how often it was emptied and who had the undesirable duty to do so.

"Who's there?" Pandora gasped, her pale hair greasy and limp, her nails bitten and dirty. Her feet were curled beneath her, tangled in the filthy blanket she'd been provided. She was a shade of what she once was. Her clothes were grimy linens, no longer was she bedecked in jewels and velvet. No longer was she keeping Jacira with that thing she did with her tongue. No longer was she playing the king.

"Hello Pandora," Valine announced in a low voice, stepping closer to the bars.

Pandora's eyes narrowed, searching the shadows as flame played across Valine's face. She was surprised and confused, and Valine smiled a feral white smile beneath the hood, but she knew the fire picked up on it.

"Valine? Wh—what are you doing here?" Pandora's voice was a quiver, her green eyes fearful.

"I'm here to offer you a choice."

"A choice? What kind of choice?"

"You face the gallows tomorrow, but I'm giving you the option of a second chance." Valine paused, Pandora's face losing color. "You can choose to work for me—finding dirty secrets, trading intel, using your charms, whatever suits my needs and whatever you feel equipped to handle—or you can choose death."

"What? What are you talking about? You speak of treason? Like you're some sort of spy?"

Valine crouched before the bars, eyes level with the woman on the ground, a subtle threat in her tone. "Something like that."

"Why me?" Pandora pressed.

"Because somehow you were fucking both the king and the princess without anyone knowing, not to mention the allegation of your relationship with Larysa Olympias. You clearly have charm, and I could use it. I hate to see talents wasted."

Pandora narrowed her eyes, not even summoning the ability to be ashamed. She was so far past that point. "You called the relationship an allegation."

Valine was thrown for a moment but didn't allow the confusion to show on her face. "I did."

"But you didn't with Jericho and Jacira, meaning you knew those relationships were true, but not with Larysa."

Valine cursed herself internally. She felt anger burn in her eyes, her lips thinning. She inhaled sharply and immediately regretted it, smelling damp wool, mildew, and piss. Pandora wasn't shackled, but there were chains in the cell, flaked with rust and what Valine suspected was blood.

"I don't see why that detail matters."

"I think it matters a great deal," Pandora said, strength growing in her voice. She stood to her height, Valine realizing for the first time that she was as tall as her. Unsettled, Valine got to her own feet. "I think you know the truth."

Her voice was an accusation, and Valine continued to stare at her, her gaze beneath her hood flinty. She wasn't sure what to say next. She was still so off-kilter from her altercation with Nylantia, she was not at her best.

"Whether or not I know the truth is irrelevant," Valine hissed.

Knowledge lit Pandora's peridot eyes. "It was you," she gasped. "You killed Jericho."

"And how would I have done that?" Valine nearly growled. "Were you not the one that woke next to his dead body? Were you not the one supposedly associating with Larysa Olympias, paying the fucking healer with Lunethian jewels to pay off his gambling debts? Were you not seen with him many times, feigning headaches to conspire? Were you not accused of blackmailing him in your quest for the crown? And was he not caught with fleur de mort? It was the perfect crime, dear Pandora. You had motive. You had opportunity." Valine curved her fingers, puncturing Pandora's supple flesh with her magic. She gasped with pain. Valine cocked her head. "How would *I* have done such a thing? I had already left Talloh long before you even went to bed with the king."

The veins stood out against Pandora's pale skin as she struggled for breath, pain wheezing through her lungs. "What are you doing to me? This isn't funny, Valine."

"I see no humor, either. I'm simply applying pressure to show you what I am capable of." Valine lifted her hand up to her face into Pandora's line of sight. Slowly, she curled her fingers inward, and the magic responded, black smoke constricting the woman's throat. She clawed at the invisible mist, but her hands only went through it. Maintaining eye contact, Valine unfolded her fingers, and the smoke receded. Pandora heaved for new breath. "Let me make this clear; I could kill you right now. I could let the gallows take you tomorrow. Or, you can pledge yourself to me and live."

Pandora was rubbing her throat with a dirty hand, staring at Valine with true fear. "Are you a necromancer?"

"I think that's a foolish question at this point. I want an answer."

"I want to ask a question before I agree."

Valine was impressed with the woman's courage that even after Valine had choked her by barely lifting a finger, she still had the spirit to negotiate. She could admire that. "Ask it then."

"Why frame me?" Angry and despairing tears pooled in Pandora's eyes. "What have I ever done to you?"

Valine offered her a solemn smile. "You were convenient. That was all. You happened to fit the requirements needed for the job I was doing."

"That's it?" Pandora screeched. "I was *there*? That's it?"

"Yes," Valine said, voice concrete. She wasn't proud of the part she'd forced Pandora into, which was why she was trying to make amends this way. She didn't deserve to swing by the neck tomorrow. She didn't deserve to be dishonored and disgraced when her bowels and bladder let go above the stones. "Which is why I'm here now."

"You can go fuck yourself," Pandora spit.

Valine sighed. "I'm offering you an out."

"I don't want your fucking job."

"You'd rather die?" Valine lifted a brow.

"I wanted more." Pandora's voice was defeated.

Valine was curious, so she couldn't help herself. "Why *were* you involved with Jericho and Jacira? I could never put together why, so I assumed."

Pandora barked a laugh. "That's just it. What you assumed was exactly what I wanted. I want to be queen. I'm little more than a bastard, but I could taste that fucking throne. I was so close, and you took it from me."

Valine considered, a plan forming in her mind, decisions marking, penning themselves in her mind, plots shifting. "What if I could get you a different crown?"

Pandora lifted her head, slowly watching. She had her attention. "How?"

Valine shook her head. "I can't tell you that now. Not when you haven't accepted my offer. But I swear to you, if you agree to my terms, I will do everything in my power to give you the crown that you so desire."

Pandora stared at Valine flatly, eyes hard.

"You have what it takes to survive in the court," Valine told her. "We can make this work, but you will not get it right away. You will have to do so much before the opportunity will come to pass. Do you agree to work for me?"

Pandora, defeated as she was, stared Valine through, resentment and hope mingling. "I'll do it."

"Okay, but first, you have to die."

"*What?*" Pandora squawked.

"I'm going to create a permanent tether between us. When you die, you will be reanimated but bound to my commands. You will maintain all the abilities of life, including bearing children and aging, as long as I live. But if at any point I sense your defiance, I will kill you, and I can do it from two feet away or two hundred miles." She snapped her fingers. "Just like that."

Valine was lying. There was going to be no tether; she could not sense Pandora's defiance, and she could not kill her from miles away. What would be her undoing was a broken command, and Valine had no direct control over those. But Pandora didn't know that, and folk knew enough about necromancers to fear the might of tethers. Valine could resort to more control, but she was not that desperate. She was going to resurrect Pandora the "right" way, as she had no interest in sacrificing a piece of her soul for the power-hungry girl.

Even so, fear was a prevailing motivator.

"Will it hurt?"

"For a moment," Valine told her honestly.

The blonde woman sat on her filthy pallet and nodded once. "Are you going to do it now?"

"No," Valine said. "It will be tomorrow at the gallows. They need to see you hang. I will ensure your body is retrieved, and I will bring you back." Valine tossed the menstrual products in the cell. The padded linen landed around her like large snowflakes, stark against the grime. "People shit themselves when they die. If you want to spare yourself the mortification, pad your undergarments with these. Your bowels will still release, but it won't end up on the pavers."

All the color drained from Pandora's face, tears rising and silently slipping down her face. "I didn't want this."

"Most people don't care for the cards they're dealt, but you make them work for you, and if you can't, you bluff."

"I will never forgive you," Pandora swore.

"I don't expect you to, but I don't need forgiveness. I need obedience."

"So, this is really it."

"It is. But don't take it too personally. You are one very small piece in a much bigger machine."

"You're a villain," Pandora hissed, her teeth still white despite it all.

"I know."

And with that, she began walking in the direction she had come from, pausing in front of a cell. Inside was Healer Das, staring at her with terrified, rheumy eyes. There was hope there, too, but Valine ignored it.

"You can swing tomorrow," she snarled, and for good measure, she drew her magic away from Pandora and lashed at the healer, severing his vocal cords. It would not kill him, but he could not speak of anything he'd heard this night.

She left the dungeon behind with the sounds of Healer Das's gurgling cries following behind her as she smiled and ascended the stairs to her king.

CHAPTER THIRTY-SEVEN

Swaying

The gallows were white-painted wood with the symbols of They, She, and He, painted in lavender on both the beam holding the nooses and on the stone below. The executioner's square was at the lowest point of the palace, closest to the city center but not a necessary thoroughfare to cross the boundary between royals and citizens. There was a separate courtyard for that. For the hangings was a designated square of gray, making the white and purple of the platform even more contrasting.

Valine was dressed in gray beside Malik, her magic already tethered to Pandora. She could feel the woman approaching already, following behind Healer Das and the guards. On the platform was the priest, who waited solemnly in starched linen and a sash of violet. He was the only one not obligated to wear the mourning shade because he was the only connection greater than the royals to the Stygian Ones.

Malik had his hands crossed reverently before him, Sarim and Freyja nearby echoing the same sentiment while Alastair comforted Jacira nearby. Amaris was directly on Valine's other side. She wore a veil of gray, but beneath it she could see the stone of her face and the tears that silently flowed from her eyes. She took no pleasure in this, but she was now a sole ruling queen and it was her duty.

Before she'd retired to Malik, she'd stopped to see Hanish, filling him in on her plan to rescue a post-mortem, soon-to-be reanimated Pandora and that she would require him to ensure she had an opening to do so. Hanish agreed, though he did so with a sour twist of his lips. She had made him do so much for her in such a short timeframe.

Pandora was approaching quickly—she could sense the tether drawing shorter. When she and the head healer appeared there was silence. There was no throwing of rotten vegetables like there would have been in Runell, there were no tossed curses like there would have been in Adraali, there was simple shunning silence. The two were meant to meet the grave in silence and banishment, forever ostracized in the eyes of the gods. That was their way, that was their final "fuck you" into the afterlife.

Pandora and Das ascended the staircase, writ with condemnation from the gods, the nooses swaying ominously in the silence. The air was thick with tension and scented with fear and anticipation, there was the sour scent of sweat carried on the ocean breeze that did little to mitigate the temperature. It was only just approaching noon and already the sun was at its zenith, bearing down with oppressive heat.

The corpse rot would be wretched in the hot day.

Despite the fact that Pandora knew Valine would rescue her, the woman had tears coursing down her face, dripping on her gray linen shift in dark circles. Das was struggling against the guard that had him, his bound hands thrashing wildly as he stared hate directly at Valine. She kept a placid expression. The guards framed the platform in orderly lines, ensuring that the convicted could not leave their posts.

As Pandora and Das were guided to their spots below the ropes, the priest came around behind them and looped the nooses around their necks. Valine ensured that the tether was firmly in place and braced herself for the oncoming death. When she was not the one delivering it, she felt its blow. It wasn't enough to hurt, but it was enough to knock the breath from her if she was not prepared.

The ropes were around their necks, and Pandora kept her freshly washed face impassive, staring blankly at the crowd without emotion. Valine could only imagine it was a sense of self preservation. Surely inside, she was screaming. Das was still trying to curse Valine out, spitting guttural sounds uselessly, his old bones already giving up on him.

From behind them the priest declared their crimes.

Murder.

Treason.

Extortion.

Theft.

Conspiracy.

"May the Stygian Ones take your souls," the priest commanded.

Pandora met Valine's eyes with conviction. Valine nodded once. Pandora closed her eyes.

Then the floors dropped out from under them.

Valine felt Pandora's neck snap as soon as the rope went taut. She did not struggle. Valine inhaled sharply at the sensation as watchers gasped around them. Hands covered mouths and quiet sounds of retching could be heard over sobs. Valine felt Pandora's life hanging on by the thread she held and silently, she slid her fingers over each digit, knotting Pandora's flickering life to her magic.

Healer Das was not as lucky as the gently swaying corpse beside him. His neck did not snap—not fully—so he was forced to gurgle and struggle as his face bloated and turned purple. His tongue swelled in his mouth; his eyes bloodshot. It was another few seconds and his bladder emptied onto the lavender moon etchings. It was several breaths and he finally breathed his last. It was moments and it was done.

Jacira let out an ugly sob, collapsing into Alastair's arms, crying desperately, heaving great breaths that she struggled to regulate. Her face was a blotchy mess, snot and tears mingling on her face. Alastair was the only thing keeping her afloat. She was in a sea of desolation and despair, and the careful manipulator was her life raft.

Amaris did not react either way. Valine could see her face unchanged beneath the veil, though tears continued to slide uselessly down her marble cheeks. She nodded once and swept from the gallows courtyard, her guards circling her immediately.

Valine stared at the execution site, watching Pandora's lovely face bloat and turn gray and swollen, purpling with ugliness. She hoped she'd saved Pandora some modesty by supplying her with the menstrual products; she could smell shit in the air already, suspicious brown sliding down Das's legs.

Before she turned to go, she saw Cersei across the crowd, staring at her directly. Her lionesses gaze was hard, resolute, dangerous. She was holding Valine with a look she could not decipher, but it made her feel like she'd swallowed an anvil. She didn't let herself think too much further about it as she ensured the tether was still in place and departed for the Vesper Wing with Malik.

It was several hours later when Hanish's message arrived. They had an opening, but it was short and it was in twenty minutes—it was close, but she was ready. Valine rushed from her suite, the palace uncharacteristically quiet in the reserved air of the executions. She made her way down to the holding area just beyond the gallows, stone cells with a row of bars. It was there that she found Hanish with a cart and the bodies.

And it was certainly bodies because there were three of them. She supposed someone had to take Pandora's place.

"Before you ask, no I did not kill anyone, but this was the best I could do on such short notice," Hanish informed her curtly. "This body was from a brothel. She contracted a pox and recently succumbed to her sickness. Don't touch her."

"Wasn't planning to," Valine told him evenly. "I admire your support reverently in this endeavor."

Valine didn't mince words, she quickly pulled up the dark wool of her wrap, the scent of clove, eucalyptus, and lemon thick beneath her nose. She'd ensured that she'd had a strong scent to counter the cloying rot of death and gases while she stole Pandora's body.

Hauling Pandora's corpse over her shoulder, she carried her to one of the many secret tunnels around Talloh's palace, weaving her way through on sturdy boots. Valine ignored the cold and wrongness of touching the body and focused on her assignment. She counted paces and peeked out from behind tapestries to cement where she was in the palace. It took thirty minutes of carrying the reeking body before she came across the nearest alcove to her room. There were no guards posted and the hallways were empty, only a curtain fluttered in the breeze. She held her breath and waited ten minutes, watching that fabric for any more movement but when none came, she darted to her door, unlocking it and peering inside. Also empty. Leaving the door open, she bolted back to the alcove and hauled Pandora's shrouded body into her suite.

When the door slammed behind her, she sighed and dragged Pandora to her ensuite, laying her out on the floor next to the tub. She ran a hot bath, scented with lavender and lemongrass, pulling fresh towels from the rack, and found a cotton shirt and pants. Tossing her cloak aside she knelt next to Pandora and pulled the funeral shroud from her body.

Rigor mortis had only just begun to set in, delayed by the tether that still flickered against Valine. Carefully, she curled her fingers, pulling magic from herself and allowing her necromancy to reanimate the woman. Color bloomed in Pandora's cheeks, a healthy pallor was restored, the harsh bruises around her neck horribly clear. Valine was only able to heal the spinal break because it was the cause of death. Had it been a preexisting injury there was nothing she could have done. A pulse restarted in Pandora's throat and Valine felt the first beats of Pandora's heart.

Pandora revived with a gasp, clutching her chest and neck, tears flowing down her cheeks, sobbing as she struggled to sit up. Her eyes were wild and animal.

"Shh," Valine cooed, reaching for her. "It's okay, Pandora. It's me. It's Valine. I'm right here."

"I was dead," she howled in a hoarse whisper, hands clinging to Valine desperately.

"You were. But you're alive again. See," Valine said, punctuating it by taking one of Pandora's hands and placing it over her own heart. "It's beating. Your heart is beating. You are alive."

"It hurt," she whimpered.

"And I'm sorry for that, but this was the only way. Just know your suffering will be worth it. One day you will be a queen."

Pandora's haunted eyes flittered to hers.

"I ran you a bath. I figured you'd like to get clean and warm up." She made a sound of discomfort. "I'll dispose of your clothing for you."

Pandora was crying silently, but she nodded, pulling off the linen she hung in. She let out a broken sound when she realized the state of her undergarments. Valine averted her eyes while Pandora dealt with that. Once the woman had tied every-thing up in the shift, she handed it to Valine from the cleanest point. Valine gestured for Pandora to get in the bath, and she did, tears still flowing.

Once she was settled, Valine stepped out of the room with the soiled garments where she found Malik standing in her suite. Shock and horror written across his face.

"I can explain," Valine gasped.

"What," Malik said flatly, the words deliberate and even, "the fuck did you do?"

CHAPTER THIRTY-EIGHT

Valine quickly explained everything and Malik took it in stride. He was displeased, but he was not furious like she feared. She told him her intentions with Pandora, and what use she would serve. Malik agreed, but hammered in the importance of informing him of these plans.

"I thought we talked about this," he said, angry and hurt. "I need you to trust me. I told you that you can do things your way, but I can't be kept in the dark."

"You're right, and I'm sorry. It's just…I—" Valine stopped herself, drawing an uncomfortable breath. "I felt guilt. I needed something to do that was mine and not predetermined by gods or patrons or kings. I'm sorry, I'm just so shaken up from Nylantia still that I just…I'm sorry."

Malik lifted her chin to meet his gaze. "Do not apologize, just don't do it again. I don't want to repeat this conversation." He brushed long, dark locks behind her ear. "Okay?"

"Okay," she breathed.

"You will have to answer for it eventually, though," he said, sultry.

"Oh, I think I can figure out some suitable punishments," she responded in kind.

"Does it involve you on your knees?"

"It certainly can."

"Perfect."

They smoldered together, threatening to let the flames of lust consume them. Valine could feel the charge in the air, like a lightning strike before a forest fire. But they could not give in because there was a recently reanimated corpse in her bathtub.

Waiting for Pandora to finish in the tub was an age, but eventually she entered in the cotton Valine had set out, hair dripping down her back and onto the floor.

"We're going to have to do something about that," Valine said, pointing at Pandora's platinum locks.

"Oh…" Pandora murmured, glancing at the floor. "Sorry, I'll clean up the mess."

"No," Valine said. "Not the water. Your hair. It needs to be different. It's like a beacon here and it will be everywhere else."

Pandora clutched her long, beautiful hair possessively.

"It's your choice what we do with it, but it has to be changed. We can stain it with ink, cut it, or shear it. It is up to you."

The blonde stared at her long hair longingly. "It's just hair, it'll grow back." She sighed. "Let's cut it and dye it."

"Good choice," Valine told her.

Pandora's hair was cut from her waist to just below her shoulders, the platinum disappearing beneath a paste of henna and ink, blending into a natural looking reddish brown that was as dark as Valine's, but the undertones followed closer to scarlet while Valine's swayed towards indigo. For good measure, Pandora's brows were dyed as well and Valine ensured that she knew how to properly apply mascara to darken her snowy lashes. She also taught her how to create deeper hollows in her face and how to subtly shift her features with cosmetics.

"We leave tomorrow," Valine said, eyeing Malik who was drinking a flavored water in one of her armchairs. "You will be posing as a servant in a separate contingency. In the meantime, you will be posted in Luneth. I will have a contact get a hold of you, and you will feed them any information you hear. Gossip, secrets, anything of note, I want to hear it."

"What am I going to be doing there?" Pandora asked, unconsciously reaching for her missing locks. She was still stunning as a brunette, but some of her etherealness was gone.

"You'll be working in an apothecary. There's a need of a new one while a certain one is raided. I will ensure you have a placement and you will learn the craft. But I need to reaffirm this; you are not immortal. You can die again, so be careful. I'm going to separate the tether and then you are on your own. Do not forget what I told you of betrayal."

"I'll be careful."

"Good." Then Valine allowed a swell of magic to build within her, tying it to the oath of her command. She allowed the smoke to soak into Pandora and once it was absorbed Valine very carefully sheared the tether.

It broke with a soft snap and Pandora scrubbed her chest as the last of the necromancy slipped into her.

"It's done."

They left Talloh the next day without ceremony, Hanish and his family smuggled onto a ship with Valine, Malik, Sarim, and Freyja. Pandora, disguised as a servant, was escorted by Alastair who'd volunteered, voicing his glee at not being a "fifth wheel" on the sea voyage. The plan had always been for half of Adraali's retinue to journey via ocean to deem the best route for the soldiers to take, but Malik, upon hearing about the Call of the Phoenix diverted their course.

"You know where to find the Call of the Phoenix?" Valine asked, brow raised in Malik's guarded cabin. The ship rocked beneath them, cutting through the waves, the scent of salt and brine thick in the air.

They'd hired the crew of the *Tempest*, the captain of which bore a striking resemblance to the murdered Captain Wallace Yarl, which Valine soon learned was because Morgan Yarl was Wallace's twin brother. They shared the same frosty beard and salt spray hair, only Morgan was cleaner and more refined without the libidinous air his brother had. He also was missing the gnarly scar that cut across the former Yarl's face. The Yarls had dominated the illegal trades across the ocean, hating each other with a fiery passion for what each specialized in. Morgan had condemned his brother for sex trafficking and slave trading, while Wallace abhorred his brother for the "cowards" career of art theft and drug imports.

"Not for certain, but all the whispers are coming from Cuuevota and I need to ascertain something else there," Malik responded as he rolled the black sleeves of his blousy shirt to his elbows. Valine was momentarily spelled by his forearms, the coiled strength, the veins, the tattoo of the athame and script, this time, she could see that it was Stygian. She didn't know he knew the language.

Ve du la vessurrae vu alla nask mylii.

Valine mentally translated.

I am the sword you will not wield.

"What could you possibly need at the black market?" Valine asked, pulling herself from distraction.

"Not a what." Malik paced. "Cuuevota is an independent country with no allegiance or alliance—I intend to secure one."

"Malik," Valine chastened. "The market operates outside of the king and queendoms, they will not agree to any terms you set."

"We will not know unless we try," Malik said resolutely.

Valine's stomach heaved uncomfortably at the prospect but she kept her mouth closed. They were traveling to Cuuevota either way. The market may be illegal, but they weren't stupid enough to kill a king there, were they?

"Right," she managed. "Well, I need to get a report from Sarim."

"Before you go…I want you to know that I don't want to follow through with the brides next year."

Valine froze and half turned. "What?" Shock filled her voice.

Malik shifted, discomfort evident in the way he held himself. "I don't want a false marriage." The king's eyes were intense and focused, but he wavered, and his eyes went to her hand—to the ring. She felt its weight grow on her.

Her heart hammered. She knew what she was being offered, the potential spoken into existence. "We'll discuss it later," she deflected.

"Okay," he allowed.

She turned to leave, but Malik caught her hand and pulled her against him, she felt the ridges of his abdomen beneath her, his hands enticing manacles on her wrists. "Stay. We never got to finish what we started. I miss the way you taste."

He dipped his head and kissed her throat, nipping it lightly and soothing the small hurt with his tongue. She dropped her head back, feeling her dark waves cascade as she opened to him more, luxuriating in the feel of a king at her mercy. She felt powerful and everything about Malik was so addicting. She'd hardly got a taste and she didn't know if she'd ever be able to stop.

"Malik," she moaned throatily. He answered with a delicious groan that caused the length of his cock to harden against her. "We can't here, there's too many people. They'll hear."

"I know ways to keep you quiet," he murmured against her collarbone.

"I'm loud," she breathed.

He chuckled, the sensation burned into her skin and she felt heat coil low in her belly, wetness pooling between her thighs. "Oh, I know."

She pulled back and pressed one forceful kiss against his lips, detaching from his steel grip. He was too surprised to fight her. "I really do need to speak to Sarim."

Malik watched her with hunger, his eyes held promise and she thrilled at the prospect. "Please attend to whatever business you need; all I ask is think of me and how I had you splayed on that bed and ready to fuck you until you couldn't remember your own name."

Valine muffled a whimper and exited the room, a furious flush on her cheeks. Oh, she was certainly imagining it, she hadn't stopped imagining it ever since the first touch of Malik's tongue on her clit. But that wasn't entirely true, she'd fantasized about him well before he'd even dressed or undressed her. Before he'd touched her at all.

Climbing up to the quarter deck, Valine found Sarim looking out over the waves, watching the ivory queendom disappear as they sailed north. He was in his regular Valmotti leathers, the crisscrossing straps of belts across his chest lined with daggers.

Sarim was positively glowing as he watched the glitter over the water. The cut and spray the sleek dark lines of the ship created, the polished rail his hand rested on. This was how Sarim was meant to be, on the sea with the briny air on his clothes. He deserved to be on the open water, not constrained to the walls of Valmotti servitude.

"He's different now, you know," Sarim said without turning around, that warrior training revealing her presence before she made it known. He turned to face her, amber eyes indecipherable. "I've never seen him like this until you."

"I think it has little to do with me and more what I'm capable of offering him," she told him, crossing the deck to lean on the rail next to him, watching ship cut through the endless blue.

"You're wrong."

She shook her head. "There's so much you don't know. So much of what you saw in Selyndyr was acting."

"Bull-fucking-shit, Valine. You think I'm an idiot? I know the difference."

Aethermancers in pale blue were scattered across the deck, working in tandem to power the sails, the wind rippling over them. Hydromancers in indigo were directing in unison, quieting the worst of the waves around them, hands outstretched and sweat beading on brows. Among them were a few other mages, Valine noted the yellow of a luxmancer and the storm gray of a fulgurmancer—one that was not Hanish, as he and his family were stowed safely down in the berth.

Valine thinned her lips in concentration, avoiding answering, and realization dawned on Sarim.

"You're trying to convince yourself. Why?" he asked, voice softened.

She drew in a breath that tasted so strongly of the ocean she wanted to fall into it.

"I fear the future," she admitted.

"That doesn't make any sense. You can choose what you do. We're constantly moving towards the future and because it hasn't happened yet, you can *choose* its course. How can you be afraid of it?"

"Forget I said anything."

"No," Sarim disavowed. "I'm your friend, I want to know what's wrong." Fear lit his eyes. "You're not pregnant, are you?"

Valine laughed. "No, I haven't even slept with him."

"*You haven't?*" Sarim was clearly astounded.

Valine cocked a brow, pointedly looking in his direction. "Does everyone think we're going at it like rabbits?"

"Honestly, yeah," he said. Valine rolled her eyes. "Weren't you found naked in his bed when Balchon and Tallulah died?"

"Don't forget Countess Magdelena, but no, I was still wearing my dress."

"So, if you're not pregnant, what's going on?"

She drew in a breath and let it out slowly. "Have you heard of the Call of the Phoenix?"

"Yes, hasn't everyone?"

Apparently, everyone but her had. "Nylantia told me I was going to find it, but in doing so I would experience a loss."

"So, you're distancing yourself to protect from the hurt. You think you're going to lose him."

That was exactly what Valine feared. She feared that she would earn the throne only from Malik's death, and she couldn't express how much she didn't want that. She wasn't striving for the throne in the first place, she just wanted him and she was too selfish to leave him entirely. And she wanted vengeance against Runell too much to take him now. So, holding him at arm's length it was.

"I know it's stupid, but I think I—" she suddenly broke off, horror arrowing through her. "*Get down*!" she screamed.

Valine tackled Sarim to the opposite side of the quarter deck just as an enormous gray tentacle slammed into the ship, wood groaning and shattering beneath the weight. Suckers warped the wood, a wickedly sharp hook impaled boards. Valine looked up, shoulder throbbing, water raining down onto her, and met the glowing red eyes of a kraken.

CHAPTER THIRTY-NINE

Child, Father, Patron

The kraken was enormous. Its dark tentacles were plated with a crab-like shell that ridged menacingly over its entire body. Its horned head dripped with more tentacles, hiding a razor-sharp maw of fangs. Valine couldn't see it, but she knew beneath the water, the beast had a beak crusted with serrated teeth as long as her forearm.

It lashed against the *Tempest* again, shattering the foremast, sending sails tumbling to the sea. A man on the ropes shrieked into the turbulent waters. Valine clawed the deck, gaining purchase on anything she could, shoving Sarim away from the brunt of the attack. The starboard side was being chewed away, exposing more and more of the ship and its hold.

People were screaming and racing in varying directions, away from splintering wood and shrapnel. Ropes and nets swayed precariously over them as aethermancers directed all their magic at the kraken, doing everything in their power to push it away. Hydromancers joined the fray, attempting to submerge the monster beneath the waves. The ship shifted, unsteady, and Valine grappled for a rail. Without the direction of the mages, the ship was a disorganized shitshow. The captain, departing his cabin, was shouting orders as his crew was ejected into the sea in increasing numbers.

The kraken swiped the deck, sending men and an aethermancer into the ocean with a crunch of bone. Valine virtually dove down the stairs to avoid the next blow, feeling the current of air stir her hair as she fell to the main deck. A second thump beside her reassured her that Sarim was still onboard.

Cannon fire erupted around them. Puffs of smoke tainted the air as the creature shrieked against the weapons. It struck with precision, spearing towards the cannons and tearing a man from the gunport, taking the weapon with him.

Valine froze as she stared up in terror at the gigantic sea beast. It was more than double the size of a sand serpent, possibly even four times as large. She didn't know if she had enough magic to take it on and survive, but they were fucked if she didn't try. The last time she encountered a beast of the patrons Alastair had saved her, but now, Alastair was weeks away and oceans apart, and she had no hope of reaching him.

Steeling herself, Valine lashed out with her magic, spreading her arms wide as she turned her fingers into claws and created as many tethers as she could handle, finding them and hooking in. She could feel death surrounding her, death bleeding into the tethers as those she chose were doomed by the kraken. Sarim figured out what she was doing and removed his Veritasium Medallion, allowing her to use him. She tethered to Sarim, and it was the strongest one she had created—both from his strength and the bond of camaraderie between them securing it. He'd taken to removing his medallion around her.

She bolted across the main deck, dodging bodies and collapsed masts. Empty sails littered the path, and still, she continued running, launching herself at the stairs of the fore deck. Valine felt the tethers trailing her like smoke, the black magic like the lines of a spider's web, each life snared and stuck to hers. She ascended the stairs and spun, watching the destruction the beast was wreaking.

Valine caught sight of Freyja on the remains of the quarter deck, straining her magic as she attempted to undo all the damage the kraken was creating. Exertion was plain on her face as time seemed to rewind, shattered sails mending, masts re-erected, planks replaced—the entire ship rebuilding. Freyja was sweating, her face flushed as her hands continued to shape and direct. She met Valine's face from directly across the decks, teeth gritted.

She reached across the ship with her magic, creating one last tether with Freyja, and she was shocked when they connected. She saw the ghost of Freyja's magic. It was a blur around everything she touched. Freyja's eyes widened as Valine's magic was revealed to her, and she followed the black smoke of Valine's necromancy, gaze darting along each and every tether Valine had linked to herself like some macabre web.

The women met eyes once again and Valine lifted her hands above her head, drawing as much necromancy from the death surrounding them, from the essence of her soul, from the doom and peril, and gathered it into a massive orb. It grew like a boiling dark sun, encompassing her arms, bigger and bigger. Freyja watched it grow, stunned as she continued weaving her ruinmancy, guiding the opposite of her gift to save their lives.

Valine groaned and sweated as the pressure became immense, her arms aching with the strain of holding so much power. She watched it almost in slow motion as one of the tentacles came down directly between Valine and Freyja, threatening to rip the ship in two.

Freyja screamed as she focused all her magic on repairing the titanic tear, furiously weaving her magic from keel to hold to berth to deck. At the very same moment, Valine let loose an identical howl, launching all her summoned magic at the kraken.

It hit squarely on its horned head, scattering over the shell and down its tentacles ripping through it like a disease. The darkness of her magic bled through as it shrieked a daemonic sound, something more unnatural than any reptilian screech the sand serpents had released.

The kraken tossed itself backward, tentacles flying into the air as it crashed into the sea, screeching and splashing. It hit the water, its violent red eyes fading as it stared Valine down. As it disengaged from the ship, the hooks slowly tore into the boards as it slipped beneath the waves.

Freyja scrambled to repair the damage as the beast created it, and Valine dropped to her knees as the ruinmancer took over as the day's savior. Head swimming, Valine swayed and toppled to the deck, watching the world spin and blur as Sarim raced towards her, a second figure in tow behind him. Valine realized with a start that it was Malik, a line of blood crossing his brow. Deliriously, she reached out for the king, wanting to wipe away the blood there.

Malik caught her hand as she reached, her mind slow, like slogging through syrup. "Did you tether?" he demanded.

She nodded but must not have done a good job because Malik repeated his question, this time a little more shrill with panic.

"She did," Freyja answered for her, suddenly at her side with Malik and Sarim. "I saw it."

"You saw it?" Sarim asked, gravitating towards her.

Freyja swallowed, wood and smoke in her hair, fine scrapes and slashes of blood all over her. "When she tethered to me, I could see her magic. I could see all the threads of her magic connecting her to a dozen people." Her eyes flashed to Valine, the necromancer blinking away fog and confusion. "I've never seen so much power before. It was terrifying."

Malik squeezed Valine's hand tighter. "Are you still with us?"

She nodded, this time more successfully. "Yes, I'm not nearly as drained as I was…last time."

Malik helped her into a sitting position, and her head wavered as she adjusted. Closing her eyes against the sway, she also reached out with her magic, seeking. She plunged beneath the waves, letting her smoke torrent down into the depths. With a net, she plundered the deep, dark sea and felt a responding twinge. Her eyes flew open, and panic lit within her.

"There's another one below us."

As she threw out her tethers, plunging into the survivors, she felt the kraken barreling for the surface. For the hull of the boat. Terror tore through her as she gathered as much necromancy as possible before she powered it through the ship and into the ocean below. She felt when the necromancy made contact, the beast stutter-stopping in the waves as it speared through its brain and through the beak below. It floated, losing motion, ending in shock and death. Her hands were claws to the deck as she felt the life leak from the beast, her own life wavering as she slumped to the side.

Sarim and Malik caught her, guiding her safely back into position. She looked at the two of them, at the tethers that she'd flung into them, ones only she—and the still tethered Freyja—could see. She blinked in realization, shock grounding her.

Valine had arrowed through Malik's tattooed Veritasium Medallion, breaking through the ward and tethered the Adraalian King to her.

Tentatively, she reached out, following the web of her tether to him, her mouth in a small O of surprise. She glanced at Freyja whose eyes were also wide, shock pure and unaltered on her face. She could see her magic and how it had broken through a Veritasium Medallion. It should not have been able to do so.

"Do you see this?" Valine asked Freyja.

"I do," the ruinmancer managed, dropping to a knee beside her.

"What?" Malik asked, brows drawn together.

Valine continued reaching, pushing open the button at the top of his shirt. The tattooed medallion was still there, but a piece of it was broken. One of the lines of the maze shattered. In the center of the maze was Valine's necromancy, undulating like shadows and into his heart.

"I tethered you," she whispered.

"That's not possible," he told her in dismay, but even so, he looked down, and due to his secret psychomancy, he saw her tether.

"I assure you, it is," Freyja informed him succinctly.

Valine had broken one of the fifteen Veritasium Medallions in existence. Malik's, though crushed and tattooed, should have been just as strong as a whole medallion. Her magic was unnatural, intense, and dangerous. Nothing should be able to break a Veritasium Medallion but another Veritasium Medallion. They were relics of the patrons; they were no creation made from man. But the evidence was staring her in the face, only further affirming Malik's theory.

She was a child of Mrithun. Her father was the Patron of Death.

It was the only explanation.

"We need answers," Malik said stiffly.

It was an understatement.

Valine, weak in the knees, assessed the damage. The loss of life was immense. They'd lost sixty percent of the crew and had one surviving aethermancer on board. The captain was trying to delegate basic tasks to new people, previous roles now unfilled. Hanish and his family were still safely ensconced in the hull, the fulgurmancer having been prepared to blast the kraken should it have come near his wife and children. Valine, after assuring herself of their continuation of life, took leave to Malik's quarters and fell into the bed, head swimming. She kept her eyes closed but stayed awake, casting fingers into the water and seeking any other krakens lurking in the deep.

The rest of the journey continued this way. Valine, listening with her magic, prepared to attack at a moment's notice as they cut through the waters further north. The air became hotter, more humid as they continued, from lack of hydromancer cooling, and also the northern route. It was a known fact that the climate became hotter the further north they went and nothing was hotter or further north than Cuuevota.

That they knew of.

There were, of course, stories of the distant land further from which the current royals of Talloh had descended, but Valine wondered the merit of it as the route to Cuuevota alone was treacherous. She wondered who would dare sail across the open waters unnecessarily.

Someone shouted that land was approaching, and Valine shot up from the bed. She didn't know how many days passed in delirious half dreaming, half waking, but the presence of land was salvation on her mind. She relaxed her magic and stepped out into the sun, seeing a large land form from the deck, green as verdant and wild as the eye could see, swaths of fabric on the beaches in tents, revealing a market. The harbor was cut into the beach, five ships at port, men milling about on the docks. The people she could see were every manner of skin and height and build, their dress giving no identity to originating kingdom. Because everyone originated from elsewhere, Cuuevota sprung from the sea.

They moored, and pirates met them on the docks. There were three of them: a tall man with wild mahogany curls and a pleasant smile, a curvaceous woman with skin the color of hickory and braids bright as blood, and another woman, this one petite to the extreme with sand-colored skin and a scar bisecting her brow. All three of them were dressed in a motley assortment of elaborate frock coats, blousy shirts, loud patterned pants, and weapons attached to their persons.

"What brings you to the Black Market, Mor?" the curvy woman asked pointedly as Captain Morgan Yarl stepped from the ship, the rest of them following down the ramp.

"Guests hailing from Adraali," he answered easily.

The woman craned her neck and took in the entourage before her, raising a brow. "Hardly any of these fuckers look Adraalian. Those two, maybe," she said, indicating Malik and Sarim.

Captain Yarl laughed. "I would hope he does. That's the king."

The woman spit on the dock. "The fuck does a king want here?"

"Ask him yourself, Ylaine."

"We seek an object we are told is here," Malik said, stepping around the captain. "Do you know where we may find someone that specializes in mythic relics?"

Ylaine twisted her lips, considering. "Yeah, not a dealer or anything, but our Sovereign, Thiandra can probably help you. But it's going to cost you."

"I'm sure I can manage that," Malik replied.

"I'm sure you can," Ylaine said disinterestedly. "Just know, they don't deal in coin."

"Noted."

"What's up with you? You seasick, or something?" Her voice was directed at Valine, who still hadn't fully recovered from the kraken attack.

"Yeah, something like that," Valine answered distractedly.

"We require new supplies. We lost a bunch at sea. Attacked by krakens, we were," the captain began, scratching his beard. "And I'll need more recruits for the voyage. I lost some."

Ylaine tsked. "I've never known you to suffer a kraken attack, Mor. You goin' soft, or are these fuckers bad luck?"

"Could be either," he chortled.

"Yeah, well, you know the drill." Ylaine waved towards the beach. "Make yourself at home, buy your shit, make your deals." She turned to the rest of the gathered. "Welcome to Cuuevota, motherfuckers."

CHAPTER FORTY

Thiandra's tent was on the cusp of the jungle, swathed in shades of flame. They sat on a tufted seat behind an orange cloth-draped table, slender and small-chested with dozens of necklaces hanging from their neck. Most were gold, but a silver piece with carved runes hung close to their navel and a bronze choker that looked like a creature wrapped around their throat.

Valine and Malik entered, the scent of incense thick and cloying in the air with the undertones of citrus. The two of them stood before Thiandra, sweating, while the person before them remained at ease, scarlet-painted nails tapping on the table.

"We can do away with the pleasantries," Thiandra said, their voice lilting and smoky. "I know what you seek. The question is, can you afford it?"

Valine screwed her brows together. "How would you know that?"

Thiandra levelled Valine with an eerie stare, their eyes ice blue and startling against their cocoa skin. "I am a divinamancer, little necro. Save your tedious questions. They really are quite trying."

Valine started at this revelation and flickered her eyes to Malik. The king was holding himself still, and she could see the discomfiture in his frame, which set Valine ill at ease. He was supposed to be in control. But they were not on the continent, and the rules they played by no longer applied.

She realized that on this black market island, though, he was on equal footing with this ruler, and all bets were off. Cuuevota cared little for the monarchs of Enneive and even less for diplomatic relations. The ways of the island were cut and dry, plain without flippancy or political maneuvering. Everything was for sale, and everything had a price.

"You want the Call, so pay for it," Thiandra continued. "And do not lie, for I will know it, and you will know my wrath."

Valine inhaled sharply and met the ice eyes of Cuuevota's sovereign. "Crown Prince Lukov Varshovski—"

"No," Thiandra interrupted Valine. "I do not care to hear of the Prince of Melusda's indiscretions and debts. I want information pertaining to you and yours. I want the difficult truths."

"If I may, the knowledge about Melusda pays handsomely. You could buy a ransom for it."

"That is not what I seek. I seek the things you do not wish to speak. I want to see you pull the darkest secrets of your hearts by the skin of your teeth. I want to know how much of yourself you're willing to betray for this." Thiandra grinned menacingly. "That is my price. That is the power I seek."

Valine took in Thiandra. The soft oval-shaped face, the wide mouth, the high and proud cheekbones, the dark corkscrew curls. They were stunning, and power burned from their very core. Valine could see the knowledge of wisdom and dreams in their eyes. They operated on a higher plane of existence than Valine. They did not care for the simple whims of men and their slavery to coin. They thrived on emotional turmoil and the severity of human nature. On greed and lust and desire.

"I watched my father kill my younger sister the day she was born. Simply because she was born with the wrong parts. And my mother let him." Valine shook her head, still at a loss all these years later. Refusing to picture it. "I never understood *how* she let him. After carrying the babe for nearly a year, laboring for seventeen hours, only to let him do that.

"I swore that day that I would never let it happen again. So, I researched, and at eight years old, I went to the market and stole mugwort, baneberry, and wombsbane and made a tincture. I meant to give it to my father, but my mother took it instead, and she collapsed within the hour." Valine swallowed down the emotion. "She bled. I remember seeing the red on her legs, and I remember that she never bled again. And she never bore my father another child."

Thiandra watched Valine's admission with a blank stare. "It is not enough."

"What?" Valine asked aghast.

"Your truth. It is not enough. You tried to make your father sterile, and you failed. It is not enough."

Valine gritted her teeth and stared at the sovereign. So many of her misdeeds and dark truths pertained to death, and she couldn't just outright admit to murder, could she? "The first time I used my magic, I killed the stable hand that tried to rape me."

"It's not enough."

"What do you want from me?" Valine demanded angrily.

"I want something you struggle to admit to," Thiandra said leaning forward, necklaces swinging. "I want something that you have to force out of your soul and drag it out, kicking and screaming. An accident and self-defense do not suffice."

Valine ground her teeth together. "You want to know who I've killed?"

Thiandra shrugged. "Only if it's painful to tell me so. Otherwise, no." Thiandra lowered their lids. "You immediately gravitate towards death and heinous deeds when vulnerability can be just as effective." Thiandra paused. "Is there anything you feel that you don't want the world to know?"

Valine would rather reveal deaths by her hand than confessions from the heart. She would pull whatever deplorable acts she'd done from the depths of her black soul before she admitted to any feelings.

"I am the blood daughter of Mrithun."

Thiandra raised a brow, surprised. "Well, that *is* interesting. Continue."

"My necromancy is more potent than anyone else I've encountered. I have killed sand serpents and kraken, I have survived a judgment from the arachne, I have been visited by Nylantia herself, Patroness of Night and Stars, and lived to tell the tale."

"Why?" Thiandra asked.

"Why what?"

"Why would Nylantia deign to visit you?"

Valine drew in a breath, eyes betraying her emotions to Malik's presence. "Mrithun has blocked the saints and daemons from moving against me. She believes that I will be a queen. She claims she has seen it in the stars."

"Do *you* believe this?"

Valine hesitated. "I don't know."

"This makes you uncomfortable."

"It does," Valine admitted.

"Good, tell me why."

"It won't make a difference."

"I assure you, it will make all the difference in the world," Thiandra told her, fingering the bronze necklace.

Valine looked at it more closely and realized that it was more than it appeared. It was a choker wrapped around their throat, a sleeping bird, head resting on their collarbones, long tail draping down their chest. There was a proud crown of feathers on the bird's head depicted in the metal, eyes closed, onyx-tipped beak hooked, claws of the same black stone curled beneath in slumber.

That bronze necklace was the Call of the Phoenix.

"Tell me your deepest secret."

Closing her eyes, Valine plunged inside of herself with a vicious hand and dragged the inescapable truth to the surface. The admission thickened her throat, the words dragging obsidian claws through her lungs. She felt her heart hammer, a blacksmith's anvil making home in her chest, fire burned inside her, a conflagration threatening to swallow her whole. She opened her dark eyes and stared Thiandra down. A darkly delighted smile was on their lips.

"I am in love with the King of Adraali."

The truth was out, and she refused to look at Malik. She kept her gaze resolute and trained on the black market sovereign. She felt and heard Malik's intake of breath beside her. She felt him gravitate towards her, a hand raising, disturbing the air.

"Valine…" he whispered.

Valine set her jaw. "Is it enough?" she bit out.

Thiandra giggled. "It is."

And with that Thiandra reached for the Call of the Phoenix draped around their neck. They removed the choker and held it out on smooth palms, the necklace laying like a tiny beast on their fingertips.

Valine plunged the object into her satchel, the metal warm, so warm that Valine wondered if prolonged contact would burn her.

Thiandra turned to Malik, face falling, losing its charmed malice. Their lids dropped, their mouth thinned. "In regards to the proposal you will no doubt exalt to me, I will spare you the breath. I am not interested, and Cuuevota will ally with no one. We are an independent nation, and I seek no alliance with kings or queens, star-chosen as they are."

"Your Majesty," Malik began, prepared to barter.

"No," Thiandra said flatly, raising a hand. "My only and final answer is no."

Malik stiffened and nodded once. "I understand." He drew in a breath. "If it wouldn't be too much to ask, is there a possibility we may acquire rooms for the night?"

Thiandra smiled warmly. "Of course. But it will cost you."

In the end, Malik paid with the truth that his father had his first lover whipped for finding them fooling around in the royal baths, the former king having lived a lie when he claimed he sought equality for all. But for none of the "deviant" behavior when displayed by his son. Malik's father thought it was fine for others to be intimate with those of the same sex, but it was immoral in the king's eyes for his kin to do the very same.

It wasn't just the lack of tolerance his father had for the relationship but the revelation that he'd forced Malik to enact the punishment, therefore defiling Malik in the eyes of his lover. Forevermore, he'd see the former prince and see the person who'd whipped and bled him.

Valine's heart panged when she realized how much of Malik's father's disgust affected him still today. How much of Saalim's hate-filled views drove Malik to the darker side of ruling.

She wondered if he killed his father, too.

Despite the revelation tearing a hole in Malik's chest, the truth only treated them to two rooms, one of which Hanish's family shared and Valine and Malik the other. The rest of their retinue remained onboard the ship or in stranger's beds for the night—aside from their guards. Their room was a small, cramped space with simple, rough-hewn furniture and sun-faded fabrics. The windows were open to let in the balmy night air, the single moon illuminating the one bed. It was generously sized and enclosed with a finely woven mosquito net; the sheets starched white.

Malik walked over to the basin of water on the pedestal, scrubbing the grime of travel from his face, while Valine stumbled to the wooden chair. She pulled off her boots and wiped her feet with a damp, citrus-scented cloth and took out a vial of lavender oil, massaging it into her aching soles.

They were quiet as they washed, unwilling to break the silence between them that hinged on the reluctantly revealed trauma and admission of love. It wasn't just their wounded truths; it was the brusque refusal of allyship that burned the king. He hadn't even gotten the words out and Thiandra had shut him down. It stung, and the embarrassment likely lingered.

Malik reined in a deliberate draw of air and rested his hands behind him on the pedestal, leaning back, buttons on his shirt open to his abdomen. "We need to talk about Thiandra."

Valine shuttered her eyes. "Yes, but not what they forced us to reveal. Not yet."

Malik was silent, and Valine saw the war wage behind his eyes. She admitted she loved him, and it was the truth. Now, he knew it. Now it was out in the open, and she couldn't snatch the words back.

"Then what are we talking about?"

"Maybe about how they shut down an alliance. You can't tell me that didn't piss you off."

Malik averted his gaze, his sharp jaw working beneath his short beard. "Of course it did," he bit out. "Acquiring Cuuevota's allegiance was part of my plan, and now I feel like it has shattered in my hands, and I'm stuck looking stupid and staring at the pieces."

"Malik," Valine said softly, rising and crossing the room, her hands shiny with oil, the scent of lavender and jasmine pervading her steps. She paused directly in front of him. "We can never expect everything to go according to plan. We must always have backups and contingencies for those backups and even more reserves. Things will always go wrong, but we will fix it." She put her palms on his chest, tracing the hollows, watching the glide of oil on his skin. It was mesmerizing, and her fatigue made everything dreamy and slow.

"You make it sound so simple," he grumbled, his eyes shuttered in pleasure.

Valine continued gliding her fingers across his pecs, her fingers tracing the lines of the damaged Veritasium Medallion. She wondered which of the patron's medallion he possessed. Perhaps Aaseayah's? What if it was Mrithun's?

"I've always had to be adaptable," she murmured as her hands crept up his throat. He let out a sound that was half moan, half growl. She let one hand creep up into his hair and tilted his head back, kissing his whiskery jaw. "This is new for you, but I will guide you through the process."

"Can we talk about what you—"

"No," she shut down the train of thought immediately, squeezing the hand that was still on his throat. "Not when you're frustrated with the sovereign and not when I am so tired."

"Soon?" he pressed.

"Soon."

Valine kept her hand in his hair, working through the styled waves. Malik kept his hands trapped behind him.

"I know it has always been the way of Cuuevota, but why must things stay for the sake of tradition?" Malik asked. "I can offer the black market a new kind of stability and legitimacy."

"I doubt they want legitimacy when I'm sure parts of it thrive on the human slave market."

"Speaking of," Malik began, eyeing her with curiosity. "Did you happen to sink a certain Yarl's ship?"

"Perhaps."

"I heard whispers here that the trafficking market has slowed with a loss of the captain that pioneered it."

"Pity."

"Yes, it seems to be so."

There was a pause. "I want to ask you something," Valine began.

"You are the only person free to ask me anything."

"If you had acquired an alliance with Cuuevota, would you still allow trafficking and slaves?"

"No," Malik said immediately and firmly. "But saying I abhor it isn't that simple. People will still do it in the dark and in secret no matter how illegal I make it or how severe the consequences of such actions would be. People will still operate rings with schemes and for those who have coin. I might abolish it, but I am not so disillusioned to think that it would not exist after the fact."

Valine was equally saddened and relieved by the answer. It was more along the lines of what she had hoped he would say, but in the same vein, the reality of it frustrated and infuriated her. She was so tired of this fight—she was tired in so many ways.

"How do you think Thiandra manages it?"

Malik sighed. "Thiandra allows it only with indentures, the problem with that is that papers can be forged, and people can be coerced. Not to mention, Thiandra's power is precarious. They are young and mostly untried, and Cuuevota's ruling does not come from bloodlines or votes, it comes from killing the previous sovereign."

"So, what would have been your plan?"

"Install a new system of election, allowing certain trades to continue and restrict others, hiring a team of mages to make travel to the island safer, integrate a new import of goods and wares between Enneive and Cuuevota, among other things."

"What about independence?" Valine asked as she swayed, her eyelids drooping. A headache from earlier was making itself known, and the throb of it was making the moonlight flare blinding white.

"Valine, are you okay?" Malik asked, hands on her hips, tightening. There was a thin lace of panic on his words.

"I just need to lie down. I'm still drained from the kraken attack."

As soon as the words were out of her mouth, Malik swept her up and carried her to bed. She couldn't summon the words to refuse, and her head was lolling against Malik's freshly oiled chest. Her signature scent of lavender and jasmine mixed with his tobacco had something primitive and feral rising in her. She wanted to sink her teeth into him and stake a claim.

Malik brushed away the netting and set Valine down. The bed was downy and soft, and she immediately melted into it. She was half dazed as Malik sank down beside her, draping a blanket across them both. He was on his side, propped on an elbow and staring down at her while she fought to keep her eyes open. She was blinking the fog from her vision while staring up at the canopy above her, trying to figure out how to string words together.

Malik brushed her hair back from her brow, stroking through the locks while her hands stayed glued to his skin, savoring the sensation and scent. She wanted to get beneath his clothes and mold her body to his. She wanted to be held and consumed.

"You're not a failure," she managed.

"What?" Malik asked, confused. His hand paused its gentle ministrations, and she made a noise of distress, which caused him to continue again.

"You're not," she repeated. "I know you won't say it, but I know you're thinking it. This is a setback, that's all. I believe in you. In us. You can't let this hang over you. Don't let Cuuevota be your guillotine."

She was speaking nonsense, but she could no longer control it, and guillotine was the last word she remembered speaking before she fell into slumber with a pounding headache.

CHAPTER FORTY-ONE

Valine slept for perhaps an hour or two when she woke. Malik was beside her—still awake with his eyes slightly shuttered. His arm was around her, fingers skimming her ribs, while the other was tucked up behind his head. She kept her breathing even so he wouldn't know she was awake, but his scent was heady and her awareness of him was visceral—and so was her arousal.

The more she lay there in silence, the more turned on she got. The more time ticked onward, the thinner her resolve became. She wasn't ready to talk about her confession, but her body had other plans. Though, perhaps she wouldn't have to.

Without telling Malik anything further, Valine sat up and swung her legs over his hips. Seating herself firmly over him, his lightly dozing eyes flew wide, and his hands went to her thighs.

"Valine? What are you—?"

She stopped him by abruptly leaning down and kissing him. Her lips were on his and he let out a low sound, half in pain and half in pleasure. Malik parted her lips with his tongue and he swept in, claiming her. Valine's hands were on his jaw and he sat up hastily, one hand on the small of her back, the other tangled in the hair at the nape of her neck.

"I don't want to talk about what I said earlier," she whispered. "I just need this."

"Can we talk about it later?" he pleaded.

"Later. Right now, I need you," she rasped.

"Then take me," he told her, nipping her lip. "I'm yours. I always have been."

Valine kissed him firmly and started tugging on his shirt. It was off before she could think twice. Malik's fingers found the ties on her shirt and pulled them apart, her nipples straining against the shifting fabric.

"Are you taking a tonic?" Malik asked lowly, kissing her collarbone.

"Yes," she gasped. "I assume you are still taking yours?"

"I am. And I have been examined by a physician, I pose no risk of disease."

He freed her from her shirt and his mouth found her nipple. He pulled the stiff peak into his mouth and let his tongue flick over it, sending a bolt of pleasure directly between her legs. She keened and ground her core down onto his pelvis—she was so wet.

"You will not contract anything from me," she told him breathlessly. She'd been tested and examined after her last partner, something she did as a precaution. As a necromancer, she generally did not fall to ails and auges, but that didn't mean she wanted to unknowingly pass something off or risk some sickness that could negate her necromancy.

Her pants were loose so she shimmied out of them quickly and Malik was all too eager to assist. In seconds she was bare atop him and grinding wantonly against the hard ridge that pressed against his sleep pants.

The friction from his thick length was divine.

Malik moaned low in his throat and his hands went to her back, massaging up and down her spine as she rode him over his pants. His eyes rolled back and his lips parted. Valine swept in and pulled his lip between her teeth, while her hands wandered to the waistband of his pants.

"Take them off," he practically growled. "Then take my cock inside that sweet pussy of yours. I want you to take everything I am."

Valine turned molten and acquiesced. His pants vanished and they were both utterly naked. She didn't spare a second's hesitation as she met his eyes and then guided his cock into her slick core. They both moaned as she sunk to the hilt, feeling him stretch and fill her as he sat up and wrapped his arms around her. Valine tossed her head back, her long dark hair a curtain behind her. She rode him hard, grinding her clit against him and seeking the friction she desperately needed.

"Fuck, Valine. You feel so good," Malik groaned, mouth going to her chest, pulling a nipple into his mouth. "Like this pussy was made for me."

"*Malik*," she rasped, bouncing against him as he sucked on her hardened peaks.

"Fuck me. Show me how badly you need me."

Valine increased her pace, headache forgotten. The bed squeaked and she let out a keening sound that matched to Malik's low groans. She was so consumed in the moment that she didn't care if anyone heard her. Everyone already thought they were fucking, there was no reason for them not to at this point.

Desire had taken the place of her blood and she felt an orgasm build low in her belly. She fucked harder and Malik thrusted up into her in return, hitting a spot within her that made her see stars.

"Oh, saints. Oh, fuck, just like that," she managed. "Don't fucking stop."

"I can feel you squeezing me. Are you close, Little Liar?"

"Yes," she keened.

"Come for me. Come on this cock—it's yours."

"*Mine.*"

"Yes, all fucking yours."

Valine felt herself tipping over the edge and when Malik suddenly flipped them and pinned her to the bed. He began thrusting into her relentlessly, hitting so deep inside her that she came immediately.

Her climax crashed through her like a tidal wave and she arched off the bed as he continued driving into her. Her thighs quaked and she felt as if lightning was dancing in her veins. She wasn't entirely sure she didn't scream because all thought had left her mind. Everything was ecstasy and Malik's perfect body—and the love between them she wasn't ready to face.

In the final waves of her climax, Malik joined her over the edge, spilling into her. She felt him throb, felt the heat fill her, and she squeezed him tighter in response. He groaned and sank his forehead to his chest.

When the final shudders passed through them, skin sweat-slickened, Malik withdrew. She gazed up at him, lust-addled, but he wore a different expression—a devious one.

He sat back on his haunches and took in her form as she took in his. She gazed at his tattoos, the serpent, the Veritasium Medallion, the blade, the script. His cock was still swollen and slick with her wetness, and Valine clenched from the way it aroused her. He visibly perused her and she watched his eyes land on her core.

And then he moved.

His fingers slid up her leg, drifting from her knee to her inner thigh. She was so sensitized that she shivered and bit her lip. His fingers did not stop until they found her core and then he swept two fingers into her center and dragged his release over her sex. He painted her pussy with his cum, and then he used it to fuck her.

Fingers wet with their combined climaxes, Malik swirled over her clit, pressing expert circles there. He was winding her up again.

"Fuck, Malik. What are you doing to me?"

"You deserve to come again and I want to hear my name fall from those pretty lips when you shatter."

Suddenly, Malik plunged those two swirling fingers into her pussy and rubbed her clit with his thumb. She arched off the bed and cried out. She'd just finished, but saints, he knew what he was doing and she was already close again.

The room was filled with the sounds of her thready breathing and the wet slick of her being pleasured.

It was all so much—too much. Malik's fingers pumped in and out and he was doing wonderous things to her clit. Her second orgasm threatened to take her, she felt it build and she chased it. Her hips thrust up and Malik guided her through it.

"Come," he commanded. Then grazed his teeth over her nipple and she fucking soared.

She shattered through her orgasm, moaning Malik's name. She was ruined, so fucking ruined.

When she came down from the high, Malik cleaned them up and then silently returned to the bed. As he pulled her against him, he smoothed her hair and whispered into her ear.

"We won't talk about it tonight, but just know I have many things to say to you."

"Okay," she whispered as they drifted off to sleep naked in each other's arms.

Valine tried to hide the thunderous headache that throbbed in her skull, but the shafts of sunlight and boisterous market belied her pain—not including the pleasant ache between her thighs. She flinched and cringed at every bright and loud exposure, and the concern from Malik and the others was painfully evident. It was only dawn, yet the pink and powdery light was enough to aggravate her.

As they boarded the ship, she stayed silent, casting anxious looks over her shoulders at Cuuevota's coastline. All the unexplored stalls and wares, all the secret beaches and waterfalls the island contained. All of it hidden from her. She was disappointed their stay was as short as it was, but she was more than grateful for how fortuitous it turned out to be, despite the alliance refusal.

It was when Hanish and his family attempted to reboard, that Valine stopped them. "This is where your journey ends for now."

"What?" Hanish said, aghast.

"For now, you need to stay in Cuuevota until I'm certain Hafsa's organization isn't attempting retribution for her failure to carry out her mission. The further you are from them, the safer you are."

"Safe?" Hanish was outraged. "This is a fucking black market, Valine!"

Behind her husband, Hafsa was cupping the innocent ears of their two children, both dark of hair and light of eye, neither older than five. They stared up in confused curiosity while Hafsa scowled, twisting her pretty face.

"I know," Valine said quietly. "But this is the best I can do."

"The fuck it is!"

"Hanish, you go no further. I am sorry."

"You're not sorry," he bit out. "And after all I've done for you? You would be dead without me."

"I know," she allowed. Closing her eyes, she sighed and dug out a satchel, handing it to someone she considered a friend. "It won't do you much good here since the market trades mostly in information, but there are wares that coin will get you. Until I return, ration this. You should live comfortably on it for a while."

Some of the fury drained from Hanish's eyes. "You'll come back for us?"

"I promise. If I am still living, I will."

Hanish was silent before he sighed. "Okay."

"Thank you, Hanish. For everything."

He nodded.

For a moment neither of them spoke, but caught up in a fit of emotion Valine reached out and grasped his shoulder, staring at him firmly and nodding farewell. Hanish did the same to her, the warm weight of the fulgurmancer assuring her she hadn't destroyed every semblance of their allyship. In that moment, she debated something before slipping Wallace Yarl's pistol into Hanish's hands.

"Keep your family safe," she whispered.

He stared at her, emotion raw on his face before he promised.

Hanish and his family turned and slipped back into the crowd on the docks, disappearing into the masses and the anonymity of the black market. Valine strode for the ship.

She patted the Call in her bag, clinking against the Veritasium Medallion she'd taken from Larysa's drug lord. She could feel the heat of it through the leather, and she wondered what magic it possessed and how it worked. Even so, she couldn't believe it had been so easy, and because it was so simple, she was unsettled. It didn't sit right with her that they arrived, retrieved and were leaving. It was too straightforward and she never trusted something so uncomplicated. Because of this, she was constantly casting looks, waiting for an attack. Waiting for a surprise.

Valine could never quite shake her suspicious, assassin ways. She always thought someone was out to fuck her over.

Captain Morgan Yarl was bright-eyed and cheery as he gazed out over the sea in the mild light. New crates were stacked near him and several new faces had joined his crew. Valine wondered if any of them had been destined for brothels and other acts of servitude, and the better Yarl brother inadvertently saved them from that fate.

Still unsteady on her feet, Valine crossed the ship to the port side and leaned over the rail, inhaling the briny air, trying to clear her head. The pain was racking up and her previous day's exhaustion plagued her even worse. Her magic was still so untried and she wasn't equipped to use her necromancy against two kraken at once. She fisted her hands on the rail, tightening her grasp on her reality, unwilling to slip into darkness.

"Valine." She turned to the sound of the feminine voice and found Freyja at her side. "Are you still weak from yesterday?"

Valine hesitated but nodded once.

Freyja cast her eyes over her slender shoulders nervously. "Would tethering your magic to me help?"

Valine's head snapped up in surprise. She waited a beat. "It would."

"Then do it," Freyja said resolutely.

Carefully, Valine pried a hand from the polished rail—a rail that only survived due to the blonde's ruinmancy—and twisted her fingers, pulling threads to the surface. Slowly, she drew them, the smoke thick like syrup, and sprawled her fingers out as they crept over to Freyja. Pointing, she allowed the necromancy slip into Freyja's chest and she inhaled sharply as she felt the connection.

Valine's headache eased and her cognition cleared. No longer did she sway or depend on a hand on the ship to remain standing.

"*Valine*," Freyja said sharply, the sound like a swear. "What are you doing?"

Valine stiffened as she met the ruinmancer's eyes. Freyja's hazel gaze was hard and astonished, following webs and lines.

"It's a contingency."

"How many?"

"You don't want to know."

"*Fucking Mrithun and Vitus*," Freyja muttered in horror, staring at the stark lines of Valine's magic. "Does Malik know?"

"No."

"Oh fuck, are you serious, Valine? Now I'm in the middle of this mess?" Freyja fussed, throwing her hands in the air.

"It's probably unnecessary, but the opportunity was there and I never do anything without a safeguard."

"Your funeral," Freyja said, fed up and walking away. "Don't get yourself killed."

Valine sighed and looked out over the waves, glancing around at the replacement aethermancers guiding the sails. New hydromancers were diverting the immediate tides to let the ship cut through the water without resistance, hands twisting, triumphant gleams in their eyes. If they kept up this speed, they'd reach Adraali in three days.

The further they got from Cuuevota, the more her anxiety lessened. That didn't mean that she'd relaxed, no, instead she was pacing the ship, eyes flickering nervously and she was sure she unsettled more than one pirate on board. She was like a wraith, haunting the ship, stalking along the edges with silent, deadly grace. Her tethers whispered against her, pulling and prodding. Every moment she hung onto them was another moment that the headaches and exhaustion were creeping back on her.

Hours passed without incident, Valine still pacing. Malik approached her cautiously.

"What are you worried about?" he asked her.

Valine jerked a look over her shoulder, back at the vanished island behind them.

"I don't trust Thiandra."

"Of course you don't, you shouldn't trust anyone."

"Including you?"

Malik cracked a sly smirk. "Present company excluded."

"Hmm."

Malik sobered against her dour mood, detecting that her inability to tease back registered from anxiety. "What about Thiandra is bothering you?"

Valine pressed her lips together, tilting her head in thought. "It was too easy. You're telling me that we got the Call in exchange for some unpleasant truths? No, I don't trust it. There was no hunt, no bloodshed, no proper negotiations. And they handed it over like it was *nothing. That,* I don't trust."

Malik crossed his arms and leaned against the rail, tipping his head forward in her direction. It created an oddly intimate bubble despite the lack of touching. "So, what do you think they'll do?"

"I don't know," Valine sighed, and stared out over the water, suddenly seeing a nightmare. And then horror clawed up her throat. "Maybe send a fleet after us."

CHAPTER FORTY-TWO

Malik turned to where Valine's eyes were trained. "*Fuck!*"

Calls and shouts went up around the ship as others caught sight of the five ships approaching them from the coast of Cuuevota, the black market's flag of a kraken flying over each of them. People were racing across the wooden boards of the ship, aethermancers and hydromancers flying up the stairs to the stern, their surviving fulgurmancer ascending the ropes to the crow's nest. At the top he harnessed himself and then Valine watched, neck craned as he summoned a storm.

Clouds rolled in viciously, the sky bruising before her eyes, the heavens opening, and then they were awash with rain. The deluge was instant, the thunder quickly following, lightning sure to come. Within seconds, Valine's hair was plastered to her head, the gray, wet world blurring her vision to the following ships. She couldn't see them, but she knew they were there.

Captain Morgan Yarl was shouting at the mages, realizing he was duped. He needed the mages—especially the aethermancers—to stay on schedule, but he couldn't be certain that they weren't double-crossing him, and still working for Cuuevota rather than him. Valine didn't know if he'd purchased slaves or if these were hired magic users, but regardless of the fact, they couldn't be trusted. The captain screamed for his original crew to hold the new mages at gun, sword, and knife-point, preparing for any betrayal.

Had the mages powered the sails slower over the hours? Did they ensure Cuuevota could catch up to them? Or were they just so unlucky that there were faster ships hidden in the market?

Valine and Malik were still frozen on the main deck, eyes locked. The downpour made their proximity feel so insular. Valine could see the water droplets on his lashes, coasting down his cheeks, beading on his lips. His gold-blue eyes were alive with fear and anger.

"In case I don't survive," Valine said, cupping Malik's jaw in her hands, his short beard slick with rain, "I love you."

She kissed him, fiercely and quickly, pressing her soaked mouth to his, pouring all her emotion into the kiss. She pulled his lower lip between hers, opening her mouth to him just enough to brush his tongue with her own. In shock, Malik clutched her face between his hands, warm despite the storm, holding her to him, as if just by prolonging the moment he could prevent what she planned.

"Protect yourself," she whispered, and broke from Malik, racing for the rear of the ship, pushing past the mages gathered there with blades aimed at them.

Time slowed as she crossed the deck. The rain lashed her in freezing sheets as her boots determinedly clomped, eating the distance between her and the sea. Her blouse was stuck to her like a second skin, her hair plastered to her cheeks and tossed to the wind.

Lighting struck the water between them and the approaching ships. With their speed, Valine could now see them through the storm. The water was working up a vigorous froth, the waves churning against the hull, water splashing over the sides. The scent of the air was thick with voltage and brine, the atmosphere of chaos palpable.

Valine approached the rail at the lowest point, staring down the five ships. They were black and sleek, built for speed and aggression, and the white and black flag was a stark reminder of the brutality of the market. The black market was reprehensible for a reason, and double-crossing was one of them.

A laugh sounded behind her.

Valine whirled to find the woman who'd greeted them on the docks, the scar bisecting her brow divulging her identity quickly. She hadn't said much of anything on the docks, but here it was clear that she was someone important. She wore hydromancer garb, but Valine deduced that was probably a guise. A pirate held her in a crushing embrace, restricting her with a blade against her jugular.

"You truly thought that Thiandra was just going to give you the Call of the Phoenix?" the woman asked, her black hair slashing dark lines on her cheeks. "You are more foolish that I thought. But you believed them so readily." She fake pouted. "Some sad secrets and you were putty in their hands."

Valine gritted her teeth. "You talk a lot for someone who has a knife against their throat."

The woman shrugged. "I'm not the one who is going to be hunted and drowned."

"Because a slashed throat is so much more appealing."

"Oh, Ula here is just pretending," the woman revealed, showing startlingly white and straight teeth. "Isn't that right, darling?"

The pirate holding a blade to the woman's throat smiled and dropped it. "It's true," she told Valine shrugging. "I belong to Alvah, and I'll follow her anywhere."

Alvah cupped Ula's cheek and she leaned into it. Ula was giving Alvah sickeningly devoted eyes, and if they were under better circumstances, Valine would've had to fight off a gag, but as it was, a storm was raging and ships were ready to attack.

"Sorry to do this, but Thiandra commanded me and I must follow through," Alvah said, stepping closer to Valine. Valine backed up while the pirates around them slowly realized the turning tables. Mages were turning on pirates, pirates turning on crew. No one was able to help as chaos broke out as steel rung loud and gunfire cracked. It quickly transformed into a blood-bath. "Thiandra saw the horror you will bring; they decided you must die for the greater good."

Valine hardly let this information sink in as Alvah lunged at her with a blade extended. Valine dodged, sliding across the deck. With panic coursing through her, she tried to untangle the threads of her necromancy, all the caught-up teth-ers, as Alvah slashed again. Valine threw herself against the rail, her lower back smarting against the pain. She gritted her teeth as rain chilled her bones.

"Tell Thiandra they can have the fucking Call!" Valine shouted as the blade came down again. She rolled across the deck, her hand sliding across a broken spindle, opening up a deep gash. Pain fired through her hand, blood pouring out and down her wrist. She hissed as she came up on her feet, digging through her bag until she found the newly familiar warmth of the Call. Thrusting it out, she offered it. "Here! Just take it!"

Alvah's eyes widened. "Don't touch that!"

As Alvah shouted, a massive wave hit the side of the ship and sent it careening to the starboard side. Valine and the Call went flying across the deck. The necklace skittered away, bumping against a rail, precariously balanced and threatening to weave between the railing and into the sea. Valine crawled for it, leaving blood on the rain-soaked deck, lancing pain arrowing through her palm as she dragged herself to the Call. She caught it before another wave could toss it further.

"No!" Alvah screamed as Valine's bloody palm made contact with the Call of the Phoenix.

Valine felt fire erupt in her veins, a conflagration exploding within her. The inferno in her blood had her rising on her toes in agony, her mouth opened in a silent scream. Her arms were outstretched, the Call of the Phoenix dangling from her bloody fingers. She thought she was dying. Everything was pain and fire and flame and agony.

"Valine!" Malik yelled, crashing onto the deck, engaging in battle.

He fought gracefully and gracelessly, formal training interspersed with blind panic. He slashed with a short sword as often as he shot with his pistol. The crack of the gun was an echo of thunder, the dropping bodies a whisper of it. Her king fought through the throng of betrayers against the tide of swords and hail of bullets.

"Starboard incoming!" the fulgurmancer shouted from the crow's nest.

It was too late. Valine was going to die, one way or another. And she wasn't ready.

A sudden force crashed against their ship, the groaning of wood hideously loud as the immensely long spear of a bow plowed through the *Tempest*. Valine was tossed off her feet and into the furthest rail of the highest deck. She hit, abdomen curving over the rail while the rest of her body continued moving, the Call launching from her grasp. The fire left her body as the Call vanished from her grip, but the wind was utterly knocked out of her. Valine collapsed backward against the deck, gasping for breath. In the space of seconds, she thought she was dying again.

Malik was tossed to the deck near her, the King of Adraali slowly rising to all fours, searching for her. His eyes were bleary, but when they caught sight of her, relief bloomed. He slipped as he got to his feet but raced for her, covering her against any onslaught.

Freyja ascended the stairs, jumping two and three at a time, blood mixing with the white blonde of her hair as she cast her hands to the destruction around them. She threw a hand at a charging pirate and tore him in half with her magic, the feat costing her greatly as the ruinmancy wavered.

"*Valine!*" Freyja shouted. "Now!"

Valine watched as Freyja's magic flowed out of her, mending the *Tempest* from the warship's attack. She had to blink away the confusion when she saw not the sleek black body of Cuuevota's ships but the blinding white and obnoxious gold filigree of Talloh's ships. The realization was cemented by the lavender flag depicted with a white palace crowned by three violet moons thrashing in the storm.

They were being attacked on two different fronts.

Talloh was attacking them. Amaris didn't believe them. Amaris allied with Runell. She had lied. They had been followed.

Valine felt her rage erupt within her, and she flashed her dark eyes onto Alvah. She was just stirring from the deck, a hand to her head. Grinning the smile of a daemon's daughter, Valine reached out for Alvah's life and simply snipped it. Alvah crashed to the deck among the bodies lying around them.

The deck was slick with blood and water, but Valine made her way, blood-soaked and drenched to the very stern of the ship, Malik following, walking backward with a pistol extended. The lantern was swinging wildly behind them, and the five black market ships were dangerously close. Freyja was doing everything in her power to mend the ship, but her power was waning, and Valine needed to act before the cannons were brought out.

Mages were killing in droves. Hydromancers were sending torrents of water down throats and drowning their crew on deck. Aethermancers were depriving them of oxygen while flashes of light blinded others. On the Tallohian ship, she saw pyromancers readying their flame, hands engulfed and ready to launch.

"You can do this," Malik told her reassuringly. She knew that he didn't know exactly what she was planning, but he believed in her regardless of this knowledge. "Whatever you need from me, I give it to you."

Emotion surged within her and she reached with her necromancy, creating another tether with Malik. Her magic probed against him until it slithered through the crack in his Veritasium Medallion and into his heart. He jolted when she made the connection, but it was slight, and she soothed the pain with a soft look of apology.

Extending her hands out by her hips, Valine pulled on the deepest tethers, swaying with the waves. She gritted her teeth and strained her jaw, working the magic, fingers twisting and curling, arms raising. She felt the awareness in her tethers snap to attention and Valine directed a cue to the tethers.

Destroy them.

As she released the order, monstrous tentacles shot from the dark of the sea, wrapping around a Cuuevotan ship and swallowing it beneath the waves. Three more tentacles lashed out at the other ships and a large, heaving body pulled itself from the water, black smoking necromancy wreathing it. Violent red eyes peered up over the waves as the kraken's massive mouth began devouring another ship, crunching as the gargantuan fangs punctured through every layer of the vessels.

Screams and shattering wood sounded, and Valine saw more than one unlucky soul throw themselves into the mercy of the sea. Aenon, saint he be, was not merciful when it came to his oceans, and with the manipulation of the fulgurmancer above them, those lives were about to be forfeit.

Tugging on a second tether, Valine directed her second kraken to the Tallohian ships. She didn't know how many there were, and the vicious rains made it difficult to deduce. Lightning shot from the sky and shattered a mast on the attacking Tallohian warship, the wood toppling into the sea, and the sails dragging down with it.

With the help of the fulgurmancer and Valine's kraken, they decimated the attacking forces. She didn't think she would get the screams of men and the shriek of wood out of her mind. It took only minutes, and all the Cuuevotan and Tallohian ships were sunk, barely there survivors clinging to shipwrecked pieces, blood staining everything.

When they had served their purpose, Valine cut the tethers on the kraken and let their monstrous corpses sink to the bottom of the sea.

All her energy left her, and she started sliding to the filthy deck. Malik caught her around the middle, his hand going to her cheek. The storm still raged around them, but seeing the king look down on her with such concern, devotion, and fear…Valine couldn't imagine a more perfect moment.

"I love you, too," Malik whispered.

CHAPTER FORTY-THREE

The Call was lost to the sea. As the bodies were hauled overboard and the decks mopped of the blood and bodily fluids, the necklace was nowhere to be found.

Valine watched from a crate on the highest deck, a woolen blanket wrapped around her shoulders, a cup of weak tea in her hands. She was so exhausted, the magic required to kill, tether, hold, and command two kraken over the course of several days had taken its toll, and she was certain that Freyja's offer of tethering was the difference between her current consciousness and all-around survival. Without the ruinmancer's strength, Valine would have been—in a word—fucked.

Malik hovered close to Valine, almost circling her like a wild cat, eyes flashing dangerously at anyone who came too close. She'd never seen the king so on edge and possessive, but at the same time, she'd never heard him declare his love for her.

He was in love with her.

She should have been able to guess that only a fool or a fool in love would offer a consort ring with the possibility of marriage. Still, the denial had been strong. She could dismiss his feelings as strong affection, lust, or simple attraction, but love…that was different. And their admittance echoed in the air between them.

In case I don't survive…I love you.

That's what she told him when she thought she was sacrificing herself to certain fate. She didn't think survival was all that probable against the kraken when the sand serpents had nearly killed her, and had Alastair not been there, they would have. It didn't make sense that she'd lived. Was she getting stronger? Were kraken weaker than sand serpents? What was the dividing difference?

It was four days later when they docked in Adraali, Valine beyond exhausted by her spent necromancy. She had filtered her magic through the water, feeling for any kraken beneath the depths and diverting them away from their path. They had sailed back with another skeleton crew, the death total at a record seventy-five percent, a number that had Captain Yarl swearing up a storm of obscenities and complaints of lost coin and information.

Months had passed since she was last in Adraali, months since Malik had hired her. Too quickly, the Blooming Season was approaching, and too soon, potential brides would arrive, and Valine had to falsely befriend them, urge them towards the king, and allow them to air their struggles. Valine didn't know if she had the strength anymore. How was she expected to cater to women who were trying to take away the man she loved?

Anger prickled at her. No. She refused.

They were herded into the castle, meeting up once again with Alastair in Malik's private study. The reunion was warm, the subject matter not. They filled in the vitamancer about the failure of Cuuevota, the kraken, and the warship attacks. They quietly informed him about Valine's power, the connection when she tethered to Freyja, and the break in Malik's Veritasium Medallion. Even though they were alone, they weren't taking chances.

"May I?" Alastair had asked, extending a hand to the king.

"You may," Malik allowed.

Alastair spread his fingers and let his cerulean magic probe along Malik, searching the medallion. His brows narrowed in concentration, his eyes brightly burning at the king's chest. Valine could see Alastair's magic only because he was allowing it. Mages with magic like theirs could elect to shield it or reveal it. Valine almost always chose the former.

"I can feel the break, but I can't get past it," Alastair said, wondering, and turned his attention to Valine. "Would you be able to show me how you do it?"

Valine's eyes flickered to Malik, Freyja, and Sarim. "Okay."

She stepped forward, bringing a hand out, summoning her necromancy, but this time she did it with the intention for it to be visible. It was an extra step, something she was less accustomed to, but she managed. The black smoke spiraled out from her fingers, slithering across the air. Sarim inhaled sharply at the sight, the Valmotti being the only non-magic user in the room— to no one else's awareness.

It gathered in front of Malik, and immediately found that break in the labyrinth-like medallion, and slipped in, knotting itself behind Malik's heart. Malik's nostrils flared as the tether secured itself.

"Fascinating," Alastair breathed. He approached the magic, eyeing it carefully, watching the smoke writhe. "It knew exactly where to go and simply slipped through it."

Valine pulled her necromancy back into her, swaying on her feet. Malik rushed to her side, steadying her and immediately, embarrassment flushed through her. She dismissed Malik's help, and with a knowing look, he backed off. Alastair attempted to breach the medallion again to no avail. It was after this attempt that Valine truly flagged in her energy. Realizing her predicament, Malik summoned for a servant to assist her, and within minutes Diana arrived.

Valine grinned as the red-headed woman appeared at the door, guiding her through the halls. She had missed Diana and was an invaluable contact during her time in Talloh.

"How was the festival?" Diana asked, arm around her as they journeyed across the black and white checkered floor.

"Eventful," Valine said on a smile.

"I hear the regards of my family were sent."

"They were."

"Thank you."

Diana opened Valine's suite door for her and she was startled to find it much the same. The linens were fresh, the fire burning low in the hearth in anticipation for her timed arrival, the surfaces free of the dust it surely accumulated in her absence. Valine eyed the bed and it beckoned to her. She swore its lure was the most attractive thing she'd ever seen.

"Would you like me to draw you a bath?" Diana asked.

"No, thank you. I think I will just take a shower."

"Summon for me should you require anything more."

"I will."

After Diana left, Valine latched the lock and stripped her travel-worn clothes off, leaving them in a pile on the tile floor. She turned on the hydromancer-powered shower, letting the room fill with steam as she slipped beneath the brass faucet. The water was hot and washed away the remaining grime she failed to scrub on the *Tempest*. It took a while, but the water ran clear once again, and Valine lathered herself in lavender, jasmine, and lemongrass soap and added blackberry-scented oil to her hair.

She didn't bother dressing again once she was out of the shower. She simply dried herself with a fluffy towel and tossed it to the floor as she climbed beneath the downy covers, falling asleep before the sheets settled.

She awoke sometime later. The light of day had since slipped below the horizon, and night hung heavy in the sky. Stars danced across the view from her window, cool air rushing through the partially open window. Dislodging herself from her nest of blankets, she went to the window, shutting it firmly, letting her head rest against the frame.

Her job was far from over, but for now, her immediate assignment was done. She'd set out to kill a king, and she had. The mission had been large—far larger than any she'd done before—and it was complete. She'd succeeded.

For a moment, Valine stared down at the city, at the final millings of people about town before bed, all so ignorant of the machinations behind the crown. They were so naïve to the plots Valine had enacted and thought out. She was a cruel creature, a false being among the masses, a savior who wielded death's scythe. This was all for the greater good, and even then, they did not know.

She had killed so many to gain control over Talloh, directly and indirectly. By her hand and by her magic. By her accidents and by her purposes. No one knew the lengths she'd gone to, the measures she'd taken. She was so isolated in her maneuverings, but she was good at it. They had no idea how good. It was a talent, and yet she couldn't share it, and it kept her so insulated in her own world.

Valine was so apart from regular life, never had she felt so disconnected from others before this. She was always slightly distanced; when she was a lady, she had to hold herself to a higher standard, and when she was simply an assassin for hire, she had to keep her secrets close. Now, she had to do both and more, and the overwhelming prospect was beginning to numb her.

She didn't know how long she stood there, staring. Perhaps it was only minutes, but her thoughts were getting away from her. Was this how Malik felt? To hold his crown and his plots with the same hand? To seek the freedom of the people while appeasing the egos of men? She wasn't sure, but the thoughts of her king had her heart aching.

She needed him.

Abruptly, she tore herself away from the window and strode over to her armoire. Inside were all the clothes she didn't pack for Talloh, including a lacy piece of black lingerie. The corset dipped provocatively low in the chest and followed the shape of her, high on her hips, barely a scrap of it against her sex. The back covered little of her ass and nothing of her back. She put on the piece, and though it covered her breasts, she could see every detail of her nipples through the lace, including how tight and hard they were.

She covered up with a long black cloak, and a pair of thigh-high leather boots and made for the door. The hood covered her face from sight, and it was probably for the best as the anticipation on her face was flashing in inescapable notice.

When she opened the door, she was shocked to find Malik already there, prepared to knock. Valine froze, taking in the sight of the king.

He was dressed all in black, the golden clasps on his corset a clear indicator as to how to remove it from his person. His lean legs were encased in leather, his boots just as finely made. His brow was clear of a crown, but a wave fell over it in one endearing curl.

"I was just on my way to see you," Valine said in a rush.

"What for?" Malik asked carefully. She could see his gold-blue eyes, trying to take her in beneath her cloak, knowledge blooming in his heated gaze.

"Because I love you desperately and I am tired of fighting it."

And then she reached for his wrist and dragged him inside, slamming the door behind him.

CHAPTER FORTY-FOUR

Malik needed no more words to understand Valine's intentions. With the door locked behind them, Malik spun them so that Valine was pinned against the cool wood, her palms plastered to it while his hands were manacles to her wrists. His lips were hot and heavy on hers, the passion burning her as his mouth moved across hers. She opened her mouth, allowing him entry, and his tongue slipped along hers, tasting and licking and dancing together.

Valine moaned low in her throat as Malik rolled his hips against hers, and she felt the hard ridge of his desire grinding exactly where she wanted him. She could feel the wetness spreading between her legs, her nipples peaking, nerves and excitement twisting low in her belly. He met her moan with a low groan of his own, rolling his hips again, this time releasing a wrist and grabbing for her thigh, finding it bare beneath the cloak.

Freezing, Malik pulled back, lips bee-stung. His eyes were liquid with heat, and she was certain hers were just as dark with desire. He didn't hesitate as he coasted his hands over her hips, around her waist, skirting her breasts before they came to the clasp at her throat. With a flick of his fingers, he released it, and the cloak fell from her, pooling in a shadowy puddle at her feet.

She stood before him in nothing but skimpy lace and leather boots.

Malik groaned. "Valine, you're killing me."

She reached for him, fisting a hand at the collar of his shirt. "Death is my specialty, but tonight, I'm much more interested in the little death than anything else."

He reacted, and so did she. She was tearing at the buttons on his shirt, flicking open the clasps on his corset, and throwing it all to the floor. Within seconds, Malik was shirtless before her, his bronzed skin on full display, his tattoos dancing across his body. Still, she didn't stop as she sought his pants. Malik fisted a hand in her hair, kissing eagerly at her throat, using lips, teeth, and tongue.

While she was wild, tearing at him, he was rapidly removing her lingerie, pulling the straps free from her shoulders, exposing her breasts. He dipped his head low, nipping her collarbone before finding a nipple and pulling it into his mouth. Valine threw her head back, letting out a deranged sound of pleasure, while his fingers worked the other one.

Pleasure was sinking through her, liquid and languid, hot and wild. It was pooling and raging within her, striking against her core, making her hips roll with every lave of his tongue. It was exquisite, and it was torment. Even more so when he wedged a thigh between her legs and her center ground against it, rubbing her clit just right.

Through her addled thoughts, she managed to get the buttons on his pants undone, and seconds later, they were stumbling towards her bed, a trail of clothing left behind them. Somehow, there was a boot left by the door while the other still remained encasing her leg. But as they crashed to the bed, Malik made quick work of that too, bending down, kissing his way down her thigh, pulling the leather free of her smooth legs. Her lingerie was down around her hips now, and his undershorts were the only things between them.

Tossing the boot away, Malik crawled atop her, hitching a thigh over his hip, his hard cock grinding against her clit through the lace. She arched in response, fisting her hand in his hair, and the other went to his back, nails dragging. Malik coasted his free hand between her breasts, palm flattening over her sternum before it glided to her throat, wrapping a gentle hand and applying the right amount of pressure to pleasure. Wetness rushed between her legs at the contact, and she writhed against the friction the wet lace was causing.

Valine arched into the hard ridge in his pants, incredibly turned on by the concern and reassurances he was giving her. No partner had cared beyond preventing pregnancy, and even then, that wasn't always the case.

Malik was thumbing her pulse, feeling the race of it beneath him, and she knew it was giving him a prideful satisfaction that he had the effect on her. The hand on her thigh went to the scrap of lace barely on her and dragged it down the side of her hip, showing just the teasing of her bare pussy. She enjoyed the sensation of hairlessness that was considered so sinful back in Runell, but there was something so powerful in making the choice and throwing it in the face of her former kingdom.

His fingertips were digging into the curve of her ass, his mouth everywhere. Valine's hands went to his shorts, pushing down the black silk.

"These fucking things need to come off," she growled.

He chuckled against her skin. "As you command."

Within seconds the shorts disappeared, and she was treated to the sight of his cock. Her mouth dropped open of its own volition as he approached her. It was proud and long with a girth that made her contemplate if it was going to fit inside her. But in a word, it was perfect.

"I like things a little rough," he told her huskily. "Tell me if I do anything you don't like."

"I'm willing to try anything with you," she rasped back.

Malik's hands grasped her ankles and dragged her to the edge of the bed, slinging her thighs over his shoulders as he knelt before her. He pulled the lace covering her sex to the side, exposing all the wetness that he elicited.

"So wet for me," Malik drawled, licking up the center of her.

She mewled and arched, eager for more. Her hands went to his hair, fisting in the waves, letting the silken strands slip through her fingers.

He returned his face to her, his beard tickling her thighs as he licked along her slit and then came to that tiny bundle of nerves and circled it with his tongue. She jolted and moaned as he began lavishing more attention to her clit, suckling and licking and nipping in a way he knew she loved.

"Fuck, Malik," she gasped, digging her hands into his hair, pulling him forward, urging him on. He acquiesced, tending to that little bud in earnest as he reached up and palmed her breast, rubbing her nipple with a thumb.

She felt her orgasm building, the pleasure rushing through her veins, begging for release. She felt the pressure below, threatening to unfold and explode from her. She clutched the sheets in her hands, wildly digging into the blankets before another hand shot to Malik's head, pushing him into her sex. Malik continued his attentions while her thrusting hips became wild, no discernable rhythm or pattern, just eager and wanton.

Valine keened a sound of intense pleasure—she was getting so close.

"Come for me, Little Liar," he murmured against her pussy. "I want to taste it on my tongue." Valine moaned at the erotic image. "That's it, so good, *fuck*."

That did it.

She shattered. She felt her orgasm erupt from her, and she nearly screamed, hips undulating, chasing the vestiges of the climax as Malik continued licking and sucking her through it. His movements slowed as the orgasm receded from her, and after she came down from the high, he gave that soaked little slit a kiss that sent overstimulated shudders through her entire body.

Her knees were weak, but she managed to surprise Malik by slithering down to the floor so that her face was between his legs, level with that lovely cock. She licked the head once, and it twitched in response, Malik's hands turned to claws in her bed curtains.

He looked down at her with burning gold eyes. "Such a tease."

She stared up at him, her dark eyes lust-addled. "Fuck my mouth."

The command sent a clear line of arousal through the King of Adraali. His eyes widened, and a tight gasp slipped from his throat as the length of him prodded forward, answering her. Begging for the sweet, wet heat of her mouth. His hand cupped her cheek, his thumb brushing her lips.

Valine licked up his shaft again, and he made a sound that was part pain, part pleasure. He closed his eyes, his cock getting even harder. She knew he must be aching.

"This looks painful. Don't worry, I'll take care of it."

She took him into her mouth, letting her tongue circle his head before drawing him in deeper. She felt him hit the back of her throat, and tears prickled in her eyes as she continued moving on him, taking him nearly out to toy with the head and the small slit. She sucked away the small pearl that beaded there and returned him once again to her wet heat.

Malik moaned and then gathered her hair in his hand, beginning to thrust into her mouth. She relaxed her throat, urging him on with one hand to his firm backside, her nails digging into the delectable flesh there. His hips rolled forward a few more times before he withdrew.

"As incredible as this is, I want to fuck this pussy first." His voice was a low growl that sent anticipation flooding through her.

Valine pushed up and crawled back onto the bed, parting her thighs, exposing her glistening sex. "It's yours for the taking."

Malik climbed atop her. "Put your hands up," he commanded.

She did as she was told, and he grabbed the lingerie they'd divested her of, using it to tie her wrists together behind the bars of the headboard. Valine met his eyes as he tied her, consenting to the restraint as she became solely at his mercy. The bonds were tight but not uncomfortably so, and when he parted her legs, she was more than ready.

It was then he spotted something on her side table, a perfect brow arching. "Do you consent to a little fear tonight, Valine?"

Valine's heart hammered, and she felt a pulse throb between her thighs. She tested the restraints and rolled her hips once. "Yes, I trust you."

Malik leaned over and picked up the viridian blade he'd gifted her for her twenty-sixth birthday. Carefully, he felt along the blade's edge, curving a finger on it. Slowly, meeting her gaze, he touched the flat of the blade to her hipbone. The blade was cool, the metal leeching from her, but heat flooded her.

She'd never been more turned on in her life.

"I won't break the skin."

Gently, he traced her navel and brought the knife around to the other hip, circled and dragged the blade back up along her side, gracing her ribs around her scars. He alternated between the flat of the blade, to the tip, to the edge, knowing just how to maneuver the weapon to heighten her sexual pleasure. But at the same time, he was using his other hand, stimulating.

His thumb pressed her clit while the flat of the blade slid along her outer thigh. He pinched her nipple as he patted her ass with the knife. She had to press her knees together to quell the raging lust in her core. He was experienced enough that he really didn't break the skin, but the light scratching brought a risk that was highly erotic, and Valine found herself moaning. Even when he made her writhe, he made sure the sharpest parts didn't cut her. He continued this controlled teasing, tracing her curves, her sharp angles, until she was panting.

"I need you now," she groaned as the flat of the blade tickled her inner thigh.

He immediately withdrew the blade, setting it once again on the stand, and parted her thighs, kissing the underside of both knees before settling between her legs.

Malik entered her, a slow, delicious thrust that had her lifting her hips to meet his movement. Taking her hips in his hands, he angled her up, pressing in and filling her with his length, thick and deep. Every thrust took him deeper, slow, letting her adjust to his length. Finally, he entered her fully and hit the hilt. He met her eyes, and she knew it was all changing.

He pulled out and slammed back into her, a cry leaving her lips as he began fucking her in earnest. His hands were tight on her ass as he pulled her to himself, pounding deep into her channel, his thickness stretching her exquisitely. She thrashed at the restraints, eager to touch him, to feel his skin, to bite her fingers into his back.

Their gasps, heavy breathing, and moans punctuated the sound of skin against skin. Malik's black orchid and tobacco scent was heady, mixing with her jasmine, lavender, the room filling with them and their lovemaking.

"You're fucking perfect," he groaned, his thrusts rolling expertly to graze her clit tantalizingly.

Her eyes rolled back in her head as she felt her back arch, stretching herself taut, ecstasy blooming through her. She was being fucked by a king. Valine was in her sexual prime.

"Harder," she moaned.

He did, his cock driving into her with perfect precision, his thumb moving to her clit and rubbing circles. She mewled, moving her hips in answer, wanting more.

Suddenly, Malik pulled from her and flipped her over. She was on her belly, arms crossed above her. Malik picked up her hips and pulled her ass against his pelvis. He smacked the swell of her cheek once, the sting in her bottom sending wetness flooding between her legs.

"Are you commanding me, Little Assassin?"

"Yes," Valine breathed.

Malik slapped her ass again, and she moaned. "Naughty girl." He leaned down and kissed the hurt. A finger glided along her spine, following the curve of her backside. "You like to be punished a little, don't you?"

"Yes," she whispered.

"Good," he said, punctuating it with another spank.

Valine was so wet, so aching for his cock to return again. "I need you," she practically whined.

He fisted a hand in her hair and brought her head back, kissing her cheek, so close to her mouth. "You want this cock back inside you?"

"Yes."

"I want to hear you say it."

"Put that fucking cock back inside me."

Malik immediately returned his length to her pussy, pounding into her while his other hand—the one that wasn't fisted in her hair—went around and made designs on her clit. He played with that nub, rubbing perfect, rapid circles on it, adding an agonizingly incredible pressure that had her crying out, another orgasm building. All the while, he continued thrusting, and she could feel his cock twitching inside her. He was so close.

When his cock pulsed inside her, she felt her climax hit her, plowing through her body and causing those inner muscles to clench around Malik, pumping him. He groaned as he came, thrusting hard and deep with final strokes. He worked her clit for a few more moments, letting the orgasm reach its full potential.

Without withdrawing, Malik turned her once again to her back, the king staring down at her with adoration. He kissed her deeply, luxuriously, his finger replacing his lips when he pulled back.

"I love you," he whispered.

She smiled against the pad of his thumb. "I love you, too."

They fucked two more times that night, falling into a rhythm of pleasure and sleep. They went at it hard and fast and rough, and then they had a gentle tumble, slow and intense, drawn out and luxurious. They lay in the bed, tangled in limbs and sheets, wrapped up in each other and blankets.

She was tracing his chest, trailing along the bronze flesh, when she stopped over his tattooed Veritasium Medallion. It was then that she noticed it was ridged, perfectly aligned with the black ink. She paused before continuing, but Malik noticed it.

"My father branded me with his medallion as a child. He had thought that perhaps a branding would offer the same protective effects—it did not. However, part of it did transfer to me." Malik sighed and ran his fingers through Valine's dark tresses. "I think that's where he went wrong. Shortly after that, the medallion broke. So, I stole it, and something in me told me to crush it. I don't know why it worked, but it did.

"I took the powder to a disreputable healer and asked them to make ink with it and cover my brand. When it was completed, I felt the medallion take effect, and I never told anyone. The healer of course was silenced, he had a slew of other problems so I justified his death with that consolation."

Valine leaned over and kissed the branded tattoo. "I'm sorry he did that to you." There was silence, and then she spoke again. "Malik...did you kill your father, too?"

It was quiet and she felt Malik pull in a slow, deep intake of air. "Yes."

"He deserved it."

Malik kissed her forehead and said nothing more, both of them falling asleep.

At dawn, Malik woke Valine with another kiss to the brow. "I'm leaving before Diana arrives. I'd rather not explain all this. Not yet, at least."

Valine was groggy but turned to him, seeking his lips. He kissed her sweetly, sweeping his tongue into her mouth. "She's going to know anyway, but I understand," she said against his lips.

"Can I come back tonight?" he asked softly.

"Please do."

CHAPTER FORTY-FIVE

Diana did know anyway, the evidence on Valine's skin was damning. She had love bites on her throat and thighs and fingerprints dancing over her hips. She said nothing, but a coy little smirk hidden when Valine's back was turned betrayed her knowledge.

"Would it be too much to ask you to send a messenger to Sarim?" Valine inquired. "I would like to know if he's willing to spar this morning."

"Not a problem," Diana said, dipping her head in acknowledgment. "Any particular time?"

Valine shrugged in the bath, lathering herself with jasmine-scented soap. "Whenever he wakes, he's an early riser."

Diana slipped away for a moment to send the message, and Valine sunk into the bath, luxuriating in the feel of the hot water unwinding her muscles. Her body had never felt so sated before. Valine smiled as she recalled last night's gymnastics, the sounds the king had made, the feelings he'd evoked in her.

When Diana returned, Valine had a dreamy look on her face.

"The Ōrdinem has been inquiring after you," Diana announced. "They wish to offer you a boon, as they do not like to leave favors unanswered."

"Oh?" Valine asked, stiffening. She continued letting the water sift through her fingers, keeping her thoughts off her face. "How come?"

"They wanted to extend to you membership, but they've caught wind of other allegiances."

"To the King of Adraali," Valine replied, deadpan.

"No," Diana corrected, voice hard. "To the Vanguard."

Valine held Diana's stare, both gazes stone. "I left them years ago."

"The Vanguard is not something you can just leave."

Valine cast her eyes away, angry and shameful. "Well, I did. I owe nothing to them."

"They trained you; they take their pay in blood."

"I am aware."

"Valine, are you in danger with them?"

The assassin was silent, and the spirals of steam rising from the water coiled like a veil between the women. Between Valine's thoughts and the words that she did not want to reveal, she'd thought she'd escaped her past. She thought her membership had been long buried and forgotten, rotting six feet down.

"I took care of it, and one day I will owe a debt," Valine managed finally.

"You left with an open bargain?" Diana was aghast.

"It was my only option," Valine bit out. "The Vanguard is not like the Ōrdinem. They are cruel and ruthless, and the contracts they take, I abhor. I will not kill unjustly or unwarranted. They do. There are reasons why I staked out on my own, why I never worked for royals. I won't tread on the Vanguard's territory,"

The largest reason for Valine's anti-royalty rules was the Vanguard, the assassin's guild's specialty. Messy, yes, but lucrative. Staying away from contracts they could gain was one of the agreements of her departure, but Malik's offer had been too much to refuse. Now, she was suffering the consequences and debating on how to dispose of her debt with her past.

Diana inclined her head in understanding. "I see."

"Do you?" Valine challenged.

"You have morals. I can respect that."

Valine didn't have a response; she just looked at Diana, her eyes leaking vulnerability. Diana was too perceptive, and noticed this, turning to busy herself with the rack of oils to salvage Valine's dignity. Blinking away the traitorous feelings, Valine submerged herself beneath the jasmine and lavender water.

She thought about staying under for a while but resurfaced. Immediately after this, she stepped from the tub and toweled off, before slipping into flexible clothing. Dressed in a long-sleeved black wrapped tunic and gray leather leggings, Valine made her way to the training yard, her favorite boots clomping on the stone floor.

When she arrived in the training yard, Sarim was already there, twirling a long staff, dressed in flowy linen and bare of feet. His hair was tied up, but loose strands slipped from its bun and were plastered on his sweat-dampened brow. He grinned when he caught sight of her, tapping the blunt end of the staff onto the dirt-spattered stone.

The training yard was an interior courtyard near the southernmost point of the palace. There were dummies and racks of weapons strewn about the place and walkways circling the space high above, serving as a vantage point as much as a balcony offered the best view at the theatre. This space was dedicated to bettering weaponry and related arts, but it was also a spectacle. The walls were gray stone, scraggly bushes attempting to grow forth from the pavers and between the cracks in the building's façade. It was a dreary space, but it was effective.

"What made you want to train this morning? We just got back yesterday," Sarim commented casually.

Valine shrugged, letting her fingers glide over the shining blades. "Nervous energy, I guess."

Sarim squinted and assessed her. Valine fidgeted discreetly, picking up and putting down knives after she examined them. The slight tang of sweat carried on the wind, mixed with the damp of stone and oil from polishing.

"You two finally fucked," Sarim said gleefully.

"Fucked?" Valine crowed, picking up a beautiful dagger with a blade of waves and a hilt of amethysts. "Don't be crass. It was making love."

"Was it?" Sarim said sarcastically. "I assume there were harps playing and rose petals all over the bed, right? And, of course, it was gentle and sweet and solely missionary."

Valine smirked. "Something like that."

Taking the amethyst dagger, Valine brandished it with a few quick strokes through the air. "Care to practice some knifework?"

She refrained from thinking about *that* kink as she heated.

Sarim chewed on his cheek, clearly wanting to make a comment about her night but deciding against it. "Sure, but you have to take your shoes off."

She bent to remove the boots, peeled off her socks, tucked them inside, and then moved the boots out of the way.

Sarim glanced over at the table of knives and picked one seemingly at random, swiping it once through the air, a ruby glinting in its pommel. He took a stance across from her in the empty ring, Valine circling the edges of it, the cold stone pricking her bare feet uncomfortably.

"Any idea the plan for the east?" Sarim asked as he darted towards her, blade outstretched.

Valine ducked and skirted to the right. "Not exactly. Adraali already has a solid alliance with Dubon, Thycca—" she leaned back from a swipe, "and Melusda. Things are a little more strained with Ixaitha."

"Because of the Tri-Region War," Sarim said as Valine jabbed for him. He rotated away from the blow.

"Yes, and the tension between Valencya and Thycca is only getting worse since Valencya started building that university to rival the one in Valos and asked Adraali for support and funding."

"That's not public knowledge," Sarim said, startled, and his momentary lapse allowed Valine to swipe his arm. A line of blood emerged, matching the ruby in his blade. Sarim hissed and parried back. He missed.

"I'm an expert assassin, Sarim. What do you expect?" Valine thrusted the blade out. "Besides, we know they're only doing it to piss off Thycca, but in doing so, they're putting us in an awkward situation. If we choose to fund the university, we are virtually siding with Valencya, but if we refuse, then we are officially aligned with Thycca."

"You sound like you'd prefer the Thyccan alliance." He twisted to the left and slashed on the turn.

"If I had to live anywhere else, I would choose Thycca,"

Valine wasn't willing to elaborate more. She wasn't willing to tell Sarim that access to medical care from Thycca drastically changed the trajectory of her life, and had she not sought the herbs she did, she didn't know where she would be today. She didn't say that because she'd already let her heart bleed her secrets once. It was enough for quite a while.

"Is there a chance my input could be of value?" Valine looked up, caught off guard to see Malik standing on the overhead decking, a smile on his face as he leaned over the rail.

"I'm not certain you're qualified on the matter," Valine teased.

"Ah, well, maybe a layman's opinion can offer new perspective."

Valine's lips twitched into a smile. "Perhaps."

Malik descended the steps to the training area, crossing the space between them, and came to a stop only feet before her. He was dressed in black leather pants and a silk shirt, gold embellishments, and a heavy cloak of suede rested on his shoulders, the lining an ornate pattern of firebirds.

"Good morning," Malik said softly, warmly.

Valine's heart fluttered unevenly in her chest. "Morning," she murmured.

They said nothing more, but their gazes did so much talking. There was heat and promise, reflecting memories of last night and fantasies for tomorrow. Valine felt herself going molten. The desire to shove Malik against the wall and have him inside her was debilitating.

"I swear to Mrithun, if you two start eye-fucking, I'm leaving," Sarim complained while wrapping a thin strip of linen around his readily bleeding cut.

Malik sighed, smiled, and shook his head. "Does anyone back in Runell know you're a necromancer?"

Valine, startled, considering the question. "No, I'm sure they don't."

"Not even your siblings?"

"I kept it hidden."

"Does anyone know you're an assassin?"

"Anyone that remembers me as a lady, does not know that I kill for coin."

"Good. We're going to attempt a truce with Runell, and I want you two to lead it. You two have the strongest excuses to be in Runell and linger or explore. You both have family there." Malik began to pace. "If you two can scope it out, figure out anything we can use, then we're one step closer to taking down Gallae and Cydra."

"So, for the sake of clarity—this is a false truce, correct?" Valine asked offhandedly, twirling the amethyst-encrusted blade across her knuckles.

"Correct, we just need an excuse to visit their kingdom. Also…" Malik looked askance at Sarim. "Valine, I'd like to speak to you privately."

Sarim rolled his eyes. "Well, I plan to continue sparring, so take your horny eyes elsewhere."

Malik quirked a smile and threw Sarim the middle finger as he put a hand to the small of Valine's back and guided her along through an archway. Valine hadn't had much time to scope out the Nyxia palace like she had Selyndyr's, but from living in Adraali for the past five years, she'd learned much about the layout. Mostly from restricted archives in the library that hosted builder's plans of the hydromancer powered plumbing system and the architect's configurations. She'd, of course, killed the guard who'd caught her, but was it really her fault that the guard decided to peer into her fake identification too closely? She'd lifted the card from a former lover, realizing what an excellent opportunity it was that the man she was fucking was a librarian at Adraali's Great Library. Serendipitous, truly.

CHAPTER FORTY-SIX

They were soon huddled into a shadowy alcove on the edge of a nearby ballroom. Valine could see the chessboard floor and the decadent chandelier, dimmed with sparse candlelight, but she knew that the fixture would be illuminated by a luxmancer to a much brighter degree during a ball. Malik pulled the viridian drape of the alcove behind him and turned, then spun the knob on a small stained glass wall sconce, sending refractured scarlets and ceruleans across the small space. The alcove was used for trading secrets, salacious encounters, or simply to have a moment alone. The latter rarely happened as couples were wont to stumble into the curtained doorway, disrupting the entire point of solitude.

"I wanted to speak to you about the arrival of the prospective brides," Malik began, a slight tone of wariness in his voice.

"What is there to talk about?" Valine questioned sharply. Fear curdled in her belly, a lead weight hovering in her throat, threatening to drop.

"How to plan this out. If we decide to do this, are you still going to act as their companion?"

"There is no if," Valine said flatly. "You are doing this and selecting a bride. That is the way of the world and the way of the crown. How else will you be able to take on Runell?"

"It doesn't have to be. And even if—it's a false alliance." Malik seemed genuinely confused. "It's to take control of their kingdoms. I don't want to marry any of them, but we agreed that I am giving the illusion."

"And when they figure out you're faking it all and fucking the help? I'm sure they'll love that on the wedding day." Valine bit out.

Malik drew his brows together in a frown. "There won't be one, you know this." He placed his hands on Valine's upper arms, brushing sweet circles on the soft fabric. "What's truly bothering you?"

Valine turned her face away, tears prickling. She swallowed thickly, staring at a shoe print on the wall. Hating herself. "You must do what is right for Adraali, including a strategic marriage. And while you may feel it is fake, they will not know it is false. They will fancy themselves in love with you. They will expect touches and gifts."

"I don't want to do this, and they can imagine all they wish, but I belong to you."

"But what if you do fall in love with one of them?" She was letting her jealousy get the best of her, and it was ruining all her plans to drive him towards a bridal alliance and ultimately destroying Runell.

"I won't."

"It's possible. I have heard they are all very beautiful."

"What need do you see in inviting them still?" Malik demanded. Valine felt a wave of jealous insecurity rush through her, and she wanted to string words together in a desperate plea. But that was not for the good of Adraali. "We don't need an outsider's marriage, not anymore. We can solidify the alliances other ways—with Thycca, we can do so by not investing in Valencya's university and purchasing shipments from Liesl's apothecary." Malik continued. "Ixaitha is already weakened by the aftereffects of the Tri-Region War, they'd be willing to do anything to establish themselves once again. And Dubon is content minding its own business, playing in its orchards and drinking mead—we have no quarrel with them."

"It will not be acknowledged. It must be legitimate."

Malik cocked his head. "I thought you understood this." He tucked two fingers under Valine's chin and brought her face up to his. "It's a lot, and you know anything with them won't be real—will not happen. I will not marry them."

Fury ignited within her. "You're putting your feelings above the needs of the kingdom. You need this for Runell to fall."

"Valine, *you* can give that power to me by marrying me."

Valine blinked in shock, feeling hope bloom warmly in her chest. "What?"

"You have the right name. You come from Runell. It's the same tactic we imposed in Talloh." His confusion was quickly shifting to irritation, but he hid it well beneath a veil of assurances. "Valine, I gave you that ring. I gave you the option, and you chose consort. You could've been my wife, and as much as I want it, I won't push it on you."

"It's not the right move. The other brides are." Her words were flat. She was trying to convince herself of this, and she was failing miserably. "The Desdemons won't answer to me. I am outcasted—banished. I am not the daughter of a king like they all are."

"You're wrong. Choosing one of them would be the biggest mistake of my life. And the ring is an open invitation. You may choose to be my wife and queen at any time, but should you decide so, I will not let you go lightly."

Malik began nipping at her jaw, drawing slow, sharp kisses along it, dipping to her throat and continuing there. She was intoxicated by the scent of black orchid and tobacco as he stepped toward her, into her, and pressed her to the wall. Valine's hands instinctively went to his chest, trailing exploring fingers over his ridged abdomen.

She was losing her resolve to convince him against her. Against them. But why was she trying to fight it? She wanted him. But she also wanted vengeance. Was her wrath clouding her judgment? What would she be left with after Runell's toll was paid? She'd be left with a yawning nothingness and nothing to fill it.

"You have no idea how much I would like to fuck my wife," he murmured, and her legs turned jelly. Him speaking about her in the position of his spouse had wetness pooling between her legs. She was shocked at how much she enjoyed the words on his tongue. "You see, she makes this divine little sound when I lick her sweet pussy, and it's the same sound she makes when I fuck her slow."

Malik's hand crept down to her breast, thumbing her peaked nipple. Her eyes rolled back, and her fingers clawed at the buttons of his shirt. She was being driven by instinct, thoughts clouded by his heady presence.

"Us…it complicates things," she managed, trying to direct the conversation.

"It shouldn't," he murmured into her shoulder, kissing the curve of her neck. "I love you, and the others are just politics."

"I cannot share you."

"You will not."

"We can't do this," she argued pitifully as he mouthed softly against her collarbone.

"We can. I can call off the bride's arrival."

"If you revoke the invitation without cause, it would be a great insult."

"Then give me cause," he riposted, punctuating it with a nip. "Marry me."

Valine caught the gasp in her throat before she could let it out, but her heart was hammering, and her hands trembled on Malik's abdomen. Fire and ice battled in her veins, hopeful panic rushing along through her. She felt like bliss, like ecstasy.

The King of Adraali proposed. To a necromantic assassin with the right name and the wrong parentage. But Valine could see very clearly in those vibrant, heavy-lashed, blue-gold eyes that stared up at her from her decolletage that he meant it, and he didn't give a fuck about any of that.

"It's too soon," she rasped.

"Is it?" Malik kissed along her neckline. "We've known each other months, probably wanted each other for just as long. I knew I needed you the moment I met you."

She wanted to say yes. Oh, all the daemons and saints, she wanted to say yes.

"Not yet," she whispered. "After the ruse."

Malik paused and brought his face up to Valine's, looking her in the eyes as if he was seeing her soul through her dark brown depths. There was relief and glee in his gaze.

"Is that a yes?" he pressed, desire and anticipation bright in his eyes.

Valine hesitated. Weighing her desire for vengeance and her desire for this man. "Conditionally. Firstly, you must play along—enchant the brides and let them think you are serious about courting them. Second, we need to keep us secret. I do not want the brides catching wind of our relationship, so for the duration of their stay, I will wear the consort ring on my index finger. You must use your psychomancy or influence to cast doubt on any rumors of us from Talloh."

Malik's smile dropped a little at this, and Valine wanted to kiss that mouth. He evidently held some possessive traits, and rather than be objectionable to the fact, she found it rather endearing—and if she was completely honest, quite sexy, too.

"Anything else?" he asked sultry.

"Yes, when you ask me again, I want you on one knee."

"Acceptable." A wicked grin came over his face. "But let me make it up to you, and I'll get on both knees now."

Before Valine could protest, Malik dropped down and undid the corset-style ties on her pants, wiggling them down her hips. She was slightly swollen and sore from last night, but it was a pleasurable, sated ache. He bared her glistening sex and groaned with desire. She was sure he was rock hard.

Leaning forward, he kissed her right above her clit, and the slight brush of his slight beard against that tight bud made her moan and fist her hands in his hair. He slipped his nose along her pussy, his lips tracing the slit, and she could feel his breath against her. She wanted to cry out from the delicate pressure, from the wanting, from the teasing. When she felt his tongue, she arched and tipped her head back against the wall.

His tongue dipped between her, tasting her very center, stroking a hot trail through. When he came up to that little bundle of nerves he circled it with the tip of his tongue, moving in faster circles. She felt her hips buck in response, and Malik chuckled against her clit, rewarding her with a nip. She cried out, pushing his face closer to her. The movements became quick flicks of his tongue and gentle suction from his lips, alternating and building her up, letting her climb toward her climax.

A hand slipped beneath her top, and Malik's fingers found her breast, squeezing a nipple with just the right amount of pressure that had her sensations heightening immeasurably. She began bucking her hips against Malik's mouth, desperate for more, and when he pinned her to the wall with a forearm and scraped his teeth on that bud, she mewled.

"There's that fucking sound," Malik murmured against her wetness. "Make it again, love."

She came hard and fast, Malik continuing to lick and stroke her through the orgasm, her legs trembling, knees weak. She steadied herself on Malik's shoulder, breath heaving, sweat dampening her brow. When she came down from the high, Malik kissed between her thighs and slowly drew up her pants once again, tying them expertly, lifting his gaze to hers. His lips were wet from her sex, and she felt a twinge at her core from the sight.

"Am I properly forgiven?" Malik asked, husky.

"Quite," Valine said, switching their positions and dipping down. "But now it's your turn."

She wasted no time, freeing Malik's straining cock from his pants. He moaned as soon as it was released and groaned deeper when Valine set her lips to his length. She swirled her tongue around the tip, licking away his excitement, and bobbed her mouth along his proud member. Her hand was at the base of his shaft, pumping him in tandem. Relaxing her throat, she let him slide deeper into her mouth, her teeth grazing him as he slowly began to thrust into her. His hand fisted into her hair, and she hummed her pleasure at him taking his. Malik moaned again and increased his pace. His movements were filling her, her jaw aching, her tongue laving tirelessly.

"I love seeing your mouth on my cock," Malik breathed, tilting his head back against the wall. She felt his fingers tighten, and she knew he was getting close. "*Fuck, Valine.*"

She took him almost completely out and then bobbed mercilessly on him, hand working in unison. Saliva was all over him, and her ministrations were making a mess of him. This made him lose control, and moments later, she felt the pulse in his length, and then warmth spread across her tongue as he moaned low in his throat. She swallowed as she took him through the last throes of his climax, gentling him as he spent himself.

When he was done, she tucked him away and returned their pants to their former position, smiling shyly as she did so.

Looking at him reassuringly, she removed her consort ring and slipped it to the other finger. She couldn't pinpoint the exact feeling, but it felt like a mix of loss and betrayal. It was the same look she watched pass over Malik's face, but it wasn't those feelings alone that showed. There was also understanding and devotion. They were united in another cause but remained loyal to each other. He was technically her fiancé, after all. And she was his.

CHAPTER FORTY-SEVEN

It was days later, Malik and Valine having engaged in numerous salacious encounters and other sexual acts, that led to hours ensconced in their chambers when curiosity struck her and didn't let go. In addition to the bedroom—and other locations—that she and the king were participating in, Valine was also using her body for training with Sarim.

The Valmotti warrior and the assassin met at the training ring each morning, sparring and sharing techniques and maneuvers, parrying blades and words, teasing each other about their newfound sexual encounters. It became abundantly clear that Sarim and Freyja were up to a similar amount of fucking as Valine and Malik were. Sometimes Malik and Freyja showed up to observe, the two of them bearing the brunt of more jokes and taunting, to the point that Freyja declared that "the onslaught of innuendoes was horrific". This had only sent them laughing.

Although she was keeping her body busy, her mind had latched onto an idea and couldn't shake it. Concerning thoughts wouldn't leave and so she took to the rookery to pen a letter. In addition, Valine had tried to slip away while Malik slept, disappearing into the forests that edged the palace and standing on a cliff face under the stars, venting her frustrations and tinkering with her necromancy, but even that didn't bring solace. She debated asking for an experiment, mixed between not wanting to show her hand, and needing to know the extent. She played this game of mental tug-o-war for days, laying abed after sex, staring at the canopy, zoning out during meals, a plate of food untouched before she managed to work up the nerve.

After a knifework session with Sarim that left the Valmotti hilariously sweaty and Valine astoundingly cool, Valine departed for a certain dignitary's chambers. Valine navigated her way through the halls until she found the door she was looking for, knocking perfunctory.

Alastair opened the door, groggy and sleep-drunk. His hair was rumpled, and he wore a half-tied emerald silk dressing gown and white pajama pants—also silk. He rubbed the heel of his hand against his blue eyes, dusting off the sand.

"Valine, what are you doing here so early?" Alastair asked, voice roughened by fatigue. A yawn punctuated his words as he rubbed his eyes again. "Is it even dawn?"

"It's past dawn," Valine said dismissively. Alastair was wont to wake up at noon if he so pleased, and while sleeping in sounded lovely, this niggling thought could no longer wait. "I want to try something. Something I've never done before."

Alastair raised a reddish brow. "You'd think coming onto a gay man would be the last thing on your mind, especially considering the sounds I heard in the courtyard the other day."

Valine resisted a blush and the thoughts that came along with it. Malik had hiked up her skirts over her bottom and pressed her face first into the wall while he'd railed her into oblivion. She'd tried to keep quiet, but Malik had been doing the most exquisite things to her clit and nipples.

"Or was that Freyja and Sarim I heard? I simply cannot keep track of your fucking antics anymore. Or rather *fucking* antics."

"You're hilarious," Valine said deadpan. "And as much as I enjoy your company, I don't want to sleep with you."

"That makes two of us."

"I wanted to test our magics."

Alastair cocked his head in curiosity. "Now you have my attention. Come in." He swept her grandly into the room, and he guided her to his sitting room.

The walls were all done up in warm shades, marigold yellow, pumpkin, rust, gold, and interspersed with some cooler tones of sage and muted blue. Alastair had taken a maximalist approach to his space, floral print wallpaper and plaster walls painted ochre, heavy wood furniture was built in chestnut and walnut, clear glass scattered throughout the room as vases and light fixtures, an elegant chandelier hung high above, reaching its arms like a kraken.

Valine took a seat on a paprika lounge chair, scraping her slowly growing nails against the velvet. Across the room, Alastair was at a drink cart, a crystal decanter in one hand, a tall, silver coffee carafe in the other.

"Which one do you take to start your day?"

"Coffee, please."

"So responsible," Alastair scoffed jokingly. "Next, you'll tell me you drink the recommended amount of water a day."

"Well…" Valine trailed off as Alastair handed her the steaming cup.

"Are you even human?"

"I mean, technically, no, I'm a necromancer."

The comment had circled them back to her original intention, leaving the perfect opening to delve into her idea. She redirected the conversation and took a sip of the hot, rich coffee, smiling at the taste of cinnamon.

"So, what brought this on?" Alastair asked, sitting across from her in a matching orange-red chair, sipping an identical cup of coffee—well, maybe not entirely identical. She was pretty sure she saw him splash some liquor in his.

"I've been thinking lately—"

"You have time to do that?"

"Shut up. Anyhow, I've been thinking about the extent of my magic, and I truly don't know what it is at this point. I've killed sand serpents and kraken, not to mention broken a Veritasium Medallion, and I'm questioning how far I can push my limits."

"So, you're wondering how far past mine, yours are?" Alastair said slowly.

"Right. We know that vitamancers and necromancers are magical opposites. While retaining some of the same abilities, it only makes sense that we negate each other, correct?" Alastair nodded. "So, with that being said, will you nullify me completely if you tried? Or only to the degree that our magic matches up? Say…" Valine brought her non-coffee hand to the side, level with her shoulder. "What if your magic is here, but mine—" she moved her hand up to her temple, "is here. What would happen if we pushed our magery against each other?"

"Perhaps societal collapse and a combustion that would rival the experimental weapons of the Tri-Region War."

"Har-har. I'm serious, Alastair. Haven't you ever wondered?"

"Of course, darling. But as you probably know, I haven't had the privilege of meeting many necromancers—willing or otherwise."

"Well, you'll be pleased to know that I've not met a vitamancer, either."

"Look at that, taking each other's magic-user-meeting virginity. How do you feel?"

"Like a new woman," she said flatly.

Alastair cocked a brow. "Did your first sexual encounter disappoint you as much as your face is telling me right now?"

"Yes, did yours?"

"Well, of course. He was a man, instinctively, they know how to take pleasure, not give it. That's why you have to teach them."

"You're a man."

"I'm an anomaly." He waved offhandedly.

"So, are we doing this?"

"Lets."

Valine and Alastair set down their cups on crystal coasters and situated themselves across from each other. They remained seated, but their feet were planted and their backs straight. Their hands were on their knees, and their eyes were level.

"On the count of three?"

"One," Valine began.

They counted, and on three Valine uncoiled her necromancy and directed it outward, seeking to tether to Alastair. The vitamancer threw out his sapphire magic and Valine watched as her shadows shattered through it an immediately speared into him. He gasped as her magic caught him, but immediately she pulled it back.

"*Bloody hell!*" Alastair cursed, hand flying to his chest.

"Come on, Alastair. I need you to actually try."

"Valine…" Alastair raised his cornflower blue, Runellian sea blue eyes to hers, fear and shock alighting them. "I did. You destroyed my magic the moment you touched it. I've never felt that…it felt like it just exploded through it."

"What?" Anxiety and trepidation flushed through her, raising the fine hairs along her body. "That's not possible."

"I assure you it is," he said haltingly.

"Can we try again? You with your magic up first?" Valine requested cautiously.

Alastair patted his chest once. "Yes, let's go for one more."

Twisting his fingers, Alastair brought up his vitamancy and pulled the sparkling light between them, allowing it to form a hazy shield. Once the wall was in place, Valine lifted her hand, tweaking her fingers delicately. Her shadows slipped between them, and she aimed once again for Alastair's chest.

His shield didn't stand a chance.

Without resistance, Valine speared through his magic and arrowed through him, knotting a tether between them. The shield dissolved between them, like paper disintegrating in a fire. It was ash and nothing. She watched his magic dissipate and flicker out in horror, the blue decaying to gray before going out.

Slowly, as if in a trance, Valine dropped her hand, meeting Alastair's shocked expression. The dignitary stared at her, taking her in for all that she was, knowledge dawning, realization becoming concrete.

"*What are you?*"

Valine looked down, drawing herself up. With resolve she felt strengthening, she pulled her midnight gaze from the floor and looked at Alastair. "I am a true daughter of Mrithun." Valine paused and then inhaled sharply. "I'm sorry, I have to go."

Before Alastair could rebuke or reassure her—if that is what he wanted—she was gone, racing for the doors. She delivered a hasty note to Malik, informing him she'd be scouting the city for the day, then she was out beyond the castle walls. She snagged the black cloak she'd tucked into an alcove for her midnight jaunts, eased her way past guards, and navigated her way through the forest. Climbing up steep terrain, Valine dug her fingers into the dirt and planted her favorite boots against roots and rock.

When she reached the top, she could see the pewter sky yawning above the treetops, shadows languishing around her, the foliage creating an air of darkness that was both eerie and welcoming. The small rock clearing on the cliff was insular and freeing. She was hidden as if she were miles away and ensconced in the deep woods, praying like the ancients to the patrons.

She sat alone for a time with her thoughts, watching the sun reach its zenith and then fall again. She sat on that ridge all day and most of the night until darkness was a velvet sheet and the moon hung like an illuminated orb in the sky.

Finally, she steeled herself, and she stood. Instead of reaching out with her magic to Mrithun, she reached inward. Into the very being of herself, into the very essence that made her, her. Past her necromancy, and past the orb of fire that wrapped around it. She dove through and in, shuttering her eyes against the night, feeling a new tether in her very soul. Then, she did something for the first time, something she intrinsically knew how to do.

She summoned her father.

Valine focused and willed the existence and when she opened her eyes, a man swathed in the very shadows that made her necromancy stood there.

Daemons were traditionally depicted with leathery wings and horns, but the man that stood before her bore neither. His skin was deathly pale, his eyes liquid pools of ink. A small smile graced his wide, pouty lips, and humor lined his sharp, angular features. He tilted his head to the side, his black waves shifting and lifting in the smoke as if the gravity of the earthly plane did not affect him.

"Daughter," Mrithun said lowly, his voice like gravel and endlessness.

Valine drew herself up to her full height, levelling the Patron of Death with a hard stare. "Why?" She demanded. "Why am I here? Why do I exist?"

Mrithun smiled and let the shadows dance between his black-painted fingers. "You were a dream, and I knew I had to make you real."

Valine held a breath in her throat and steeled herself for her next question. The answer to it would shift her perspective and understanding of herself, should it be the response she abhorred. She wasn't sure she entirely wanted to know. It was as they said, ignorance is bliss. But the not knowing was almost worse. Her heart hammered, but she finally spoke through the anxiety.

"Was I created through deception?"

"No," he said calmly. "Your mother knew who I was. She sought a lover when her husband forsook her for others. She was so sad, Little One, and I was glad to bring her joy, if only for a short while."

Valine deflated in relief. She wasn't the product of rape or dishonesty. She wasn't the product of violence and power and fear. And she wasn't the product of Dáinn Desdemon.

It sounded odd coming from a necromancer, but death was demanded and warranted in certain situations. She could not name one that called for unwilling sexual violence. Death could save, death could be mercy, death could end. There was no excuse for the other.

"You have grown to be more incredible than I ever thought you could be," Mrithun said, approaching her. He tucked two fingers beneath her chin and tilted her face to his, admiring her. She realized, through the smoke and shadows, that they had the same eyes, the same slope to their nose, the same full pout of lips. But somehow, she still looked like Dáinn Desdemon. "And as any father, I have hopes for you."

"Such as?"

Mrithun smiled a white, cheery smile. "Have you not figured it out by now? There is a path set before you, drawn by the saints and daemons of old, from their prophets and seers."

"You want me to be queen."

"No," he corrected. "I want you to be empress. Can you not see your lover's vision? You are creating a deathless empire."

There it was again, a deathless empire.

"That doesn't make sense. I've killed so many to be here."

"You misunderstand. *You* are deathless. *You* are undying."

An undying queen.

"I cannot die?"

"You can, should someone decide to forcibly take you from this world, but you have contingencies for that, don't you?" Mrithun's voice was filled with pride. "You stopped aging on your twenty-sixth birthday. You will not grow old; you will remain immortal and a master over death. It is the gift that patrons give their children."

"I will outlive everyone?" Valine despaired.

"Not if you properly tether those you care about. Create an indominable legacy and a generational legend. And should you have children with someone you've tethered, your children will be immortal, too—a dynasty. You are so close, daughter, so soon you will be infinite and unconquerable."

Mrithun was smiling at her so proudly, his cool fingers on her chin an affectionate and paternal touch she'd never known before. It was reassuring and comforting, it rang of safety and care. Dáinn Desdemon had never ventured this gentling of behavior.

"I'm not just a dream, though, am I? I'm a weapon. A weapon you created against—what? What do you fear so much that I exist?"

"You think highly of yourself, don't you?"

"I am not stupid."

Mrithun sighed. "It has been foreseen that forces will one day come to the shores of Enneive, and only a child of the earthly plane, with the blessing of a saint and a daemon, can stand against it."

"When?" Valine demanded.

"That, I truly do not know. But you will be alive to face it, and it will be your battle to be won."

"Can't you ask Ayyubia or Nafiza, or whoever has power over clairvoyance to figure it out?"

"I cannot."

"Why?"

"She and I only have so much power, Little One. We are not the only patrons, there are patrons on other continents."

Valine's blood went cold. "What do you mean?"

"The northern continent, Eilassor, possesses three powerful patrons with powers unlike those of the mages here. They are like us—like the saints and daemons—but also *other*. They do not have the power of the elements or storm, or life and death, or even over the mind. Their powers are unknowable to us."

Eilassor. The continent the original Mayar family came from?

"They're gods?"

"No, patrons. They are of the same caliber as myself or Nylantia or Dunia."

"But you're afraid these other patrons will influence their people to wage war from across the sea?"

"It has been foretold they will come, but not what their reasons are. It could be war, or curiosity, or something more banal, but I do not know, and I dare not risk my world to find out. I only know them by one name, so do you—their reputation falsely praised here."

Valine didn't even need to ask. In that moment she realized and her world began to crumble down around her, raining ancient monoliths and cathedrals within her mind. The construction and civilization of her beliefs falling into disrepair.

"The Stygian Ones."

"Yes," Mrithun confirmed. "They are not gods, but I do not wish to stoke their wrath. I need you to be powerful when they come, which is why it is so imperative that you do not fail your quest. It's not just destroying Runell. You must conquer. You must let the power of Adraali spread and consume Enneive. Do you understand me?"

"Yes, I—I do," Valine stuttered, "but I can't be the foretold one. I'm not blessed by a saint, only a daemon."

"Think again."

So close she could see flames in her father's eyes, Valine came to a startling realization. A memory of a story and bonds that could not be broken. She stepped back from her father, understanding growing on her face.

"I thought it had burnt me and left a mark on my magic," Valine spoke softly. "But that's not what it did. The Call of the Phoenix was not lost. It is inside me."

"The necklace was only a temporary vessel. When the blood of one of Seraphina or Mrithun's own touched it, it unlocked. You are connected to the Call at the very core of your essence. You are the new vessel."

Valine blinked several times trying to clear the fog that was threatening to settle on her. She had awoken this morning under an identity she'd known and understood for most of her life, but now she was encountering a stranger with her face. She was unrecognizable from the person she was before.

"Heed my words, Valine Mithra, if you do not continue on the path you have taken, Adraali will fall to Runell, and when those foreign forces come, they will be able to take it all. Some of our patrons stand against us, heralding their own champion from Talloh, urging them to side with Runell—you must not let that come to pass, even if some do not want to see a crown upon your brow." Mrithun reached out and stroked her hair. "You are so very young, and immortality yawns before you. One day, you shall understand. Until then, I must depart."

"Wait," she said, reaching. "Who is the other?"

"I do not know. The others bar me from this knowledge. You must discover it."

"Please don't go, I need you."

"I cannot stay, Little One. I wish I could."

Mrithun kissed her brow delicately and backed away.

"You are my best creation," he said and then disappeared into the ebony.

CHAPTER FORTY-EIGHT

The winds of night chased through Valine, every cold kiss and harsh bite from the zephyrs forcing her to contemplate if they were sent from restless spirits. She was struggling to wrap her mind around the fact that the Stygian Ones existed, even if not in the fashion Tallohians believed.

The wind nipped her again.

Just then, she heard the shuffle of feet and whirled with her necromancy raised. There, swathed in a gray traveling cloak, golden hair wild and unbound with a lioness gaze, was Cersei.

"So, you figured it out?" Cersei asked, an edge to her voice.

Valine inclined her head. "You are from Eilassor."

"I am."

Through secrets and snooping in Talloh, Valine had discovered Cersei had no history or witnesses pertaining to all of

Enneive. Everything she'd heard had been fabricated and easily unraveled after a little inquiry. It was through thorough watching that she'd deduced the truth. What she's also gleaned was that Cersei was a mage—and now confirmed through Mrithun, her father, she didn't even know what kind.

Upon arriving back in Adraali the concern wouldn't leave her, and so, she wrote a coded letter to Cersei and asked her to meet in the woods outside of Nyxia. Finally, she'd arrived.

"How?" Valine queried.

"Magic. And much risk."

"Why?"

"I knew too much, and I did not agree with their ideals. I sought change and thought I found it in Talloh, but I was wrong about their morals. I'm hoping Adraali has what I am looking for."

"So, you came here with what purpose? To liberate us from their attack? To find peace in a new life?"

"I don't think I can trust you yet, Valine Desdemon."

"The feeling is mutual." Valine was unsettled by the fact she couldn't address Cersei in the same fashion. "But, if you dislike some methods of Talloh's operation, perhaps we may speak of an understanding. That is, if you do not betray me."

There was a lingering breath of silence between them. Where the two stared each other down and remained unmoved.

Could Cersei be the one sent from the unknown patrons? Could she be Valine's opposite in the coming conflict?

The silence held a moment longer.

Finally, it was broken.

"I was not the one who killed during the Tri-Moon Festival," Cersei said without any prompting.

Valine hadn't thought so, but the confirmation was nice. "I know." Valine took a step forward. "Do you have magic, Cersei?"

Cersei froze, eyes flickering, despite the way she controlled her emotions.

"That would be a yes," Valine continued. "What is it?"

"Something that will haunt your dreams."

Valine twisted her magic in her hand and manifested it for Cersei to see. "I would encourage you to tell me."

"I'd rather show you," Cersei said without fear, and then stepped back. "But in the meantime, think if our morals align—if they do, let me know, because you may have gained yourself a dearest ally."

And with that, Cersei dispersed into smoke, leaving not a trace behind.

She'd completely vanished.

Valine stared in shock, standing on the cliff, suddenly alone with all her new revelations. Mrithun, Cersei, Stygian Ones…

Valine shivered in her cloak, weaving her way back into the palace, taking a shortcut that ran through the throne room. It was empty and flickered with weak candlelight and abstract shafts of moonlight through the glass ceiling. It was when she entered the dark stone space that she stopped.

This was where her journey was cemented. It wasn't inside that basement, nor when she killed Captain Ishaq. It was here, after she thought she'd saved Freyja from her own magic, where Malik lounged on the dais. She'd revealed that she killed her father, and he didn't flinch. The serpent was still embossed in the floor, the chandelier still hung, the skylights still fractured stained glass, and the throne still stood.

Dark and elegant on the dais it beckoned to her. Valine stepped forward and slowly ascended the steps. She took measured breaths and measured steps. Finally, with the throne before her, she looked down at the gold and iron and velvet. Tentatively, she reached down and touched it with a finger, the very finger that held her consort ring. A ring that could be the symbol of her marriage.

Knowing of the Stygian Ones and their forces changed the game. Changed the stakes. It wasn't just her vengeance that fueled her, but her love for Malik and the life she wanted to lead with him on *their* terms. Not on the whims of the unknown powers. Not on the terms of invaders.

She stroked the arm of the chair once and then turned. Looking over at the sea of jet, at the snake and orchids on the floor of the cathedral-like space, Valine slowly sat, set her hands on the arms, and crossed her legs.

Just then, Malik entered the throne room and approached curiously, garbed in black, devotion shining in his eyes.

"Valine?"

She inclined her chin. "We have much to discuss, My King." She smiled. "And you and I are going to get exactly what we want."

Malik slowly grinned and crossed over to her.

This was her kingdom.

This was her throne.

And she was going to be the undying fucking queen of it all.

THE END

PRONUNCIATION GUIDE

CHARACTERS

Valine Desdemon: Val-Leen Des-Dee-Mon
Malik Amir: Mal-Lik Ameer
Sarim Kahlil: S-Air-Im Ka-Leel
Freyja Nahara: Frey-Ya Na-Hara
Alastair Whitechurch: Ala-Stair Whitechurch
Larysa Olympias: Lare-Rissa Oh-Limp-Ee-As
Jacira Mayar: Jack-Keera May-Yar
Jericho (Mayar): Jer-Ree-Ko
Amaris (Mayar): Am-Maris
Hanish: Han-Neesh
Hafsa: Haf-Sah
Tallulah Illise: Ta-Loo-La Ill-Lees
Balchon Raziche: Bal-Kon Raz-Zee-Chee
Cersei: Ser-See
Liesl Ryniel: Lee-Sul Rin-Ee-El
Thiandra: Thee-And-Dra
Alvah: Alva
Ylaine: Ya-Lane
Ishaq: Ish-Ack
Dáinn (Desdemon): D-Ah-N
Mareek Das: Mar-Reek Da-Ahs

PATRONS

Mrithun: Mree-Thuun
Nylantia: Nil-Lan-Tia
Nafiza: Naf-Feeza
Atifa: At-Teefa
Aenon: A-Non
Dunia: Doo-Nia
Barak: Bare-Ahk
Charna: Char-Na

Vitus: Vee-Tus
Seraphina: Sara-Feena
Aaseeyah: A-See-Ya
Ayyubia: I-You-Bee-Ya
Anvindr: Ann-Vin-Deer
Lucian: Loo-Shee-En
Styrmir: Steer-Meer
Bela: Bella

PLACES

Adraali: Ad-Draw-Lee
Runell: Roo-Nell
Thycca: Thii-Ka
Dubon: Doo-Bon
Ixaitha: Ix-Ay-Tha
Cuuevota: Q-Eh-Vo-Ta
Astra: Astra
Bastia: Bast-Ya
Gallae: Gal-Lay
Valos: Valos

Talloh: Ta-Low
Luneth: Loo-Neth
Valencya: Val-Len-Se-Ya
Melusda: Mel-Loos-Da
Pravo: Pravo
Nyxia: Nix-Ee-A
Selyndyr: Sel-Len-Deer
Ophette: O-Fet
Cydra: Si-Dra

OTHER

Veritasium: Veri-Tasi-Um
Robursium: Row-Bur-See-Um
Valmotti: Val-Mott-Ee
The Ōrdinem: Oh-Rid-In-Em
Stygian: Stig-Ee-En

GLOSSARY OF TERMS

In alphabetical order.

AASEAYAH: (Saint) The saint of telepathy, first psycho-mancer. One of three sisters who were the original mind mages. Once triplets that became one entity after Aaseayah was fatally injured and her sister Ayyubia (Clairvoyance) saw they needed to combine to save her or else the ability and her life would be lost.

AENON: (Saint) The saint of water, first hydromancer. Sworn enemy of Seraphina.

AETHERMANCER: Air/wind mage. Controls all that is in air, can summon and take element. Different levels and complexities. Common. (Daemon—Anvindr)

ADRAALI: Growing to be the most powerful and influential kingdom, ruled by King Malik Jirani Amir—previously ruled by Saalim Halil Amir. Characterized by gothic architecture, stained glass, and dense forests. Wet climate, severe seasons, often foggy and rainy. Royal colors are viridian and gold with snake and spider motifs. Notably progressive.

ANARMANCER: Chaos mage. Controls and creates chaos, anarchy, and misrule. Draws power from disruption. Only one ever to have existed. Extinct. (Daemon—Mara)

ANVINDR: (Daemon) The daemon of air and wind, first aethermancer. Neutral ally to Aenon (Water) and Seraphina (Fire), will help or hinder either or both and known to have fought battles on different teams each time.

ARACHNE: Carriage-sized female spiders, black carapaces, two violet eyes. Weavers of dreams and desires, and deliverers of justice. Live in the Muravo Mountain Pass and doles out justice on travelers. Will kill if found guilty for crimes, very rarely do they give pardons.

ASTRA: Second largest city in Adraali.

ASTRA'S EDGE: Road demarcating the edge of Astra and Nyxia.

ATIFA: (Saint) The saint of empathy, first pathomancer. One of three sisters who were the original mind mages. Once triplets that became one entity after Aaseayah was fatally injured and her sister Ayyubia (Clairvoyance) saw they needed to combine to save her or else the ability and her life would be lost.

AYYUBIA: (Saint) The saint of clairvoyance, first divinamancer. One of three sisters who were the original mind mages. Once triplets that became one entity after Aaseayah was fatally injured and her sister Ayyubia (Clairvoyance) saw they needed to combine to save her or else the ability and her life would be lost.

BARAK: (Daemon) The daemon of lightning, one of the first fulgurmancers. Conjoined twin of Styrmir (Storm), younger sibling of Lucian (Light).

BASILISK: Large serpentine beasts, scaled and feathered, two wings, four legs, blunt snake's head with a razor hooked beak, and horns. Native to Runell and remote mountains of Thycca, Valencya, and Adraali. Only royals of Runell can ride them.

BASTIA: Capital city of Luneth.

BELA: (Daemon) The daemon of destruction, first ruinmancer. Consort of Nylantia (Night and Stars), daughter to Dunia (Earth), unknown father.

BLACK ARBORS (THE): Line of black trees and mist that connect in arches at the southernmost point in Thycca. Rumored to be the resting place or doorway to the saints and daemons.

CHARNA: (Daemon) The daemon of darkness, first umbramancer. Mother to Nylantia (Night and Stars), soulmate to Lucian (Light).

CURRAM: Capital city of Dubon.

CUUEVOTA: The black market island ruled by sovereign, Thiandra. Located in the north and characterized by jungles, bright colors, excess decadence, and pirates.

CYDRA: Second largest city in Runell. The Desdemon lands.

DAEMON: Patron characterized by perceived evil. (Mrithun, Anvindr, Dunia, Barak, Charna, Nylantia, Bela, Mara)

DIVINAMANCER: Mind mage—clairvoyants and prophets. Can see the future to varying degrees. Uncommon. (Saint—Ayyubia)

DUBON: Southeastern kingdom characterized by rolling hills, orchards, and farmland. Notably peaceful and renown for their festivals.

DUNIA: (Daemon) The daemon of earth, first terramancer. Mother of Bela (Destruction). Neutral ally to Aenon (Water) and Seraphina (Fire), will help or hinder either or both and known to have fought battles on different teams each time.

EILASSOR: The northern continent from which the royals of Talloh and Stygian Ones heralded from.

EMERALD (THE): One of three great rivers between Runell, Pravo, and Luneth. Colors indicate name.

ENNIEVE: The southern continent from which the patrons herald from. (Setting of A Deathless Empire.)

FAYLA: Capital city of Valencya.

FLEUR DE MORT: Rare and deadly poison derived from roses which Mrithun's lifeblood fell upon. Grown only in

Luneth. Characterized by being the most painful poison that forces one's heart through their chest.

FULGURMANCER: Lightning and storm mage. Can summon both elements or draw from. Notoriously volatile. Uncommon. (Daemon and Saint—Barak and Styrmir)

GALLAE: Capital City of Runell.

GODSBREATH: Poison that swells blood vessels and makes hearts and lungs explode. Victims suffocate and drown in blood. Made from distilled blackwort and vervain mixed with absinthe and arsenic.

HYDROMANCER: Water mage. Can summon water and control it. Drawn from element. Different strengths and levels, complexity varies on individual, one of the easiest elements to master. Common. (Saint—Aenon)

IXAITHA: Northeastern desert kingdom, once a powerful empire. Very hot climate and prone to flash floods. Characterized by vast sands and sandstone buildings with steeply-pitched roofs.

KORTHA: Capital city of Pravo.

KRAKEN: One-hundred-foot-long squids with tentacles whose suckers have hooks and end in talons. Ridged with natural armor, horned head, glowing red eyes, fanged beak beneath body, and a secondary maw covered in tentacles on head. Native to the open seas and oceans.

LAPIS (THE): One of three great rivers between Runell, Pravo, and Luneth. Colors indicate name.

LASKAVA MOUNTAINS (THE): Mountains in Adraali.

LAZULI (THE): A river that branches off the Lapis and cuts through Luneth.

LUCIAN: (Saint) The saint of light, first luxmancer. Father of Nylantia (Night and Stars), soulmate to Charna (Darkness), oldest brother of Barak and Styrmir (Lightning and Storm).

LUNETH: Western kingdom ruled by the Olympias family. Characterized by hot climate and mixture of desert and temperate land with a famous garden.

LUXMANCER: Light mage. Can use light as a weapon (can blind, etc.), draws magic from sun and light sources. Can nullify umbramancers. Common. (Saint—Lucian)

MARA: (Daemon) The daemon of chaos, first and only anarmancer. Daughter of Bela (Destruction) and Vitus (Life), Mrithun was suspected of fathering due to a tryst that occurred at the same time. Due to the fear of her ability Aenon, Seraphina, Anvindr, and Dunia (Water, Fire, Air, and Earth) combined powers to destroy her.

MELUSDA: Eastern kingdom characterized by short, ornate buildings, frequent temples, cherry blossoms, and villages. Prone to quakes and tsunamis.

MRITHUN: (Daemon) The daemon of death, first necromancer. Star-crossed lover of Vitus (Life). Killed in Luneth and his blood fell on the rose gardens and produced the potent and fatal poison—fleur de mort. Oldest friend and ally of Seraphina (Fire), bearer of the phoenix as he stood by her and her rage known as the Great Flame. Once had a tryst with Bela (Destruction) during which time Vitus also had a dalliance. A daemon of chaos (Mara) was produced and in fear Aenon, Seraphina, Anvindr, and Dunia (Water, Fire, Air, and Earth) combined powers to destroy Mara.

MURAVO MOUNTAIN PASS (THE): Mountain pass to Talloh created by ruinmancer Ilyas Muravo through slave labor. Was killed by the arachne upon the commencement of the pass's creation.

NAFIZA: (Saint) The saint of mind, first psychomancer, pathomancer, and diviniamancer. Name of the three sisters who were the original mind mages. Once triplets (Aaseayah, Ayyubia, Atifa) that became one entity after Aaseayah was fatally injured

and her sister Ayyubia (Clairvoyance) saw they needed to combine to save her or else the ability and her life would be lost.
NECROMANCER: Death mage. Magic powered by death, bones, poisons, venoms, instruments of death, etc. If above are unavailable it draws from the necromancer themselves, bringing them closer to the afterlife. Can kill with magic and resurrect. Can perform ability incorrectly and bind a soul to the mage as a slave. If a resurrection is done incorrectly and the mage does not want a mindless slave, the necromancer can sacrifice a piece of their soul to give them autonomy. If resurrection is done correctly the necromancer will have had their magic tethered prior to individual's death. Vitamancer is their true opposite and can nullify. Very rare. (Daemon—Mrithun)
NILAX: Capital city of Ixaitha.
NYLANTIA: (Daemon) The daemon of night and stars, first stellaemancer. Daughter of Charna (Darkness) and Lucian (Light), consort of Bela (Destruction).
NYLANTIA'S TEARS: Extremely potent poison. One drop for sleep, three for death, two is a mistake.
NYXIA: Capital city of Adraali.
NYXIA'S EDGE: Road demarcating the edge of Astra and Nyxia.
OPHETTE: Third largest city in Runell.
ŌRDINEM (THE): Order that trains assassins and healers, acolytes must choose path (death or healing) at fifteen years-old and graduate at eighteen. Acolytes learn same skills until they decide. Characterized by opal/moonstone for assassins and amber/sunstone for healers.
PATHOMANCER: Mind mage—empaths. Can feel/manipulate feelings. Common. (Saint—Atifa)
PHOENIX: Flaming birds the size of a horse, long tail feathers, reborn out of their own ashes after a week and one day. Loyal to other phoenixes and will never attack each other. Cre-

ated by Seraphina (Fire) and bonded to her and Mrithun (Death). Native to Talloh.

PRAVO: Western country, and only country without a kingdom—ruled by a community. People originally hail from Cuuevota before pirates took it over.

PSYCHOMANCER: Mind mage—telepathy, mindreading, and thought manipulation. Different levels and strengths, varying abilities, can be thwarted by mental blocks and tells. Can manipulate thoughts into false memories. (Not mind control.) Rare. (Saint—Aaseayah)

PYROMANCER: Fire mage. Can summon fire and control it. Drawn from element. Different strengths and levels, complexity varies on individual, one of the easiest elements to master. Common. (Daemon—Seraphina)

ROBURSIUM MEDALLION: Magical artefacts that protect from physical attack.

RUINMANCER: Destruction mage. Can destroy objects in a controlled or uncontrolled manner. Can also put back together. Experts in explosions, disintegrations. Rare. (Daemon—Bela)

RUNELL: Southwestern kingdom, renown for power. Characterized by towering buildings, high arches, waterfalls, filigree designs, statues, blackberry fields, and gardens. Coast on three points of kingdom, mild climate. Notably restrictive.

SAINT: Patron characterized by perceived good. (Nafiza—Aaseayah, Atifa, Ayyubia—, Vitus, Aenon, Seraphina, Lucian, Styrmir)

SAND SERPENT: Titanic snakes with five foot wide mouths, four sets of fangs, a secondary mouth with a rotating maw, fanged teeth, frill around head that detects vibrations and is used for intimidation. Two arms with three claws, scales blend with the sand they burrow in. Extremely venomous and deadly. Native to the Twilight Sands, have been known to travel to Luneth. Endangered species.

SAPPHIRE (THE): One of three great rivers between Runell, Pravo, and Luneth. Colors indicate name.
SELYNDYR: Capital city of Talloh.
SERAPHINA: (Saint) The saint of fire, first pyromancer. Sworn enemy of Aenon, oldest friend and ally of Mrithun (Death). Creator and bearer of the phoenix, created from her rage known as the Great Flame.
SHIREEN: Capital city of Melusda.
STELLAEMANCER: Night and stars mage. Can read the stars and sense patterns and prophecy. Higher intuition at night, powered by the stars and night. Uncommon. (Daemon—Nylantia)
STYGIAN: Language and religion.
STYGIAN ONES: Entities that Talloh worships as gods (religion), consisting of He, She, and They. Religion dictates all but devout nobles are equal and deserve the same treatments as another. Devout nobles consider themselves blessed and enlightened, therefore, better than everyone. The Stygian Ones are symbols of peace, protection, and prosperity—respectively. Hailing from Eilassor. In reality they're not gods, but equal to the patrons.
STYRMIR: (Saint) The saint of storm, one of the first fulgurmancers. Conjoined twin of Barak (Lightning), younger sibling of Lucian (Light).
TALLOH: Northern kingdom ruled by the Mayar family, having usurped the original rulers. Mayars hail from Eilassor. Hot climate, characterized by three moons, white stone and gold architecture. Surrounded by purple sands.
TERRAMANCER: Earth mage. Can manipulate the ground and environment. Soil, rock, and raw/untreated metal. Common. (Daemon—Dunia)
THYCCA: Southernmost kingdom, ruled by the Ryniel family. Characterized by mountains, lakes, forests, and severe weather. Notably progressive and known for diversity and a safe haven.

TWILIGHT SANDS (THE): Purple sands that stretch from the borders of Luneth to the entirety of Talloh. Home to sand serpents. Crossing the sands is the most dangerous of the three ways to access Talloh.
UMBRAMANCER: Darkness mage. Can remove sources of light and blind (temporarily) and drive individuals to insanity. Can nullify luxmancers. Common. (Daemon—Charna)
VALENCYA: Southern kingdom just north of Thycca. Climate and landscape similar to Thycca. Values are notably restrictive.
VALMOTTI: Specially trained warriors devoted to a country or kingdom of their choosing unless otherwise sold. Common in Runell and Adraali. Selected at five years-old, taken from family when showing battle affinity or sold to the warriors by family. Rumors of outright stealing/kidnapping. Training is rigorous and deadly, many die or are maimed. Taught to use every style of weapon and final test involves marksmanship, sword fighting, unique weapon capabilities, blind defense, and escaping a maze.
VALOS: Capital city of Thycca.
VANGUARD (THE): Ruthless assassin's guild.
VERITASIUM MEDALLION: Medallions from the patrons that protect from magical attack.
VITAMANCER: Life mage. Magic powered by life and recharges it, can extend other lives by proximity up to 200 years. Notoriously long-lived. Can heal severe wounds and bring back to life if recently deceased depending on degree of fatality. Cannot kill others with their magic. True opposite to necromancers, can nullify. Ultra rare. (Saint—Vitus)
VITUS: (Saint) The saint of life, first vitamancer. Star-crossed lover of Mrithun (Death). Once had a tryst with Bela (Destruction) during which time Mrithun also had a dalliance. Father of Mara (Chaos).

ACKNOWLEDGEMENTS

I want to start by saying this was the first book I wrote after having my first daughter and it was a testament to me staying me after becoming a mother. It was powered by the want of retaining my identity and all the rage of those whose rights were—and continue to be—taken away. And with those feelings came a lot of dark thoughts. I love this book, but many times it put me in a bad headspace and it became important to have something not so dark to work on—which will be the norm for the rest of the A Deathless Empire books.
Onto the thanks.
Always and forever, endless thank yous to my husband, Michael. You constantly believe in me and push me to keep writing. It was you who convinced me to self-publish and you are what keeps me going. I love you.
Thank you to Fay Lane for this gorgeous cover and all the subsequent ones—I can't wait to show them off. You nailed it.
Thank you to Indigo Melanson for the gorgeous line art in this book and for your endless love for my books. You are genuinely one of the sweetest people I've met and I'm so honored you've chosen to read my stories.
Thank you to Cassidy Hudspeth for editing this and truly humbling me with my comma usage.

Thank you to my discord groups for supporting me and celebrating my wins and putting up with my loses. Thank you for believing in me.

My babies, Vivienne and Rosalie, you afford this life to me and make my heart so happy. I would take on the world for you both. I love you so much.

To my friends and family, thank you so much for being excited about my writing journey and hopes and dreams.

Thank you to every person who shared any graphic or anything related to my books, I appreciate you all.

And as always, thank you eternally, Dear Reader, for picking this book up. I would be forever grateful if you left a review on Amazon and Goodreads.

Until the next one! I hope you stick around to see what I have next.

ABOUT THE AUTHOR

Kayla McGrath has been writing since the age of thirteen out of spite, having read a book with a love triangle that didn't go her way. After that, it became a passion. If she's not writing, then she's reading, or drinking endless cups of chai. Kayla lives on Vancouver Island with her husband, two daughters, and two boxers.

She is the author of the Cold as Iron trilogy, the Infernal Curses series, A Deathless Empire series, and the inter-connected standalone Love and Other Tropes novels. A Deathless Empire is her sixth book.

You can find her mostly on Instagram/Threads (@kaylamcgrathbooks), TikTok (@kaylamcgrath_), and sometimes on Twitter/X (@KaylaMcGrath_).

OTHER BOOKS BY KAYLA MCGRATH

THE COLD AS IRON TRILOGY
This Broken Memory
These Ruined Dreams
Our Shattered Fates

INFERNAL CURSES
The Nightmare Curse
The Hallow Curse (10/29/24)

A DEATHLESS EMPIRE
A Deathless Empire

LOVE AND OTHER TROPES
Love & Other Tropes (Emmett & Illiana)